SINFUL
LIKE US

BOOK 5 IN THE LIKE US SERIES

KRISTA & BECCA
RITCHIE

CHARACTER LIST

Not all characters in this list will make an appearance in the book, but most will be mentioned. Ages represent the age of the character at the beginning of the book. Some characters will be older when they're introduced, depending on their birthday.

The Cobalts

Richard Connor Cobalt & Rose Calloway

Jane - 23

Charlie – 21

Beckett – 21

Eliot – 19

Tom – 18

Ben – 16

Audrey – 13

The Hales

Loren Hale & Lily Calloway

Maximoff - 23

Luna – 18

Xander – 15

Kinney – 13

The Meadows

Ryke Meadows & Daisy Calloway

Sullivan - 20

Winona – 14

The Security Team

These are the bodyguards that protect the Hales, Cobalts, and Meadows.

SECURITY FORCE OMEGA
Akara Kitsuwon (lead) - 26
Thatcher Moretti - 28
Banks Moretti - 28
Farrow Keene – 28
Oscar Oliveira - 31
Paul Donnelly – 27
Quinn Oliveira– 21

SECURITY FORCE EPSILON
Jon Sinclair (lead) - 40s
Tony Ramella - 28
O'Malley - 27
…and more

SECURITY FORCE ALPHA
Price Kepler (lead) – 40s
…and more

A NOTE FROM THE AUTHORS

The Italian used in this book is an Italian-American language developed by Italian immigrants. It is an incomplete language and uses Italian, English, or both. Different Italians speak different dialects in certain areas, and what is used in the Like Us series is prominent on the East Coast. Words may vary in pronunciation and spelling in different communities. A glossary with pronunciations for *Sinful Like Us* is included at the end of the book.

Sinful Like Us is the fifth book in the Like Us Series. Though the series changes POVs throughout, to understand events that took place in the previous novels it should be read in its order of publication.
Sinful Like Us should be read after *Tangled Like Us*.

LIKE US SERIES READING ORDER

PROLOGUE

Jane Cobalt

LATE IN THE QUIET night of the lake house, I'm curled up on a leather sofa. Eyes raw from crying, pastel purple stationery paper lies on my lap, and I lift my ballpoint pen off inked words, my stomach sunk low.

I stare faraway at my messy scrawl. "This isn't the end," I whisper, grabbing at any leftover optimism.

I'm all alone and talking to myself. It's certain then: happy or sad, I can't shut up.

My cousins, brothers, and bodyguards are in their bedrooms for the night—while I'm in the living room, staying warm in flannel pajamas beside a lit fireplace.

I don't love the solitary quiet, but the crackle of flames fills the silence a little. Light flickers against the dark walls, and I blow out a breath. "Come on, Jane."

My heart has been broken. Just recently.

Torn to bleeding shreds, and I'm trying not to sit with these painful feelings. "You can withstand anything," I murmur. "You're a Cobalt."

A lump lodges in my throat, and I bite the inside of my mouth to quell emotion—*emotion* that pierces all the armor I've ever built.

I'm not sure I want to be a Cobalt these days, and even the thought feels sacrilege. My family is my everything.

But I never prepared to be hurt by the people I love. By two *Cobalts*. By my parents.

Aren't they supposed to believe me and trust me? When I've done nothing devious in my life to elicit their doubt. Yet, they're the ones who believed I could be in a forbidden relationship with my best friend.

Oh, and that best friend—he happens to be my *cousin*.

It's unthinkable. Never in my *life* have I ever even imagined…

My face starts to twist in a cringe and then morphs into a grimace as I remember how my parents will be at the lake house tomorrow. I'll have to confront them face-to-face then.

I can't say that I'm ready. Not when I'm wallowing. More pitifully than I like.

I sigh at myself. Where is the fierce roar of a lion? "Where are the claws?" I mutter and tuck a piece of wavy hair behind my ear.

God, I feel kicked down and meek. As the firstborn Cobalt, I'm supposed to be the fiercest, the most vicious and courageous of them all.

Not a puddle that people can splash in.

My voice falls to a softer whisper. "Buck up." Soon, I'll be on a tour bus and on the path to rebuilding my tarnished friendship with Moffy.

I nod. *We'll be okay.*

It's the bright side of an awful December. I take another breath and focus more on the stationery paper.

My fingers brush along my handwriting, a few words scribbled at the top:

For Thatcher Moretti.

I continue writing out a list.

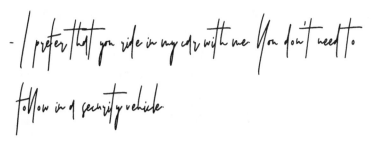

- *I prefer that you ride in my car with me. You don't need to follow in a security vehicle.*

- *Fans can approach, but if you feel they're possible threats, please don't let them near me.*

- *I talk a lot. (If I bother you, please let me know.)*

I spend a few more minutes making notes for my brand-new bodyguard, and I end with just three words.

I write: *keep me safe*

Once I pick my pen off the paper, I look around. Half expecting one of my cats to keep me company. They're not here at the lake house in the Smoky Mountains.

I really don't love being alone, and these rumors have wedged something between me and Moffy. Pushing him further out to sea while I'm standing on a lonely island.

I take an umpteenth breath and pull out my phone. Without second thought, I text my new bodyguard: I have the list you asked for. We can go over it now if you're still awake. I'm in the living room.

It's late and it's highly likely he's fast asleep. But as I lower my phone to my lap, a message lights up the screen.

I'll be down in a minute. — Thatcher

A small smile tries to tug my lips. Thatcher coming at my call is new to me. Lately, and very slowly, it's been dawning on me that he's been transferred to my detail.

Just temporarily.

He's considered my secondary bodyguard, you see. Quinn Oliveira, the youngest SFO bodyguard, is still on my detail. I'll have two men protecting me during the charity FanCon.

I look up as floorboards creak.

Thatcher walks across the third-floor balcony towards the stairs, moving with grave authority. A sort of domineering confidence. Like he's on a single life-or-death mission. It lures me in for a much longer moment, an even longer minute, reminding me that he's a *leader* among security, and this is the first time I've ever been protected by a lead.

His shoulders are bound strictly, a radio in his fist, and his serious gaze sweeps the living room—he sweeps *me*.

He zones in on my eyes, which must be red and bloodshot I'm guessing. Mostly because he lingers on my gaze for quite a while. At the same time, he's hiking down the steps.

And he nears me.

I leave my notes on the couch and rise to my feet. I plan to extend a hand in greeting, but his sheer imposing *height* seizes my attention.

Oh…

My eyes slowly widen.

He's an archangel. Sent to protect me. And I doubt it'll be the first time I think it—because, dear God, the analogy fits.

I lift my chin to meet his gaze, my hands naturally perching on my wide hips. "We've obviously met many times before," I say aloud.

He nods. "Yeah. We have." The corner of his lip almost lifts, I think, but then he rubs his mouth. Not much else passes through his stoic features. He attaches his radio to the waistband of his black slacks, also dressed in a black button-down while I'm in pajamas. "But this is different."

My brows jump. "How so?"

He rakes a firm hand through his brown disheveled hair, longer pieces curled under his ears. "I'm here to protect you, Jane. You're my first priority now."

"Even though you're a lead?"

"Even though I'm a lead," he confirms. "Your safety is what matters most to me." He holds my gaze.

I don't want to look away. I lean closer, even.

He asks, "Do you prefer I call you Jane?"

"I do," I say softly, entranced by him. Thatcher might be hard to decipher, but I realize that I'm finding his strong presence extraordinarily comforting. His whole protective demeanor envelops the room and wraps around me—as though silently commanding: *I am here for you.*

Warmth spreads through my limbs, and I could bask in this safe feeling for eons of time. Maybe that's why I keep my eyes on his eyes, even as my neck aches.

"And I should call you Thatcher?" I make sure since I've called him *Mr. Moretti* before (I was a little drunk) and he said, *Thatcher is fine.*

He nods. "*Thatcher* works. Unless you feel more comfortable calling me something else."

"No," I say quickly. "I like your name. It's unique to you. I don't know any other Thatchers." We're still staring intently at each other, and I can't tell if he's reading into my bloodshot eyes. Knowing that I've been crying.

"I don't know any other Janes," he admits.

I nearly smile. "I always thought Jane was a common name. There were five in my grade in high school. But most people just referred to me by my full name anyway." I rock forward on my feet. "I was *the* Jane Cobalt. Still am, I suppose." I think of my family.

I think of my mom and dad, and a frown drops my lips.

My eyes burn.

Thatcher never breaks my gaze. "Look, it might not be my place to say something, but you should just know that you'll get through this."

I clutch the comfort in his eyes. Earlier today, Thatcher told most everyone here that he knows what these kinds of accusations feel like. So I say, "As a twin, you said you've received rude questions before?"

"Yeah. That and more." He weaves his arms over his chest. "Guys in high school used to say that my brother and I did some...*things* together for fun."

Things.

I assume it verges on incestuous *things*, which is why he can relate to me now. I do wonder if he's censoring himself to remain professional or because the past is hard to talk about. Either way, I won't pry.

I tilt my head. "Did it change your relationship with your brother?"

He's nodding.

And my hands fall off my hips, and my heart plummets. It's what I feared. That this rumor will forever destroy my relationship with Moffy.

"It made us closer," Thatcher says. "We got stronger."

Stronger.

I inhale. "I want that so terribly for Moffy and me." I stare off at the burning fireplace logs. "I think our odds are 50-50."

His brows draw together. It takes him a second to ask. "You're that unsure?"

I smooth the wrinkles of my cat-chasing-yarn-balls pajama top. "I know that you know me and my family better than most ever will because you're a bodyguard, and I might never fully know you—and that's okay." I speak quickly. "But I'm not my mom. I'm not always so sure of myself, even when I wish I were, and I'm not a warrior *goddess*, even when I wish to be. I have to take that into account when constructing probabilities."

Thatcher stares at me in a way that causes my pulse to speed, heart to pound, and my lips part as I find more words to fill the quiet.

"Do you agree?" I wonder.

He almost shakes his head, but I see how he cuts the movement off. And he just says, "I think you're really hard on yourself, Jane."

I like how he says my name so softly at the end, and I wasn't searching for reassurance, but I didn't mind that at all—in fact, I think I liked that too.

"Not 50-50. 70-30 then," I say. "Moffy and I come out stronger."

"90-10." His eyes *almost* drop to my neck, but again, he stops the movement mid-way—and then he nods to the couch. "You want to take a seat?"

Heat blazes my cheeks for some reason. "I can sit." I return to the couch, splaying the papers on my lap. In the quiet, I steal a few glances at him.

Thatcher looks back at me before he pulls a leather ottoman over.

I have trouble focusing on the notes. Sitting pin straight, I fold my palms over my paper. "Were you sleeping before I texted?" I wonder if I woke him.

He takes a seat in front of me, his posture rigid, still quietly commanding. "Not that long."

So he was in bed. "How come you didn't come down in your pajamas?" I raise a hand. "I'm sorry if I'm being nosy. I'm disastrously curious, which you may already know."

Bodyguards talk. Of course workplace gossip exists, and security's workplace is me and my family. Plus, Thatcher knew the names of all my cats when he wasn't even *on* my detail.

That fact alone is highly attractive. And it means that he's paid attention to my life before being assigned to protect me.

Thatcher cups his hands together, elbows to his thighs. "You're fine, Jane." He takes a short beat. "It's inappropriate for me to be around you in anything that I wouldn't wear on-duty."

Interesting. I lean forward some. "But you'll be on a tour bus with SFO and my cousins and brothers soon, so the lines will inevitably blur?"

He never flinches. "SFO will maintain professionalism while we're in close quarters with our clients. We're having a security meeting before your parents arrive to discuss these details." He's not a buddy-guard. He's not about to fist-bump me or lounge on the couch beside me.

I understand.

"Right," I breathe, and I tie my hair back in a pony, warmer all of a sudden. "Professionalism is important to you?"

He runs a hand over his mouth, nodding.

I tense, unable to read him. The air thickens with a new sort of heat. "I respect that. Very much."

"I appreciate it." His husky voice might as well rake hot coals over my body.

I've been trying not to notice how physically handsome Thatcher is, but he exudes powerful masculinity just *sitting*. As though he could lift me up in his arms and carry me to heaven. Somewhere safe and beautiful.

I clear my throat. "If you're tired, we can make this quick."

"I'm awake," Thatcher says. "And it doesn't have to be quick. I want to make sure we're squared away before we leave the lake house." He starts to reach a hand towards me, and my shoulders arch. I eye him in curiosity.

What's he about to do?

Thatcher suddenly goes still, his hand a couple inches from me. "Can I?" He nods to the purple paper.

"Oh…yes. Yes, of course." I lift my hands off my lap, and he takes the stationery paper. *He wants the notes, Jane. Not to touch you in carnal ways.*

Which would be too orgasmically good to be anything other than a fantasy. And we've just solidified what we are to one another.

Professional.

Respectful.

Bodyguard and client.

I lace my fingers together. "My handwriting can be illegible, so I'd be happy to type out the list for you."

He concentrates on the notes. "I can read your handwriting."

I can't help but smile. "You must be able to read all chicken scratch."

"No," he says, multitasking well by talking to me and doing his job. "It took practice to read yours."

Fact: *Thatcher Moretti taught himself to decipher my handwriting.* He didn't have to do that. My old retired bodyguard never did.

My pulse skips. "You know," I say, thinking aloud, "I've known *of* you since I was seventeen."

He looks up at me.

"Which you already know," I add quickly, flush creeping up my neck. "Because that's when we met. I was seventeen…" Oh my God, why am I repeating this fact? "And you were twenty-two. Now you're twenty-seven." I waft my pajama top away from my sweating breasts. "You look older, very much a strong…twenty-seven."

Shut up, Jane.

He sees that I've stopped talking. "Jane—"

"How does this work exactly?" And there goes my big mouth cutting off my new bodyguard after I just word vomited all over him. "I've never had *two* 24/7 bodyguards before, though I know this is just temporary. You're temporary, I mean." I shake out my jumbled thoughts. "I mean, you and I—we're temporary."

I'm rarely this flustered, and I'm breathing heavily.

Too heavily.

Thatcher stays quiet for another second, which helps ease me a little. I take a few more breaths.

He keeps his eyes on mine. "I'm working alongside Quinn, so if you need anything, you can come to either him or me."

Thankfully he skipped over my extraneous ramblings. "Merci." I pause. "Do you know French?"

He returns to the notes. "I'm trying to learn, but I can't promise I'll be able to pick up more than simple phrases."

"It's okay if you aren't fluent. I don't mind translating whatever you need."

He nods, scanning the notes again. "Do you have a preference on who drives?"

I scoot forward a little. "That depends. Would you consider yourself a good driver?"

I swear he almost smiles. "Yeah."

My lips rise. His one word answer carries so much confidence. "Then I'd prefer we switch off on driving."

Thatcher nods. "Copy that." We discuss several more of the preferences I listed out. Mostly how I react towards fans, crowds, and security at home—which is really *the bus*.

"I might grab onto your back in large crowds," I warn him.

"That's what I'm there for." Thatcher looks over at me. "If there are hostile threats, I'll need to touch you. Are you okay with that?"

"Yes." *I'm more than okay with that.* I swallow a knot in my throat, trying not to pulse between my legs. I cross my ankles instead. "So...I think that's it?"

He pockets the paper.

I rise.

He stands so much taller.

I look up, and I just realize something...I realize it out loud. "This is actually the very first time we've been alone together." The air pulls deathly taut.

Thatcher hardly blinks.

My breath shallows. "I'm..." I shake my head, scrambling for more words.

"Are you alright being alone with me?" Lines crease his forehead.

I whisper, "I am." I know it'll happen ten times as much now that he's on my detail. "You...make me feel very comfortable." I open my mouth to say more, but a yawn fights its way forward, and I cough into my palm.

He nods, arms crossed, then he uncrosses them to click his mic. "Keep your eyes on the weather." One pause. "Roger." He stares down at me. "You should get some sleep. I think we're good for when we push out."

I take a few steps back towards the staircase. He watches me go, and once I reach the banister, I mime a tip of a top hat. "À la prochaine," I tell him. "It means *until next time*."

His face is all hard, professional lines. Caged of emotion, but he doesn't look away either. He nods and says, "Goodnight, Jane."

Until next time. With our boundaries cemented and solidified and permanently set.

1

Jane Cobalt

"YOU'RE GIVING ME TOO much, honey," Thatcher tells me, completely serious like I've bought him a Rolls-Royce and diamond-encrusted watch.

I have the means to gift both to my new boyfriend, who is also my *ex*-bodyguard, but I actually haven't purchased anything extravagant for Thatcher yet. That's not what's happening here.

I stand absolutely confused in my bedroom, and his quiet, bold dominance bears down on me. Reminding me that he's a former Marine, he's twenty-eight to my twenty-three, and he carries the severity and focus of an experienced leader. Despite not being on my detail anymore, Thatcher Moretti still looks at me like his sole mission is to shield me and ground me and build a fortress of peace around me.

It's one of the greatest feelings I've ever felt. His love is raw, bottomless safety that deserves as much as I can give in return.

But he's already rejecting the little, infinitesimal, bitty *nothing* I've offered.

I frown at the closet, then at him. "You think this is too much?"

"Yeah, it is." His strong arms are crossed, not in defense. It's just his usual sturdy posture.

My flannel pajamas heat up my body, along with the growing pile of pastel blouses, cheetah vests, and tulle skirts I'm hugging. Hangers still attached to the clothes.

"I've only cleared out 30% of the closet," I tell him, "and you're allowed 50% now that we're living together."

Thatcher rubs a hand across his mouth, and we seem to glance at his duffel bag at the same time. His packed belongings are propped against my nightstand. Ophelia, my white cat, sniffs the bag while my two hyperactive calicos scamper around our heels.

It's sinking in, for us both. How my room is now *our* room.

We've only been an official couple for two days. Just two, and he's already moving in with me. But if I calculate our time spent fake-dating in public, we've been together for much longer.

Yesterday was Thatcher's last night in security's townhouse, and only a half hour ago, he came into my room and threw his duffel bag down.

Our gazes return to each other, and he says, "I don't even need 20% of the closet."

My face falls at that microscopic number. "I'm most surely giving you more than 20%. I don't have a dresser for you to put anything in." I only have room for my vanity, and when I offered to donate the vanity and buy a dresser, he also said *no*.

"That's fine. I don't need a dresser." Thatcher takes a few of my blouses from my arms and places them back into the disorderly closet.

"Wait, Thatcher," I say before he grabs more clothes out of my hold.

His hard gaze fixes on me. "I grew up with one drawer, then I lived out of a fucking rucksack. I don't even have enough shit for 15% of that closet."

My eyes widen. "Stop decreasing your percentage."

His lips almost lift. "Jane—"

"The fact that you've lived out of a single drawer, then a bag for most of your life is precisely why you deserve the whole closet. At least let me give you 50%."

Thatcher is about to shake his head.

"It's imperative," I add.

He brushes a hand across his unshaven jaw. Carpenter swats at a hanging tassel near my hips, cutting into our talk. Thatcher picks him up under his furry belly and places him on the nearby vanity.

I notice how Thatcher eyes the zebra-print notebook on my pink bedspread. He's been far more interested in that notebook than unpacking.

Protecting me is still a priority of his, even if he's not allowed to be my bodyguard.

From a few feet away, my gaze traces the beautiful gold horns of his cornic', the necklace resting against his shirtless chest. Natural hair tracks down his muscles and draws my eyes lower.

To his sculpted abs and V-line, even lower—to his gray drawstring pants and the outline of his...*large* cock. I linger on his bulge, and an awkward amount of silence passes.

"Um..." I look up, his attention already on me, but he's relatively stoic.

My cheeks blaze. Thatcher catching me staring shouldn't cause any sort of red-hot flush (he's already been inside of me) but I'm set to broil.

I smooth my lips together and then clarify, "It's distracting." *Why am I clarifying at all?* Hands full, I nod to his package. "Your dick." *End this quickly, Jane.* "You're big, which you know—we both know." Oh my God.

He goes to speak, and I cut him off, "It's just that you're not wearing boxer-briefs." He's my boyfriend; I shouldn't be this flustered around him anymore.

Thatcher nods, looking me over from head-to-toe. "I almost never wear them with drawstring pants."

"And the fabric is thin," I add for some reason.

I swear a smile is in his eyes. But then he leaves my side and goes to his duffel.

I study him more curiously. "What are you doing?"

He crouches down and glances back at me. "Getting dressed."

"You don't have to." I adjust the clothes in my arms, a hanger poking my small boob. "I like this quite a lot." My heartbeat flutters a mile a minute. "Seeing you in pajamas just reminds me that you're here in the early morning and not for security reasons or *secrecy*."

He's here because he's truly with me, and the world and the security team and our families know we're really romantically together. Some learned more recently than others.

Not all are thrilled, to say the least.

Still squatting, Thatcher rests a forearm on his knee. "You can't even know how much I want to be here with you." He skims my features from afar, as though tomorrow I could disappear and he needs me in his mind for a second more. "But I'm not gonna be a distraction for either of us." His South Philly lilt fights through, and he digs for clothes in his duffel.

A smile tugs my cheeks. "I distracted you?" His seriousness draws me closer to the bed.

Thatcher grabs a pair of boxer-briefs and slacks, then he rises to a commanding stance. "The longer you stare at my cock, the more I want to push inside of you."

My hip knocks into my bedpost. I ache for him to lift me in his arms, to *fill* me. I'm tempted to drop my clothes and step into his towering build. "Why don't you then?"

"Because you're not a normal girl." He pulls off his drawstring pants, no hesitation or pause. His naked, muscular body resembles epic warriors in fantasy novels, and somehow he's *my* protector—and so much more. I expect him to come forward and hoist me up, but he steps into his boxer-briefs.

I draw forward. "What does that mean exactly?"

"It means you have a recent unknown threat who broke into your townhouse, a new bodyguard who acts like he's a descendant of Hercules but is more like a fucking Potato Head, and you're supposed to be giving him your preference notes this morning. Which you haven't finished yet." He lifts the elastic band to his waist, then picks up his slacks. "You need someone to have your six right now. Putting my cock in your pussy pretty much hinders that."

I love him.

The sudden abrupt feeling wells up inside of me like a balloon filling with helium. Followed closely by bubbling fear. My pulse skips.

I readjust my grip on my clothes again. "You realize I'm more used to the sexual aspect of a relationship—seeing as how I've only had friends-with-benefits." My voice drops to a whisper. "Anything else is entirely new to me."

Thatcher nods. "I know." He puts on his black slacks. "If it means anything, it's not like I've dated an American princess before."

I nod back.

But it's not exactly the newness of a relationship that scares me. I'm frightened of loving a man to an overwhelming degree—to where I'd *need* to be loved by Thatcher. Necessity is life, and I'm afraid to need his love like I need air.

I can't tell him this. I can't say, *Oh, Thatcher, I'd rather only fall mid-deep in love with you because I don't want to need your love like water in the Sahara.* Part of me longs to feel that un-reversible depth of emotion with him, but the other part resists completely.

Regardless, I need to prioritize and focus on what's in front of me—*no*, not his dick. But rather his luggage and the closet. I toss the armful of clothes on my pink duvet. Pastel blouses land in a wrinkled heap.

A worn library copy of *The Outsiders* peeks from his unzipped duffel. I've already asked Thatcher about the book—not just because it looks like it was due back to the library eons ago—but because Thatcher has admitted more than once that he's not a big reader.

What I know: the book belonged to Skylar Moretti.

Thatcher's older brother would read it every night, and in the end, he never returned it to the school library. Skylar's name is even still scribbled on the card inside the flap.

The bigger fact: the book is Thatcher's only possession of Skylar's, besides his cornic'.

Thatcher buttons his pants. "I'm putting my duffel under your bed. All of your clothes can go back in the closet."

I crinkle my brows. "You're not living out of a *bag*."

"It doesn't bother me—"

"It bothers me," I rebut. "Greatly." I think quickly while he sidles next to me. "So you'd prefer not to unpack? Would you rather live somewhere else?"

"Hell no." Skin pleats his forehead. "I already said I want to be here." More strongly, he emphasizes, "I want to live with you, Jane."

I nod, believing him. But we're both still frowning, and I hear his voice from before saying, *you're not a normal girl.* "Are you trying to give me the whole closet because I'm obscenely wealthy—because you think I'm used to this humongous amount of space and need it?"

I did grow up in a mansion that is regal enough to be a modern-day American castle. But I've lived in this modest townhouse for four years, and I've loved every minute here.

Thatcher stares into me. "No. I wouldn't want any girlfriend of mine, rich or fucking poor, to shove her clothes under a bed to make room for me."

I hate that I almost smile, and I hate how my heart swells. He makes me feel…doted on. It feels quite nice, and it shouldn't. Because he can't give me everything while I give him *nothing.* My parents are equal to each other in every measure of their lives.

It's what I saw growing up.

It's what I know works. It's been proven to succeed.

So I have to stand by my decision, and I tug a frilly purple blouse off a hanger. "I'm not putting this back." I fold the blouse very messily. *It'll do.* As soon as I set it down, my boyfriend picks it up. "Thatcher—" I cut myself off. Because he's not slipping the frilly sleeves onto a hanger so it can be returned to the closet.

He refolds the blouse into a much neater square.

Our gazes meet, and he says, "Don't take out more than this."

He's accepting 10% of the closet. Far less than I wanted for him, but I suppose it'll have to be enough for now.

I extend my palm. "You have a deal."

Light touches his stern eyes, and his large hand engulfs mine as we shake.

We don't let go.

In a quiet moment, his other hand finds the small of my back, and Thatcher dips his head down so slowly...

Our lips collide in a scalding, sensual kiss that melds me against his chest. I rise on the tips of my toes. Electricity spindles up my limbs, from each toe to my head. My fingers descend to his ass, and his tongue parts my lips. *Yes.*

A high-pitched noise tickles my throat, and his hand slips beneath my flannel top. Scorching my skin. We are overflowing magma. Heat gathers, and our bodies scream blistered pleas for skin-on-skin contact *everywhere.*

And then, he breaks the deep kiss, his forehead nearly pressed to mine, and I scrounge my lungs for lost breath.

"You're..." I breathe hard, words scattering into oblivion. *You're very good at kissing and very good at stopping. You're more and everything.*

He straightens up, resting a hand on top of my head. Our eyes still hot on each other. I eagerly search his gaze, and he tells me, "We're still kerosene."

Flammable.

Combustible.

I smile. "Sounds disastrously right."

He kisses my temple, and we work together to sort through our clothes. He unpacks and slips his button-downs on hangers that I remove from vests and blouses.

"I called the Tri-Force earlier this morning," I admit.

His gaze tightens. "About Tony?"

"Oui." Twenty-eight-year-old Tony Ramella is unfortunately my new 24/7 bodyguard.

And it's not everyday I speak with the Tri-Force: Price Kepler of Alpha, Akara Kitsuwon of Omega, and Jon Sinclair of Epsilon. The three leads are essentially Thatcher's superiors. My four-way phone call with them didn't last long, but it felt necessary.

I pass him a hanger. "I thought if I requested Tony to be transferred *elsewhere*, they'd be more open to the idea."

Thatcher shakes his head, already knowing they wouldn't be. He used to be a lead, so he would have a very good read on the Tri-Force. But I had to see if I could do something more to change this situation.

I turn more to his chest and look up. "It's not right that they listened to Beckett's request for Donnelly to be transferred. But yet, when I ask for one, they say, *give Tony a chance.*"

My brother has been secretly using cocaine, and once he heard about Donnelly's family history with drugs, Beckett decided to have him moved. Quitting his drug use to keep Donnelly around wasn't an option, apparently.

Thatcher rakes a hand through his disheveled brown hair. "Donnelly has been with Beckett for a long time. Tony hasn't been with you for even a day yet. In their heads, that's the difference."

I consider this. Softly, I say, "I still wish Price would take my unease into account."

He nods a few times. "I do too." He stares off for a split-second, then focuses back on me. "You know since Tony is my stepmom's brother, Price thinks my issue with him is just some family horseshit that's affecting a client."

And I'm not supposed to be aware of feuds in security.

I'm supposed to just be an heiress to a billion-dollar empire, and he's supposed to only be a bodyguard, one hired to protect my family.

But now that he's more to me, the curtains inside the security team have been pulled back, and I can see the in-fighting and the unprofessional conflicts that the Tri-Force would rather stay hidden.

We stare deeper at each other, more knowingly. We both *know* that part of my unease does stem from his feelings.

You see, bad blood seeps between Thatcher and Tony, originating from adolescence, and I can picture this darkness crawling and festering while Tony is on my detail. Not to mention, his pompous personality is particularly grating to be around.

Thatcher adds, "It shouldn't matter why you feel uncomfortable, just that you *feel* uncomfortable at all. That's enough. In any other circumstance, it *would* be enough for a transfer, and it's my fault it's not."

"You're not to blame," I defend.

"I fucked them, Jane," Thatcher says strongly. "Price is punishing me—"

"Precisely," I interject. "Price is the one who's not taking my feelings into account."

Heavy silence drops.

His features are grave. "Price took that action because of what I did. I'm not telling you who to blame, but I have to accept my part in this."

I study him and his solid, unwavering self-assurance. Thatcher is used to trekking forward with weight. He's always quick to carry ownership for the team's decisions and mistakes like it's just what should happen. Like "strapping on blame" is included in a morning routine, right after making the bed and brushing your teeth.

I realize it's engrained in his DNA the same way that rallying at someone's side with blades and armor is written in mine.

"Okay," I nod. "I asked the Tri-Force how long of a chance I'm supposed to give Tony."

Thatcher keeps his protective gaze on me while he hangs up his last black button-down.

"They said he could be on a two-month probationary period with me, and afterwards we'd reassess to see if it'd work long-term."

Thatcher narrows his eyes and walks to the closet, hanging up his clothes. "I don't want you to feel like you're trapped. If Tony does something out of bounds, the Tri-Force would cut the two-months shorter." His jaw clenches at that thought, and he returns to the bed, his stride incredibly strict.

The idea that something "out of bounds" could happen is disconcerting. I try not to cringe. Thatcher went to high school with Tony, so he knows him better than I do.

"Has Tony ever made an unwanted pass at a girl before?" I ask.

"No," he says sternly. "...not as far as I know." His red-hot gaze pins on the wall. "I would've already broken his hands if he did."

I store our folded clothes in a plastic bin, which Walrus promptly hops into. I smile, a small one, and I lightly bop his wet nose with my fingertip. "So what we do know about Tony: he's obtuse, he can't tell you and Banks apart, and he's capable of having sex with another man's girlfriend."

Evidence: he slept with Thatcher's high school girlfriend.

I continue, "That alone makes him an awful person and a prick." I pause. "Anything else pertinent?"

He shakes his head, neck stiff. "Banks would tell you Tony mostly just spews shit without thinking." He grabs my notebook off the bed, and we both check the clock on the nightstand.

I'm supposed to be at security's townhouse by 8:00 a.m., just to briefly go over my notes with Tony since he's new to my detail. I still have time, but if I'm late, I worry he'll show up in my living room unannounced.

Thatcher meets my gaze. "Can I check your preference notes?"

I nod. "But I don't have a lot written yet. I wasn't sure how specific I should be."

"I can help you." He flips open the spiral notebook, his severe focus like a loaded gun. Deadly when needed.

Thatcher is my most powerful catnip. I'm transfixed to him, all the while dazedly placing my bin, with Walrus, under the bed.

He stops on the right page. "You'll need to type this out and either email him or print it. He can't read your handwriting."

My stomach twists. "...I forgot he couldn't." I've been so spoiled having Thatcher, who made a huge effort when he started on my detail. Learning to read my illegible handwriting and all. "I might as well type it now."

I take a seat on the edge of my bed and open my phone's notes app. Thatcher remains standing, reading my list, and his brows pull together. "Jane." He says my name with intensity.

"What's wrong?"

"Your number three." His shoulder muscles pull taut. "You wrote: *do not touch me under any circumstance.*"

I sit pin straight. "It's called a preference list. I *prefer* that Tony doesn't touch me." I cringe picturing his hands even hovering near my body.

"He's your bodyguard, honey."

"I don't know him."

Thatcher seizes my gaze, much harder to read. "You didn't know me, and you still trusted me to touch you."

My eyes burn, hearing Thatcher relate himself to Tony.

Thatcher might be all stoic, hard lines, but I know he wouldn't push me into another man's arms. I can't let fear or insecurity distort his intentions. *I can't.* He's just trying to rebuild trust between me and my new bodyguard—someone he can't stand. It slices a knife through my lungs.

Very quietly, I ask, "Is this as hard for you as it is me?"

His nose flares. "I'd rather be chugging battery acid."

"Pass the jug," I quip.

His lip almost rises, but seriousness darkens his features. "Under certain circumstances, your bodyguard will need to put their hands on you."

I wince.

He squats so he's eye-level with me. "He won't hurt you. All seven of us on Omega are triple-checking Tony when it comes to you and your family."

"I'm not afraid of Tony. The things he says just make my skin crawl, which is my number six." I point to the notebook.

Thatcher glances at the page. "*Six, do not converse with me.*"

"I'm covering my bases," I tell him.

"You need to uncover number three."

"Is it so terribly necessary that Tony touches me?"

"He can't protect you if you don't let him." Thatcher cups my cheek, and I can practically hear my heavy heartbeat. He tells me, "There'll be times where you have to rely on Tony. I can't be with you when I'm on-duty protecting Xander, and you're not always going to be around Banks, Maximoff, and Farrow." He trusts them to look out for me when he can't. "Your safety is what matters. Above everything."

I loosen my grip on my phone. "What if I request *minimal* touch? Only when absolutely necessary?"

Thatcher nods once. "That works." He stands up, his hand never leaving my cheek, and he places a knee on the mattress.

My phone lights up next to his knee and buzzes on the duvet. A text message blinks on the screen, but it isn't from Tony.

Your mom and I are on our way. We need to talk. — Dad

2

Thatcher Moretti

THIS IS A WEIRD position to be in. Days ago, Connor Cobalt and Rose Calloway knew me as a professional, stringent bodyguard. Nothing more.

Today, I'm the man that's been dating their daughter.

Flipping that switch isn't just turning on and off the lights. It's going from pitch-black darkness to a neon-fluorescent disco.

I've been mentally preparing to face two pissed-off parents just looking out for their kid. Hell, if I had a daughter, I'd probably lay into the fuckbag who secretly hid their relationship from me. Sneaking around—not a great look to impress the parents.

I just want to make it right.

Unfuck this fucked situation and start on solid ground.

But I'm standing in front of Connor Cobalt—a man who literally was on the cover of *Forbes* this month—and I realize that anything I say could bury me deeper.

The fridge hums, ice machine gurgling in tense silence. The cramped kitchen feels more compact with another man over six-feet here. But I have three-inches on Connor.

And still, I don't think a single person could walk in this room and tell.

Jane's dad stands like he owns the world. Expensive slacks and navy-blue button-down, a Cartier watch on his wrist that probably costs more than my uncle's row house. He has billion-dollar energy that screams *I'm better than you.*

Arrogant.

Poised. All the way down to the look in his eyes and posture. How he leans back against the cabinets, hands casually careened on the counter.

In the past, in a professional setting—conversing over security matters—Connor has been approachable and easy-going. But I understand he's no less deadly than the woman he married. The only difference is that Rose shows you her dagger, and he keeps his behind his back.

Silence mounts.

I'm in foreign territory, but it wouldn't be the first time. I check on Jane. On instinct. I glance through the kitchen archway and see her on the pink loveseat, talking quietly to her mom. Jane catches my eyes and gives me an encouraging nod.

"Do you want to offer me a drink?" Connor asks, pulling my attention. "Water, lemonade, bourbon? You live here now, so I'm to assume you can act as a host."

Fuck all things to hell. I nod towards the fridge. "Would you like a drink?" I ask. "I can get whatever you want."

"Not right now. But I appreciate the offer, even delayed and obviously coerced."

He's not going to make this easy.

That's fine. I can shovel myself out of the grave I'm in, and I add, because I think it's an important detail, "I've only been living here for less than an hour, sir."

Connor doesn't even pause. "You've been sleeping with her for much longer than an hour."

Holy fuck.

My features harden to stone.

I knew he'd run me over the fucking coals, but I didn't think he'd do the job so bluntly and without hesitation. "Yeah," I say, not denying that fact. "It's been consensual."

"I know," Connor says. "You'd already be in jail if it weren't." He says the words casually, like this is everyday conversation. Somehow, his calm tone sounds more threatening than if he were screaming in my face.

"And I would want the same thing," I say and then shake my head. "That's not true, actually."

Connor tilts his head, but his stare is blank. "You wouldn't want someone who forced themselves on Jane to be put in jail?"

"No, I wouldn't." My voice is deep and assured. "I'd want them dead." I'd also like to be the one to carry out the murder, but I don't add that fact. I'm not sure Connor would appreciate how easily I could kill someone, even if it'd be for Jane.

Connor sizes me up for a second. "Coffee?" He's the one who moves to the pot and starts pouring liquid in a pastel pink mug.

He hands me a cup.

"I can get yours," I tell him, but he's already filling up another one.

My grandma is at home clucking her tongue in disapproval. I should be feeding a guest, not making them do all the fucking work.

I'm an assertive man, but something about Connor is slowing my reflexes.

He raises his cup to his mouth. "Jane is many things, but I would never call her irrational nor spontaneous. So when she told us that her boyfriend of—" he gives me a look "—how long have you two been together?"

My hand tightens on my mug. "I can't calculate an exact number."

He arches a single brow. "You can't?"

I hold his gaze.

In my head, Jane and I didn't wake up one morning and decide that our fake relationship was real. It was gradual, and the feelings inside the fake-dating op were never fabricated. But Jane was slow to let me in, and she'd say that we were "pals who fuck" for most of that time.

The technical answer is two days ago.

The answer I feel is more ambiguous, and both are wrong ones to tell her dad.

Make a decision, Thatcher. Steam billows from my cup and heats my face.

"It's felt like a long time," I say.

"Feelings tend to blur rationality." He rests an elbow back. "Since Jane seems to care a great deal for you, let's say that you two officially became a couple when you started sleeping together. That would be when?" He takes a sip from his coffee.

"Over a month ago."

"Four months?"

"No."

"Three?"

I shake my head. "Less than that. Just…over a month"

He inspects his coffee, then me. "Let's *also* consider that you were her bodyguard and around my daughter for longer periods throughout a day. That increases the value of time you've spent together. So we'll round up 'over one month' to three months." He sets his mug on the counter behind him. "So when Jane told us her boyfriend of *three months* was moving in with her, I thought it was fast. What do you think?"

It's not slow.

Don't fucking say that, Thatcher.

"It's the speed that works for us, sir."

"But you didn't think to wait to move in until you met her parents or told her siblings you were dating their sister."

No.

Because I'm apparently really damn good at moving out of order. I grind down on my teeth. "Respectfully, sir, I'm not going to apologize for following my heart. And Jane was just following hers."

His unreadable expression puts me on edge. He stands straighter and grabs his coffee. "You remind me of someone."

Before I can ask who, Rose slips into the kitchen. Black dress. Black nail polish. Diamond earrings and the coldest, piercing glare in her yellow-green eyes. Rose Calloway's reputation of being an Ice Queen runs throughout the world, but among the security team, bodyguards know the warmest thing about Rose is the love she has for her family.

That extends, most especially, to her oldest daughter.

Jane squeezes into the archway with wide-eyes. No room in the kitchen.

I'd like to believe I'm handling myself fine.

Rose gives me a long once-over. "You're still alive, so I take it Richard didn't do a good job annihilating you. Did he tell you that you're moving too fast?"

Jane's mouth drops. "Mom."

I nod. "Yes—" I stop myself from saying "ma'am" because Rose has always requested security not to call her that. "Connor did tell me we're moving fast."

Rose eyes me. "Did he tell you that your cock will be on the end of a skewer, if you so much as hurt a hair on her head?"

Jane mutters, "Oh my God." She mouths to me, *I'm so sorry.*

I shake my head, telling her it's okay. I'd be more upset if her parents didn't love her. To Rose, I say, "We didn't get to that yet." *That,* as in cock-skewering.

"And we never will," Connor says. "Hyperboles are your affliction, darling."

Rose purses her lips. "Affliction? I think you mean *gift.* Talent."

He grins. "I meant what I said, but if you need more synonyms for talent, I can also provide those."

She lets out a frustrated growl and her yellow-green eyes land back on me. "Look at these, please." She passes me the photo album.

"Don't do it," Jane tells me. "It's a terrible, awful trick."

Rose rolls her eyes. "Gremlin, I'm not tricking your boyfriend." She waves me on, and Connor extends his coffee to his wife.

Jane puts her hands to her eyes, scissoring her fingers to see me.

Can't be that bad if she's not stealing the thing out of my grip.

The title on the photo album reads: *The Evolution of Jane Eleanor Cobalt's Style.* I flip open the hefty album and realize it's a scrapbook. Neatly organized with patterned paper and cursive handwriting.

Each photo is of Jane.

Most when she's just a toddler. I almost smile. Her style is still as Pepto-Bismol pink, mint-green and mind-boggling eccentric in the past as it is today. Bold. Colorful. But I can't miss the blatant photos of tear-streaked Jane. Sobbing in the bathroom. *Actually…*

I keep flipping.

A lot of them are of her crying.

I narrow a look on Jane in the kitchen. Her hands have dropped to her side, and she smiles. "I was a fussy toddler."

Rose sips her coffee. "You had the loudest cry. It was earsplitting. Look at those photos and remember that all babies cry. They will wake you up at odd hours of the night. They are not cute little squishy things. They are menaces." Her fiery glare drills into me. "So when you're thinking about having unprotected sex with my daughter, remember these photos."

"Oh…God, *Mom.*" Jane's eyes are full orbs. "He's not going to think about me as a *four-year-old* right before we're about to have sex!"

Not that I need to mention the fucking obvious, but I agree with Jane.

"We don't need to bring God into this conversation," Connor says calmly.

Rose skips over Connor's statement. "If Thatcher wants to keep his life, he will be thinking about that scrapbook." She points to the album, still in my hands. "Page seventeen."

I flip to the page. Another crying photo of Jane. This time she's in her childhood home and at the foot of her bed. Face beet-red and mouth in an opened scream. She was a cute kid—even crying. My lips begin to really lift.

"Why are you smiling?" Rose snaps at me.

My mouth flattens. "Because I think my girlfriend's baby pictures are cute."

Jane brightens like radiant sunlight.

Rose nods strongly. "She was a very cute baby." She squints at me like I'm up to some alleyway, goblin-sniffling plot, and I'm not.

Hopefully one day she'll see me as a straight shooter.

"Dramatics and props aside," Connor says, focused on me. "You need to keep our daughter safe. Your job is to protect her from the person she's sleeping with, and since that man is now you, you have a bigger responsibility to Jane." He's talking like I'm still on her detail.

"I'm not her bodyguard anymore, sir."

"Last time I checked, you also weren't her bodyguard when she was choked in her own bedroom. But now you are her boyfriend."

The kitchen sobers at his words.

My jaw tics, muscles flexed, and a blood-red fire burns in my veins. I hate thinking about what happened to Jane. I was just an Epsilon lead at the time of the *Chokehold Incident*, and I had enough power to erect more protections but not enough to actually talk to Jane, to ensure that she was okay.

"I would never hurt her," I say strongly.

"You're six-seven."

"I know."

"She's five-seven. And if you choose to prioritize yourself over her during intercourse, she could get hurt in an instant, and I wouldn't call that an accident."

Him referring to sex as intercourse doesn't make this interaction any better. Jane is wincing, but she doesn't seem surprised. Her family is open about sex.

Common knowledge.

"I know," I tell him, not shying. "But I've been six-seven all of my adult life, and there's not a single time I don't think about the power I have in bed. Her safety is always on my mind. In every aspect of our relationship. Especially when we're sleeping together."

"This is true," Jane says like this is a business meeting. "I can confirm, but I'd like to keep the details of it private. Thank you."

Connor and Rose smile, clearly in admiration of their daughter.

This conversation is easier with Jane here. Maybe because she glances at me and gives me a small, reassuring smile. One that pushes me to say more.

"If something happened to Jane and it were my fault," I tell them, "I don't know if I could live with myself."

And that's just the honest truth.

Silence blisters.

Rose flips her shiny brown hair off her shoulder. "I'm going to try to believe you, even though you've given me no reason to. Which is really your own fault for breaking our trust before you've even built it."

I nod. "I appreciate you hearing me out, Rose."

She spins on her heels to Jane. "The holidays are going to come and go before you know it, and if you still want a job I might have another assistant position at Calloway Couture—"

"No, no, no." Jane raises her hands. "I am retired from fashion design. I'm still certain it's just not in my blood."

Good call, honey.

"That is both tragic and wonderful all at the same time." Rose rests a hand on her hip. "What are you going to do then?"

Jane takes a deep, measured breath. "I don't have a passion. I've run out of time to find one, so by the New Year I was thinking…" She turns to her dad. "Is there still an opening in the financial department at Cobalt Inc.?"

Connor cocks his head. "You still think you're running out of time?"

"Yes, I'm *still* jobless and twenty-three."

Connor softens his gaze on his daughter. "I'll look into it, but I can't make you any promises, mon coeur."

She smiles. "I wouldn't want you to."

Rose plucks a buzzing phone out of her Chanel purse. "Your Aunt Lily is calling. I have to take this." She struts off, heels clacking on the floorboards. "No, I'm not doing another bake sale for that school. They've insulted my baked goods enough." She pauses. "Yes, they were from Whole Foods. That's not the point."

Connor says a short goodbye to me, and then speaks in French to Jane. Something that downturns her lips before he follows his wife out.

Jane stares dejectedly at the sink.

Maybe I shouldn't ask—but I do anyway. "What'd your dad say?"

She takes a shallow breath. "He said you're not invited to Wednesday Night Dinner. Not yet."

3

Jane Cobalt

"SOMETHING HAPPENED?" Maximoff scrunches his face at me while he enters the townhouse from the garage, a towel around his waist, pool water still dripping from his dark brown hair.

Farrow kicks the door behind them, carrying two bags of Chinese takeout.

I've been ever-so-innocently brushing Toodles near the rocking chair. But I must be staring off into space more than usual. Recounting what occurred this morning.

"Is it Tony?" Moffy asks, already glaring at the adjoining townhouse door. Where security lives.

I did give Tony my preference list, but luckily, I skirted out of the interaction before I had to stare at his smug face for long. And Thatcher was with me.

Farrow raises his brows at Moffy. "I thought you didn't 'hate' Tony." He uses air-quotes.

Moffy gestures to the door. "If he hurts Jane, I'm going to *more than* hate him."

I already know that Farrow isn't a Tony fan.

You see, all of SFO hates Tony after he let Xander Hale participate in a pseudo boxing match at the Halloween party. They believe he should've intervened and pulled my fifteen-year-old cousin to safety.

Of course I wish he had, but Moffy and I—we can't blame bodyguards for our mistakes. There is immense guilt in doing so. The security team is our safety net, but they can't be our scapegoat or moral conscience.

Xander asked to fight, so we can't pin fault on Tony for being "hands off" at my cousin's request. It's why our parents still believe he's an asset to the team. He's just not the right fit for Xander.

Farrow and Thatcher know the complexities behind our feelings—why Moffy can't hate Tony for those recent events. And why I can't either.

"It wasn't Tony," I tell Moffy. "My mom and dad were here this morning." I stroke my cat's tuxedo fur. "It was as frightening as expected."

Moffy gives me an empathetic wince. "That bad?"

Farrow has a boot on the chair. "Moretti is still alive." He eyes Thatcher who leaves the kitchen, carrying kibble in little cat bowls. Walrus and Carpenter make a mad dash to him, jumping at his calves.

"It wasn't that bad," Thatcher says seriously.

Curiosity pools, and I bow forward like he is gravity, a magnetic pull—all things that wrench me to him. "You really weren't scared when my dad started talking about how you're six-seven and could hurt me while we're having sex?"

Farrow almost chokes on a bite of Lo Mein.

Maximoff laughs like he just beat his fiancé at Rock 'Em Sock 'Em Robots.

The best (and quite frankly, sexiest) part: Thatcher is unperturbed and unflustered by the tiny grenade I flung. "No," he tells me. "I wasn't scared."

I help him fill water bowls for the cats. "You think it went well then?" I wonder.

He glances at me, before wiping up a small spill. "Better than I thought it would."

But he's still not invited to Wednesday Night Dinner, and I can only hope my family welcomes him into the fold. I don't want my boyfriend to feel ostracized.

"Jane," Farrow says after a swig of water. "Maximoff has something to ask you."

"You do?" I cap a water jug near the unlit fireplace.

Moffy gives him a tough look. "I thought you said after dinner?"

"Now's good too." Farrow is completely at ease.

And Maximoff is a rigid statue.

Farrow lifts his brows. "See, that's called changing your mind."

He shakes his head. "No idea what you're talking about. Changing your mind? Is that like a thing people do?"

Farrow smiles from cheek-to-cheek. "Okay, smartass."

Maximoff tightens the towel around his waist and runs a hand through his thick hair. I'm more concerned that this is *bad* news, and I hug the water jug.

"Do I need to sit?" I wonder.

He swallows. "No—sure. Maybe. I don't know."

Farrow looks him over. "Take a breath, wolf scout."

Maximoff glares instead.

Farrow almost laughs. "That's not how you breathe, but nice try."

"I'll sit." I lower on the rocking chair, swaying a little when my butt hits the seat.

Thatcher almost steals my full attention. He's *brushing* Ophelia, and my white cat is absolute mush on the floor.

Yes, Ophelia, he has that affect on me too. I know the feeling deeply well.

"Janie," Moffy calls.

I realize that Thatcher did indeed steal *all* of my attention. I flush and focus on my best friend. "Yes, old chap."

"I trust you with my whole life," Maximoff tells me.

The fact warms me completely, but I'm also on the edge of a cliff. "I trust you with mine too."

He licks his lips. "As you know, I'm getting married, and the amount of people I trust to have their hands in the wedding is pretty much... not a lot. And when I think about who I want to remember being involved in this whole process, I always think of you first."

I start to smile.

"So...what I'm trying to ask... is if you could...would you want to...?" He stumbles on his words, and it isn't often that he does.

My smile fades.

Farrow glances between me and Maximoff worriedly. Mostly because we can all sense Moffy's nerves.

"You can ask me," I say softly, having a small guess about where this is leading.

His shoulders are braced as though I'm about to reject him. "Would you plan our wedding for us? I know it's a big undertaking and a ton of work—"

"Yes," I cut him off, my smile already reappearing.

"Yes?" he asks in disbelief.

"Yes, of course. I will plan your wedding. I'd love to." My heart swells just at the fact that they would *want* me to be such a big part of this. "Though, I don't understand why you'd be so nervous to ask me."

"I know we've talked before about you being involved in the wedding, but planning the entire thing is a big deal. And I don't want this to interfere with *your* life." He gestures to me. "You put everything on hold for me, and this is just another thing. I shouldn't even be asking you—"

"Please stop." I rise to my feet, setting the water jug aside. "You're not interfering. There's nothing to interfere with. I am a jobless, aimless person right now, so it's the perfect time to ask me."

He grimaces. "No, you should be focusing on *you* and finding your passion." He looks to Farrow. "I shouldn't have asked her."

"We wanted her help. You already asked," Farrow says coolly. "And she said yes."

They wanted my help. *Farrow wanted me too.* I smile even brighter, and with an agreeing nod, I also remind Maximoff, "I said *yes*."

He lets out a distressed breath and looks to Thatcher. "Please tell me you at least see where I'm coming from." It feels like Moffy is actively trying to include Thatcher more, and my heart flutters.

Thatcher stares up from Ophelia, brush in hand, and he tells Maximoff, "She's excited and she'll be good at it."

He thinks I'll be good at it. I breathe in. "Three against one," I say to Maximoff. "You've been outvoted."

He sinks onto the loveseat in his wet towel. "Je te dois beaucoup, ma moitié." *I owe you so much, my other half.*

We exchange a smile together, excitement brewing.

"You'll need to talk to Farrow about details," Maximoff says.

I frown. "Why not you both?"

"He's been dreaming up his wedding since he was a kid. I never thought I'd get married."

Farrow passes him a to-go container. "Just because I've dreamed up shit doesn't mean I don't need your opinions. We're not doing everything I want…" He grins. "Even though that would be nice."

Maximoff lets out a dry laugh and they start teasing each other.

We talk for a while about wedding destinations, and I propose a scouting location trip. To pick the perfect spot.

"How about a vacation in December?" I ask them. "We'll be back before Christmas."

Farrow smiles at Maximoff. "You know where you want to go?"

He says he'll have to think about it, and after a few more minutes, I stand and cross towards the kitchen. Thatcher sidles next to me.

He dips his head down to whisper, "You're going to have to leave the house, if you're planning this wedding."

My stomach plummets.

A part of me wanted to hole up inside for Tony's two-month probationary period. If I don't go out in public, then he doesn't need to be around me. It was a win-win.

But Thatcher's right. I'm not going to be able to become a two-month hermit, and while he's on Xander's detail, I'll have a pompous asshole on mine.

We share a long look.

It's going to be a horrible two months—and the worst part—maybe I am hoping I get hurt. Because if Tony is actually bad at his job, those two months could be cut short in an instant.

4

Thatcher Moretti

I HAVEN'T SEEN JANE since *early* this morning. Hell, we've barely talked all day. I missed four of her texts while I was on-duty. She's missed three of my calls.

Don't think about it.

Fuck that—she is *all* I'm thinking about.

Jane Cobalt is still in every compartment of my brain, and I'm not looking to cut her out. I'm not looking to shut down or shove off without her, but ever since I moved in a week ago, we've been zigzagging in the fucking opposite direction and not meeting at the same point.

Missed calls.

Brief texts.

Gaping silence.

I'm not her bodyguard anymore. Distance between us is territory I expected to cross, but I'm afraid this isn't due to our fucked circumstances.

I stand next to a wooden stool at an old South Philly sports bar, too tensed to sit, and while I change the frequency on my radio, my breath tightens in my chest. Like an iron fist squeezing my ribcage.

Banks smacks my flexed abs before sliding on a barstool. "She'd call you if something bad went down. Just take the silence as a gift."

I narrow my gaze on my radio. "It's not a gift. Silence from Jane is a fucking omen." I tune into Epsilon's frequency, and I look over at my twenty-eight-year-old brother.

Banks Moretti.

My identical twin, my soul and conscience, someone I couldn't live without. The sun could be crashing down on the world, and Banks would be right by my side burning alive to push it back into the sky.

He leans forward on his stool to tie his boot. Dog tags clink together around his neck, which he's worn since the media and security team discovered we were in the Marine Corps. "You think something's wrong?"

"I have a bad feeling." I shake my head, neck stiff, and I keep my voice low. "Since we got together, I feel like she's holding me at a distance." I re-clip the mic on the collar of my black shirt and fix my earpiece.

He sticks a toothpick in his mouth, frowning. "You two haven't had sex since you moved in?"

I meet his eyes. "We've had sex every night."

"Then what are you worried about? Because it seems like she's holding you pretty fucking close." The corner of his lip rises but then falls at the sight of my dark frown.

The physical part of our relationship was always going to be easy. But to push through the bad in her life, she closes off emotionally to a lot of people. So do I, and I've struggled to be emotionally available to girlfriends in the past.

But while we were fake-dating and sneaking around, we found an indescribable solace together. Point-blank, I wanted to tear myself open for Jane. No matter how brutal and gut-wrenching.

I wanted and *want* to keep her safe from every cruel thing.

I'm the only person she's confided in that intensely about Nate, her fucking ex-friends-with-benefits. She's the *only* person I've confided in that deeply about Skylar, my older brother who passed away.

I'm head-deep, un-fucking-believably in love with this girl, and I would do anything for her. What's been gutting me is that I can sense her nerves. Jane is confident as all hell, but in the past week, sometimes she'll drop her gaze from me. I can't tell if it's what her parents said about moving in together too fast or if her brothers have questioned her decisions and she's doubting everything.

This kind of commitment isn't easy for Jane. I know that, at least. She's used to keeping men at arm's length, emotionally. I think it's partly why she's only had friends-with-benefits.

Just sex.

No potential to fall in love, but she's fallen in love with me.

I want to calm whatever fears she has about us. I want to be *emotionally* available to Jane in a way that I've never been before in a relationship.

But I just don't know how.

There is no protocol for love. No orders passed down to me, and I'm walking through this blindfolded and with my hands tied behind my back.

I stare hard at Banks. "I'm worried she feels like we moved in together too fast."

"You were basically there every night when you were fake-dating," he whispers. "It's not that different now."

I'm about to reply, but in the short beat, I zero in on the toothpick he chews. "How do you feel?"

He seesaws his hand. "Menzamenz." *Half and half.* "I could use a cigarette like a prostitute could use a stiff dick." He bites on the toothpick with a half-smile. "But you're not gonna help me out."

I nod strongly. He's not wrong about that.

I'm not fueling my brother's vice.

I tell him, "I never understood how you crave nicotine but I don't." In the military, we smoked about the same, but I quit easily coming home and I recreationally smoke a hell of a lot easier than him. He has one cigarette and he's hungering for the entire fucking pack.

"Probably because you're used to denying yourself life's greatest pleasures." He rests an elbow on the bar. "To make Dad happy, someone had to take most of the shit in our family, and you were good at it." He winces in a thought. "He made you clean his Chrysler with a toothbrush, and all you said was, *yes, sir.*"

"I must've been ten. "It wasn't that bad.""

Banks cracks a quarter of a smile. "I'm pretty sure you liked living in hell and have no clue what heaven looks like."

I instantly picture Jane at the mention of heaven. *I'm trying to get there.* I cross my arms. "Where do you think you'll end up? Heaven or hell?"

He raises a shoulder in a stiff shrug. "I just know I want to be wherever you are." He smacks my chest again. "And you'll be chain-smoking in the afterlife with me."

"Hell no."

We smile, but it fades fast. My phone buzzes, and I take it out, expecting a text from Jane. Instead, I find a message from her brother.

Where are you? — Charlie

I reread the text with tightened eyes. Any text from Charlie to me is a thousand meters out of the ordinary.

Something's not right. Carefully, I show the phone screen to Banks.

His brows furrow. "Haven't the Cobalt brothers been icing you out?"

"Like a fucking arctic wind." I text Charlie Cobalt my location, slip my phone in my back pocket, and tinker with my radio for better reception. Once her five brothers learned that I'm their sister's *real* boyfriend, I thought they'd all have something to say to me.

Cobalts aren't known to holster their opinions.

Instead, I got tumbleweeds.

Somehow that was worse.

My worry for Jane escalates, and the bar grows noisy as more people walk inside. Banks tries to flag down the busy bartender, and then he turns to me and asks, "What if your bad feeling about Jane is actually about Tony?"

Tony. His name rakes hot coals against my eardrums. "What do you mean?"

"Maybe Jane isn't telling you how much of a douchebag he is during the day, which is why she hasn't called you back. She's trying not to cause conflict between you and him on the team." He turns more to me. "She's protecting your job."

My deltoids pull taut, shoulders constricted. Jane isn't really a peacemaker and terminator of *conflict.* She's the co-pilot, the second-in-command, and she unites side by side with whoever the hell needs another pistol in the fight.

But I hesitate to say *no* to my brother because… "That's something a wing-woman would do?"

Banks nods. "Fuck yeah."

Goddammit.

Fuck Tony. "I need to talk to Jane." I send her another text about meeting at the sports bar. "I don't even know where she is." Last we checked in, she was taking Ophelia and Licorice to get annual shots, but that was hours ago. Way before I got off-duty.

Banks glances at my radio. "Any intel over comms?"

I drop my voice another octave as more people pack around the wooden bar. Mounted televisions play football, drowning out our conversation. "Other than Eliot and Tom heading to Philly tonight, it's been quiet on Epsilon's line."

It'd be easier if Tony Ramella were an Omega bodyguard. Akara, the Omega lead, would know where he is, and I could just ask him. But there's a problem with that:

I fucked Akara over, and we're not speaking. *My fucking fault.*

I thread my fingers through my brown hair. "There's no chance SFE will tell me Tony's AO if I ask." Epsilon were my men, and very few respect me after I slept with a client.

I'm Farrow 2.0 in their eyes.

Banks touches his waistband for his radio, but it's not there. He left it back in the car since he's off-duty.

Once Xander was in for the night, I got off-duty too. Not long ago, I drove Xander home after a boxing session at Studio 9. The kid still wants to fight, even after his dad told him, "Not over my dead decaying body."

Xander asked Farrow, Banks, and me to convince his parents to let him box again, and we agreed to be his advocates and to keep training him if he made a promise to stick to throwing punches *in* the ring. Or else, we're out.

The only reason we're not siding with his parents is because we all know how much boxing can help Xander feel empowered. Especially in situations where he feels helpless.

My brother leans back, realizing he has no radio on him.

"They wouldn't have responded to you anyway, Banks." My eyes sear, hating this part of being an identical twin. I slide a grave look to him. "My sins are your sins."

He bites harder on the toothpick. "Not everyone is a knucklefuck who treats us like one person."

"Not everyone is Akara," I sling back since Akara is still speaking to my brother.

A rock lodges in my throat. I want to unburden Akara after the hole I sunk him in with the other leads, but I'm not in charge. I can't help him anymore, and not being able to do anything of worth—that fucking suffocates.

I swallow hard.

Banks points to my radio. "Let's just see. Pretend to be me and ask Epsilon for intel on comms. We practically have the same voice." *They won't be able to tell the difference.*

I nod once, and I click the mic at my collar. "Banks to Epsilon, anyone know Tony's AO?" I ask for his area of operations.

Static crackles in my ear.

And then the Epsilon lead cuts in, "Not your business, Banks."

I glare at the wall. Jon Sinclair shouldn't be dismissing my brother *that* quickly. Banks protects Maximoff Hale often, and Maximoff is close to Jane. My brother should be able to ask about Jane's new bodyguard.

"Fucking horseshit," I mutter under my breath, switching a knob to Omega's frequency. I tell my brother what happened.

Banks exhales his irritation out, pissed.

"Excuse me?"

Our heads turn as a middle-aged woman leans on a stool and taps the bar counter near me. Skin sags on her face, teeth yellowed. She reminds me of a neighbor we used to have who smoked three packs a day.

The sports bar is crammed with South Philly locals.

She gestures between me and Banks. "Are you two twins?"

"Yes, ma'am," we say automatically.

Her face lights up. "And you spoke at the same time!" She laughs.

I try to remember this is routine. Before we even stepped through the doors, we were asked the same thing. Twice.

It's aggravating me since I'm not in a great fucking mood. Banks ignores her completely and orders a beer. Leaving me to handle this interaction, which usually I don't mind. It's how we operate.

I lead.

He follows.

"How old are you two?" She places a hand on my forearm. "Do you do the same thing for work?"

Apologize. Move out. I start, "Sorry but we're—"

"Mom," a young girl cuts me off and whispers to the woman. We make eye contact, and quickly, she averts her gaze and blushes.

On any day, I'm intimidating, but I bet I'm glaring into every ring of hell right now. I rub my face, then drop my arm to my side.

Where are you, Jane?

I glance at the door that creaks open, an old man filing in and patting his buddies on the shoulders near a dirtied high-top table. I stay alert and keep track of movement in the bar. *Habit.* There aren't famous ones here I need to protect.

Not yet.

She's not here yet.

"Paige, look, they're twins." She beams at her daughter. "Aren't they handsome?"

"*Mom,*" Paige hisses, eyes popping. "They're the Moretti brothers."

People at the bar start to overhear and plaster their gazes on us.

But the one thing we're used to is *staring.*

"The who?" her mom asks.

"They're the bodyguards to the Hale, Meadows, and Cobalt families—and Thatcher is *dating* Jane Cobalt." Paige speaks in a nervous rush.

Banks rotates to me. "You want something?" The bartender is still in front of us, waiting for me to order.

I nod. "I'll take a water."

Banks frowns slightly at me. He must've thought I'd order a beer. We speak in short glances, and I give him a look like, *I'm still staying sober.* He knows why.

A target broke into the townhouse last month, and with no evidence, it's becoming more probable that we won't know who broke in until a second attempt happens.

I have to be vigilant. I can't lose sight of what matters. Of *who* matters. *Everyone in that townhouse.*

The intruder could've been Nate.

It could've been a stalker.

I don't know who—I just have to be ready for them.

"Water?" the bartender repeats and assesses me with a long, incredulous stroke. His snide tone puts me on edge.

"Yeah," I say concretely. "Water."

He wipes his hands on a towel. "You aren't gonna find sparkling water here."

"We're from *here.*" I scowl, acid running in the back of my throat. I'd take a punching bag and gloves right about now. Nothing grates on me like people trying to shove me out of the place where I grew up.

This is my fucking home. I'm South Philly born and bred.

"Doesn't look like it to me." He tosses his towel aside.

I don't break his gaze. "Tap is fine."

He quirks his brow. "You're with a Cobalt, aren't you? You're probably drinkin' some gold-infused sparkling water seven days a week."

I glare, unblinking. What makes him think I'd tell him *anything* about the Cobalts?

"My brother doesn't drink bougie water," Banks says coldly to the bartender.

Banks has always thought even knock-off brand *bottled* water is bougie. Which he knows I drink a fuck ton of, so he's just trying to push the bartender off my ass.

Somewhere on the other side of the packed bar, a man shouts, "Yeah, he's just been fuckin' a bougie girl!"

My narrowed eyes swerve and find the voice. Grease stains his white shirt, his middle-aged face weather-beaten and antagonizing.

He leers over the bar. "Women around here aren't good enough for you? You gotta go eat that expensive pus—"

"You want your head inside your asshole, keep fucking talking," I growl, blood coursing hot through my veins.

Banks chews his toothpick and stands threateningly off the stool. His arms crossing over his firm chest.

The guy looks between us and our towering heights and cut builds. His smile recedes with a breathy laugh, and then he raises his hands. "Just sayin' what everyone is thinking."

Banks says frostily, "No one asked you."

He opens his mouth again, but people nearby yell at him to shut up and just drink. We all reroute our attention, and the bartender slides an ale to my brother and a glass of tap water to me.

Banks sinks back onto the stool. "What a fucking stunad."

I nod, knowing he's calling him a *drunk idiot*. I check my phone.

No new messages.

Charlie hasn't replied. With a rough hand, I rub my sore jaw that I've been clenching. I push back some apprehension and grip my glass of water.

Banks has been waiting for Friday Night Fight to start, a pro-wrestling match that plays weekly. But as I look at the TV, entertainment news airs first with some blonde hotshot, Hollywood-looking anchor—and the current topic is *me*.

I can't look away.

JANE COBALT & HER BODYGUARD BOYFRIEND –
HAVE THEY SPLIT?

Fake.

Rumor.

Still, I'm reading the slow closed captions with a knot in my throat.

> Where is... Thatcher Moretti? Fans are wondering... why Jane Cobalt... has a new bodyguard. Trouble... might be brewing between the... 23-yr-old American princess... and her towering, rugged protector... make that ex-protector. This November, Jane has barely... been spotted with Moretti in public. If you thought they'd head down the altar... before Maximoff & Farrow... maybe you should... rethink your bet.

I stop reading, and I take a tense sip of water. "I'm fine," I say, sensing Banks staring. I try to pack away most ass-backwards, eye-roll-inducing commentary from the media, but this one slices at the neck.

Because it's not all wrong.

I hang onto a fact: I'd rather take a million strangers critiquing me than have Jane take the unwarranted, toxic rage they shoot. Even when she's used to this shit.

Banks swigs his beer. "Ever since you've switched details, you two really haven't spent much time together in public."

"I realize that." I set down the water with accidental force, the glass clanking harshly.

"And that vacation next month to wherever Maximoff and Farrow pick, you won't be with Jane then either."

I give him a hard look, then survey the bar. "Try not to throw your back out pouring all that salt on me."

He smiles and wipes moisture off his glass. He's lost in thought and sips his beer with a contemplative stare.

I rest my back against the bar to face my brother. Concern grips my shoulders. "What is it?" He has something on his mind.

Banks licks beer off his lips. "I'm supposed to go on this trip and help protect Maximoff, and you're supposed to stay behind and protect Xander." His lip rises. "Switch places with me."

I think I hear him wrong. I know my twin brother is like a strong wind. He can adapt to any fragged mission and fly through hellfire. But he can't be suggesting *that*. "Say again?"

"You get to spend more time with Jane and keep an eye on Tony, and I get to have some quality time with Xander." He speaks hushed. "Just for the trip, you pretend to be me, and I'll be you."

He's lost his damned mind. "No," I say strictly. "*Hell* no."

Banks lets out a short laugh. "You're such a fucking gabbadost'." He can call me a *hardhead* all he wants.

I'm just more rational about the optics of his idea. "You're acting like you're suggesting we play *patty-cake* on Tuesday," I say under my breath, arms woven tensely over my chest. "This is a big deal."

"It's just one week, Thatcher." He stands off the stool so we can talk more quietly. "We tell the truth to who we trust. We'd just lie to whoever would snitch to the Alpha and Epsilon leads."

Tony.

Any Epsilon bodyguards.

I can barely entertain this plan, for so many reasons. "I'd have to lie to Price and Sinclair again. After I just got buried by a lie." All the honor that I had like a vessel to my heart was crushed under my actions.

I lied to my superiors. I became romantically involved with a client. I chose Jane.

"They won't find out," Banks says with so much assurance. "When has Tony ever been able to tell us apart?"

I take a long pause and then shake my head at myself, pissed that I'm even considering this for half a second. "Consequences aside, the fucking ethics of switching places, Banks, should be enough to say *no*."

He leans forward. "You just radioed in as me, Thatcher."

"You know that's not the same as impersonating each other for days." My voice is severe, and the darker look my brother wears and the short nod says, *I know.*

I add, "You can act like we're in some candy-coated twin movie and suddenly swap, but this is real."

He puts a hand on my stiff shoulder. "But it's not like you're falling in love with someone pretending to be me, and I'm not kissing Jane pretending to be *you.* Should we really feel that guilty fooling *Tony?* That prick treats us like dogs, man, and I'm tired of Epsilon acting like he's God's greatest creation."

What Banks says, I feel, but if we're caught deceiving two leads, I'd be putting my brother in a broiler, and he's my responsibility. I'm about to shake my head, but my phone rings.

Banks watches me slip it out, and I breathe in when I see her name on the screen.

Cell to my ear, I say, "Jane?"

"Thatcher. I just pulled up to the sports bar." Her voice is higher pitched. Strained. "Can you meet me in the car?"

I'm already walking out the door.

5

Thatcher Moretti

HER BABY BLUE BEETLE is nowhere in sight. I push forcefully out of the sports bar. Rain pelts the cracked sidewalk and the umbrella that Tony is holding. He guards the door of a black stretch limo, parked against the curb.

Her dad's limo. For the past week, Jane has been borrowing the limo, just so she can block out Tony with the screen divider.

She's in there now, and I don't waste a fucking second. I jog forward, surrounding paparazzi yelling my name.

"THATCHER!"

"THATCHER! THATCHER!"

"WHAT CAN YOU TELL US ABOUT YOU AND JANE?" Cameras click and flash.

I stay deadlocked on my objective: *the limo.*

Jane.

Jane.

Jane.

I reach Tony, and his thick eyebrow rises with the most fucking annoying self-importance. His slicked back, dark-brown hair accentuates his jawline and short stubble. He postures himself in his expensive suit like he's somehow better than me, and I hate how he tilts the umbrella away from my head just so I stand soaking in front of him.

I hate how he smiles smugly.

And I fucking hate how he's keeping me from her.

"Move," I order.

"Move? No, *hey, paesan*?" He puts a hand to his chest in mock hurt.

I wouldn't call him my paesan' if someone paid me five grand. I use that Italian term for men in my family that I love, and he's not one of them.

"Move," I repeat, rainwater dripping off my eyelashes.

He cocks his head. "Is that really how you're gonna treat your uncle?"

I love that my mom married Nicola. I hate that Nicola is his older sister, and I can't stand that he's related to me *on paper.* Thank fucking God it's not by blood.

Under my breath, I growl, "I'm going to treat you a lot worse if you don't move your ass."

Tony rolls his head back like I'm a joke and he's some kind of king. "You sure you don't want a progress report on your girlfriend first? I've been with her all day. Want to know how many times she mentioned you?" He mouths the word, *zero.*

I grit my teeth.

Don't grab him. I force myself not to shove him. Not with cameras flashing, not with paparazzi in view, and I stare at this piece of shit. Blistering inside out.

I tap into the last sliver of fucking willpower I have just to suppress a hotheaded reaction.

Don't deck him.

"Move," I order *again.* I'm not playing around. "Or else I'll radio your lead and let him know you're disobeying a direct command."

His mouth forms a line. "You're not my superior, Moretti."

"No, but I'm the boyfriend to *your* client." I glare through sheets of rain. "And I'm allowed direct access to my girlfriend, so I'm telling you one last time. *Move.*"

Tony lifts his chin like he thinks I'm bluffing.

I touch my mic almost instantly, and I open my mouth to speak into comms—and just then, Tony finally sidesteps.

Jane is all I care about, so I don't even acknowledge him again as I grab the handle and open the door.

6

Jane Cobalt

I HUG A MESSY BINDER that contains budget spreadsheets and vendor information for Moffy and Farrow's wedding, and my heart patters at an uneven, queasy speed as the limo door swings open.

I need Thatcher—no.

No, I'm an independent, self-sufficient woman, and I don't need any man for affection and love and emotional support. I can still provide all of this to myself now that we're together.

Do not fall into his lap like a bird without wings, Jane.

You're born from lions.

I lift my chin, holding breath, and I watch as Thatcher slides his long legs into the limo and shuts out the thunderstorm behind him.

"Thatcher." My face falls. "You're soaked." I couldn't hear much outside with the raucous storm or even see with Tony's body obstructing the tinted window.

Thatcher's black shirt suctions to his abs. Rainwater drips from his hair and soaks his shoulders, and after he locks the door, he pushes the damp strands out of his face.

"Do you need…?" I begin to ask, but he's already shaking his head.

His strong gaze tunnels through me, his grave concern like a safety net that I could so effortlessly collapse into.

How easy it can be—to be swallowed by all of what Thatcher offers me, and I claw for equal ground where I can engulf him just as fully.

I open my mouth, but words stick for a second.

"What happened, Jane?" He tries to edge closer to me on the leather seat, but with my binder to my breasts, I shift back against my door, further away from him.

Air vacuums out of the limo. As quick and powerful as a shotgun blast.

He goes rigid.

I inhale but can't exhale. My knee-jerk reaction of adding distance between him and me causes an unbearable amount of strain. I'm making a terrible mess out of this, and I don't mean to.

"Wait," is all I manage to expel as I gather breath and courage.

Thatcher grips the top of the seat and rubs his mouth with his other hand. His protective gaze never abandons me.

In our silence, I hear the *ping, ping, ping* of rain on the limo's roof.

I glance down at my lavender tulle skirt, my arms hot beneath a rainbow blouse and leopard faux fur coat. I'm not supposed to cower or unravel this way. "I'm not unraveling," I whisper to myself, but he surely hears.

"Just talk to me, honey." His deep voice practically cradles me and pushes me to a metaphorical stance.

As I raise my eyes, I linger on the stretched leather seat we share. "I was born right where you're sitting," I realize aloud, and my cheeks heat.

He looks at the seat, very briefly, then back to me. He's so stoic; I can't even begin to guess what he's thinking.

"It's just a fact," I mention unhelpfully. "My birth." I roast from head to toe and waft my blouse. "And I'm sure this is what my parent's pictured twenty-three-years later," I quip. "Their daughter struggling to *talk* to the man who she…"

Loves.

I withhold the word, even though I've said it once before. My body floods with the sentiment that overwhelms my senses, that rips breath from lungs and pricks my eyes.

Love is a violent emotion. Full of fortitude and might, and I'm going to be destroyed under ours, aren't I?

I clear a ball in my throat. "Now you're probably thinking about my limo birth."

He takes the earpiece out of his ear. "No, I'm thinking you might regret that I moved in with you."

My eyes widen. "No," I say quickly. "No, not at all. That's not what I feel." I set my binder aside. "I'm glad that we're living together." Panic creeps into my bones. "Do you have regrets about it?"

"No." He never pauses, so assured that I ease a little. Thatcher keeps his eyes on me while he unclips his radio and tries to dry the device. "Something happened?"

Yes.

I tuck a piece of frizzed hair behind my ear. "I tried to text you that I was on my way to the bar, but none were going through, and I thought I'd just tell you in person."

His brows draw together. "Tell me what?"

Usually I bask inside the intensity of his gaze, but in this moment, I can't meet him head-on. I blink and look down at my lap like a cowardly lion. "I've never been good at diffusing two sides of conflict—I never could with Moffy and Charlie, and I shouldn't be surprised that I can't now." I speak in a rush. "This past week, I've just kept awful things Tony has said to myself, and I thought it'd make your job easier. I wanted to give that to you. I wanted to give you *something*. But I feel like I'm hoarding secrets from a ride-or-die, and it's made me quiet around you, and I think you can tell."

He nods, his muscles tensed.

I ramble on. "And whatever I tell you now could cause friction between you and Tony. It feels selfish to share. But maybe you don't even want to know; and in that case, we can ignore this conversation and just go about our days—"

"No," Thatcher cuts me off, which is rare. "Whatever *Tony* said or did, I need to know. You're not dealing with that fucking tool alone." His South Philly lilt fights through. "I hate that you already have been." He clips his mic to his collar, like he's seconds from reporting Tony to a lead.

I want to tell him absolutely everything. I want inside his head, and I know he wants inside mine, but in the same breath, what I have to say will just stoke his anger and aggravation towards Tony.

Tell him.

"Okay." I try to take a readying breath. *You can do this, Jane.*

Nervous heat builds, and I slip off my leopard coat.

Thatcher stares so hard at my movements, I think he's going to pop a blood vessel in his eye.

My heart races. "What is it?" I ask.

His gaze darkens on my coat. "Tony shouldn't have been anywhere under your fucking clothes." He grips his radio, about to kick into action.

I hold up a pointer finger. "I'm removing a *coat*. A single article of clothing that is nowhere near a shirt or a bra and has absolutely *nothing* to do with Tony other than I'm sweating... a lot." I ungracefully tug and tug at my sleeves to free myself from this heat trap.

Thatcher rubs a rough hand over his face, then he edges closer to help me.

I jerk backwards. I go deadly still, elbow sticking out of my coat.

He stops suddenly.

We both breathe hard. We both stare at each other in binding silence, every inch of space between us slashing at my lungs and heart.

He raises his hands to show me he's not nearing. "Can you answer me something?"

"Anything."

"Are you afraid of me?"

I shake my head fiercely, a lump in my throat. "God, no." I long for Thatcher in ways I've never longed for a man. With one more tug, I finally free myself from the fur coat. Cold air barely washes over my burning limbs. "It's the very opposite."

He threads his fingers through his wet hair.

I can't read his hard features. My pulse won't slow, and I have to ask, "What are you thinking?"

He looks me over. "You keep me on my toes." He lets out a laugh. "And it's driving me nuts, and it's un-fucking-real how much I want you."

"You have me," I remind him.

Thatcher nods a short nod, and in a long beat, he looks deeper into me. "When I was your bodyguard and we were fucking, you'd let me help you no hesitation, and now that I'm your boyfriend, you're frozen."

My eyes flit down.

Thatcher shifts uneasily. "You're confusing the hell out of me, and I want to walk with you through this, honey. But I don't know where you're going."

"I want you to hold me so badly," I admit. *I want you to swallow me whole.* Fear pinpricks me, and I hate that I'm unwilling to drown in his comfort right now and yet I hate that I want to be completely and wholly consumed by him. "But I feel like I have to stand on my own first." I cling onto my autonomy by my fingertips, and he's there, reaching a hand out and asking me to grab hold, to pull me up.

And I won't let him.

Not entirely.

I glance out the window. "And I feel so guilty."

"Why?"

"You sacrificed everything to be with me, and I can't even let you help me take off my coat."

His gaze narrows in severity, and he shakes his head over and over. "You owe me nothing for what I did. If you'd rather not be touched, I'd rather not touch you, Jane."

I love him.

It chokes me. It throttles me. I don't want it but I want it, and that is my tragedy.

He adds, "I'm going to match whatever pace you set."

I breathe in. "What if I pull you at a million different speeds? What if I slow and speed and stop and speed and slow? Are you prepared to grow exhausted of me?" My eyes burn.

Thatcher doesn't recoil. "I'm prepared to be with you at every speed, and there's no way you'll exhaust me."

I arch my brows. "How can you be so sure?"

He is all confidence and man. "Because I don't tire that easily."

I exhale, face flushed, and I rest my shoulders on the limo door. We hold each other's gaze for some time, and I try to squash some of my insecurities. I smooth my lips together, and then I say, "You keep me on my toes too, you know. Quite literally."

He almost smiles. With his forearm, he wipes a droplet of rainwater that glides down his temple. "About Tony—you don't need to mediate any shit between him and me."

I nod. "I'm glad not to play that part," I admit.

Maybe there is good in sharing the bad with Thatcher. Nothing strengthens a bond like a common enemy, and we both dislike Tony very much.

"What I say will just fuel your hatred," I warn him. "It has little to do with me and more to do with you." If it were about me, I could run to the Tri-Force and have Tony fired, but mostly, he's been a decent bodyguard. I haven't feared for my life in crowds, and he's deescalated more than one rowdy fan interaction.

This is just bad blood between them. What they'd consider security in-fighting.

"I want to hear it," Thatcher confirms.

I lace my fingers. "I, um…" I unlace and reach for an expensive champagne bottle in an ice bucket. "Maybe we should drink first."

He grips his knees. "I can't."

I remember and shake the cobwebs out of my head. "Right. The break-in." *He's wanted to stay clear-headed and focused.* "I probably shouldn't drink either. It's a bad distraction tactic, drinking alcohol. That can go awry quickly." My eyes grow. "Not that I'm trying to distract myself from you, from this—I mean, I am, but…"

Merde.

Thatcher brushes a hand along his unshaven jaw and nods to me. "It's okay."

"It's not," I wince. "I'm being unfair to you."

"Because you can't get the words out? Welcome to the fucking club."

I want to smile, but everything I need to say weighs on me. I put the champagne bottle back in the ice bucket. "It's been hard this past week hearing Tony say things about you, and the more aggressively I defended you, the more he'd smirk like he got a rise out of me."

Thatcher glowers out the rear window, and when he looks back at me, he says, "He's a piece of shit."

"Je suis d'accord." *I agree.*

The corner of his mouth lifts a fraction. He leans his side more into the seat, already fully turned towards me. "What else?"

I rehash the past week to my boyfriend. All the little biting comments. Tony restrained a heckler from approaching me, and afterward, he said, *"Bet Thatcher would've struggled with that. Probably would've broken a sweat."*

I snapped back, *"He never has."*

Tony had that grating conceited smile and haughty swagger.

Every day, I heard:

Moretti can't do this.

Moretti has half a brain.

You realize no girlfriend has ever wanted to be with him. That's why he's been cheated on a hundred times.

I tell Thatcher, "If there'd been a 'shut up' button on Tony, I would've risked touching him and pressed it a thousand times by now."

"I would've decked him," Thatcher says plainly.

I scrutinize his left hand that clutches his knee, tiny scars mar his knuckles and his ring finger is crooked like the bone shattered and healed poorly. "Is that how you fractured your finger?" I wonder. "Hitting Tony?"

He opens his hand and rubs his knuckles. "I've punched him before. But this is from bar fights and protecting Xander."

I scoot nearer, the air winding around us as I do, and he looks down at me and I look up at him. Our breath coming heavier.

He holds out his hand, knowing why I moved. Gently, I take his palm in mine and inspect the healed wounds. Thatcher has been through grief and war. His hands have carried the body of his brother and my badly beaten cousin, and if he could, I'm sure he'd carry more.

"What he's said, it gets worse," I murmur.

His jaw hardens and he nods me onward. "I'm ready."

I explain how I overheard Tony talking when he was on a break. I had stopped by my dad's office in Center City, which is a secure location. Bodyguards aren't required to enter.

"I was about to leave," I tell him, "and Tony was waiting for me in the lobby just outside the women's restroom. Through the door, I could hear him talking on the phone." My stomach roils, and I shift closer, my knees knocking into his leg.

I freeze again.

He assesses me in a sweep, and I clutch my elbows, looking at his lips more than a few times. Once he notices, our breathing switches tempo. Desire pulses between my legs, and I imagine his large hands knowing exactly how to please the aching, building need inside me.

Wrong time.

The body wants what the body wants, and I suppose so does the soul. I'm just struggling with feeding the latter.

Thatcher keeps us on track. "You heard Tony talk on the phone?"

"Oui." I straighten up and tuck a flyaway hair behind my ear. "He mentioned you and your brother."

Lines crease his forehead. "Which brother?"

"Skylar." I shake my head hotly and cringe. "He said, *Thatcher never even visits his dead brother's grave, and he wants everyone to be sympathetic about that shit.*"

Thatcher mumbles an Italian curse word and almost rolls his eyes. "He's unbelievable." He looks back at me. "I visit Skylar's grave."

I bristle. "So he's inaccurate and cruel."

"He got us confused," Thatcher clarifies. "Banks is the one who never goes to the cemetery."

I wonder why.

If I could classify my relationship with Banks Moretti now, it'd be filed under *new*. Simply, he's been more of a bodyguard to me and I've been more of a famous client to him. Whatever we know *personally* about each other has been what Thatcher has shared.

I whisper, "Tony has no empathy for you or Banks."

Thatcher scowls. "He wouldn't. To him, we're a punch line and fucking twin gag like Thing 1 and Thing 2."

I understand being dehumanized by internet trolls and media outlets. But Tony isn't a nameless internet user. He grew up with the Moretti brothers, and I can't even imagine how much worse that would hurt.

"He's like an impenetrable, grinning Cheshire cat," I say softly. "I think it's easier when we both shut him down together." We're frowning because under our current situation, Thatcher can't help me this way.

He dips his head, his voice low. Eyes serious. "I should be next to you."

We both know he has to be with Xander. "It's two months," I breathe. "Once the probationary period is over, he'll be transferred."

Thatcher glances down.

At my hand.

That's been on his thigh. "Oh," I say aloud, warmth spreading throughout my body. "I didn't realize I was..." *touching you*.

"You can keep it there." We're impossibly close now, and I don't move away anymore. I don't freeze, and his large hand hovers next to my cheek. Sensitive places tingling, electricity sparking, and an ache pulses harder and begs for him to just pick me up and devour me whole.

I whisper, "Thatcher."

His forehead nearly presses to mine.

My eyes scald. "I can't believe I'm going on a trip without you." It'll be strange. He was my bodyguard for almost a year. With me every day, and now...

I drop my gaze.

His hand encases my cheek. "Fuck it." He's a breath from my lips. "We're switching places."

"What?" I shake my head, utterly confused.

"Me and my brother. I'll explain everything."

7

Jane Cobalt

"YOU CAN'T BE SERIOUS," I whisper to the Moretti brothers, and I can't believe I even ask. Both are *very* serious men, Thatcher more so than Banks. They're definitely not playing a practical joke on me.

My bugged eyes dart between my boyfriend and his twin brother in the noisy South Philly sports bar. So crowded here that only one barstool was unoccupied.

Thatcher has taken the stool. And while I clutch a pint of beer, I sit across his lap, his strong arm around my waist—and I've been really, *really* taken with our seating arrangement. Especially the nearness of his chest, his body heat flushing me all over, and how my arm brushes against his abs.

That was, until, they dropped a Mary-Kate and Ashley sized bomb on me.

"It's just one week," Banks says with a slight smile, one teeming with confidence that Thatcher matches in a shared glance. "This is nothing for me, even less for Thatcher." He cocks his head to his brother. "Pack me up and ship me out, I'm ready."

I begin to smile, sensing their energy. "You're both excited about this, aren't you?" Thatcher enjoys his job, and it's often a high-octane, high-risk one, and I suppose this will jolt them with more adrenaline.

"To spend more time with you," Thatcher says, looking down at me. "Hell yeah."

A smile explodes across my face, and I sip my beer, feeling like my thirteen-year-old easily smitten sister. But realities take hold, and my smile starts to fade. "If you're caught..." I trail off as they shake their heads.

"It won't happen," Thatcher assures.

It makes me sad to think they truly believe very few people can tell them apart. It makes me sadder to think it could be true.

They said they'd be fooling a small number of individuals. Mostly Tony, which should be easy enough.

I take another sip of beer. Thatcher keeps a hand on my binder that I placed on the bar counter, as though someone might snatch it and leak Maximoff & Farrow's wedding plans.

It is a possibility, and I love how he ensures that all parts of my life are safe.

Thatcher looks into me. "You're going to help us."

My lips rise. "I like the sound of this." I doubt I could sit idly backseat to this plan. I want to make sure the risk is low for them. With the tilt of my chin, I stare up at my boyfriend. "How can I be of service, Mr. Moretti?"

His palm slyly disappears under my robust, tulle skirt. The better to hide my boyfriend's hand with.

I smooth my lips together and try to subdue my shallow breathing. His warm hand tracks hot lines up my thigh. Thatcher kisses the nape of my neck before whispering, "Okay?"

"Yes." *Oh my God, yes.* If I blink three times, I feel like this raw, sexual, warrior of a man will disappear in a poof, and I'm wide-eyed and too eager.

Banks... is staring right at me. He nearly laughs.

Am I panting? Am I childishly head-over-heels?

My face is on fire. "I like your brother," I state outright.

"Right on." He smiles and swigs his beer. He's been standing and shielding bar patrons from reaching me. People pack in tight to watch football and a pro-wrestling pre-show.

I sweep Banks more curiously. Whereas Thatcher carries himself like a commander in a mythic warzone, Banks is a primed solider who would fill every frame of a documentary. He's background that can't be unseen.

I glance back at Thatcher, just as he tells me, "Banks and I need an objective eye when it comes to our similarities and differences."

"That's where I come in?" I ask.

Banks nods. "My four," he suddenly says to Thatcher.

"I see them," Thatcher replies, but he never shifts his gaze or hand off me.

I just now notice a few men ogling me from afar. Not nicely either. I'd say *snidely* is more like it.

I lean more of my weight against Thatcher. He pulls me closer to his chest, and I feel his heavy heartbeat that thumps in a calming rhythm.

Thatcher and Banks are off-duty. Yet, they're still watching. Still surveying our surroundings.

Tony, my actual bodyguard, is seven-stools down the bar, and I make a concentrated effort not to glance at him. Though, I'm sure he's observing everyone and also pompously gawking at us.

At least he's not in earshot.

I sit more upright. "From what I've seen, Tony can't discern your personalities, so the biggest risk might be mannerisms and physical traits."

We go over a few technicalities in the next five minutes and screech to a halt on glaring problems.

"Your tattoo," I whisper to Thatcher.

"It's on his ass," Banks says.

Yes, ladies and gentlemen, that's right—my boyfriend has a tattoo on his ass. SFO, namely Paul Donnelly, inked script on Thatcher recently, and I wasn't present. It happened under the cloak of *Omega Brotherhood* and I just saw the result.

They didn't write "hypocrite" on his butt like I thought they would. Like Thatcher said they *could*. Instead, SFO decided on something that "better fit" Thatcher.

And so they tattooed the word, *Cinderella*.

The cursive lettering and placement is actually quite beautiful. When I first saw the tattoo in bed, I was overwhelmed. Thatcher has always been the one living the rags to riches story. He's been the one with everything to lose.

Banks finishes off his beer. "Just don't get buck-naked, Cinderella." Thatcher glares and motions to him. "You also have a fucking tattoo."

My brows jump. "You do?"

Banks pats his right thigh. "The ink is blown out. If I could kick my fourteen-year-old self in the ass, I would."

Thatcher explains to me, "Free tattoo in a friend's basement."

"Is it a design or script?" I ask.

"Roman numerals." Banks places his empty beer on the bar. "Which should've been tattooed over years ago."

Thatcher hones in on his brother. Banks stares directly back. Neither one blinking.

Tension pulls uncomfortably, and I look between them, something unsaid gripping them and the air.

"You want me to tell her?" Banks asks.

I freeze.

Thatcher is dead-set on Banks. "She already knows."

"Yeah? She knows that everyone in our family blames each other for his death, but no one thought to point a finger at him?"

A chill slips down my spine, and I realize this is about their older brother.

"Fuck him," Banks says with bite.

Thatcher's nose flares. "Don't."

"I love him, but Mary Mother of God, I *hate* him like a thousand pounds in his direction, and my dumb ass has to live with his death on my thigh."

My stomach flips.

Roman numerals. A date.

The day Skylar died.

His words drop heavy. Like a small implosion. Banks looks everywhere but at us, and Thatcher drills a pained expression on the wall. I can *feel* how infrequent they discuss Skylar, and my big mouth might lead all three of us in a sinkhole, but I just speak.

"It could be worse." I offer my beer to Banks.

He takes the glass, his brows knitting. "How?"

"You could've tattooed it on your ass."

Thatcher laughs first, the sudden noise deep but light.

Banks smiles into laughter too, and I brighten and realize how somewhere deep down, I knew Thatcher would find humor in this exchange. He's become less of a mystery, and I'm so incredibly fond of the man next to me.

Or rather...the man I'm sitting on.

I blow out a breath, my heart beating wildly.

He presses a kiss to the top of my head.

I'm in love.

Don't be frightened, Jane.

I'm trying.

Thatcher nods to his brother. "See that, you had some common sense at fourteen."

"Yeah. But still less than you," Banks says, lips upturned. Happy that Thatcher is smarter, but Thatcher already shakes his head like his brother is brighter and better. Their pride in each other and for each other is as deep as the Bering Sea.

Banks swallows a mouthful of beer, then passes the glass back to me. "What else should we worry about?"

He means the twin swap.

"Piercings?"

"None," they say in unison.

Thatcher let out a frustrated breath.

"That question was for *me*," Banks says to him. "She already knows you have no piercings."

He scowls. "Statazitt'."

"You shut up," Banks rebuts.

I smile into another sip of beer, finding their relationship the sweetest as can be. "What about scars? Thatcher has quite a few."

He actually has *many*. Most are small and scatter his chest.

Banks lifts a shoulder. "I have some, but Tony won't be able to tell us apart from them."

Thatcher nods in agreement.

"Your hand," I mention to my boyfriend.

He removes his left hand off the binder, just enough to touch his bent ring finger. Thatcher looks concerned.

Banks shakes his head. "Barely anyone notices that."

"Yeah, let's hope," Thatcher says strictly. "Or I'm going to kick *my* twenty-five-year-old self in the ass for re-breaking the same knuckle."

We all conclude that it shouldn't be much of an issue, and I think about another angle. How Banks will be left in Philadelphia pretending to be Thatcher.

"We aren't planning to tell my parents or aunts and uncles about the twin swap, are we?" I ask. "Because I can't be certain they won't tell the Alpha lead." They're all very close to Price Kepler. He's been Aunt Daisy's bodyguard for over twenty years.

Thatcher frowns at me. "If you asked your parents to keep this a secret, you don't think they would?"

We, Cobalts, are notorious secret-keepers and loyal to the very death, so I understand his confusion.

"I do think they would," I say softly, "at least 98% of me does, but there's 2% uncertainty."

Banks asks, "Where's the 2% coming from?"

Uneasiness sinks my stomach. I glance up.

Thatcher rubs his mouth a couple times and then nods. "Me."

"I'm the first Cobalt to be in a relationship," I explain, "and I just can't predict whether my mom and dad will challenge you or profess immediate fealty. It's too soon to tell, and in my mind, there's not enough substantial data."

Thatcher and Banks lock eyes and speak through a long look, and then Banks shrugs. "It's not like you're supposed to be around Connor and Rose. You're on Hale duty. I can pretend to be you and protect Xander. Easy."

Thatcher looks grave. "If you run into her parents—"

"I won't. It's only a week."

I nod. "Since it's such a short timespan, it's easier just not telling them. We don't need to add in more variables."

Just as they agree, the bar quiets to murmurs, and I follow gazes as the door clatters shut.

Snow and cold air blown inside, Maximoff lowers the hood of his Eagles sweatshirt, and Farrow combs back his bleach-white hair. Hand in hand, they weave their way between nosy looks and side-eyes to reach our spot. I instantly smile.

Maximoff lets go of Farrow and nears me. "Bonsoir, ma moitié." His forest-green eyes sparkle with happiness. There's nothing less that I'd want for him.

I stand off Thatcher to hug my best friend. We breathe deeply, and Moffy kisses both my cheeks. Attention presses on us, but thankfully some bar chatter reignites.

"It's just you and me, old chap." I smile more. "And my boyfriend, your fiancé, and my boyfriend's brother." My cheeks hurt at this declaration, but his smile drops faster and he glances over at Tony.

I prickle. "Yes, he's *unfortunately* still here."

Maximoff grimaces. "I think he's smirking at me."

"I don't even want to look." I pay more attention to the bodyguards we like. Subtly, they shift around us. Thatcher rises from the stool and positions himself next to Banks. Farrow does the same, all three creating a semi-circle barrier between us and bar patrons.

Moffy and I are pushed up against the sticky counter. Where I'm sure is the safest place to be. I excitedly grab the messy binder, stuffing loose papers back inside. "I found some great cost effective vendors, especially for flowers."

"Before that," Moffy whispers, "did you talk to Thatcher about He Who Must Not Be Named?"

Tony has reached Lord Voldemort levels of evil for Maximoff ever since he overheard my bodyguard crack a "joke" about Thatcher *and* Banks sleeping with me.

Something along the lines of, *she likes that two-for-one action?*

I've been venting to Moffy about how much I hate Tony and how much I wish I could vent to Thatcher, and it was eating me inside out.

"I told him everything," I whisper and breathe out a lighter breath.

Maximoff smiles, able to see that I'm at a better place. "So Janie Dark Ages is diverted?"

"Sufficiently."

"Forever."

"We can only hope." I lean my hip into his side, and he wraps an arm around my waist. Our backs to the bar, we stare ahead.

His fiancé and my boyfriend speak under their breaths to one another, seeming very civil, and that is *profoundly* new.

Maximoff squints. "Are we in the same universe?"

"This feels unfamiliar."

"If they hug, we took a wrong damn turn somewhere." He watches more closely as Farrow bites the tip of his black leather glove with casual ease, pulling it off. Maximoff's Adam's apple bobs.

I stifle a laugh.

Farrow has put a spell on him, and it would be the millionth-and-one time. I watch Thatcher say one more thing to Farrow, then he speaks into comms with authority. His gaze—all bold hardness—rakes the bar.

I ache to step into his arms.

"Why did God have to make gloves?" Maximoff asks, forcing his face into a scowl.

My dad would not appreciate that mention of *God*. I don't mind as much. "God didn't make gloves," I whisper. "But they've been around since the Romans, and it's not *gloves* you're drooling over."

"You're right," he says with an exhale, "I'm drooling over the floor."

I laugh.

When Farrow bites off his second glove, he catches Maximoff staring. His knowing smile causes Maximoff to glower. 9 out of 10 for hiding his affections. I'd wave pompoms if I had them.

Farrow raises his brows in a teasing wave, and all Moffy can do is flip him off.

I smile less when I see a vocal middle-aged man behind the SFO bodyguards—he's yelling drunkenly at Thatcher's back. I can't distinguish the words over the loud bar chatter.

Thatcher shakes his head sternly at me, as though to say, *ignore him*.

I try to.

Once we begin discussing wedding details, we crowd closer to each other. I open the binder on the bar and we go through the spreadsheets.

"The florist said I could have a 50% discount if I advertise on Instagram."

"No," Moffy says firmly. "Even if you weren't still in a Cobalt Social Media Black-Out, I don't want you to have to do paid advertising."

"The exposure helps local vendors," I remind him. "It's good for their business, and my brothers, sister, and I plan to end the Black-Out tomorrow. I'll be back on Instagram."

Maximoff cracks a knuckle, thinking longer. He loves the idea of helping others, but I know he's weighing this against a million other factors. "Or we could just pay full cost, Janie. It'd give more money to the vendors."

"In the short-run," I tell him. "Long-run, advertising would help."

He turns to his fiancé. "What if we do both?"

"Free advertising?" Farrow tucks his gloves in his back pocket. "See, this is a wedding, not a charity party."

"Sorry, man. I totally forgot you've thrown a hundred weddings before ours." His sarcasm is thick. "How were all those divorces?"

Farrow rolls his eyes into a widening smile. "You mean the ones that don't exist, smartass." He speaks faster before Maximoff jumps in. "This is going to be the biggest, most selfish event you've ever thrown, and you're going to have to be okay with that."

Moffy stares faraway in thought.

I glance at Thatcher. I thought he'd be looking between Maximoff and Farrow, but his eyes are on me.

Butterflies flap in my stomach, and I fumble as I file the florist contact list, then I clear my throat. "Um…" I shake my head. How strange and wonderful it feels to be seen—but for the right reasons. Not maliciously or perversely but adoringly. Lovingly.

Protectively.

Carefully.

I grab onto words that flit past my brain. "You still have time to decide, Moffy."

"Yeah." He nods, focusing back on us.

Thatcher threads his arms. "Have you two picked a date yet?"

Last I heard, they were still up in the air.

Maximoff rotates his stiff shoulder. "Farrow has always wanted a winter wedding, so we're thinking a couple years from now. It gives us time for this." He gestures to the binder.

I tell him, "I can simplify for you."

"He'll need that," Farrow teases.

Maximoff groans. "You'll need that more than me."

He smiles with the tilt of his head. "You can think that all you want, wolf scout."

Before I close the binder, we talk a little more about vendors, and then we land on the topic of the upcoming trip to scout a wedding location.

"Hawaii?" I repeat the fake destination as Maximoff stealthily shows me his phone screen with the real location.

Scotland.

Behind me, Thatcher and Banks lean forward and see the country's name too. A winter retreat in the Scottish Highlands with my boyfriend—I take a breath and smile. Brimming with excitement, I rock back on my heels and collide into Thatcher's hard chest with a *thud.*

I freeze.

This is all allowed, Jane. We're together, and the security team doesn't have to sign off on our public interactions as part of a ploy anymore.

He clutches my hips, and my lungs expand. While I lean against his body, I weave my arms behind him and slide my hand down his back pocket.

His peach-perfect ass is all mine.

Maximoff sends me a confused look. "I thought you were sad about leaving him during the trip."

I crane my neck up at the Moretti brothers. "Do you want to tell them or shall I?"

"You," they say.

Banks curses under his breath as they speak at the same time again. And quietly, I unleash the twin swap plan. By the end, Farrow is grinning so wide that his smile reaches cheek-to-cheek.

"Just say it," Thatcher cuts in.

"You like breaking the rules for her," Farrow tells him matter-of-factly.

Thatcher looks only at me, and my heart swells. No man has ever made me feel like a rare beauty worthy of sacrifice. He's never sought after my fame or fortune.

He's just sought after me.

I open my mouth to speak. "I—"

A drunken fool *plows* into my boyfriend's back.

"Merde," I curse.

Thatcher hardly sways. He's quick to take my hand out of his pocket, to pull my arms safely in front of me, and just as the fool barrels into him with purpose *again*, Thatcher swerves onto this twenty-something man and shoves his chest. Like the violent rip of caution tape, the packed bodies explode with rowdy, hostile force.

Pushing.

Yelling all at once. "Get outta here!" can be heard above the jumbled, slurred mess.

My heartbeat spikes.

Banks is suddenly facing me and back-to-back with Thatcher. *My boyfriend's brother is guarding me.*

I see Tony out of the corner of my eye. Squeezing through the mosh pit of a crowd. "HEY!" he yells. "Knock it off, Gio!"

He knows one of these assholes?

"Morettis can't come in here actin' like they own the place!" Gio yells back.

Male voices from all directions drown out his complaint. Thatcher and Banks included, shouting over him.

Curiosity nearly goads me to *stay* and watch. Thatcher is more willing to argue here than if we were somewhere else. He outwardly blazes, and he glances back and communicates with his brother.

I swallow my speeding pulse. "We need to leave!" I shout to Moffy, and I grab my fur coat off the stool. Once I look up at my best friend, I pale.

His red-hot fixated glare is all too familiar. He's hyper-focused on three young guys in green Eagles merch. They berate Farrow, who's as cool as can be. He couldn't care less, only a hand outstretched to keep them from shoving. But he shoots Moffy a warning look to stay back.

And then they spit on Farrow.

"Moffy, *no*."

He launches forward. I drop my coat and clasp his waist.

"MOFFY!" He barely even notices me pulling him, and so I leap onto his back.

"Janie?" He stops in place.

Someone hollers, "Look, cousins screwing cousins!" My stomach lurches, but I try not to listen because if I let go of him, he'll—

Tony suddenly tears me off of Maximoff.

"No!" I scream and kick my feet out.

I've been ripped off my best friend plenty before; it's protocol—and every time, I yell about not leaving him behind. But in this moment, only one word escapes my lips.

No.

I yell it again.

Tony cages me to his chest. I squirm against his stronghold, and my panicked eyes land on Thatcher.

He's already coming towards me.

He heard me scream.

Moffy sees me struggling. "Let her go!" he shouts at Tony.

I flail my feet, and my heel makes contact with my bodyguard's crotch. Tony grunts, "*Fuck.*" He sets me down and doubles over.

"Moffy!" I bolt to catch his arm. Now that I'm fine, he's already leaving for Farrow, who does a fantastic job restraining the pushing crowd.

"Jane!" Thatcher cuts off my path and shields me. "*Jane!*"

I lose sight of Moffy. "I can't leave him!" I put my hands on his chest to push him backwards. But my strength doesn't outmatch his, so I use all my weight and jump on my boyfriend.

He catches me in a front piggyback. My legs instinctively wrap around his waist—his hands cup the backs of my thighs.

Hoisting me higher on his tall build.

Oh.

My.

God?

I hold his neck, and our eyes sink into each other. As though the world falls hush around us, as though meeting the safety I've always craved has the power to stop time and grow impossible gardens. As though we're Adam and Eve and whatever sinful deed we commit, we'll commit together.

Wild pieces of my hair stick to my lips. His narrowed gaze is full of purpose and potency.

He breathes hard.

I breathe harder. "*Thatcher.*" I can't leave my best friend. *I can't leave him*, and I'm not ready to be dragged out of this bar like I always am when Maximoff fights.

"You're my eyes," Thatcher says strongly. "Watch Banks. He's helping Farrow and Maximoff. Copy?"

"Yes." I inhale. "I'll be your eyes." I scrutinize Banks. His arms are extended, and he barricades the angered bar patrons from physically confronting Maximoff and Farrow.

My pulse decelerates for the first time, and I realize it's because I'm in Thatcher's arms.

He takes charge and yells at Tony. "Tell your friend to mind his own fucking business! Or take him out of here!"

"My friend?!" Tony unleashes a bitter laugh. "Gio and I haven't been friends since we were sixteen! If it were up to me, I wouldn't even be in this shithole!"

I can practically feel Tony gesturing to the rustic green bar sign above the televisions.

The one that reads: *South Philly Brew.*

Thatcher has spent countless nights at this sports bar with his family. He's told me about how his uncles would buy Banks and him beers when they were teenagers. Yes, even underage, and they'd watch football and blow off steam.

He's rigid against me, boiling. "You grew up in this shithole like the rest of us!"

"And I made it out! Unlike you!"

I cringe, hating every little jab that Tony loves to take. South Philly is a beautiful place, and I want to turn and defend Thatcher to the death, but I made a promise to watch Banks.

Not coming to my boyfriend's defense—it hurts like a billion blades in my stomach, but I force myself to stay pinned to his brother.

Ohh...

No.

No.

My eyes grow as a thin guy in a winter beanie stands on a chair, a plastic shopping bag in hand. What did he buy?

For what purpose?

"Gio, sit down!" Banks yells.

"Thatcher," I warn.

He swings his head, and immediately, he lowers me to my feet, his towering height shielding me.

Zeroing in on the target, Thatcher yells, "Che cozz'!"

He's taught me enough Italian that I remember the translation: *What the fuck are you doing?*

"Just bought this for you, Moretti!" Gio digs his hand in the shopping bag. "So you can tie up your rich bitch!" He chucks an object at us, but Farrow intercepts first and catches what looks like restraint cuffs, meant to tie a submissive to a bed.

I boil. "I do *not* like BDSM!" I shout at the top of my lungs, as though the whole world will hear me.

"Prove it!" He points from me to Thatcher, as though we'll *fuck* in front of everyone.

My face twists in disgust and ire. I loathe this redundancy more than anything, how I always find myself here, shouting the same phrase and meeting the same unwelcome result.

It is *infuriating*.

"Are you fucking kidding me?!" Maximoff almost charges at the guy.

Farrow puts Moffy in an arm-lock and whispers rapidly in his ear. Banks is pushing other men back from us.

And Thatcher—he could spark infernal damnation in a single glare. "She has nothing to prove to you." He projects his voice without yelling.

I touch a slow-growing smile on my face. *I can't believe I'm smiling.* I perch my hands on my wide hips, chin raised, and then—

Boom!

I flinch.

Thatcher clasps my hand and draws me behind his back. Every head whips to the noise behind the bar as an older gray-haired gentleman bangs a baseball bat to the counter.

"EVERYONE OUT!" he yells.

Complaints gather from whispers to shouts.

"I SAID OUT! I OWN THIS DAMN BAR. I SAY YOUSE GO, YOUSE GO!" He points the bat at the door. People begin to shift, and I snatch my wedding binder before another pair of hands do.

"You wanna lose business, Jerry?!"

"I'm losing *nuthin'*. I get ten grand just to get you shitheads outta here!" He suddenly aims his bat towards me and Maximoff. "Youse can stay. Everyone else, go!"

Ten thousand dollars?

I go cold. This makes little sense.

People shoot us nasty glares and huff on their way out. I hear *rich bitch!* yelled at me, as though this is my doing. Snowy gusts blow inside as bodies exit, the bar slowly clearing. Leaving behind a beer-spilt floor, crooked chairs, and littered tabletops.

Moffy and I exchange a tentative look, and I sense our bodyguards talking amongst themselves and hawk-eyeing all the passing, disgruntled people. I hug the binder and lean into my best friend. "Did you pay the owner to clear out the bar?"

"No." His fingers weave through his thick, dark brown hair. "Did you?"

"No. I wouldn't. It'd be easier to just leave." We're uneasy, and I say what we both know. "Our bodyguards wouldn't spend *ten grand* to evacuate a room full of assholes. There are only a handful of people who would."

His shoulders square, ready to protect and defend even though he's not a bodyguard.

"Charlie," I declare. "He would."

Maximoff licks his lips. "As cool as it'd be for telepathy to be real, Charlie isn't *telepathic.* Your brother couldn't have known *this* mayhem broke out at this moment."

"What if it's online?" I theorize. "Someone could've recorded and posted everything." I take a seat at the bar, setting my binder back down, and we take out our phones and do a quick social media search.

My frown deepens.

No peep. Nothing about the eldest Cobalt and eldest Hale in a South Philly bar fight.

Banks plops down on the stool beside mine. He just intercepted the path of a drunk middle-aged man, who probably would've sat next to me.

"Thank you," I whisper.

He just nods and reaches over the bar for a beer bottle. He motions to the owner, who gives the okay for him to take the beer.

"It can't be Charlie," Maximoff concludes. "Jesus, does he even know we're here?"

"He does," Thatcher says, coming closer to the bar with Farrow.

I rotate on the stool. "What do you mean?" I rush to obtain whatever knowledge they've acquired.

"Charlie texted me earlier." Thatcher squats and collects my trampled fur coat off the floor. *Dirtied.* He splays the filthy thing on a vacant stool. "Your brother asked where I was. So I told him."

I'm wary. "That was all he wanted?"

Thatcher nods.

My neck elongates, tense and very cautious of what's about to occur. "Charlie is coming here."

Maximoff shakes his head, uncertain. "It doesn't make any damn sense, Janie."

"I know my brother," I say. "He's bought out this particular bar, and he'll be here in dramatic glory."

It has to be Charlie.

Maximoff turns to Farrow. "Ask Oscar if Charlie is coming here." Oscar Oliveira is Charlie's 24/7 bodyguard, and so he'd know more than just where Charlie is.

He should be with him.

Beside him.

Protecting him.

Farrow blows a bubblegum bubble and pops it in his mouth. "You're five steps behind me, wolf scout."

Maximoff growls in frustration. "Farrow—"

"I already tried. Oscar is off comms. Most likely because Charlie asked his bodyguard not to share with the whole class."

Thatcher looks grim, from the door to us.

"What is it?" I ask.

"Earlier, I heard that Eliot and Tom left New York and have been heading to Philly."

"It could be a coincidence," I note.

Farrow rests a boot on a stool rung. "Or your brothers are up to some shit."

"They're not up to some shit," I defend, more hotly than I mean to. He raises his hands.

Thatcher's concern bears down on me. "What's wrong?"

I take a strained breath. "I'm afraid my siblings are being coy in order to give you a hard time." Admitting this is difficult because I would *love* to just roll out a beautiful, luxurious red carpet for Thatcher.

But this is not the Cobalt way.

It's very possible Thatcher's introduction into my family will be grueling, taxing, and of the most theatrical, over-the-top caliber—and I need to save him from this, don't I?

Possibly that's what I can offer him, an open window into my family that he can easily crawl into. But how?

Life is chess. And I need to be ten moves ahead of Charlie.

"Jane." Thatcher draws my gaze upward. "I can handle whatever they throw at me."

Even if this were true, I have to help him. "Ensemble," I say deeply, a word meant for my family, and I want that to include him.

Together.

His chest rises, and he nods.

I type on my phone, my sibling group chat relatively quiet tonight.

I send: How many of you are coming here?

"What in the ever-loving fuck…? Where's everyone going?"

I look up.

Sullivan Meadows, my twenty-year-old cousin, suddenly arrives. Her bodyguard Akara Kitsuwon safely leads her against the grain, and they enter the bar while masses barge outside.

Sulli unzips her puffy teal jacket. "Are we supposed to be here?"

"It seems that way," I tell her. "Someone's bought out the bar for us." Much earlier, I invited Maximoff, Sulli, and Luna—my three cousins who live with me in the old townhouse—to join Thatcher and me at the bar. I haven't heard back from Luna, so I suppose she's busy tonight.

Akara fixes his mic on his red windbreaker. He speaks in short glimpses to the other bodyguards. Including Tony who hovers far too close. His proximity might as well light Thatcher's eyes on fire.

My phone buzzes.

Have I missed something? Where is everyone going? —Audrey

If my little sister has no clue about what's happening, then it's likely that Moffy is right. Charlie isn't coming here.

None of my siblings are.

"Oh hey, you don't have to get up for me." Sulli knots her long brunette hair in a messy top bun. "Really, I can just fucking stand or take another stool."

Banks has already risen. "It's not like you'll block my view or anything." He's six-seven to her six-foot. "Go ahead." He's offering her the seat beside me.

"Thanks." As Sulli sits, she watches Banks and Akara clasp hands and pat each other's back in greeting. To me, she says, "I heard we're going to Scotla—I mean, *Hawaii*. Fuck, I suck at code names."

I smile and scoot closer. "Have you decided on whether you want to bring Will Rochester along?" Sulli and Will have been dating privately, and she's admitted that they probably would've kissed at Hallow Friends Eve if the party hadn't been cut short. Will hasn't pressured her to move faster or made her feel badly for ending the party early—a party that he threw for her.

So far, he seems honorable and decent.

Yet, surfacing his name suddenly silences the bar. The door bangs shut, the last stranger leaving.

She catches a look that Banks and Akara give each other. "What? You don't think I'll invite Will? That I'm chicken shit scared?"

Akara grimaces. "No. That's not it, Sul."

Banks tilts his beer to his mouth. "Why would you even want to invite the Rooster?"

"The Rooster?" Sulli and I say in unison.

I swing my head to Thatcher. He rubs his temple and shoots his brother an annoyed look.

Security Force Omega. They must've jokingly coined a code name for Will Rochester. I shouldn't be too surprised.

Sulli gawks. "What the fuck is that? The Rooster?"

Akara has trouble restraining a smile. "It's for comms."

"It's for comms?" Sulli stands and slugs his shoulder. "He's not a cock!"

Banks laughs.

Sulli lands a fist in his arm too, and he hardly sways and just grins into a sip of beer. Akara smiles more and places his hands on her broad shoulders. "You're not the butt of a joke."

"Yeah but Will is, and he's not a fucking *cock*, Kits."

Banks tips his head. "We're just callin' it like we see it, mermaid."

She huffs. "Yeah? And his cock is probably ten fucking times bigger than both of yours."

Akara and Banks try not to laugh, and then Banks says, "No way in hell."

She goes still and glances down at their crotches. I can't blame her. My curiosity has piqued too, but Sulli flushes a deep red, her breath shallow. She turns to me, an *SOS* signal in her green eyes.

I pipe up. "Don't listen to them, Sulli. They're just jealous that you're bringing a hot date to Scotland."

Maximoff crosses his arms, not a fan of Will Rochester. He's told Sulli to *be careful* about a hundred times and counting.

"Is that it?" Sulli asks Akara and Banks. "You're both just jealous."

Banks raises his shoulder in a shrug.

Akara's muscles are flexed. "No." He puts his fingers to his earpiece, as if comms chatter is louder. "I'm your bodyguard and you're dating someone for the first time. That's it."

Sulli frowns. "So you won't care if I bring Will?"

It takes him a second to say, "If that's what you want."

"That's what I fucking want."

The door whips open, and I hear commotion outside like the bar patrons are loitering. They yell at whoever comes through.

Instantly, I recognize the chestnut-haired, blue-eyed bodyguard. A plastic bag is hooked on his elbow.

"Suck my dick!" Donnelly shouts at the crowds, then shuts them out with the kick of the door.

Akara pushes back his black hair. "Donnelly."

He spins, noticing me and Sulli. "Sorry, boss." I can tell he's off-duty, no radio, and plus, his client isn't present.

After Donnelly was taken off Beckett's detail, the Tri-Force transferred him to a Hale.

Xander Hale, to be exact. He's been working alongside Thatcher this past week. Two bodyguards on one client.

"Smokes?" Donnelly procures a package of cigarettes from the bag, plus a carton of cheesecake.

Banks groans. "Don't tease me, man."

I text my sister back while Donnelly greets everyone and slings an arm over Farrow's shoulders.

I thought some of you were headed to this bar tonight. My mistake. I send the message.

"You don't know what you're talking about," Farrow says coolly to Tony.

I missed something.

Tony smirks, too pompous. "We all know Donnelly shouldn't be going to Hawaii if his client is staying back home."

Thatcher retorts, "Donnelly is a groomsman, and Farrow wants him there."

"Was I talking to you, Moretti?" Tony snaps. "Didn't think so."

A bad taste floods my mouth. "Are you four?"

"Twenty-eight, actually." Tony rests an elbow on the bar and his creeping eyes track down my body.

God.

Thatcher steps forward, and Banks pulls him back.

Tony cocks his head. "And isn't Xander going to be a groomsman, so does that mean *you* don't want him there?" He points at Maximoff. "Or does Xander just not want to be around you?"

More shots fired. That direct hit hurts.

Moffy is stewing. Smoke is coming out of his ears. The truth: Xander requested to stay home so he could go to therapy. He said it's been helping lately, and he doesn't want to miss a session.

Farrow has a calming hand on the back of Moffy's neck.

"Hey." Akara comes forward and motions for Tony to step aside. He ushers him towards the corner and sneers, "You can't talk to a client like that."

Donnelly digs into his cheesecake. "Been waiting for someone to put away Tony the Toolbox."

"If only permanently," I sigh.

"Murder with the Cobalt fam," Donnelly says through a mouthful of cheesecake. "Those who slay together, stay together."

I eye him. "I meant *metaphorical* murder." I pause, curious. "Did you?"

He puts a hand to his chest, grinning and not saying one way or the other, and that's when the door rips open again.

This time, camera flashes cast shadows on the walls and wind whips through the entryway and more than one body struts inside the sports bar.

First come the bodyguards.

I count five.

And then *five* famous faces bring up the rear.

Charlie, Beckett, Eliot, Tom, and Ben.

Every single one of my brothers. They're all here, and they're far too fixated on *Thatcher* like he's tonight's five-course meal.

8

Jane Cobalt

I SPRING OFF THE stool and clasp Thatcher's muscular waist. Panic shoots through me, and he curves his arm around my shoulders. Bringing me to his chest before I can swerve in a million frantic directions.

"Jane—"

"I haven't properly prepared you for the avalanche you're about to endure," I whisper rapidly. "It's my duty to strap you with as much ammo as humanly possible."

Though, every counterattack of ours will be aimed at my brothers, which is possibly why his eyes darken.

It feels wrong.

So incredibly *wrong*.

But if they're coming for my boyfriend, then I'll have no choice.

"Do not cower," I coach quickly. "Do not avoid their eyes. Do not show fear. They're little fiends that will chew you up like you're nothing more than a three o'clock snack."

A shadow of a smile plays at his mouth.

"You smile now but they can smell blood in the water, and the second you cut open a weakness, they will poke and prod until you're bleeding out." My mind whirls inside a new sort of apprehensive alarm. I've never been in this position with my siblings. I've never felt like we're on a battleground and I stand opposite all of them. "They could make you jump naked over a fence for all I know."

He cups my hot cheeks, his large hands cocooning my face, and it helps me breathe somehow. I curl my fingers over his strong wrists.

"Five teenage boys can't hurt me, point-blank," Thatcher proclaims. "I doubt a hundred could."

I ease some. "Your cockiness is helpful." *Because the sky and Earth know that most of my brothers are tremendously arrogant.* "But you do realize that Charlie and Beckett are twenty-one?"

He nods once. "I'm all good. I have this." He drops his voice lower. "They can't make me do anything that I don't want to do."

I quirk my brows, lips parting. "You would jump naked over a fence for me?"

His complete unwavering, sexy self-assurance says *hell yeah.*

I rest my chin on his chest, looking up. Could I do the same? I'm not 100% sure, but I want to believe I can make this equal. I have it in me—I know I do.

Somewhere.

And so I say, "As I would for you."

He gives me a stern look, his hand tracking down my back. "You'd be in tabloids. *Naked.*"

"A sacrifice," I whisper, my heart flops on a treadmill set at the highest speed. "One I'm certain I can make."

He shakes his head, his thumb stroking my cheek. "One you'd be *uncomfortable* to make. Tell me I'm wrong."

"You're wrong." I lie, for some reason. I shouldn't lie. It feels morbid and nauseating, and I'm not positive he can tell I'm being untruthful.

He just stares at me. "We're not competing for jack shit, you and me."

"We're not," I agree. "This is just something we do together."

"Getting naked and jumping fences?"

"Oui."

He blinks and breathes hot breath through his nose. He's straight-forward and direct. I talk like I'm taking every roundabout, side-street, and detour on a map, and lately we haven't always crossed paths. He's trying not to be lost inside metaphors and subtext.

"Dude, it's like a morgue in here."

Tom.

We turn, just as Tom trots closer with buckles clinking on a black rocker jacket. Golden-brown hair artfully styled, mouth in a corkscrew smile, charm and mischief melded together.

He's eighteen and I've seen him grip a microphone like a second heart. Singing with every ounce of power and feeling inside of him. Captivating a screaming, frenzied audience with such tremendous ease.

But in this moment, he's not a lead singer of an emo-punk band.

He's just my little brother.

One who put toothpaste and shaving cream on our dad's pillow, thinking he wouldn't notice. (He did.) One who was so afraid of *Jurassic Park* as a child, he crawled into my bed for the whole month of July.

Tom swings his head to Eliot with a laugh. "You think it's us?" He means the dead quiet.

Eliot grins. "If it's not, I'd be offended." He unbuttons his expensive pea coat. If the God of War and hedonistic Dionysus birthed a child, they'd spit out my nineteen-year-old brother.

It's best not to confront Eliot and Tom. They'll joke around the truth like they're batting an inflatable ball over my head, and I need answers.

So I do the sensible thing and approach Ben. "Pippy." I use his nickname.

My sixteen-year-old brother lingers near a dirtied high-top table. He offers me a warm smile while he takes off his Dalton Academy beanie and unzips his letterman jacket, one for ice hockey. He's grown into his height, and at six-five, he stands like a confident athlete.

I touch his arm. "Que se passe-t-il?" *What's going on?*

He winces a little. "Demande à Charlie." *Ask Charlie.*

I frown. "What'd he put you up to?"

"Nothing. I want to be here," Ben says strongly. "It's important." I wonder why our sister isn't with them, but it's a question for later.

My voice is soft as I ask, "Then why do you look pained?"

"Parce que. Je ne pense pas que cela te plaira beaucoup." *Because. I don't think you'll enjoy this very much.*

My stomach drops out of my butt.

I glance over at Beckett. He leans calmly on the bar and eats a carton of Wendy's fries. Tonight is a rare night where he doesn't have a ballet performance, and I bet that's why they chose today.

So he could be here.

His lips are noticeably downturned and face sullen. He locks eyes with Donnelly, his former bodyguard.

I mutter under my breath, "It's like a break-up."

More than just me notices their silent, uncomfortable exchange. With an equally morose expression, Donnelly stuffs his cheesecake in a plastic bag and waves goodbye to Farrow and Oscar before he leaves the bar altogether.

Beckett is a heartbreaker, I've come to realize.

"Which mailman lost my invite this time?" Charlie asks dryly.

I locate him, just as he stands up on the bar with unkempt sandy-brown hair and mysteries behind yellow-green eyes. He has no coat, just an askew white button-down that sticks halfway out of black slacks.

The media talks about how we, Cobalts, are intelligent and witty. Poised and confident. But very few mention how deeply we *feel.*

How Eliot can summon tears out of cold-hearted eyes. How Beckett can make your awed gasp feel like the last breath you'll take. How Ben can harness your empathy so you do the right thing. How Tom can wake the dead things buried inside you. How Audrey can bottle love and *romance* like it's life's greatest necessity.

And Charlie—everyone thinks he has no soul but his is just the darkest, deepest of them all.

I sidle to the bar. "It was housemates only, but if I'd known you were in town, I would've invited you all."

"Where's Luna?" Eliot asks.

Tom looks mildly worried at the lack of Luna.

I frown. "I thought she'd be with you," I say honestly, and I look to Maximoff. He puts his phone to his ear and heads further back into the bar. Farrow follows. I trust that Luna's older brother will find her.

I look up at Charlie. "Are you here to drink and watch a wrestling match?"

A coy smile inches up his lips. "You know I'm not." He leans slightly on his cane. He hasn't needed one in a while, but the cold weather has stiffened his healing leg, which he had surgery on back in May after the car crash.

I zone in on the ornate head of the cane: a gold lion eating a snake. I whisper up at him, "Why does this have to be a war?"

"It's only a war if you make it one."

"Then what is this, Charlie?"

He sighs out an annoyed breath. "You know what this is, Jane."

A test of loyalty. Interlopers beware. The Cobalt brothers will not let you through. Farrow endured a lukewarm version. Beckett took it upon himself to grill Farrow at every turn.

I hiss, "He's proven *enough*. He sacrificed his job for me." I'm trying desperately to open up the window for my boyfriend.

Charlie is slamming it shut. "Hundreds of men would follow suit if it meant they could date you. He's not special."

"He is when his career is his entire purpose and reason for *being*," I combat. "Let's just all go out to dinner and talk." For once, I would like my family to shelve the dramatics.

Charlie squats and rests his forearms on his knees, our eyes parallel. I'm just as smart, just as capable, just as strong as my dear brother.

I don't back down. "We don't need to do this, Charlie."

"Yes we do." He leans forward. "Just remember we love you."

Heat builds in my body, and I whisper back, "I hate you right now."

He smiles. "It'll diminish in time." He rises.

Eliot is the one to clamp a hand on Thatcher's back. "Follow us, boyfriend-in-law."

Thatcher seems unruffled and ready for any hell. He swivels a knob on his radio and glances over at his brother.

Banks upnods to him. "Get some."

I recognize the military lingo, but not all my brothers do. They send each other wary looks, and it creates a new tension. A new divide between them and Thatcher.

As though we belong to two vastly different worlds, and it'll take blood and sweat to pull him into ours.

We can do this. I try to bolster courage as I come up beside my boyfriend.

Thatcher clasps my hand and threads our fingers.

We can jump over fences naked together.

Don't be afraid, Jane.

9

Thatcher Moretti

COBALTS ARE A TORNADIC force you don't want to fuck with. Out of the three famous families, they have the most power and can wield it with the snap of a finger.

Should I be afraid?

I think if I were someone else, I might shrink at the eye-popping, slack-jawed sight: all five Cobalt brothers strewn across a U-shaped booth like they're Apollo, Zeus—godly figures—posing for an oil painting to be immortalized.

Among tabloids and fans, Xander Hale is considered the "prettiest" boy. Maximoff Hale is in a league of his own. And the Cobalt brothers— they're cited as the "sexiest," oozing some kind of ancient, sensual allure.

But as I lower on a chair next to Jane and face her brothers, I can't flinch. Or shy. It's not in me. I've seen and lived through the worst hell, and whatever conditions they set, I can survive.

I just can't make an enemy out of them, and lately I've been way too good at making those.

My objective: *don't piss off my girlfriend's brothers.*

And behind that objective lies another: *take care of them.*

Her brothers are in their teens and early twenties, and I'm still a bodyguard—I'm not here to cause harm. I want to defend and protect them, and the sooner I'm on their side, the easier this'll be.

But Christ, I have *no* idea what they want me to do. So I'm in recon-mode. Attentive. *Frosty*. I assess each guy in every passing beat. Trying to determine which one will be the flat-out hardest to please.

Charlie Cobalt? He's a wild card. Could be helpful, could be antagonistic. Could be something that I've never confronted before.

He lounges like he's about to be fed grapes: his foot on the cracked leather cushion, elbow on his knee. His yellow-green eyes puncture me. "You were fucking our sister during the fake-dating ploy."

I don't blink.

"*Charlie.*" Jane's face is beet-red.

I've listened to men talk crasser about so much fucking worse. Hearing this should be like popping a jellybean in my mouth. *Too easy.* But a sharp taste sears my throat, and I rake a hand over my hardened jaw.

"I was respecting your sister." I will *always* respect Jane.

Eliot hoists himself on top of the booth frame. He uncorks a bottle of wine between his legs. It pops. "Did you hear that, brothers? Thatcher, here, was respectfully fucking our sister."

Starting off just great.

I stare blankly.

"Dear God," Jane mutters under her breath, wide-eyed like a freight train just smacked into her face.

Concern flexes my muscles. I watch Jane out of the corner of my eye but keep fixed on her brothers. "I didn't say that."

"It's what I heard, dude." Tom slouches back, lip upturned.

"All Thatcher said was that he was respecting our sister," Ben argues.

I nod once. I'd angle towards the idea that Ben Cobalt already likes me, but with his long legs tucked to his chest and head tilted back, he's sizing me up.

Haven't won him over.

Beckett brings a cigarette to his mouth with a graceful hand. Not saying a thing yet. Based off past history—Beckett trying to nail Farrow down—I'm guessing he'll be the last to come around on me.

Eliot fists the neck of the wine and tells Ben, "It was said between his words."

"Subtext." Tom drums his fingers on the table.

I adjust my earpiece, static crackling with comms chatter while Akara tries to locate Quinn Oliveira, Luna's bodyguard.

Empty bottles and half-eaten baskets of wings are cleared off the table. Familiar scents of cheesesteak and beer linger. I shouldn't be surprised the Cobalt brothers wanted to stay at South Philly Brew since Charlie bought out the bar.

But they could've easily just taken me to some upper-class, blue-blooded, rich-prick place where I'd have to feel my way in the dark to the finish line.

It puts me on a steep edge. Like they're up to something more unexpected. Something worse. My senses hum on a taut vibration.

Jane's collarbones jut out, and she slips each brother a warning look.

The security team is going to talk about this shit for years. Not because I plan to run my mouth about it.

Anyone who isn't a Cobalt—like Maximoff, Sullivan, my twin brother, like Omega and Epsilon bodyguards, like fucking *Tony*—watches us from the bar. Not even pretending to be disinterested.

They're all turned towards this table like my ass on this hot seat is a nine o'clock blockbuster. And they're viewing it for fucking free.

"Thatcher Alessio Moretti," Eliot says with the raise of his wine. *He knows my middle name.* It's a public fact. But his drawn-out, embellished delivery snakes a chill down my spine.

I stare him down. Remembering the night I picked his drunk ass off the floor—Eliot is destructive. Most of her brothers are like ticking bombs on the verge of explosion.

Just don't set one off.

If he were my nineteen-year-old wild-hearted brother, I'd rip the bottle out of his hand.

Jane shoots out of her seat and careens forward. "Eliot. You promised you'd be better about this." She tries to steal the wine.

He yanks back. "I'm not drinking in excess, Jane."

She reaches further.

He lifts the wine over his head and gasps. "Why so edgy? We're all just talking. *For now.*" He winks at me.

I'm not scared.

But I also can't tell if he's bluffing. There could be nothing but smoke behind the curtain. For as intensely as they're studying my stern features, I'm guessing they can't read me any better than I can them.

Jane snaps at Eliot in French. He responds with less heat in the same language, and while they argue, Charlie tears the wine out of Eliot's hands.

"Brother," Eliot glares.

Charlie ignores him and puts the bottle to his lips.

Comms sound in my ear. "Take the wine from Charlie," Oscar instructs. "He'll appreciate it."

Copy that. I listen to Charlie's bodyguard and extend my hand towards the Merlot.

Charlie scrutinizes me for a long oxygen-caging second. He wipes the corner of his mouth with a finger, his intrusive eyes crawling down me. And then he passes me the wine.

"You have to drink it," Oscar says.

I almost stiffen. *Don't freeze up like a motherfucking shitbag.*

I try to kick my ass into gear, but a nagging voice growls, *stay sober.* Adding to the mess upstairs in my head, Eliot and Tom's Epsilon bodyguards start spewing shit on comms.

"Stop helping Thatcher."

"This shouldn't be easy for him. He *fucked* the team."

They want me to hear their complaints. Or else they'd forget the radio and just turn to Oscar who's beside them at the bar.

Guilt hammers my ribcage, but I shove it down. I've got an objective to see through.

Make a choice.

I swig the wine, and then I lower my radio volume a notch before handing the bottle to Jane.

"Thank you," she says softly to me and takes the heftiest gulp. Scratch that—*three* gulps, and just when I think she's done, a second from taking the bottle, she holds up a finger and swallows more wine.

She has a high tolerance. She's not approaching drunk. Probably not even buzzed, and I'm glad one of us can down that much right now.

I curve my arm around her chair. Waiting for when she's ready.

She finally shoves it in my opened hand. "Liquid reinforcements," she whispers to me, wine trickling down her chin. I wipe the red liquid off with my thumb.

She blushes, and our eyes attach deeper.

Blood pulses in my cock, and I could kiss Jane. I'm a millisecond from dipping my head down—

"Do you have anything to say?" Beckett asks, stealing my attention. He blows a filmy line of smoke upward.

I nod a few times.

He's calm, but I can't discount the threatening look in his eye. They're all protective of their older sister. And I understand how they'd want to guarantee no harm invades her life. Fuckbags after targets after shitheads surround her on a daily basis, and if they need me to prove that I'm not one of them, they don't even need to command me to *jump*.

I'll already be off the ground.

"Yeah," I nod, about to start talking in length. "Look, I love Jane—"

"That's funny," Charlie cuts me off. "Considering a week ago, none of us thought you were even attracted to her."

It throws me back. Not physically.

I'm mentally wrenched to a moment I shared with Jane.

To the night she told me her brothers and little sister wanted her to "open herself up" to *love*, and subsequently heartbreak. Because they thought her feelings were one-sided, un-fucking-reciprocated, and that I'd never be interested in her sexually or romantically.

She gushed all of this to me.

And then as I was tying my boots, she said, "I can't blame them, really."

I knotted my lace. Thinking she'd mention how I wasn't easy to read. That I was too stoic for her siblings to conclude anything but *disinterest* on my end. Or at the very least, that I was a professional bodyguard and I would've forced my dick down during the fake-dating op.

But she said, "Your type doesn't usually fall for *my* type in popular culture."

It struck me hard. Painfully. I sent a narrowed look over my shoulder. "Why wouldn't my type be into you?"

She rolled on her side, pink sheet draped over the curve of her wide hip and belly. Wavy brown hair frizzed wildly around freckled cheeks. Her small breasts exposed and nipples perked—and my cock twitched with an aggressive, primal hunger.

If she was a lion, then I was the animal that wanted to mount the fuck out of her and play around with her until she was one beautiful *whimpering* mess. Spent and safe and satiated in my arms.

I didn't want to leave her room. I wished I could listen to her talk while the sun rose and set. Every second. Every day.

But I had to go.

Zero three hundred hours. On the dot. Or else my fucking carriage would morph into a pumpkin.

"It's just that…" Jane trailed off, giving me a long once-over. Her aching breath pushed her lips apart. She fixated on my dark hair tucked behind my ears and my jawline and my tall, muscular build. "You're blatantly hot and fit in the realm of Vikings and billboard jocks. I'm—"

"Gorgeous," I interjected. Not hesitating to cut her off there.

A soft noise left Jane, eyes melting. "I…" Flustered, she sat up slightly on the headboard. "We've been through this. I have a strong love for myself, you know, but I recognize that classically, I'm not the world's definition of beauty."

"You're mine," I said with power and force. Feeling pissed off, I shifted my glare onto the wall and grabbed my black button-down off the ground. I was boiling.

Not at her.

But at the media outlets, tabloids, and spineless pricks that constantly critiqued Jane's appearance. That pitted her against whatever the popular body type is of the fucking millennium.

It was horseshit.

Jane went quiet.

I finished buttoning my shirt, and I trekked stringently to the end table. Collecting my things. I holstered my gun on my waistband. "There shouldn't even be an ideal woman."

I caught her smile.

She cleared her throat. "I agree."

We stared at each other for a long time, unsaid things reinforcing more tension and strength between us, and I broke the silence. "If your brothers and sister are assuming that I can't be attracted to you because I'm *classically* hotter, then that's outright fucked up."

Her siblings never met any of her friends-with-benefits. Including *Nate*, who looks like an A-list Hollywood actor that spent time shoving kids against lockers in high school. But even if Charlie had shaken hands with Nate, I was sure he'd say that he'd been using Jane.

"My siblings would weigh all probabilities, I think," Jane said softly. "And maybe it hurts them to assume this. But we're all smart enough to know that the emotion inside a fact doesn't make the fact any less true."

I tried to process that, and I held her gaze in a vice. "It doesn't make it any less fucked up."

She tipped her head with a nod. "Vrai." *True.*

I'm not like the Cobalts. Her brothers and sister did everything they could to help Jane tear down walls, knowing romantic *pain* was on the other side, but I'd want to protect her from heartbreak. Not guide her towards that feeling.

So at the sports bar, Charlie's words are like a rubber band snapping against my eardrum: *A week ago, none of us thought you were attracted to her.*

I bottle heat in my lungs. "I wasn't allowed to be attracted to my client publicly, not beyond the op." I shouldn't ask the Cobalt brothers anything.

As a bodyguard, it's inappropriate. But I'm off-duty and her boyfriend. To breach the fortress of this family, you can't be timid.

And I know I'm not that. "Why were you all so sure that your sister's feelings were one-sided?"

Jane whips her head to me, smiling. *I'm not easy to push over, honey.*

"I just didn't think you'd be into her," Beckett admits, and to Jane, he says, "I owe you an apology, sis. I'm sorry."

Ben drops his feet beneath the table. "Me too."

"It's okay," Jane says with a warm smile. "Thank you."

Charlie pulls at his messy hair, his annoyance visible and on me. "You gave us no indication of liking our sister. I'm not apologizing for that."

I nod. "You don't have to."

Eliot grabs something from behind his back and tosses it down to his brother.

Tom catches what looks like a gold statue, a twinkle in his eye. He flashes a smile in my direction. "For you."

Muscles stiff and hot, I reach forward and collect the statue. I turn it over in my palm.

I breathe in through my nose. *What the fuck.* I'm holding a trophy shaped like a *snake*. The plaque reads *Master of Deception* with the year engraved below.

Comms crackle. "Flash it to us, Moretti," Oscar banters.

No chance.

If I acknowledge SFO, the Cobalt brothers will think I'm choosing security over them. I set the trophy on the table and hear Farrow, his voice picked up on Oscar's radio. "Cobalts are extra as fuck."

He's not wrong.

Donnelly enters the line and starts asking questions since he's not at the bar anymore. Their chatter escalates and starts drowning out Akara, who's still searching for Quinn.

I click my mic and speak hushed. "Shut the fuck up."

Comms quiet.

I add, "Thank you." Then I drop my hand.

Tom leans back with a grin. "You even fooled our mom and dad."

Weight situates on my strict shoulders. I blame myself for how my relationship with Jane started out on a bed of dishonesty. Us lying to her parents and siblings.

I could've pulled the trigger earlier.

I should've. Even if they don't care.

Eliot threads his palms behind his head, lounging back. "You could teach a master class on How to Deceive a Genius."

My brows cinch in confusion. *He's impressed?*

Tom lifts a finger. "I'd enroll."

They both are. I glance at Jane for confirmation.

She leans in and whispers, "They're devious little devils."

Right.

I should be happy that two out of five brothers already *somewhat* like me. But I'm not jumping for fucking joy that they see me as a third devil in their merry gang of terrors.

Eliot grins. "As would I, Tom."

Ben lets out a pained sound. "Stop sucking his dick—"

"It was just the tip," Eliot laughs.

"—he's a *liar*," Ben continues.

One of them cares that I lied.

Eliot is serious in a sudden flash. "Ben—"

"A liar is dating our sister!" Ben motions to me. "That should worry *everyone.* Why am I the only one in this family who's upset about that?"

Eliot and Tom share a glance I can't decrypt. Maybe they're concerned about Ben or they're more suspicious of me.

"Hey, kid," I say.

"He's not a kid," Charlie chastises.

I forgot the Cobalts hate that.

I nod, raking a hand down my mouth, and I tell Ben, "I'm being straight forward with you now. I'm sorry I couldn't before." I'm lost on how else to right this wrong and rebuild my integrity. But I'm trying.

His eyes redden. He pounds his head back, chin lifted higher. When I'd been the Epsilon lead, I was in charge of protecting the minors. Of *Ben.* He has a big heart.

He fights for what he feels is right.

But I lost count of all the times I had to inform bodyguards that Ben would be staying late in detention. For fuck's sake, I'm not even a lead anymore, and I just heard on comms that Winona and Ben got in a fight at Dalton Academy. She jumped on a senior's back because he called Ben a crybaby pussy.

Jane scoots towards her youngest brother and gathers his hand in hers. "I lied too, Pippy. If you fault Thatcher, then you have to fault me."

Ben lets go of her hand. "I don't know *anything* about him, Jane."

"We're about to fix that," Charlie says smoothly.

Beckett snuffs out his cigarette on an ashtray and then fans out a deck of blue cards on the table. Gold lions are hand-drawn on each one.

Can't be ordinary playing cards.

For all I know, this could be tarot and Beckett is about to read my future. Rich, poor—I don't care. I just want *her.*

Jane steeples her fingers to her lips in focused thought.

"What are these?" I ask them.

Charlie flashes a half-smile. "It's a game called *What Would You Do for Jane Cobalt?*"

I cross my arms and nod. I'm Oscar Mike. Ready to move out in whatever direction they point to. But honestly, this isn't my normal.

Where I come from, we'd throw some punches then crack a beer and laugh about the old rift. Or we'd just never talk again. Grudges have detached friends and family like broken 1000-piece puzzles. Pieces missing or edges too worn to fit back.

At least they're offering me a shot.

Jane screeches her chair forward. "I request a modification." She folds her arms on the table. "I'd like it to be called: What Would *We* Do for Each Other?"

She wants in.

I almost smile. I'm not stepping on her toes or holding her back. Not unless this spins into a place that scares her to death.

"It won't be easy, sis," Beckett warns.

"I'm prepared." She waves to the cards. "How do we play?"

Eliot slides down onto the seat. "Pick a card and complete the instruction."

Sounds too simple. "That's it?" I ask.

"You won't flip all the cards tonight," Charlie explains. "Whenever we tell you to turn over one or two or five, you'll do it. Until you've gone through the entire deck."

I get it. I finish the game and I gain their respect or trust or both, and without wavering, I turn to Jane. "You pick."

She drums her lips, then slides out a left-center card. She flips it over, and I narrow my gaze on the gold script.

Tell us the number of people you've had intercourse with.

Unholy fuck.

I rub my mouth.

She intakes a sharp breath.

I haven't even told Jane my number, and she hasn't told me hers. Now we're about to announce this shit in front of security, her cousins, and brothers.

But based on the NDAs her sexual partners had to sign, I can estimate her number. Which is probably why this task exists.

To put me on the same footing.

Eliot squints at the card. *He has trouble reading*—it's one of the first things I had to tell new bodyguards on his detail. His dyslexia screws with how he sees letters. In the booth, he whispers in Tom's ear, and Tom whispers back.

"Really?" Jane snaps at Charlie and Beckett, the two oldest.

Charlie taps the card with his cane. "If Thatcher can't complete *this*, then he'll drown every time he's with our family."

"Around forty," I announce my number. Suddenly. Just like that.

"*Around* forty?" Ben glares. "You can't remember the exact number of girls you've slept with?"

"*People.*" Beckett calmly corrects his brother and lights another cigarette. He's being inclusive.

I'm straight, and I've only slept with girls. But I don't feel a need to emphasize this, so I just tell Ben, "I didn't keep count. Around forty is my best guess." *That's all I've got.*

Tom rests his arm on his brother's shoulder. "Higher than yours, Eliot."

Eliot holds the back of Tom's head in some kind of brotherly affection. Salt scalds my eyes, a glimpse of my childhood surging hard. And fast.

I see Skylar.

He's cupping my head, his smile rising. "Thatch."

I blink, and he's gone.

My pulse jack-knives. A sheen of sweat built under my shirt. I take a measured breath, and I nod to Jane when her hand touches my knee. She's silently asking if I'm okay.

I'm good.

She nods and turns to the booth. "My number is *eight*, and I want to footnote that it'd be even higher than Thatcher's number if I felt safer with more one-night stands."

I thread my fingers through my hair. Ignoring how my ribs constrict. Mention of her safety and sex reminds me of the *Chokehold Incident*— and my frontal lobe blisters, my knuckles craving to slam into a bag.

She should've never had to deal with that.

Her brothers go quiet, and a wave of concern flows towards Jane.

She sighs softly. "I didn't mention this to gain sympathy. It's just a fact."

"It's a sad fact." Eliot pries the card off the table. Pinching the corner, he whips open a Zippo lighter. A flame licks the paper and eats through the gold lion.

We watch the card torch between his fingers, and Eliot never blows out the fire; it just dies in his hand. Nothing left to burn.

"Flip another," Charlie orders.

Jane says, "You choose this time, Thatcher."

I pick the card on the far right and flip.

Tell us your favorite part of Jane's body.

My face almost screws up. I must've read this shit backwards or ass-fucking-sideways. Because in my head, there's no way *brothers* would want to hear this shit about their *sister.*

Jane has her knuckles to her lips, analyzing the card like it's a chess piece.

"She's your sister." My voice is stern. "You really want to know this?"

"It's not for our pleasure," Charlie retorts in a tone that says, *you're a fucking idiot.*

I'm feeling pretty fucking stupid.

Eliot outstretches his arms. "'Though this be madness, yet there is method in't.'"

"Hamlet," Jane whispers to me.

Hamlet? I would've never guessed that he just quoted Shakespeare. But I'm starting to think that how I respond to the cards is telling them about who I am as much as my actual answer. In a tense beat, I mentally file through all of Jane's body parts I love:

Her pussy.
Her hips. Love handles.
Stretchmarks.
Ass.
Freckles. Cheeks. Legs.
Arms.
Hands.
Breasts. Nipples.
Curve of her neck.
Brain.

I race down literally every inch of this girl. I love every part of Jane, but I can't say that. They'll just see it as a cop out.

Goddammit, hurry up and choose.

I land on safe non-sexual territory, and I answer, "Her heart."

Jane smiles.

Beckett makes a *what the fuck* face. "So you're not physically attracted to her?"

I shake my head, a hot breath coiled in my chest. I'm not seeing the *exit* sign inside this burning building. "You want me to embarrass your sister and say a body part?"

"Jane's fine," Tom defends. "Right?"

"I am," she nods, but she's tense as hell beside me.

I'm not shouting that I love her pussy. Not with *Tony* in earshot. Not so he can shit-talk to Epsilon about her body for the next however many months.

At the risk of pissing off Beckett, I never retract or backtrack. "I said my favorite."

He looks concerned for Jane. Like her sexual needs aren't being met. *He has no clue.*

I would love to carry her out to the limo and fuck her in the backseat for three hours.

Jane cups her hands. "His ass is my favorite."

I kiss the top of her head, and after Eliot incinerates the card, they tell us to flip a third one. We decide on a middle card together.

Jane overturns it.

eat the hearts of many rabbits.

Gut reaction, I almost laugh. "Real rabbit?"

"One pound each," Charlie says in reply.

Tom drops a plastic takeout carton on the table. Gotta hand it to the Cobalts. They don't fuck around. It also dawns on me that these cards are an elaborate, twisted game of Truth or Dare.

I can put down a 48oz steak no problem. Jane, on the other hand, isn't as big of a carnivore. She eats burnt hockey pucks for burgers.

Jane mutters to herself, "It's just a little rabbit. You like cooked goose." I listen to my girlfriend's pep talk while I pop the lid.

I grit down, the gamey stench of meat hitting my nostrils like a slap to the face.

Jane pinches her nose. "Is it raw?"

"It's cooked enough," Eliot assures.

Fresh road kill would smell and look better than what stares back at us. Blood drips off rare, greasy pieces of heart. Collecting in pools at the bottom of the carton.

Jane ties her hair back. "Where's a fork?"

"Wait," Ben says, anger hacksawing his blue eyes. He pivots to Charlie. "You said you'd *throw out* this card."

"Oh fuck," Sulli says too loudly, her voice audible from the bar.

"I said I'd think about it." Charlie flips his phone in his palm.

Beckett places a comforting hand on Ben's shoulder. "Thatcher and Jane aren't vegan like yo—"

"It doesn't matter!" Ben yells. "You should all respect my feelings on the consumption of *animals*. This didn't have to happen!" He points at the hearts and then whips around on me. "Don't eat it."

Sulli was right.

Oh fuck.

I need to make a hard call. Eat the rabbit and piss off Ben. Will he hold this against me forever?

Or I could just not complete the card and irritate Charlie, Beckett, Eliot, and Tom. Before I even move, Ben tells his brothers, "How would you like it if I cracked your ribcage and tore out your heart?"

Charlie rips open the last buttons of his white shirt. Bare chest and toned abs in view. "Go ahead."

Eliot unpockets a switchblade, twirls the knife, and stakes it on the wooden table near Ben.

"No," Jane scolds.

I tear the knife out of the wood and snap the blade closed with a quick hand. I shove the weapon in my back pocket.

"Murder-blocker," Tom quips.

"The worst," Eliot jokes.

I nod and breathe out of my nose. "Symbolic death and brothers might be your afternoon tea, but it's my nightmare."

They don't know it's one I've met. Sky's death still isn't public fact. But I have another brother, and that nightmare exists for us. If I lost Banks...

Just kill me.

You'd think Eliot and Tom Cobalt are all humor, but they can turn a switch quickly and they voice their understanding.

Ben goes to steal the rabbit carton.

Charlie pushes him back. "Let Thatcher decide."

I look between the Cobalt brothers.

Choose.

I dip my head down to Jane. "I'm eating it."

"Me too," she whispers with a wince. She feels for Ben.

I tug the plastic container closer to us.

Ben makes a noise like I impaled him. "Don't eat it, *please.*"

I shake my head in apology, my muscles tensed up, and Eliot starts telling us that we need to eat with our hands and divide the meat in half.

Ben swerves towards the bar with urgency. "Moffy!" He speaks in fluent Spanish to Maximoff, and I can't translate that much.

I wouldn't be able to list off which other Cobalts know Spanish. Not all of them advertise the depth of their knowledge.

I'm just positive that Jane only knows French.

Charlie rolls his eyes in aggravation. "Maximoff can't change this, Ben."

We're heading towards a clusterfuck.

Behind me, I sense Maximoff standing up from the barstool. He talks to Ben in Spanish, and Beckett is rubbing his younger brother's back in soothing circles.

"Can't you just skip this card, Charlie?" Maximoff gestures to the table. "Ben is uncomfortable—"

"Life is uncomfortable," Charlie sneers. "Stop trying to save him."

Maximoff glowers. "Jesus, man." He tries to cool off before igniting a war with Charlie that they've put to rest this past year.

Jane leans in and whispers to me, "We should eat before this worsens."

"Copy." I pinch the bloodied heart and pop it in my mouth like candy. *Gristly.* I grind hard. It's not filet mignon, but I'm not slow to chew and swallow. I grab another heart before Jane can even touch one.

Ben slumps back, sullen, and he angles into Beckett. Me eating also diffuses a Charlie and Maximoff feud.

Jane plugs her nose while dropping meat on her tongue. She squirms. "Eh, that is…not… pleasant." She coughs in a fist. "The odor is *foul.*"

"Hold on." I pop three more nugget-sized hearts in my mouth and stand up. I chew on my hike to the bar. I have blinders.

I'm not looking at Tony. But I hear him snickering. *Fuck him.*

I mime *water* to my brother.

Banks extends his body halfway over the bar. Reaching the fridge beneath. On stools, Farrow and Oscar start clapping for me. Like I'm in some fucked-up, backwoods hot dog eating contest.

The corner of my mouth almost lifts.

"Fucking SFO," an Epsilon bodyguard snarls under his breath.

I swallow down the meat, a lump left in my throat, and after Banks throws me a water bottle, I return to Jane. Unscrewing the cap, I pass her the water.

"Merci." She drinks, and I notice that she's only eaten one heart.

I finish off mine in under two minutes. Wiping my fingers off with a napkin, I'm forcing myself not to touch her portion. *Don't do it.*

But I want to put my girlfriend out of her fucking misery.

Her eyes water. "God. I despise this," she mutters under her breath.

I reach for the carton. "I can eat it—"

"No, no," she says quickly, then pauses, palm to her mouth. "I can… I can do my share."

Jane is an alpha. I love that she's in this with me. But she has limits like everyone, and the fact that she's ignoring them *concerns* the holy hell out of me.

My brows knit. "What about delegating?" She likes to delegate tasks on strengths and weaknesses. She can't stomach bloodied rabbit. I can.

"This is different." She chews slowly, then swallows. "I have to do my equal part."

She washes down the heart and then picks up another with a heavy breath. Quietly, she asks her brothers, "What happens if I vomit?"

Eliot grins. "You'll have to eat it."

"No," I say at the same time as Beckett.

"You'll lose if you puke," Charlie says. "The game stops for you, but Thatcher will continue."

Jane looks simultaneously determined and afraid. "I'm finishing." Pinching her nose, she places another heart in her mouth.

She gags instantly. One more gag and she's puking—she starts to.

I cover her mouth with my hand.

What I do for love and pussy.

Jane has to force down vomit. Her blue eyes flit to me with relief and appreciation. She swallows. Her cheeks radiate heat against my hand, and I'm more in love with this girl today than I was yesterday.

I didn't think that was possible.

She has five hearts left to eat. I kiss her temple, and it takes ten minutes for her to eat the next two.

Three more to go.

I wipe her watering eyes while her dirtied hands hover mid-air. And then her phone rings, and I eye her breasts.

She stuffed her phone in her bra. Eating a mouthful, her eyes spark with panic and rest on me.

Her brothers are going to have to deal. I reach down into her rainbow-hued blouse. My fingers brush against the soft flesh of her breasts, and volcanic tension bubbles between me and her—our eyes latched.

Our breaths caught.

And I pull out her cellphone on the fourth ring.

"What was that about *respecting* our sister?" Charlie cocks his head.

I grind my teeth. Whatever I say will be another shovel of dirt and deeper grave I'm digging. Lord fucking knows I can't find the perfect words.

Jane tries to speak with a mouthful. Mumbling.

"The ears can't understand thy tongue," Eliot says.

She enunciates better. "I asked him to grab… my phone." She swallows, then nods me on to answer the phone.

Audrey Cobalt is calling. Back when I was just Jane's bodyguard, her thirteen-year-old carrot-orange-haired sister would gawk up at me while I was on-duty. I'd wait for her to say something, and she'd just let out this wheezy sigh.

Easily smitten, I'm sure she's had a crush on half the team, but the one that grew strong was towards Oscar Oliveira. She'd bake him cookies, up until the Hot Santa video leak.

Audrey sent the footage to a friend, who leaked the video and screwed all of Omega.

It wasn't her fault. I was a lead. That was on me. The video should've never existed in the first place.

I put their sister on the line.

"Jane?" Audrey says tearfully.

Jane frowns at the phone and clears her throat of food. "Audrey, what's wrong?"

"I heard all six of you are there and I'm not. You've all left me out." Her voice cracks, nearing a sob. "Us, Cobalts—we're a *seven*. Not a six. Yet you…you kept me from joining tonight, why? Is it because I'm untrustworthy? Because I leaked the bodyguard video? I promise you can trust me! *I promise.* Please, give me another—"

"Stop," Charlie groans, pinching his eyes.

Jane shoots him a nasty look and then tells her sister, "I trust you with all my heart, Audrey." It sounds more than sincere. Like if she could, she'd die with those as her last words.

I stare at Jane, my chest rising with a powerful jolt of emotion.

Audrey sniffles. "Why then?" Her voice rattles. "Why not include me now?"

"Very important question, Audrey." Jane glares at her brothers. "Why keep out our *trustworthy* sister?"

"She helped with the cards," Tom defends.

Beckett answers coolly, "She was with Winona and Kinney. We didn't want all the little girls here—"

"I knew it!" Winona Meadows shouts.

Kinney Hale comes onto the line. "You're all a bunch of ugly trolls! We don't even like you—"

"Hang up." Charlie orders me since I'm gripping the phone.

No way.

Jane gapes. "Thatcher will *not* hang up on the youngest girls of the family." She eyes the phone. "Girls—"

They all yell over each other. I can't pick apart a thing.

"We'll talk later, I promise," Jane says quickly. "I know they're dreadfully annoying boys, but we'll work this out later."

They voice their love of Jane, and she nods to me. I hang up.

I focus back on my girlfriend, and she's already grinding on another heart, her eyes wrinkling at the taste.

"Water?"

"Please," she grimaces.

I put the bottle to her lips, and she takes a small sip.

"Am I sweating?" She tries to elbow a piece of hair.

I tuck the flyaway behind her ear. "No." *You're beautiful.* Eating bloody rabbit hearts.

Comms crackle, the signal distant. "Donnelly to SFO, I found the space babe."

Relief strikes, then confusion. How the hell did he find Luna Hale? Look—a part of me suspects that Donnelly eating Luna out wasn't a one-time thing like they told Jane, but we're both still keeping that secret for them.

Akara is in my ear. "Where is Luna?"

"Shake Shack. Her phone's dead."

I breathe in a strong breath. *Not good.* Quinn should've rogered up on comms and given the Omega lead her AO. He's been turning off his radio more frequently. At this point, I think he admires Akara as a leader, but he'd rather be like Farrow.

"Tell Quinn to get on comms," Akara says, voice tight. He's pissed.

"Sure thing, boss."

Oscar asks, "How'd you figure out where she was?"

"Some fandoms posted pics of her in the area."

"Nice work," Akara says, and once Quinn enters comms, Akara tears him a new asshole. I tune out the reprimand.

In front of me, Tom is busy texting, but I catch Eliot's attention. "Security found Luna."

Tom looks up. "Where?"

"Shake Shack. Her phone died."

Eliot runs a hand through his hair, then he grins. "Tell her bodyguard to tell Luna that we'd like to place an order."

Tom's face lights. While Jane powers through eating, I use comms to place two orders of cheese fries. This is the most normal, routine thing they've asked me to do all night.

Letting go of my mic, I help Jane who struggles with the second to last heart. She starts sweating, her eyes downcast while she concentrates on chewing.

I hand her a napkin, and we exchange a knowing look. If she needs to spit the last one out and hide it, I'll help her cheat.

Partners in crime, she once called us.

That's not long gone.

Eyes brightening, Jane nods in agreement.

Tom groans. "Come *on.*" He crashes back against the booth, exasperated. He drops his phone on the table. "My band," he explains to me.

"They've been auditioning new drummers," Eliot clarifies. "And Tom refuses to pick the *best* drummer for the job."

"He's just the hottest," Tom refutes.

Eliot mouths to me, *he's the best.*

"Can you play without a drummer?" I ask since I've seen some two-man alternative bands before.

"I wish," Tom sighs. "Our label wants *three* members." Everyone's attention veers to Jane as she gags again.

I cover her mouth with one hand, and grab the wine with the other. I whisper in her ear, "You're okay?"

She nods.

"Kick my foot if you want the napkin." I'll need to create a diversion.

She nods again. But she's not whacking my shin. For Jane, it's a last resort. I lower my hand from her mouth. Quickly, she swallows down the organ with a swig of wine and then picks up the last heart.

I draw attention off her and ask Beckett, "How do you like your new bodyguard?"

"O'Malley?" Beckett shrugs, eyes dropping. "He's fine." He sucks on his cigarette.

I would've never assigned him to Beckett's detail. It has nothing to do with his skills as a bodyguard. We all know O'Malley thinks Donnelly is white trash, and this transfer is just another slap to SFO.

My fault.

I massage my strained deltoid.

Charlie is watching me.

I nod to him. Confused about whether he hates me or likes me—two extremes. That's what I feel from Charlie, and it's strange terrain.

He just smiles, then looks to Beckett. His twin brother passes the burning cigarette to Charlie. He takes a drag and blows smoke to the side before handing it back.

Jane gulps more wine. "Done!" She pounds the bottle on the table while her brothers applaud. My lip lifts and a bright smile overtakes her features. "We make a good team, don't we?"

"Hell yeah." I eye her pink lips.

Flush sneaks up her neck, and she almost touches her skirt, forgetting her hands are bloodied. I catch her wrist.

Her breastbone caves. "Oh."

My cock almost hardens. *Fuck.*

"That's all for tonight," Charlie tells us and tosses Jane more napkins. He stands up, cane in hand.

I let go of her wrist, and she wipes at her fingers. Beckett gathers the spread cards into a single stack. "You should take the cards, Charlie."

"No, you keep them." Charlie slowly sinks back down and places his cane on the table.

The air strains.

Beckett makes a confused face. "Besides Jane, you're the only other Cobalt going on the trip. I can't make her and Thatcher play the game if I'm in New York."

Charlie glances to Jane, and she gives him a tense nod. I understand the clandestine exchange.

I'm *in* on this plan that we've all been constructing. So are Banks, Maximoff, and Farrow. I didn't think it'd be implemented tonight, but I'm prepared for the fallout.

Shit is about to get tense.

Beckett doesn't realize it yet, but he's going to Scotland.

10

Jane Cobalt

"YOU'RE TAKING A WEEK off ballet and coming on the trip," I tell Beckett, my rabbit-filled stomach in a blender and my pulse racing at a million miles per hour. Yet, I can't let up on him.

I won't.

Charlie has an arm across the back of the booth behind Beckett, and Thatcher angles more towards me. My wingman.

My right-hand.

My partner in crime.

My protector.

My boyfriend.

It feels terribly good to have him next to me, especially in case this all backfires.

Beckett tilts his head, his befuddled expression cinching his brows. "I can't just *take off* an entire week. You know that, right?"

The booth is quiet. Really, the entire sports bar is deathly still and silent—no one from the bar makes a peep. Even the ones who don't *truly* know what this is about seem to imprison oxygen.

Dry Merlot and pungent meat sours my mouth. "You took off months for the FanCon tour," I remind him.

Beckett sets down the lion-decaled cards, straightening them into an even stack again. "I was between major productions at the time. I can't miss a performance now." He dances six nights a week in Cinderella, and his days are crammed with six-hour rehearsals and hour-long morning classes.

I know very well how hard he works.

How much he's sacrificed for ballet. It makes this next part that much more painful.

"You can stay here and dance, but if you continue to *use*, then Charlie, Moffy, and I will force you on this trip."

Beckett freezes cold. Fury lances his yellow-green eyes. I've seen his calm exterior rupture and explode quite a few times in my life, but mostly it's only ever been to protect Charlie.

"*Use* what?" Eliot asks, breathing hard. "Beckett?"

Tom gapes. "Dude." New York hedonism, they're all surrounded by the lifestyle of debauchery, riches, and fame.

Ben stares haunted at the table.

I glance backward at the bar, and Sulli mouths to me, *what the fuck?* Beckett is her best friend. None of them knew.

Not until now.

Beckett lets out a blistering breath. "Thanks, *sis*." He glares at Thatcher. "Fuck your brother—"

"He didn't do anything," Thatcher snaps.

"I know *Banks* saw me do a key bump, and I know he told you. Half of Omega already found out." Beckett pins his glare back on me. "I use so I can dance through minor pain. That's it."

"A key bump in an alley helps you dance?" I combat.

"It was *before* rehearsal." He snuffs out his cigarette on the ashtray.

I lean toward him. "You'll hurt yourself more if you dance with injuries."

He throws up a hand. "You think I'm the only one who does? *Everyone* pushes their bodies to extremes. I'd *love* to just pop Adderall like half the company, but I can't!"

My face twists. "Why can't you? *Not* that you should do that either," I add quickly.

Beckett shifts backwards, then forwards. He turns to Charlie. "I'm not doing this here."

"Yes you are."

"*Charlie*," he pleads. "Let me go."

Charlie can't look at his twin. He eyes me, in need of an assist.

I come in. "Beckett—"

"Adderall terrorizes my OCD! *Okay?*" Beckett rubs his palms together, then clutches his thighs. "Cocaine doesn't."

"You don't have to use," I say gently. "You have a choice."

Sudden quiet slices the bar into a billion little pieces.

Beckett shakes his head, and then he tells me, "That's easy for you to say."

I bristle, hurt gripping my insides. "What does that mean?"

He's blunt and honest, and I don't expect Beckett to hold back— but he does this time. He just keeps shaking his head.

I'm not an idiot.

I clutch the table and careen forward to be closer to him. "You think I have no room to talk because I've never strived for anything like you? Because I have no talents and no ambition like you?"

His reddened eyes lift to mine. "I give *everything* to ballet. My time, my body, my *life*. What have you ever given to something you've loved?"

"I've given *all of myself* to my family," I retort, tears burning my eyes. I'm the older sister. I carry the torch that lights the way, and if I drop it, no one behind me can see. "And I don't care if you can't see that—but there is a reason you never told your *best friend* you use." I turn in my chair.

Sulli is already approaching the booth. Disappointment all over her face. "What the fuck, Beckett. How long?"

He looks pained. "It's not a big deal—"

"You're using drugs!" Her eyes bug. "We said we'd *never* take the easy out and use performance enhancers!"

"Ballet is different than swimming."

"Fuck that," Sulli cringes. "Jane is right. You didn't tell me because I'm the one person who chose a sport over a childhood and I'm the *one* person who can tell you *fuck your excuses.*"

Beckett shoots to his feet. "What about you? The second you retire from swimming you're all of a sudden drinking alcohol and passing out—at least I'm not pointlessly destroying my body."

I wince.

"Cold, brother," Eliot says sadly.

Sulli grits her teeth. "Fuck you."

"No, fuck you," Beckett snaps.

We did not plan for a friendship to blow to smithereens tonight. I spring to my feet. Thatcher stands, and Maximoff is already at Sulli's side, ushering her backwards while I talk to Beckett and repeat the same ultimatum.

Beckett holds out his hands like he's at gunpoint. "If I leave, the company will replace me in Cinderella with *Leo.* He's already being called the *blond* version of me." Leo Valavanis is the same age, same height, same build, and same costume measurements as Beckett, and he's also another male principal dancer. Unfortunately, their rivalry in the company has created good buzz for the ballet.

"You can stay in Cinderella," I remind him. "Just stop using."

Beckett massages his palm. "And if I don't? You can't force me on a plane."

I quirk my brow. "I'm your big sister. I can do anything."

He takes a few tense breaths, still on his feet.

Charlie rises, leaning his weight on a cane. "What have you learned, children?" This is a classic Cobalt word game.

What have you learned, children? Whoever asks this directs the game to those younger than them.

Beckett is next in age and supposed to pick a line of poetry, the others will then add to his opening line.

He stares at the table. "I'm not playing."

Eliot rises. "It was all decaying."

Tom leans back. "I can feel us fraying."

Ben opens his mouth to finish the poem. His eyes start filling with tears. And he buckles forward and cries into his palms.

My heart tears to shreds. Usually Beckett is the one to console our youngest brother. But his face contorts in pain, and he pushes out of the booth.

Leaving.

Charlie follows, their bodyguards leading the way. I worry that Beckett will go out tonight.

But quickly, I slip into the booth and hug Ben. He cries into my shoulder.

"He'll be okay, Pippy," I whisper, and I look up at Thatcher. He crouches so we're more eye-level.

"I've asked Akara to put my brother with Beckett tonight. He agreed."

Banks is doubling up on Beckett's detail. I breathe easier. *Banks will look after Beckett.* I know Thatcher's brother has been drinking, but definitely not enough to be more than buzzed.

"Thank you," I say, my torn heart mending in a strong beat.

He nods and then holds out his pinky. "I promise we won't fuck this." He means forcing my brother on a plane. It's going to take strength and terrible might. Together.

One hand on Ben's head, I use my other and hook my pinky to my boyfriend's. He kisses my knuckles, and my heart rises with a smile that shouldn't exist.

Yet, he's summoned one out of my soul. Reaching deeper inside me than anyone ever has or could.

And it's terrifying.

11

Thatcher Moretti

ONE MONTH INTO THE twisted *Truth or Dare* game, and some of the "tell us" questions have been like slogging through knee-deep cement.

Tell us your last sexual fantasy

Jane horizontal on a kitchen table while I pound my nine-inch dick inside her pussy.

I politely answered, *sex on a table.*

I got reamed for not including, *with Jane.*

It feels like I blow my shot to hell with every card flip. I piss off or irritate at least one Cobalt.

Jane's response was more graphic, and I almost smiled when she described me pinning her against the wall. My hands cupping her ass, her legs hooked around my waist, my cock filling her to the brim with each thrust. Her face was bright red by the end of answering, but she did it.

Bolder and better than me.

The *dares*, on the other hand, are a cakewalk.

Strip to your underwear and watch Titanic four consecutive times.

Easy.

It took me back to Marine boot camp. Holding my piss while running a ridiculous amount of miles under 20 minutes. Having four Drill Instructors spit-yell insults and nonsense in my ear, their noses rubbing up against my nose while I couldn't flinch.

Couldn't talk.

I played this warped game of Simon Says where I'm never right, even when I am, and I still have to jump when I know the smarter route is to stand.

I'm fit for hell.

Semper Fi.

But Jane, the sweetest thing my arms have ever held—she's fit for heaven. She was restless after the eight-hour mark but she persevered. The good: she was beside me.

The fucking weird: she had to strip in front of her brothers. But it's not like they planned for her to be a part of the game. And she wouldn't let them alter the tasks for her.

The cards *almost* made me forget about the parasite attached to my girlfriend.

Tony.

We're 4 days out from Scotland, 4 days from executing the twin switch, and security prepping for departure shouldn't be a war, but it feels like one.

"Back the fuck down," I growl at a dark-haired, pale twenty-seven-year-old.

O'Malley has strawberry pink lips and snow globes for eyes: round, glassy, and full of shit. Bodyguards always talk about how he resembles that one actor in some airplane horror movie. Cillian Murphy, I think.

I've only really known O'Malley since he joined Epsilon four years ago—and no matter what, I would've protected him to the end like all the men on SFE. But right now, he respects me about as much as shit in a ditch.

He raises his hands in surrender. Like he didn't just throw a grenade in Studio 9, the gym lit with fluorescent lights at oh-six-hundred.

"Nah, say it again," Donnelly snaps, tossing his blue gloves on the mat. Everyone is dripping sweat in workout gear. But this call time isn't social hour. We're here to discuss security protocols for Scotland. Which won't happen until the Tri-Force arrive.

O'Malley stews, a twenty-pound dumbbell in his fist.

I narrow my gaze on him with intense warning. If he repeats what he just said, we're going to have a fistfight before this meeting even begins.

Tension splits the air. Silence taut and uneasy.

Banks glances at me, cautious. We stand between the physical divide inside the team. On my nine, two Epsilon bodyguards hover near the boxing ring and free weights.

Tony and O'Malley.

The only ones who aren't in on the twin switch.

On my three, red boxing bags hang from the rafters, and Oscar, Farrow, Donnelly, and Quinn just finished sparring.

Epsilon vs. Omega.

I feel the fracture between the two Forces more heavily because I'm the one who cracked a cavern between them.

Hurt flares in O'Malley's eyes as he reroutes his lasered anger onto me. "Back the fuck down?" He repeats my earlier words and throws his dumbbell on the mat. "You're telling *me* what to do." He jabs a finger at his own chest.

I deserve his rage. I deserve a lot of bad shit coming at me, but my insides broil. Without breaking his gaze, I tighten my loose black handwraps. Biting my tongue.

"You're not my lead anymore, *Thatcher.* You have about as much room to bark orders as a Doberman Pinscher."

My face hardens. Guilt hammering down on me.

"Relax, O'Malley," Banks says. "Thatcher's just trying to avoid a blood bath."

O'Malley clenches his jaw and mutters under his breath, but loud enough for me to hear. "And if he were better at his job, he would've thought about that before sleeping with his client."

All month.

These comments have been chucked at me all *fucking* month. November into December, Epsilon bodyguards are now just the "shit on Thatcher" brigade.

I don't care.

They can call me names.

They can curse me out.

I don't fucking care. I did break a rule, and if this is one of the many consequences, I plan to bear the onslaught for as long I need to. But if someone wrenches Jane into this, I will end them.

That's my line.

Clear in the motherfucking sand.

It hurts even knowing that months ago Farrow was in this exact position. And I was the asshole on the other side, berating him. Karma—it's got its hands wrapped around my windpipe.

I want it to choke me.

Tony squints at O'Malley. "It's not that big of a deal. Thatcher slept with a client. Who cares? Get over it."

Bile rises to my throat. Tony defending me right now feels about as good as being run over by a cement truck. On any other topic, maybe it would be a bridge to rebuild our relationship, but him being calm and nonchalant about bodyguards sleeping with clients—it tweaks my nerves.

And I can't even call him out on it without sounding like a raging hypocrite.

O'Malley frowns. "You're new, Tony. You don't understand how things work around here."

Tony shrugs. "It has nothing to do with me being new. In my opinion, sleeping with a client shouldn't even be a rule."

My blood temp skyrockets, and I can't shut my mouth. "I don't need you defending me."

Tony sets a glare on me. "The fact that my opinion leans in your favor does *not* mean I'm defending you, and what the fuck are you even doing here?" He motions to me with an angered hand. "This is a meeting for Scotland, and you're not going on the trip."

That's what you think.

"Akara asked me to be here." My voice is like hard cement. "You're still on your probationary period with Jane, and I want to make sure you're squared away before you leave."

Fuck you.

Fuck off.

I force these back. Professional, stay fucking professional.

Tony crosses his arms, sweat staining his blue tee. "You've been breathing down my neck all month, Moretti. At this point, you either trust me to do my job or you don't."

A part of me does trust him—I hate that I trust him.

It's why I can't rip him away from Jane's detail, but I'm not even here to triple-check Tony (though it's a perk). I'm here because I'm the one traveling to Scotland, not Banks, and I'd rather be in this meeting than have Banks regurgitate everything back to me.

But Tony and O'Malley can't know this.

Farrow and the rest of Omega whisper at the boxing bags. In their own conversation.

"It is what it is," I tell Tony *professionally*. "In another month, your probationary period will be over, and you won't have anything to worry about."

Donnelly laughs at something.

My senses are ringing, hyper-vigilant to any movements and sounds. I catch O'Malley looking past me and my brother. His eyes blazing on Omega.

Honestly, I wish O'Malley wasn't here, but he's Beckett's bodyguard. And Charlie has confirmed that Beckett is still using cocaine, so the plan to make Beckett go to Scotland is intact and waiting to be executed.

Banks whispers to me, "This is gonna be a shit show."

I stay alert and uncap a water bottle. "Dealing with shit shows is what we do." I take a swig and wipe my mouth with my wrist, then I hand him the water.

His lip quirks. "What you and Akara do," he corrects. "I'm just your cowboy." He swallows a gulp, and we hawk-eye Epsilon. "Incoming," Banks says under his breath.

O'Malley takes an affronting step forward.

I block his path. "Don't."

He ignores me and raises his voice. "You shouldn't be here either, Donnelly!"

Laughter dies.

Farrow pops his gum, Oscar's hand freezes in a bag of Bugels, and Quinn solidifies midway in a sit-up.

"What'd you say?" Donnelly glares.

Oscar removes his hand from the snack bag and clutches his friend's shoulder. Keeping him back. Farrow leans casually on a boxing bag, tattoos inked on his neck and chest. Intimidating in his relaxed demeanor. He pops another bubble with his gum.

"I said, you…shouldn't…be…here…either," O'Malley repeats annoyingly slow. "Your client is *Xander Hale*. He's staying in Philly, so you'll be in Scotland as a friend of Farrow's, not as security. And this is a *security* meeting."

Farrow cuts in, "Donnelly has to be here in case we need extra hands. It's that simple."

This shuts up O'Malley for half a second. "The team isn't paying for your travel expenses, Donnelly," he yells. "How are you even affording this?"

"My good looks," Donnelly quips.

O'Malley laughs with Tony, then nods back to SFO. "Still working that street corner?"

Christ.

"He gave that corner to you, O'Malley," Farrow says easily.

Oscar chimes in, "We heard no one even wanted your free blow jobs."

Donnelly smirks. "Need tips?"

"From someone who's had ten different STDs, I'll pass," O'Malley retorts, then outstretches his arms. "You want to keep going? It's not changing the fact that Beckett is *my* client. It's not changing the fact that I'm always—"

"O'Malley," I growl.

I've already heard him say *I'm always cleaning up Donnelly's messes.* And I'm not letting him unleash that twice. I nail a patented stern look on him *again.*

He cuts his gaze to me.

And in a split-second, I become the target.

Good.

"You remember what you told me on my first day?" O'Malley asks, trekking closer. Feeling how hot my blood is running, I cross my arms and step back.

Again.

And again.

"You said this was a brotherhood."

I nod, my lungs burning, and my deltoids hit a punching bag. Nowhere to go, I stop in place.

He edges nearer, much shorter but he lifts his chin. "You said that we put the clients first but the people who have *our* backs are the guys to our left and right. You said that if I couldn't be dependable, then I needed to pack my bags and leave. You remember that?"

I do.

Because as a lead, I gave that same speech to every man who joined SFE. My jaw hurts from bearing down on my molars, but I have nothing to say. Nothing to make this right.

I can't apologize for falling in love with her.

I can't call what happened a mistake. Gun to my head, I'd repeat every moment so I'd have the boldest, smartest girl next to me—a girl I shouldn't have.

But she's *mine,* and I might not deserve her but I swear to God, I'll never harm her, and I'd give my life to protect her. I know I'm not a prince.

I'm not a king.

But I'd treat Jane like she should be treated. She's my princess, my angel, and my queen. Every morning and every night. I'd kneel at her feet and stand by her side.

"It was all bullshit in the end, right?" O'Malley is up against me, chest to chest. "You're a *fucking* liar. I should've known that when we learned you're a Marine. But I was stupid enough to defend your ass to SFE."

"Leaving out some facts isn't lying." Banks sticks up for me, but I shoot him a look across the gym.

I'm not putting him in this mess.

He shakes his head and lets out a frustrated noise. He doesn't want me to take the fall for all of it, but I'm ready to go all the way down.

"*Leaving out some facts isn't lying,*" O'Malley repeats with a dry laugh. "You've got to be shitting me."

With our height difference, I stare down at him. Hating how he keeps bumping up against me. My flexed arms stay woven over my chest, biceps bulged.

"I bet your new friends don't even really know you." He glances past my shoulder and zeroes in on Farrow, Oscar, Quinn, and Donnelly. "Did he ever tell you we both went to Saint Joseph's High School?"

Strain stretches the air. Omega doesn't give O'Malley the satisfaction of wearing surprise.

"Why would that come up?" I ask him. "You were in a grade below me. I barely knew you." We had different social circles. I was a football player who worked church functions to get tuition.

He was well-off and voted student body president.

"I don't know, Thatcher," O'Malley snaps. "Maybe I thought my lead cared about other things than finding roundabout ways to fuck Jane."

Hearing her name causes my muscles to tense. Like my body is triggered into defense-mode.

SFO starts launching insults at him, either on my behalf or Jane's—I can't tell.

"Let him talk," I say loudly, silencing Omega, and then I nod O'Malley onward. "You have shit on your chest. Get it off."

He cranes his neck more to look up at me. "Admit what you did was wrong."

"I can't do that." Flat-out.

I can't.

Being with Jane is the most right thing I've ever done.

"Great." He'd be in my face if he could reach it. "So you're saying that if I find myself in a room alone with Luna Hale, and she comes onto *me*, I'm in the clear to fuck her. Right there. Down and dirty on the floor."

I almost snap.

I almost yell, *she's nineteen!*

But Jane is only twenty-three. SFO rustles behind me, fuming. I take a short glance backwards. Oscar looks murderous.

Farrow straightens up more than usual. He places a hand on Donnelly's chest. "Ignore the fucker."

"He's been asking for a fight." Donnelly boils. "He's gonna get hit—"

"Come here then," O'Malley goads, but his attention veers to Luna's bodyguard.

"You can't talk about my client like that," Quinn growls.

He raises his hands. "I'm just using the precedent Omega has set. If they're of age and willing, then it's fair game, right?"

"No," I say harshly. *Deescalate this shit.* I try to take a breath. "You were Luna's bodyguard when she was sixteen," I remind O'Malley. "Jane was twenty-two, an adult, when I was on her detail. Maximoff was twenty-two when Farrow went to his. I'm not saying it's right, but it's fucking different."

His jaw drops, like he can't believe I'm rationalizing this. "Who the fuck are you?"

"The same person who spoke to you your first day."

"No, that guy is dead. You chose pussy over your own integrity," he sneers. "Hope it tastes worth it."

I see red.

It's a switch, but all I want is distance. I want him out of my perimeter. I want him to stop bumping against my fucking chest.

Like a reflex, I uncross my arms and shove him back. He careens into a punching bag. It sways, but he barely loses balance on his feet. He charges at me.

I see the fist coming.

I can't move. My feet are forced to the fucking mat. Cemented by guilt and blame, and his knuckles smash into my lip.

Bitter iron of blood floods my mouth. People yell around me.

"Heyheyhey!" I hear my brother.

My head spins, the surrounding chaos and my bottled emotion igniting boxes in my head. Boxes that I've stapled shut for years. Senses tweaked, my eyes are narrowed, unable to close.

I hear rounds firing in violent succession. My pulse ratchets up. I turn my head, but I have tunnel vision. This—this hasn't happened before. Not while I'm awake.

Fuck me.

"Back up!"

"Let go, O'Malley!"

I blink into focus and realize O'Malley is fisting my damp black tee. Banks tries to shove between me and him, and I react like I've pressed *play* on a paused movie.

I block my brother and let O'Malley crush another fist into my body. Pounding into my shoulder. *Fuck.*

Banks tears him off me.

My adrenaline accelerates, chest rising and falling.

Farrow and Oscar drag me from the fight. My brain is screaming to protect my brother, who's standing on the firing line.

"Banks!" I call out.

Banks.

O'Malley shoves my twin brother, and Banks pushes him angrily back.

"What in the fuck is going on?" That harsh-edged voice comes from the doorway, Sinclair and the other leads entering the gym.

Hands drop to sides. We all go still.

Akara looks from O'Malley to me, his eyes descending to my fat lip. He shakes his head in disbelief, like he, too, doesn't even know who I am anymore.

My nose flares.

O'Malley is just one person I hurt. But he's one of many. Everyone on Epsilon feels like I betrayed their trust, their respect, but the person I betrayed the most is standing right there. And the look Akara gives me now—it cuts me open and spills out my insides.

It hurts the absolute worst.

Price, the Alpha lead, glares at everyone. "Who punched Moretti?" He's asking who should be fined three-grand.

Bodyguards can't hit other bodyguards without punishment.

No one speaks.

No one points fingers.

With an inhale, I announce, "I started the fight." I touch my lip. It's already swelling. "You can fine me."

Banks gives me a hard look like *you idiot.*

O'Malley frowns.

Akara wears even more disappointment.

Price nods. "Will do."

Sinclair nears and weaves between boxing bags. "You ladies done having a tea party, we need to get down to this Scotland business."

My mouth is full of blood, and I'm not about to spit it out on the mats. Quietly, I excuse myself to use the gym bathrooms.

Showers and toilet stalls are empty. I immediately spit a wad of blood in the sink basin. My pulse is racing.

I swivel the faucet and splash water at my face. *Come on.* I squeeze the edge of the sink, staring at myself in the mirror. Droplets trickle down my temples and slip off my jaw.

My eyes are bloodshot.

I can barely blink, and I can almost feel her curious hands sliding across my waist. I can almost see her rising smile peek around my body, and her chin perched on my side. Her eyes glimmering up at me with uncommon strength.

I want to turn around and lift her in my arms. To press my forehead to her forehead and stare into the bluest depths of her gaze.

But she's not here. She's back at the townhouse.

The sound of a leaking shower bleeds into the quiet.

Drip.

Drip.

Drip.

It drives me insane. I scrape a palm down my wet face. My hand is shaking. Christ, I just want to hear her voice. I should compartmentalize my feelings and shove off.

But I pull my phone out of my pocket.

Without much thought, I'm calling Jane. Like this is an ingrained reaction.

Jane picks up on the second ring. "Thatcher? Is the meeting already over?"

I can't move. I stare at the faucet.

"Thatcher?" Her voice pitches in worry.

"It hasn't started yet." I grip the sink with one hand and swallow a rock. And then I rehash everything that happened with the team.

I promised myself I'd never hit another bodyguard, and even if I was provoked, I shouldn't have pushed O'Malley.

With every word I say out loud, I'm sure that I'm painting myself as the biggest villain. "It's good that he got a punch in," I continue. "I just don't want my brother in the middle of it."

I don't want her in the middle of it either. But she's on the phone, and I don't want to hang up. I just want to hear her.

"You don't deserve to be punched, I hope you realize," Jane says fiercely. "I know you want to take fault for what's happened, but this won't make you feel any better."

My chest caves. I can't speak, but she fills the quiet.

"And I'm terribly proud of you."

It knocks the wind out of me. Slowly, I shake my head. "Why?"

"You handled everything well, especially under stressful conditions. It could've rattled you more, and you could've said worse to provoke him. You tried your best I truly believe. So…um, I…" She sounds flustered, and I almost smile because she's mostly only like this with me. "I'm very, *very* proud of you. Which I've already said, but it doesn't hurt to say twice."

I hear her blow out a measured breath.

More quietly, she asks, "Are you still there?"

"Yeah." My pulse slows. "Thanks, honey."

I can practically feel her smile. "Talking is my specialty."

"It's my weakness," I say bluntly.

"You're not so bad," she whispers. "And we even each other out. It's why we make a disastrously good team."

I exhale and release my tight grip. We start saying our goodbyes. "I love you," I tell Jane.

"I…" She sucks in a sharp breath.

It's okay.

Still, something stings. Her hang-ups shouldn't hurt because she warned me that she'd be pushing and pulling, but I feel like I'm fucking up. Unable to be there for my girlfriend the way that she was just here for me.

"You know how I feel." Her voice is higher-pitched. "What I feel for you is…" Her words carry the swell of emotion that could topple buildings, but she stops herself from adding more.

"I know, and you don't have to say *I love you* back every time," I remind her.

She's silent.

My pulse thumps in my throat. "Jane?"

"Je suis désolée." *I'm sorry.*

"You don't need to apologize," I say strongly. "I love you, that's it. Nothing else has to happen." My chest tightens. I'm not sure what she needs from me. She's someone who rarely looks to be reassured, but I feel like I need to console her.

How?

"I'll let you go, Thatcher," she says in a whisper. "Um, I'm…you know…" She sighs in frustration at herself. "À la prochaine." *Until next time.*

I stare at my reddened eyes in the mirror. "See you, Jane." I feel like a jackass. Should've stopped her. Should've said more.

We hang up.

And I could rattle the sink and scream. Instead, I stay in a lunge, clutching the life out of the porcelain.

I smother the sound of the shower *drip* by turning on the faucet again, and I rinse out my mouth, blood washing down the drain. As I splash more water at my face, cooling off, the bathroom door swings open. I expect to see my brother.

But it's someone else.

12

Thatcher Moretti

THE WHITE-HAIRED, TATTOOED bodyguard saunters inside the bathroom. Shutting the door behind him. Farrow's barbell piercing rises with his brows. "You look like shit."

"You must love this." I wipe water off my face with my bicep.

"Eh, I don't hate it." He smiles.

It causes my lip to twitch in $1/1000^{th}$ of a smile, which is more than usual. Especially around him.

Farrow leans on a stall door. "See, I know what it's like to be decked in the face for sleeping with a client."

I almost laugh. Yeah, I'm the one who punched him. I can't find any words, and we end up just staring awkwardly at each other.

He combs his inked fingers through his hair. "You okay?"

I nod once.

"Your eyes were glazed back there." He touches his dangling earring. "It's none of my business, and prying is not my favorite thing but I just remember you saying you only have nightmares." Farrow Keene has become one of the only people on the team I feel safe enough to talk with about PTSD, because he's experienced some form of this shit too.

I nod again. "I don't know what happened," I admit.

"Okay." Farrow thinks for a second. "Could you tell if there was a trigger? A sound or maybe a feeling?"

"I don't know for sure." I curl longer pieces of my hair behind my ears. "Could've been me getting punched. But I've been hit before and not been thrown back like that."

He rubs his lip piercing, tilting his head from side to side.

"What?"

"You let O'Malley hit you."

I'm quiet.

Farrow nods a couple times. "Have you dropped your hands before?"

Not like that.

I shake my head. "No."

"Your natural instinct is to survive." Farrow stands off the stall. "Putting your body in a panicked state could potentially throw you back."

Makes more sense, and this fog starts clearing. He didn't have to come in here and talk to me, but I appreciate it. "Thanks."

"No problem." He's scrutinizing my face.

I skim my tongue over my swollen lip. *I taste blood.* Glancing at the mirror, I clearly see that I busted my fucking lip open.

Farrow sticks a new piece of gum in his mouth. "That's not healing in four days, by the way."

Fuck. Shit. "Mannaggia," I curse out loud, and I rake my hand across my unshaven jaw. The twin switch—I can't pretend to be Banks if I'm the one with a visible wound. This isn't a bruise I can conceal with makeup.

I should've been thinking.

An apparent, unspoken solution hangs between Farrow and me. My muscles flex and eyes tighten. "I'm not punching my brother."

Farrow chews his gum slowly. "Will he be thrown back if you do?"

I take a beat. "No. Banks doesn't have PTSD." *Just physical pain.* My brother still hides his frequent migraines from everyone. Hell, he covers up most injuries.

Just then, the door cracks open. Banks slips inside the bathroom, concern cinching his brows.

"I'm snapped to," I tell him.

He nods, and I explain how Farrow doesn't think my lip will heal before I fly out.

Banks cuts me off midway through. "Those idiots are as sharp as marble—they won't be able to tell a difference if we both have busted lips."

Yeah.

"So someone needs to hit me in the mouth," Banks states.

I barely nod, neck stiff.

"It can't be you, Thatcher." Banks sounds adamant.

I stare hard at my brother.

We've wrestled and sparred each other plenty before, but I can't lie—this feels different. Maybe because I just got my mind right.

I turn to Farrow.

His lip rises, entertained at the absurdity of this situation. "You really want me to hit your brother?"

"I'm not forcing you," I tell him. "But yeah." I trust Farrow.

I've always trusted him. And I need him.

"Okay." Farrow slides off his silver rings from his right hand. His smile grows. "Shit, this is not how I thought today would be going."

Banks begins to smile and kneels on the tile. "Just don't knock my teeth out."

Farrow has a strong right hook, but the Oliveira brothers were pro-boxers and would do worse damage in a single blow.

"You're not the Moretti brother I've wanted to uppercut," Farrow says lightly. "Your teeth are safe." His joke alleviates some tension.

My lip wants to lift.

Banks makes the sign of the cross, and I weave my arms over my taut chest. Watching as Farrow forms a fist.

One breath later, he slings his knuckles at my brother, landing with precision on his mouth. His head whips to the side, lip broken open.

I force back a stabbing pain. *We planned this,* I remind myself. But seeing Banks hurt will always hurt me to some degree.

Farrow shakes out his hand. "Good?"

Banks touches the spot, blood on his fingertips. He cracks a quarter of a smile. "What do you think?" he asks me.

"Yeah." I nod. "Should work." I clasp his hand and help him to his feet. I upnod to Farrow in thanks on our way out. We return to the mats where the meeting is taking place, and the team quiets and zeroes in on my brother's swollen mouth.

Sinclair grimaces. "Which one of you shit-tickets hit him?"

"I fell, sir," Banks lies.

SFO is smiling. I focus more on the Alpha lead, Price's glare drilling me with fueled disappointment.

I hear Jane. *I'm very, very proud of you.*

Remember that.

I'm trying. My chest rises.

"You fell?" Sinclair knows my brother is bullshitting, but he nods and says, "Stop tripping over your damn feet, gent."

"Yes, sir."

13

Thatcher Moretti

ONLY 2 DAYS UNTIL Scotland, and there's another loose thread that needs to be tied.

Comms active, gun holstered, I stand on guard against the doorframe of a familiar *geeky* bedroom, triple the size of any bedroom I'd ever seen as a kid.

A six-foot-four armored knight lords over a four-poster bed. Beanbags surround an expensive game console, fantasy paperbacks spilling out of a bookcase. Boxers, tees, and jeans pile on a dresser—more messy than clean, but I've seen this place look like a hurricane ripped through.

The bed is made and most empty cans of Fizz and Sprite are actually *in* the trash bin.

What's new: the dumbbells in the corner, handwraps and boxing gloves on a desk, hiding a stack of 10th grade homeschool textbooks.

Xander Hale gawks like I just laid out a mission to Mordor. Jaw hanging, eyes wide—he slowly shakes his head. "What?"

My brows pull together. I didn't expect *this* reaction from him.

All I can think is: *unfuck this before I fuck it completely.*

I need Xander on board with the twin switch. Because pretending to be my brother while my brother pretends to be me is a type of manipulation.

A twin swap for a one-day prank is different. Easy. Harmless. To swap with the intention to fool others for my own benefit, not just for shits and giggles—it's wrong.

Clear-cut.

And the only way to make this *okay* in my head is to ensure we're not tricking people who matter to us. Her parents—Banks can't run into Rose and Connor Cobalt.

And Xander—he has to know the truth. Hell, even if we didn't tell him, I think he'd notice that Banks isn't me.

We decided that I'd tell Xander the plan only a couple days before the trip. Less time for him to agonize over the details, the better. But now—staring at his slack-jawed, wide-eyed expression—I'm afraid we miscalculated.

He needs more time to process.

My stomach clenches, and I repeat the first part of the plan. "I'm switching places with Banks. He'll be here next week to protect you, then I'll be back."

Xander is balancing on Maximoff's old skateboard. Fizz soda in hand, he sinks down in a daze and sits on the board. "You can't be serious…" Brown hair hangs in his eyelashes.

"I trust Banks with you," I say with everything I have, "and right now, I need to be with Jane." It's never felt more necessary. I can want and desire my girlfriend, but I *need* to be the man at her side come Scotland.

Not Tony.

Not her brothers.

Not Maximoff or Farrow.

That man has to be me. She wants a teammate, and she needs to see that we're meant to stand at the end of the line together. That no matter the circumstances, I'll rip through shackles and be there for her—always.

Forever.

That word stuns my churning brain and ripples through me like life-threatening voltage.

Forever.

I'm barely hanging onto *now* with Jane. I can't think about more.

Xander flicks his soda can tab. "That'll never work, Thatcher—you switching with Banks, I mean."

"Are you against it?"

"No, *no way*. I'd do anything for you and Banks. You guys know that." His amber eyes soften on me. For a single beat, he's that nine-year-old kid that I carried to safety. Fragile and innocent.

But he's not nine anymore.

Tissues and lotion are on his nightstand, his voice has dropped, and if he were still standing, he'd stand tall at six-two. His biceps are cut, gaining more strength.

He'll be sixteen this month, on Christmas day, and I've been waiting for him to make it there.

Because my older brother never did. And if I do anything in my life, Lord, let me have this. Helping Xander live when I couldn't do the same for Sky.

You should've biked harder.

You should've biked harder.

You should've fucking biked harder.

My jaw tics.

I shove down my dad's crushing voice, and I nod to Xander. "We'll be able to execute the plan. You don't need to worry about it."

His mouth falls. "You really don't think you'll get caught? You two don't look that much alike, man."

The corner of my lip inches upward, just slightly, because Xander genuinely believes Banks and I look different. "That's probably because you grew up around us. For other people it's harder to tell the difference. Even worse when we're not standing together."

"But my parents will definitely know."

"They won't." I don't dig into those details, but enough confidence encases my voice that Xander starts frowning.

"Wait, did they get you two wrong?"

I don't want to lie to him, so I say, "A few times." I don't mention how one of those was last week.

Xander immediately springs to his feet and steps away from the skateboard. Aiming for the door like he plans to hunt down his mom.

"Hey." I extend an arm and block the door before putting a light hand on his elbow. "It's normal—"

"That's not alright." A thousand emotions pour out of his expressive eyes. "They've known you and Banks for *years*."

"My uncles have known me my *whole* life and some still call me Banks on accident." I reassure him. "It happens, kid. It doesn't mean they don't care." If I let that shit hurt me or affect me, I'd be in pain every week.

But when people see me—truly *see me* and not just *the twin* that I am—it's a rush. Like drinking the coldest ice water on a scorching summer day, and I feel that every moment I'm with Jane.

I almost glance back at the shut door.

I miss her.

And I've only been on-duty for an hour. She's busy handling the logistics of maneuvering too many people to Scotland. Plus scheduling meetings with local wedding vendors while we're there.

I'm good at multi-tasking, but that girl could surpass the hell out of me every time. I linger on that thought and almost smile.

Together we could juggle the world.

While I focus solely on Xander, I wear seriousness. He's processing what I said. And he's wincing.

"I'm *your* bodyguard," I remind him. "*You've* known me for years. It makes sense that you can tell us apart better than your parents can."

Xander bites his thumbnail, catches himself, and rubs his hand against his jeans. "Yeah you're right." He backs up and lowers to the edge of his bed. After a gulp of soda, he asks, "So how many people know about the twin switch anyway?"

"You want the whole list?"

He snorts out soda in surprise, then wipes his nose. "There's a list?"

I go ahead and rattle off names.

All of SFO, Jack Highland (an exec producer of the docuseries), and the older famous ones: Jane, Maximoff, Charlie, Beckett, Sullivan, and Luna.

Mainly everyone who joined the FanCon tour.

Xander blinks. "Uh, that's not a secret if that many people know. *It's information.*" He crunches the can in his hand. "As the great Varys would say."

He's referencing *Game of Thrones.* Honestly, I wish I could go back in time and tell my stone-cold-serious teenage self how much I'd know about George R.R. Martin and Tolkien and trolls. I'd probably smile more than I ever did.

I fix my eyes on my client. "Then it's information you need to keep secret."

He licks soda off his lips. "I can do that."

I nod strongly, confident in this kid, and I watch his features lighten.

Comms crackle. "Donnelly to Thatcher, coming in hot with lunch."

I press the mic. "Copy." To Xander, I say, "Donnelly's on his way up with food."

"Awesome." Xander stands on the skateboard and rolls to the window.

I leave the door and grab my water bottle off his desk.

He pries down a single blind, just enough to peer out of the slat. "Do you think Donnelly is bored? Being on my detail, I mean."

My brows knit, caught off guard. "Why would you even think that?"

Xander releases the blind and glances back at me. "Because he used to be *Beckett's* bodyguard. And before that, Tom's. So he's used to hanging around ballerinas and musicians rather than just sitting inside all day and staring at a wall." Xander shrugs. "And like I don't even go to Dalton Academy, so there's no high school drama he can soak up. I'm just boring, so by process of fucking deduction he's probably bored."

I squint because he's seeing something I don't see. Something I can't see.

He's the son of billionaires, a teen spectacle that fans fawn over and media stokes into a worldwide phenomenon—his life is way out of range from *slow* and *average* and *ordinary.*

I shake my head. "I'm not bored, and you're not boring." That's it. End of story. I'm about to twist open my water, but his chest collapses.

I plant 120% of my concentration on him.

"You have to say that. You're my…you're my *bodyguard.*" He runs a hand through his hair.

I go still.

He can barely meet my eyes. What I feel for Xander…it's as deep as blood, but I'm not his brother. I'm not permanent to his life in that sense, and I've tried…

I've tried fucking *hard* to make sure he understands this.

I'm replaceable.

Banks is replaceable. We should just be nameless bodyguards on a team to Xander, and one day another bodyguard will stand here and take our post. He shouldn't bat an eye or even notice a real difference. His life should continue at the same rate without misstep or back shuffle.

Being on his detail again—I'm blowing a fuse that I already struggled to tear out of a bomb. Confusing him and *me.*

Swiftly, I act on instinct and scrounge up *professional* facts. "It shouldn't even matter what Donnelly or I think. We aren't here to be entertained by you. We're here to protect you."

Xander opens his arms wide. "Exactly. 99% of the time, you're protecting me *inside* my own damn room. And we both know that the threats are mostly just *me.*"

I unscrew my water, muscles stiff as we ride down this road.

I've seen Xander at some of the lowest points. I've tried to pull him up. I remember him at eleven. How he couldn't get out of bed one morning. He was crying, sobbing, and could barely breathe as he said, *"I don't want to be here."*

I had to call his parents. I stayed with him. I held his hand.

It's true that most clients don't ask for their bodyguards to be in their room with them all day.

Every day.

But Xander Hale has different demons that he needs us to fight off. It's why I'm here. What I'm made to do.

When he stays inside the Hale mansion, his security detail is often posted in his room with him. Mostly for his peace of mind…and so that he's not alone.

The times when he's not doing well, we'll split shifts so he has a bodyguard around-the-clock, even when he sleeps. It's one reason why he's usually assigned two men and not just one.

Right now I don't want Donnelly to interrupt this conversation, so I whisper quickly into my mic, "Thatcher to Donnelly, standby for five before coming upstairs."

The line crackles. "Copy that, Thatch."

Thatch.

Heaviness pounds my chest, but I force myself not to correct Donnelly this time. I'm more concerned about the kid in front of me.

Xander continues, not noticing that I radioed anyone. "I don't know; maybe if I went out more, it'd be more interesting for Donnelly." He hangs his head, then swallows the last of his soda.

"Are you trying to impress him?" I take a swig of water.

"No." He wipes his mouth with the heel of his palm. "I just don't want anyone else to leave."

I breathe out through my nose. That hits me hard since Banks and I were the first to really leave him. "I'm not going anywhere."

Fucking A, Thatcher.

The words leave before I can stop them, and I fucking *hate* that I just made a promise we both know I can't keep.

I'm going to go where Jane goes. I want to. I need to.

I have to. Everything in my soul wrenches me in that direction. Hell, it's been wrenching me for a while. Before I was even her bodyguard.

Xander huffs. "You can't say that. If they let you back on Jane's detail, you'll take it. And I get it. You should." He inhales a sharper breath. "I just…you know I thought if you were going to be a part of the family, you'd be a Hale." He shrugs. "Marry Luna or something."

I tense.

I'm fighting through a steel castle just to be welcomed into the Cobalt Empire, but the closer I am to them, the further I am from the Hales. Every time the three families have trivia nights, sandcastle competitions, relay races—I want to be on my girlfriend's side. And it'll be a feat to make it happen.

Team Cobalt.

Team Jane.

But I can't stand hurting Xander.

I slowly screw the cap onto my water. "I wish you were my little brother, but you're someone else's." It kills me to say that out loud. "Maximoff and even Farrow will be there for you for the rest of your life when I can't be."

He has to let me go.

I have to let him go. *I shouldn't be on his detail.* It's not good for either of us.

His eyes redden. "Yeah." His Adam's apple bobs. "I just wish I could have all of you. Moffy, Farrow, you, and Banks. I know it's selfish."

I rub my mouth, bruise and cut visible from O'Malley's punch, and then I drop my arm. "I didn't plan on loving Jane."

I couldn't stop it from happening. And now I'm doing everything I can to keep her in my arms.

"I know." Xander shoots his empty can into a trash bin. "'*Love is the death of duty.*'" He quotes *Game of Thrones* again. "I always figured you'd eventually break the rules for someone you love. I just thought it'd be for Banks."

I take a tight breath.

I was never put in a position where I'd need to break rules for my brother, but I guess we're breaking them together now.

"Just so you know," Xander quickly adds, "I like that you and my cousin are together." He picks at his fingernail nervously. "I was hard on Moffy and Farrow, and I hated that I was—and I don't want to do that again. I know Jane looks happy. You seem happy too, and I can handle this." He mutters under his breath to himself, "I can handle this."

"You can," I reinforce.

Xander nods more, then hops back on the skateboard. "Hey, can you not mention to Donnelly that I'm worried he thinks I'm boring?" I hold back a small, fleeting smile. "Yeah." Donnelly might actually be good for him. Even if Xander goes outside just to impress a bodyguard, it means he's braving the world.

We chat more about the twin swap, and then Donnelly arrives with hot hoagies from Wawa.

For lunch, we stay professional and keep quiet near the desk. Xander slouches on a red beanbag, reading a fantasy paperback and biting into a meatball hoagie.

I peel the paper off mine. "Where'd you rack out last night?" I whisper to Donnelly. I heard Epsilon threw his luggage on the lawn, and ever since he hooked up with Luna, I feel accountable for what happens to them. Almost like a fucking accomplice, and I can't report him to the Tri-Force.

I wouldn't risk his career.

I just want to make sure they're both safe in whatever they're doing. Just like Jane does.

He sips a fountain drink. "Couch in security's townhouse."

"You can room with my brother."

"Nah." Donnelly picks up his hoagie. "He already offered, and Farrow even said I could crash in his room. But the couch is *fire*." He takes a huge bite and mumbles, "Just like this hoagie."

I lean on the desk and lower my voice. "So you didn't sneak into Luna's bed?"

He chokes a little, then shakes his head. "Nah, man." He glances quickly at Xander, then back to me. "It was just that one time—"

His voice slices in half as boxing gloves topple off the desk. Probably from my weight against the wood, and as he picks them up, more shit starts falling. I set down my hoagie and crouch.

I start gathering items, and I move slower as I find a *Celebrity Crush* tabloid and three *Famous Now* magazines.

Donnelly frowns. "I thought he's not supposed to read that."

"He's not." I fan open a *Famous Now*, worried he's hiding something. I land on the Alphas Like Us column series—the one that documents Maximoff and Farrow's life.

Their couple pictures are haphazardly cut out. I don't know what the hell he's doing.

Donnelly flips through the *Celebrity Crush*, the tabloid also clipped and sheared. He pauses on an article.

> The Hales, Meadows, and Cobalts—they're like us! They read books. They love movies. They go shopping!

The title: **Sexy Like Us**

This photo isn't missing. I'm with Jane. We're leaving a cat shelter, and I'm putting my brown leather jacket on her shoulders.

She was cold.

I wish I could just drink in *us*, but my eyes instantly narrow on Tony. In the photo, he's out in front with a shit-eating grin. He was an asshole that night.

It's starting to become routine, and I don't want to be desensitized to his bullshit. Because I don't want him to stay her bodyguard.

Get your head on straight.

We sift through the other tabloids. Only pictures of Maximoff and Farrow are cut out.

"I can explain."

Our heads swerve to our client.

Xander stands close, breathing hard. "Those aren't mine. They're Kinney's—she had this *great* idea for Moffy and Farrow's Christmas present this year. And it requires *that*." He points at the tabloids.

I frown, confused as all hell.

Donnelly grins. "You're making a collage?"

"Yeah." Xander cringes. "I know, it's dumb—"

"It's dope, man." Donnelly rises with me. "Farrow will love this shit." He laughs.

"Oh…right. Awesome." Xander starts to smile.

I stack the magazines back on his desk. "Why not just use personal photos?"

"Luna said we should *branch out* or whatever." He shrugs. "My sisters just think it'll be cool to use pictures they probably haven't seen."

They shoot the shit for a second, and I zero in on the cover of *Celebrity Crush.*

A tagline: *read inside to find out which other Hales, Meadows, and Cobalts are dating their bodyguards!*

Fuck.

My jaw tenses, and I flip to page twelve. I'm not aware of what the leads know anymore because Akara is sharing jack shit with me. I can only hope they're on top of rumors.

Quickly, I read the article.

HOLY SECRETS, BATMAN!

Security Force Omega is a total sham. We've learned from a reliable source that the bodyguard hotties, hired to protect the famous families, are nothing more than a front hiding their real purpose.

Two bodyguards have already come clean, and we're waiting for the rest—but it's clear to Celebrity Crush and our source that every bodyguard is actually the boyfriend to who they protect.

The couples:

Sullivan Meadows & Akara Kitsuwon

Charlie Cobalt & Oscar Oliveira

Beckett Cobalt & Paul Donnelly

Luna Hale & Quinn Oliveira

They've forgotten about Banks, and I have to grab hold to this useless fucking fact or else I'll burst a blood vessel in my neck.

This isn't good.

This is bad.

Really bad. We'd been speculating fan theories to come to light if I stayed with Jane past October, but not *this* theory about SFO as a whole. The media believes we're *pretending* to be bodyguards.

For fuck's sake.

I read more.

> Clearly these couples are trying to hide their tracks! Thatcher is no longer protecting Jane just to throw us off, and Paul is no longer protecting Beckett. But our source says they're all still together.

I hang onto that last line.

We're still together. Jane and me.

I breathe out, not realizing how good it'd feel to hear the media change their position on my relationship. Even if the rest isn't true.

I decide to text Akara rather than use comms.

Did you see the "holy secrets" article? I press send.

A minute later, I get a reply.

But instead of answering me by text, he responds to everyone. "Akara to Omega, if you see the article in *Celebrity Crush* about SFO, ignore it. Protect your client and keep your heads up. Prove that this means nothing."

Roger that.

14

Jane Cobalt

I'M AFRAID.

I'm so very afraid that I'll be too soft on my brother. I'm afraid that Maximoff will have to be the strong-hand and it'll create unnecessary tension between him and Beckett when that should be my burden to bear.

I'm afraid that I won't be enough to help him.

That I will fail in epic glory, as I always seem to do in the end.

Fears commandeer my mind and rattle my core. We've packed our bags and left them in the Range Rover outside the Hell's Kitchen apartment complex, the world quiet and still at 3:30 a.m.—our flight for Scotland departs today.

And we've come to gather a passenger.

The ritzy elevator feels compact and ominous as we ascend the floors to my brothers' bachelor pad, and I know my apprehension is apparent. Concern spills out of Thatcher, Farrow, and Moffy. I sense them looking at me as the numbers tick and we rise.

At least I was able to convince Tony to take another elevator. Most likely because Banks stayed behind with him. Before we leave Hell's Kitchen, the Moretti brothers plan to swap clothes in a restroom, and when they come out, Thatcher will pretend to be Banks and Banks will be Thatcher.

Igniting the twin switch.

But right now, only the four of us are in the elevator, and Thatcher is still entirely himself.

I blow out a controlled breath. Hot beneath my cheetah-fur coat and pastel jeans.

"We're right here with you, Janie." Maximoff has squared shoulders and these tough green eyes that say, *we can power through anything*. And with Farrow at total ease next to him, that resilience doubles.

Thatcher is behind me, his sculpted arm protectively wrapped around my collarbones while I lean back against his chest. I look up, and he looks down.

His narrowed gaze carries unadulterated confidence that washes over me. Like we're standing beneath a steaming shower in a faraway land, alone together. Like we're naked.

Bare.

Vulnerable, and I'm syphoning his assurance and composure. My chin rises, my shoulders lifting. I'm a leech, I realize.

I'm *leeching* his strength, and I don't want to rely *solely* on him. Or anyone for that matter.

Not my parents, not Maximoff and Farrow, not bodyguards, siblings, cousins, or strangers—I need to offer something and be of use and value. Yet, I can't move.

I can't push Thatcher away. It hurts even thinking about stepping out of this embrace. I inhale and reach behind me, gripping his waist.

Eyes still fixed together, his lips lower and meet mine. In an upside-down kiss, brief and explosive. Detonating an emotional meteor in my heart, my body swells, and I breathe and breathe.

We break, and I look ahead.

Eyes wide in the same thought.

I'm a leech.

But is it so bad to leech another man's confidence?

Yes.

No, because possibly he leeches a great deal from me too.

Does he?

What if he leeches nothing, Jane?

I don't know anymore. I've never questioned my confidence so deeply, and these insecurities weigh a fifty-ton pressure on my chest that I don't need today.

Think of Beckett.

Think of your brother.

Think of your goal.

I drop my hands off Thatcher, and I find strength to move. Whether it's the right kind of strength, I'm not certain. I'm so confused, but I step out of his hold anyway.

His arm tears off my collarbones.

It hurts.

I can feel the air slice painfully, and I struggle to even look him in the eyes. I glance over at my best friend, and Maximoff shakes his head with a wince. Feeling my unease, possibly.

Farrow is eyeing Thatcher, then me. I think he sees a strain that my leech-insecurities just created.

"Jane?" Thatcher says.

I clear a pained knot in my throat. "I hate that we're forcing my brother to join us." I adjust the strap of my fuzzy mint-green purse, the unusual contents inside weighing on me. "I wish it didn't have to be like this." But none of us could formulate a better solution.

Silence thickens, the floor-numbers still increasing.

I finally look up at Thatcher.

He rubs his mouth, brows knitted. "Do you not want us to be here?"

"No," I say quickly. "Not at all."

"Do you not want *me* to be here then?"

"*No,*" I emphasize, my stomach lurching. "You have no idea how much…" I exhale, my pulse hiking to devastating speeds. "…how many times it's dawned on me and overwhelmed me—that Moffy and I have fallen for two men who fight to help us protect who we love." My eyes burn. "Not just half-heartedly or out of loyalty to us, but because you deeply love our siblings and cousins. And if we weren't here, you'd still fight for them as *deeply* as we would, and that is priceless to me."

I love him.

Say it, Jane.

His eyes cradle mine, offering comfort from afar. His chest rises in deeper breath.

I open my mouth. "I—"

Ding.

The elevator doors slide open. We've arrived.

"TRY NOT TO WAKE ELIOT AND TOM," CHARLIE

whispers, letting us inside the lavish and sleek apartment. Dark, no lamps or lights turned on, I skulk ahead of everyone and reach Beckett's bedroom.

I tie my wavy hair back with a velvet scrunchie.

Don't let up.

Confidence.

I pull back my shoulders and gently open the door. Quiet, I tiptoe on the dark hardwood and into the cleanest, most organized space. Books sit in neat rows on a polished shelf, pencils perfectly lined on a desk, and a fern is situated in the precise corner, near ironed curtains where navy fabric is pleated in straight lines.

Beckett sleeps soundlessly beneath a tucked-in, blue comforter. He holds the pillow beneath his head, colorful floral tattoos sprawling down his right arm. Donnelly inked every single one of Beckett's tattoos, and all are flowers from roses to daisies to lilies and poppies, as homage to our mom and aunts.

It reminds me that he loves our family so greatly, despite having such little time to spend with us.

I walk closer to the bed. He looks peaceful.

And I hate to wake him. But I must.

"Beckett," I whisper. "Beckett." I reach the bed and lightly jostle his arm.

He jolts and flinches, eyes snapping open. But he instantly relaxes when he sees me. "Sis," he exhales, rubbing his tired face. "What are you doing here?"

"You're coming with us, little brother," I remind him.

Horror freezes him, eyes like saucers. "No." He notices Thatcher, Farrow, Moffy, and Charlie filling the bedroom, then his head whips back to me. "*No*. Jane, I told you I can't go—"

"And I told you that if you used, we'd force you."

"You can't." He uses his elbow to prop himself up.

"Are you naked?" I ask.

His face scrunches like *what the fuck*. "No—"

I fling the comforter off his body.

"*Jane*." He's just dressed in gray Calvin Klein underwear. And for his privacy, I keep my gaze above his neck, thank you very much.

"Get up. Get dressed. Pack a bag. Let's go. You have an hour." I perch my hands on my wide hips. *Please, Beckett, make this easy.*

He glares. "I'm *not* goin—"

Charlie flicks on the lights.

Beckett squints, hand shielding his eyes. "I'm twenty-one. I control my life, and all five of you need to get the fuck out of my room."

None of us move a muscle. No one speaks.

Beckett lies back down, smoothly like silk resting on an idle lake. Even in his anger, he's graceful.

I peek over my shoulder. "Thatcher."

My boyfriend rips the rest of the bedding off, piling sheets and the comforter on the floor. Farrow comes closer and snatches the pillows, dumping them too. Charlie rolls in a suitcase, and Maximoff is careful with Beckett's clothes as he opens each drawer. He tries to maintain the crisp shape of each folded item.

They pack his things.

Slowly, Beckett sits up against the headboard, aghast. He rests his elbows on his bent knees, fingers interlaced on his neck. Staring down at the bare mattress. If I pushed him over, he'd be in a fetal position, and it makes me terribly sad.

"Beckett, please," I whisper. "We just want to help you."

He pushes back curlier strands of his hair. "You're hurting me." His eyes are raw and red.

"I'm sorry." I am.

I am.

Don't cower.

He wipes his mouth before sliding off the bed. He's finally cooperating. I let him pass. "Can I help with your toiletries?"

He ignores me and nears the dresser, squeezing beside Maximoff. We all watch him collect gray sweatpants from a drawer. He tugs them over his waist, and then he grabs his leather wallet.

"You're not leaving without us," Charlie says hotly.

Beckett lets out a pained laugh. "You're one to talk, Charlie. How many times have you ditched this family?"

Charlie looks to *me*, needing an assist.

I hike over to Beckett and tear the wallet out of his hand.

He tilts his head. "How am I supposed to fly without my license, sis? I need that."

"So you do plan to come with us?" I question.

He stays quiet. Fuming.

Maximoff treks past us towards the bathroom. "I'll get his toiletries."

Thank you.

I unzip my purse.

Beckett pinches his eyes. When he drops his hand, he zeroes in on Thatcher and Farrow who block the doorway. I can tell he's hurt and confused. "You plan to have your boyfriend drag me onto a plane? Is that it?"

I slowly shake my head. "No."

He frowns. "You *can't* force me—"

I snap a fuzzy blue handcuff on his wrist, and the other end, I lock onto mine. "Congratulations, you're now very much attached to me."

Beckett looks slightly impressed but mostly resigned and upset. He sighs. "Jane…"

I smile a sympathetic smile. "Time to go to Scotland and be with family."

15

Jane Cobalt

BY THE TIME WE board, my brother is still shirtless, just in sweatpants, and sufficiently handcuffed to me. With disheveled brown hair and his arm tattoos in view, he looks more unkempt than usual and more like the "bad boy of ballet" the media often portrays him as.

Beckett holds up his wrist, displaying the fuzzy handcuff that links me to him. "You can take this off now," he says pointedly, but annoyance clings to the words. "I'm obviously not going anywhere."

"The plane hasn't taken off yet," I note.

Our parent's private jet is slowly filling with SFO and the two Epsilon bodyguards: Tony and O'Malley. Plus, Jack Highland, Maximoff, Charlie, Luna, Sulli, and Sulli's boyfriend Will Rochester. They became an "official" couple last night, but only privately.

Sulli said she'd rather eat fertilizer than publicize her relationship. That it's easier for the world to believe she's with Akara. Just like the world thinks the rest of SFO are dating their clients, and I saw that most clearly when we were heading to the airport.

Paparazzi and fans were yelling at the top of their lungs.

"OSCAR, CHARLIE, WE LOVE YOU! Oslie for life!!"

"DONNELLY, BECKETT—KISS, KISS, KISS!"

"LunaQuinn! LunaQuinn! LunaQuinn!"

"KITSULLI IS OTP!"

Each one is a completely fictional pairing, and thankfully Omega was able to ignore the chants and maintain their duties. Their steadfast nature is a saving grace. I just hope my siblings and cousins can withstand the rumors.

In the rear of the plane, I lower onto a cream, plush double-seat. Giving us enough privacy to speak alone.

Beckett is forced to sink down beside me. "Where'd you buy these?" He touches the handcuff. "A sex shop?"

"Yes," I answer, unabashed. "The girl working there was very sweet too." I might've also purchased a new vibrator, Thatcher in attendance with me, but I don't need to mention this. *Clearly, Jane.*

Beckett leans back with a sigh. "They are softer than tactical ones."

I smile. "Precisely."

Charlie wanted to use metal handcuffs. He thought Beckett would enjoy the fuzzy ones too much, but I couldn't bear to physically hurt him. We're already puncturing his emotions enough as it is.

Beckett stares ahead in deeper thought, and my lips gradually fall to a line. He takes a tight breath before turning to me. "So you really believe I'll run down the aisle past your six-foot-seven boyfriend and bum-rush the only exit that has more than three massive bodyguards climbing on board?"

"Yes."

He gives me the umpteenth *what the fuck* face, brows scrunched tight. "*Jane,*" he whisper-hisses and yanks my wrist toward his chest. "I'm not a fucking addict."

I want to believe him, so terribly. I want to.

"So maybe you wouldn't bum-rush the exit." My voice lowers. "Maybe I believe you in that instance. But the only reason you wouldn't go for the door is because you'd be afraid one of those *massive* bodyguards could accidentally break your leg or your arm stopping you, and then you'd be out of ballet. Tell me I'm wrong about that."

He doesn't deny a thing. He just leans back, staring ahead again, away from me. And so softly, under his breath, he says, "I hate you, you know."

My stomach sinks. He keeps unsheathing the same sword and plunging it straight in my gut. Knowing those words wreak an agonizing amount of damage on me.

Am I doing the right thing?

Maybe he doesn't have a problem.

What if I'm keeping him from his career, his life's goal for no reason at all? Ballet has been his sport, his art, his love and passion for over seventeen years.

He's right—I don't know what that's like, not in the slightest.

I hate you, you know. His words ring hollow in my head. He hates me because I forced him here, handcuffed him to me, and he should, I suppose. I blink back emotion that tries to throttle its way to the surface.

I have to remember what Charlie said, *"He's going to be an asshole. A real dick. Don't listen to him."*

Beckett and I rarely feud, and so I pictured a Charlie spat. Some flowery insults with added flair and then a cold-hearted bomb.

But I should have known better. Beckett has always been honest and pointed. But he's still my little brother, even if he's just two years younger. I have an obligation to protect him, and no matter how many blades I take, I'll keep going.

I also have to remember—he's a Cobalt. Beckett is cunning and smart, and he'll use my emotions and love for him against me. Maybe he doesn't *really* hate me. What's more probable: he's just trying to manipulate his way out of the handcuff.

Packing on my battle armor, I straighten up and channel a surge of confidence. *I am a motherfucking lion.* I am my mother's daughter.

Even if I only have one-tenth of Rose Calloway Cobalt in me, that's one-tenth of fire and brimstone that I can wield.

"You'll thank me later," I say.

"Keep telling yourself that." He uses his cuffed hand to scratch his jaw, taking my hand with him. I don't try to resist.

"I'll uncuff us once the plane starts." That was always the plan at least.

He looks straight ahead, not at me, while he speaks. "You mean, you're not afraid I'll find a parachute and jump out mid-air?"

"Well, now that you mention it," I banter, trying to lighten the mood.

Beckett doesn't acknowledge me or my poor attempt at a joke. I suppose a smile from him would be too much to ask.

My attention detours as a towering man strides down the narrow aisle. I skim him far too eagerly. Dog tags lie against his form-fitting white button-down, his brown hair tucked behind both ears, and a closer shave makes him appear a year or two younger.

He still has the commanding gait of a leader.

Still possesses grave sternness in his locked shoulders and tightened eyes.

Still resembles a brooding, handsome Thatcher Moretti. To me at least.

My smile rises, a rush of *hope* cascading over me. Helping subdue the pit in my stomach. Despite all my hang-ups and personal fears, I'm so very glad he's here. I want him beside me.

More than anyone.

His stoic eyes stay on mine, which most likely display tangled affections and curiosities. Thatcher does a much better job of acting like I'm his brother's girlfriend. Nothing more, nothing less.

"Banks," I greet from my chair.

Beckett slips me a weird look. Most likely for pretending my boyfriend is his twin brother when Tony isn't even around to fool at the moment.

But I'm practicing.

Practice is important, and Thatcher nearly smiles. I'd say we both enjoy being in cahoots again. It isn't so bad this time because all the people we love are in on the secret.

"Jane," Thatcher says strongly. He reaches the rear and holds out a water bottle to me, then another to Beckett.

"Merci." I take the bottle gratefully and twist open the lid—Beckett shoots to a stance, forcing my hand with him.

Merde—the bottle tips backwards, spilling onto my breasts and soaking my zebra blouse. Thatcher has quick reflexes and rights the bottle before I'm completely doused, and I stand up and glance at Beckett.

A fraction of remorse flits in his eyes.

"That was quite *unnecessary*," I tell him.

He frowns. "You're the one who wants to be cuffed to me."

"I don't want to—"

"I have to take a piss." Beckett interrupts me. His voice has changed, almost panicked. "Can you please…?" He extends his wrist.

Thatcher and I exchange a look, one full of apprehension. Something isn't right. My brother hasn't been this hostile since I spoke to him back in the apartment.

And then I notice the change: the door to the airplane. The flight crew has finally boarded, which means we only have about ten minutes before takeoff.

If Beckett were to make a move to leave, it's now or never. Thatcher must see this too because he narrows a look on me and shakes his head. Silently telling me *don't do it.*

I touch my brother's arm. "We can go together."

"No we can't," Beckett snaps. "I'm not peeing in front of my sister. Just uncuff me. I'll be in and out in two minutes." He looks to Thatcher. "Guard the door if that'll make you both feel better."

I want to trust him, but not at the cost of ruining all the progress we've made just to have him *here.* We've come this far, and I don't want to lose my leverage in the end.

"Counter offer," I say. "How about you wait to use the restroom until the plane takes off?"

Beckett stares me dead in the eyes, frustration creasing his forehead. "I have to go now, Jane." He usually calls me *sis.* My name sounds like a thousand-pound brick on his tongue, weighted with anger.

"I won't look. I'll close my eyes," I say quickly.

More bodies pile onto the plane than before, and since we're both standing, people start to turn around in their plush leather seats and stare. The attention feels too hot for comfort, and it's not so smart to draw an audience while Thatcher is supposed to be Banks.

He sticks a toothpick between his lips and surveys the area.

Beckett lets out an annoyed breath. "Just put the handcuff on Charlie. Problem solved."

"I can't," I sigh out.

When we were devising this strategy, Charlie refused to be handcuffed to him. He said he couldn't do it. That it'd be five minutes before he uncuffed his twin brother. Instead, Charlie looked at me and said, *"It has to be you."*

He trusted me with this task, and I worry if I hand this off to Moffy, it'll just fester some sort of resentment within Charlie. For once, there is another person, another option, another someone who has nerves of steel and who stands so close to my side.

I eye Thatcher.

His strong gaze returns to me.

For some reason, my heart is beating wildly, uncontrollably, and I can't slow the pace. "Would you mind…" *Breathe.* I inhale. "…being handcuffed to Beckett for the next ten minutes?"

Thatcher is already nodding. "I'm good to go."

I look to Beckett. "There. Banks can go to the restroom with you. As far as I know, he's not your sister."

Beckett stakes me with one final glare before hanging his head and saying, "Let's just get this over with."

16

Thatcher Moretti

SOMETIMES I FORGET JUST how fucking rich Jane's family is until I meet the wealth head-on.

Like right now.

I've never seen a gold tissue holder until this moment. Let alone one in the bathroom of a *plane*. Salt scrub is in an opal dish with a spoon that looks more expensive than my salary, and ornate light fixtures cast a dim glow on the porcelain toilet.

Fit for royalty.

I have enough room to do push-ups, sit-ups, and throw some jumping jacks into the mix, and usually, I'd ignore the luxuries and focus on my duty.

But Jane is my girlfriend. This is the Cobalt *family* jet, affectionately nicknamed Heathcliff by Audrey, which outsizes all the other private planes and can comfortably carry all three famous families. It's also outfitted with four bedrooms, five lounges, a twenty-person dining room, cinema *and* fitness area.

Where Jane comes from feels leagues different than where I'm born and bred. I'm staring at the Tiffany blue walls, the two sinks, and the fucking shower with thundering caution.

They'll never accept someone like me.

I exhale out of my nose. That out-of-place feeling wants to beat me down, but I have to push forward.

Her brother is what matters here.

I face him while we're cuffed together. "I can turn around and give you privacy while you piss, or I can uncuff you and stay forward." I don't trust Beckett, and I haven't exactly patted him down for drugs.

He shifts his weight and stares everywhere but at me. "I just need to use the sink." He seems antsy.

"I thought you needed to go the bathroom?" I'm tentative because Jane always talks about Cobalt 4D chess games, and I'm not about to be duped by one of her brothers.

Beckett scratches underneath the cuff. "No. I just need the sink." He still can't meet my eyes. "Please." His voice is a sincere whisper. "I didn't want to worry her, but I have to wash my hands. It's really bothering me…" He expels a taut, anxious breath.

I realize his distress isn't some deceptive thing. He's uncomfortable being this vulnerable in front of me.

I make a choice, and I fish a tiny key out of my pocket. "Don't do anything your sister wouldn't want you to do." I unlock his handcuff.

Beckett nods, and while I stand guard near the door, he rubs his wrist and approaches the sink. I watch him pump the soap dispenser three times. He methodically lathers his palms, in between his fingers, his forearms—all the way to his elbows.

He scrubs his hands, turns the faucet on and off five consecutive times, and glances back at me. "Can you…please just look at the wall?"

I shift my narrowed gaze onto the toilet, his nerves suffocating the bathroom, and I feel badly that his OCD is riding him this hard. I have no experience helping Beckett with this, but I understand brothers who want to keep their troubles hidden and private.

Jane will want to know.

I'll tell her, and she'll blame herself for pushing Beckett there—but I'll lift her as high as I can and carry the guilt. It's what I'm good at.

He repeats the routine three more times, and when he finishes washing soap suds, he curses under his breath and starts all over again. His skin is starting to grow red and inflamed.

"Is there something I can do?" I ask.

He shakes his head, then after another five minutes, he dries his hands on a monogramed towel. "When you mention this to Jane, can you add that this isn't serious?" He comes over and extends his wrist.

Carefully, I snap on the cuff. "Why don't you just tell her yourself?"

"Honestly…it's hard for me to talk to her right now." He's still upset that she dragged him here.

"I'll mention it," I promise.

"Thanks." He stares nervously at the door, like the latch is haunted. I notice how he twiddles his fingers, and I step past him, our wrists connected, and I open the door for Beckett.

He exhales in relief but avoids my eyes.

We exit, and I peer into the main lounge. Almost everyone has already boarded. Total headcount for the trip: a staggering 17 people.

Leave it to Maximoff Hale to transform the work of scouting a wedding location into a vacation for *other* people. He invited his family, security, and any plus-ones who wanted to journey to the Scottish Highlands for a week.

We'll be back by December 20th, just in time for the holidays. My grandma has been begging me to bring Jane home for Christmas Eve. Every phone call is the same, but the most recent one was on speaker-phone in Jane's bedroom.

I was packing my duffel and her suitcase for Scotland.

"Youse twos are still coming for dinner on Christmas Eve?" my grandma asked.

On the bed, Jane smiled at the phone in my hand while she brushed Licorice. The gray cat had just come out of hiding.

"We're still planning on it," I confirmed.

"The whole family will be there," my grandma said excitedly. Proud of the family, and Jane beamed up at me, understanding that feeling of pride in a lineage. "And I want to give Jane her baby blanket I'm crocheting. I should be finished by then."

I didn't flinch.

Jane went wide-eyed. "Oh, I'm…I'm not pregnant."

"It's not for now," my grandma said. "I already made Thatcher one, but now youse can have two for the day you marry and have babies. I might not be around."

"Grandma," I said. "Don't talk like that."

"Hush now, I'm old. When I go, I'll go, and you'll have these things to remember me by." She's been preparing the family for her death since she was in her early sixties. Saying, *I'm old. I'm gonna die soon.*

She's still healthy.

After we said our goodbyes and I hung up, Jane looked more curiously at me. "Has she crocheted your past girlfriends baby blankets?"

"Hell no."

"Oh."

I didn't expect that reaction.

My pulse ratcheted up. "She likes you." *She can tell I love you.*

"I like her a great deal too," Jane whispered, but her brows bunched in concern. "What if…" Flush stained her freckled cheeks. "What if you dislike me in six or seven months and we break-up? Or possibly we might just mutually feel we're not a perfect fit? These are rational probabilities." She spoke in a single breath.

I realized then that Jane believes there's a greater chance of us being a short-term couple than a permanent one.

"How is it rational that I'll dislike you in six months when I love you now?" I asked point-blank.

She smiled, then frowned, then winced. "Anything could happen…I suppose."

I nodded stiffly.

I can't see the future any better than she can.

Mathematically maybe that shit adds up in that direction, but we're dealing with emotion.

Unwieldy, un-fucking-quantifiable, *frightening* emotion—and I just want to be *her* safety net. I want her to feel like she can fall into these feelings, and I'll catch her.

"Look, there's no pressure," I said strongly. "The blanket is just a gift, not a binding agreement."

"It's not to say that I wouldn't...I mean, I..." She buried her face in her palms, and I sat on the bed beside her and drew her to my chest. I hugged Jane, and she mumbled against my body, "This is all so..."

"Soon," I finished.

She looked up at me. "I was going to say *new.*"

"Right." My muscles tensed. Unsure of where her fears exactly stemmed.

She felt me flex, and she swallowed hard. And then Carpenter stole our attention as he knocked perfume off her vanity. We dropped the topic after that.

I hadn't thought much about Jane being pregnant. I hadn't thought a lot about marriage or our children—and I shouldn't be remembering any of this now.

We need to crawl through the first round of barbed wire before we can contemplate what lies ahead of us.

The cards, this twin switch, and *Tony.* If we can haul through this together, then maybe that door will open.

On the plane, Beckett stalls near the bathroom door. Not ready to return to his seat yet, and while I wait for him to move, my radio crackles with static.

Donnelly whispers on comms. "The Rooster has chosen his flock. I repeat, the Rooster has chosen his flock."

I regret staying on the SFO line.

For the trip, we all agreed to be on the same channel as Tony and O'Malley, and I planned to switch over once we land. Listening to Tony's voice is about as high on my priority list as chewing a bag of nails.

"He can't be serious," Oscar responds.

I scan my surroundings, and I zero in on a blue-blazer-wearing, gold-brick-shitting rich white guy: the Rooster (aka Will Rochester). He's prep-school manufactured, birthed and raised in WASP society. Even his teeth look expensive.

He laughs with Tony and O'Malley at a four-person table.

Will might be Sulli's new boyfriend, but he was the one person Jane and I were hesitant to share intel about the twin swap with. Now that he's *best friends* with Tony, I'm glad we told him nothing.

He can be in the dark the whole trip.

I lower the radio volume and focus on Beckett Cobalt. "Where do you want to go?" Until this plane takes off, I'm still attached to him, and I'll follow him wherever he wants to sit. But I'm hoping he chooses next to his sister.

He fixes his bed-head hair. "Back to New York."

"I meant on the plane."

"I know," he says softly.

I catch movement in my peripheral, and our heads veer towards curtains that conceal the front of the plane.

An athletic-built girl pushes through the fabric, her dark brown curls bouncing as she looks around. I recognize Joana Oliveira instantly. Not only because I attended her Catholic confirmation, but because she's Oscar and Quinn's nineteen-year-old little sister.

Joana carries a nylon backpack over her toned shoulder. Black leggings and a crop top show off her abs, and as soon as she sees me, she gives me a nod. "Hey, Banks." She grins, knowing I'm not my brother.

Unlike Will, I trusted Jo not to blab this fucking secret to Tony or O'Malley. There was no reason to trick her too.

"Jo," I greet. "Glad you could make it." She's tagging along to spend time with her brothers before she has a professional boxing match in London.

"Me too." She lingers and eyes the tattooed, shirtless, and lean but muscular ballet dancer next to me.

He rests against the bathroom door. "I'm Beckett." He nods in greeting. "I'd shake your hand, but…" He hoists his cuffed wrist and tries not to jerk mine.

Jo's brows rise. "Kinky."

He speaks calmly. "If it were kinky, I'd be enjoying it more."

She snorts and readjusts her backpack strap. "How many times have you used that line?"

"It's not a line." He studies her in a quick sweep. "Believe me, you'd know if I was using a line on you."

Intrigue sparks her brown eyes. "Why is that?"

"Because you'd already be in my bed."

My muscles bind. Very few men on the team have younger sisters, and Jo is one of them. I need to end this before he signs his death warrant, and under my breath, I whisper to Beckett, "You want to keep your balls, don't hit on Oscar's little sister."

"It's okay, Banks." Jo fits on her other backpack strap and stares right at Beckett. "I don't speak douchebag so I didn't hear a thing." She walks ahead of us and searches the cabin. Only glancing back to ask me, "Where's Maximoff? I want to thank him for inviting me."

"He should be with Jane in the fourth lounge. It's the rear of the plane."

She mouths the word, *fourth*, with huge eyes before heading that way.

All the while Beckett watches her ass as she goes.

"Don't," I warn.

"I wouldn't hurt her."

"I never said you would." He might think I'm protecting Jo, but I'm trying to protect him. He doesn't need SFO on his ass. "Oscar and Quinn are going to kill you if you even look at her sideways."

"Yeah, well…" He exhales a deeper breath and steps away from the bathroom. "We're preparing for a wedding, might as well have a funeral too."

17

Jane Cobalt

THE PLANE RIDE SEEMS to last forever, but I enjoy the furtive glances Thatcher and I share and the stolen moments as we wander the plane to stretch. He kisses me in the narrow bar, pumping adrenaline in my lungs and a fire beneath my heart, and then we part as though we were strangers in...love.

I smile all the way back to my seat, and the dance we play happens more than once, more than thrice, more than I can count—and by the time we land, I long to be back in the air with him again.

Five rental cars later and a four-hour drive through a picturesque landscape of sprawling hills and valleys—grass a blend of brown and burnt green hues for winter, and the air chill with every crisp breath— we've finally reached our destination.

Everyone carries or rolls their luggage into an old, family-owned inn called Mackintosh House, complete with turrets and worn burgundy stone. For one week, it's all ours.

Charlie meanders towards the garden, studying the relic of a building. He has a quiet love of old architecture.

I glance behind me before I enter. Beyond our parked cars on the gravel path.

Land stretches as far as my eye can see. Sheep roam with leisure, and if I strain my ears, I can almost hear the babble of a stream passing through this calm little hamlet.

I begin to smile. I'm truly happy that this is a viable option for my best friend's wedding. It's peaceful here. Maximoff and Farrow also chose this remote spot in the countryside because it'd be an absolute pain for paparazzi to reach.

It wasn't even easy for us.

Figuring out how to shuffle vendors and guests to this location is a brainteaser. But I love a good logic puzzle, and I haven't been this excited in a while. Something must be in the Scottish air or the fact that Thatcher keeps stealing glances as we head inside.

His boldness should heat me head-to-toe like a boiling furnace. It usually does, but there is a glaring issue with Mackintosh House.

It's hellishly *cold*.

I shiver as I wheel in my suitcase.

"This place is super creepy," Sulli says under her breath, the wallpaper deep reds and greens, a winding banister leads to the dark upstairs, and old black and white photographs hang on the walls. Doily cloths are absolutely *everywhere*.

"I love it," I announce.

Oscar passes me. "Retro Granny Realness." He raises his hand for a high-five, and I tap his palm with a smile before he treks upstairs.

"I bet it's kinda haunted." Luna snaps photos on her phone. "Kinney is gonna love this." She inspects the picture she just captured. "Or she'll hate that she's missing out." The young girls couldn't ditch their last week in school before winter break.

Sulli and Luna leave to go unpack, but I don't follow.

While footsteps and voices echo around the drafty eight-bedroom house, I'm on a hunt in the rustic kitchen. Knees on the icy hardwood, I fumble through a crooked junk drawer, searching for any manuals to the heaters.

None will turn on, and Mackintosh House is far too large to be heated from a single living room fireplace.

I reach the bottom stack of papers.

"Any luck?" Thatcher saunters into the kitchen.

I blow a frizzed hair off my lip. Oh…

He's…exceedingly tall. While I'm down here, on my knees.

His white button-down and dog tags also take me aback for a second. Even if he appears like his brother, I could never mistake him for Banks like Tony and O'Malley already have.

Neither one batted an eye on the plane.

I skim him a little more, a sweltering breath in my lungs. I suppose Thatcher seeing me dressed in all black would be just as jarring for him.

I shut the drawer. "The only manual I could find was for the washer/dryer." I stand, a chill biting my neck, and I pull my zebra coat tighter around my breasts.

Thatcher switches on the gas burner and oven. Flames lick the stovetop grates. "Come here." He motions me closer.

He is incredibly inviting. All six-foot-seven of him. Oh-so-warm and…hot.

So eloquent.

I follow his direction. More cautiously, I land next to him but keep my distance. A dreadful six inches separate our bodies.

That should be enough.

I'd normally stand this far from Banks.

Thatcher stares down at me, as though assessing my temperature from sight alone, and I look up at him, aching to step a little closer.

"It should heat up soon," Thatcher says, standing sturdy next to the oven door. He glances from the kitchen entryway to my arms that hug my body. "Can I?"

My lips pull higher. "Can you…?"

He reaches out and his fingers run gently along my wrist, tingling my soft flesh. I pulse between my legs, and I inhale without the ability to exhale. Warmth pricks my nerves like he's carried me to a roaring fire.

Our eyes dive deeper, and when I nod him on, his clutch strengthens. He guides my palm over the flaming stovetop, and his hand lingers on my wrist, not letting go of me.

I don't want him to.

My hip brushes his stoic body, the six inches now shrunk to *zero*. Thatcher and I risk the nearness, and he's so perceptive of his surroundings that I trust his instincts if we go too far.

He subtly checks the entryway.

I check more blatantly.

Clear.

Attention returned to each other, I whisper, "I'm glad you're here with me." I've said so a few times already. "I like you—I mean, I more than *like* you, which you know…" Nervous flush bathes me, and I stare at him, panic-eyed.

He seems so put-together in this moment, and I'm still frazzled like an awkward mess. Yet, I love how he makes me feel utterly unraveled. As though he's the only man who can reach a rare piece of me and pull and undo me at the seams.

"You know," I add unhelpfully.

"I know," he confirms.

"Good." *God, he's hot.* His whole unfaltering demeanor. His whole being.

He nods back, tension brewing. Thatcher studies me a beat longer. He has that look again. Like he's staring directly into the brightest, hottest sun. "I want to ask you something that might be hard for you to answer." He eyes the entryway, then me. "Later tonight?"

Curiosity has latched its sharp claws into me. "You can ask me now." I whisper even more quietly. "If you think it's safe to talk." We hear footsteps above us and chatter in the distance, but the kitchen is ours in this second.

He sweeps our surroundings one more time, then nods. "We can now, if you really want."

"I want to know." I cage a breath in preparation. "Go ahead."

His mouth dips towards my ear, his voice low and gentle. "Why are you afraid to love me?"

I shake my head on impulse, and a cold pain stabs my lungs. "I don't…I'm…" I lean to the right.

"Watch out—*Jane*." Thatcher lifts my hand higher. I nearly pressed my palm to the iron stovetop.

Hairs stand up on the back of my neck. I can't blink or close my agape mouth, and I realize I'm pressed up against his chest.

I ran into his body for safety.

It overwhelms me, my throat swelling.

My wrist is still in his grasp, and he keeps my hand raised in the air. We both breathe heavily, and I manage to say, "Usually…I can articulate what I'm thinking, but what I'm feeling—what I *feel* for you is so inexplicably complex and I feel like nothing is coming out quite right. Just that alone…scares me in the best and worst way." I wince at myself. "And that was a terrible non-answer."

"No," he refutes, his chest tightened like he's controlling himself not to hold me. To touch me further and greater. He looks to the right, then back to me. "I understand." He softens his gaze on me. "Look, I'm crawling through this with you—" He cuts himself off and his features lose all emotion, completely professional. "Be careful, Jane." He's still clutching my wrist.

I frown, about to respond, but another voice slices into the kitchen.

"Whoa, Banks." O'Malley rolls to a halt with an armful of firewood, and Quinn bypasses him with another bundle. The Epsilon bodyguard eagle-eyes Thatcher like he's lost his mind.

Thatcher is surprisingly calm and casual. Like Banks would be. He lowers my arm to my side and steps back from my body. "What do you want?"

O'Malley lets out a soft laugh. "You're three inches from your brother's girl and that's not *bizarre* to you?"

"I had to grab her before she touched the burner. She didn't realize I turned it *on*." He lifts a shoulder. "That's it."

I shoot O'Malley a look. "Why? What'd you think Banks was doing?" I'm still a client, and he treats me with more respect than he does Thatcher.

Apologies fill his eyes. "Sorry. My mistake, Jane. I didn't mean anything by it." He disappears towards the living room.

Alone again, worry bunches my brows. "Did he buy it?" I whisper. "Or was he just placating me?"

"He thinks I'm Banks." Thatcher sounds assured. "Whether he thinks Banks could be into you—I don't know."

I cringe. We knew it'd be a risk, but I don't like the idea that Tony and O'Malley could believe I'm sleeping with *both* Moretti brothers. "Do you think we should be more careful?"

He shakes his head. "They'll think what they want no matter what they see."

I appraise our distance apart. "We aren't *that* close," I rationalize under my breath.

His lip nearly lifts, his arms woven over his chest.

I realize something horrific and my mouth falls.

His muscles contract. "Jane?"

"How are we going to have sex?" I whisper. "We can't sleep in the same bedroom."

He opens his mouth to reply, but Maximoff hikes into the kitchen, cell clutched in a gloved hand. "I just got off the phone with the owners."

"And?" I turn more towards him.

"The heaters are broken, and no one can come out here for another couple days. So we'll have to work with whatever's here until then."

"We'll survive," I say confidently. "There are enough brains and brawn here to make it two days in a cold house."

He nods, slipping his phone in his back pocket, and his forest-green eyes ping from Thatcher to me, back to Thatcher, then me. Under his breath, he says, "You two should..." He makes a motion with his hands for us to separate.

Thatcher backs up and adds more cold space between our bodies.

I try not to shiver. "We're not *that* close," I tell Moffy.

He makes a face like I'm no longer residing on Earth.

Possibly Thatcher is a magnet and I'm pulled in no matter the occasion, and I've really lost all sense of reality. And measurements. Spatial measurements.

Because three inches from him to me doesn't feel close enough. God, even *zero* inches is far too little. I desire him closer, deep in the epicenter of my soul, and it's absolutely...

Petrifying.

"Janie," Maximoff says. "You look flushed."

Oh no.

I'm wide-eyed on my boyfriend.

"She's okay," Thatcher assures my best friend. "We have this handled."

I perch my hands on my hips and take a more confident breath. "Yes, we do."

"Alright." Maximoff trusts us, and he smiles at me and leans in close to whisper, "Have fun with your boyfriend."

I smile brighter. "I will. You have fun with your fiancé."

He grimaces, crinkling his nose. "I won't."

I laugh. Maximoff looks lovesick and Farrow isn't even in the kitchen.

He stops at the doorway before he leaves. "How are we on groceries?" He gestures to the fridge, tapping into his survival-mode.

"Stocked up for about two days. We'll have to go to the store again." The nearest market is about an hour drive from Mackintosh House, so it'll be a trek.

"Moffy! Where's my duffel bag?!" Luna calls from upstairs. Maximoff excuses himself to go help his sister.

Thatcher faces me. "What you were asking before." He speaks vaguely, but I remember. *Sex.* "We'll work it out."

My brows jump. "So it's going to happen?" I raise my hands. "Just for clarification. Because it's important that it does happen—I want it to happen, I mean." I'm word vomiting, and I stop as Donnelly strolls into the kitchen.

He carries two woolen tartan blankets, plaid with a red base and deep green lines. "Want what to happen?" he asks us.

"Nothing," I say. "Absolutely nothing to happen. It was a figure of speech."

Donnelly frowns. "Really? 'Cause I thought you were talking about sex." He walks off ever so casually like he didn't just explode a miniature bomb at my feet.

Thatcher shakes his head, watching him leave. He mumbles an Italian word under his breath and glances back to me. "For clarification," he tells me. "It's going to happen." He reaches an arm closer to me, and I breathe in sharp.

Our eyes lock as he switches off the burner, his fingers brushing against my elbow. I'm still warm, and his body emits rolling waves of heat. I think he might lean closer.

I think he might whisper something dirtier like, *my cock in your pussy.*

His gaze consumes mine and holds me and hoists me and pushes up against me—but we aren't touching. We aren't speaking.

I ache and ache, soaked and ready for him. I swallow, cross my ankles, and I lean further away from my boyfriend.

He notices and nods like I'm doing well. This is the plan. But as he departs for the pantry, his body heat is replaced with a sudden biting cold.

18

Thatcher Moretti

BEING ICED OUT BY Akara Kitsuwon feels like subzero winds barreling down on exposed flesh. It's different than the silent treatment that Jane delivered last summer. This one is layered with baggage and un-mendable things.

And pretending to be Banks—it has major downsides. Namely, I can't sleep in Jane's bedroom, and since my brother has no bad blood with Akara, room assignments played out like the invention of a new circle of hell.

My flaming hellscape consists of ugly burgundy wallpaper and two brass twin beds assigned to me and Akara.

I close the door, shutting out voices downstairs.

Akara drops his duffel on the floorboards. He wears a baseball cap backwards and unzips his red winter jacket. I watch him shift aside the heavy, floral drapes. He assesses the window.

Security has already swept every inch of this house, but double-checking gives him an excuse to turn his back to me.

You'd need a fucking jackhammer to dent the tension in this room. I'm the world's worst at apologizing. I should unlace my boots and place them against the nightstand.

I should rack out and give him space.

But fuck it all. I'm tired of shutting up when I crave skin-and-fucking-bones to make amends.

Akara spends an extra long minute running his fingers down the window's seal.

"We're going to have to talk at some point." My voice sounds too loud in the quiet.

He goes still. "We probably shouldn't make that point today."

My muscles tense. "You need to get something off your chest? I can handle it." I'd much rather him just ream me the fuck out. I'm used to superiors spit-yelling at me. I'm used to shackling on the blame, but I can't do that until he gives me the weight.

Akara turns around finally and leans back against the windowsill. He crosses his arms over his chest, and his expression is one of profound discontent. "Like I said, you don't want to do this today."

"What if I do?" *Just yell at me, goddammit.*

He shrugs. "It's your funeral."

I nod, ready for it.

Akara takes a breath and sizes me up. "Normally, I'd love this twin swap. Pulling one over on Epsilon—classic." His eyes land on mine in a glare. "But I honestly hate this whole thing because I could have had a week without you. Joke is on me, per fucking usual."

"What do you want me to do?"

"Go back in time," Akara says coldly. "The moment you started fucking your client, you come to me and tell me you crossed that line. *That's* what I want, but we're too late for that."

I grimace. "I didn't want to put that on you—"

"I'm your *fucking* lead." He steps away from the window in hot angered movements. "You, out of everyone, should understand what that means, but instead of giving me the same respect I would've given you, you decided to shackle me and dump me on the bottom of an ocean. We could have come up with a solution together because that's what friends do. But you and me, we're not friends, are we?"

Hurt claws down my back.

I can count on my hand the amount of real, honest and good friendships I've made over the years. Ones where people don't treat me and my brother like one person or an object or something to poke fun at.

Akara might have been the most real friendship I've ever had, and I feel it slipping through my fingers, already obliterated to dust.

"I blew it," I tell him, my chest on fire. "I didn't know how to tell you about Jane without implicating you." I inhale sharply, bottling a stronger emotion. "Akara, I thought I was sparing you the blame."

"You're on my Force. You're one of mine." He removes his baseball cap and bunches it in a tight fist. "Your mistakes are my mistakes. What you were trying to do isn't even possible. And I feel like such…a fucking idiot." He sighs in frustration and throws his cap onto the mattress.

I'm rigid, muscles strained. "Are Price and Sinclair still giving you hell?"

He glances over at me and raises his brows. "That's what we're not going to do. You lost the privilege to talk with me about that shit."

"You're really going to shut me out?" I lower my voice. "Banks isn't here. Who else do you have to talk to about *that shit*?"

It was always him and me. My brother couldn't give a rat's ass about the lead position, but Akara and I were bred for this.

"No one," he says. "But lucky for you, we don't have to spend another minute together." He bends down and grabs the strap to his duffel. His eyes ping to the bathroom door. It's a Jack & Jill style that leads to another bedroom where Jane, Sullivan, and Luna sleep.

I shake my head, fucking confused. Maximoff and Farrow handed out room assignments, and they intended for me and Jane to use the bathroom as a way to secretly switch during the night. They also put O'Malley, Tony, and Will on the furthest side of the house, so they wouldn't overhear Jane and me.

But that plan involved Akara agreeing to it.

He didn't.

"I don't understand." I rest my hand on my taut shoulder. "If I remember correctly, you said *fuck no, I'm not letting you get laid every night.*"

He nods. "You don't deserve it. But I realize in this moment that I don't deserve having to share space with you. Have whatever sex you want, I'm out." He aims for the door.

My pulse hammers, and I take a couple strides to intercept him. "Wait." I grab onto his arm.

He stares at my hand and then at my eyes.

I don't move. "If I had told you I was sleeping with Jane, do you really think the outcome would have been different? There was no way out of this, Akara. You: on this shit-end of Price and Sinclair's judgment, and me: axed from her detail."

His face breaks into pity, and it's like being swallowed by a black hole. Endless nothing on the other side. "You spent less than a year on Jane's detail," he says, his voice softer now that we're closer to the door. "Do you realize that I spent more than three years as a bodyguard to a Cobalt? Two of those were on Connor's detail. And you know what I learned from that time?"

My stomach twists, a sickening feeling surging all at once.

He looks up with that same pity. "There's *always* a way out. You don't have to fall on a sword because it's sitting in front of you, waiting. You put together the team that's going to find the right exit. You sidelined me. That's on you." He pushes my hand off his arm. "Move." He reaches the door, gripping the knob, and leaves.

AKARA JUST COCK-BLOCKED MY MIND.

When he leaves and Jane enters, I wrestle with two conflicting sides. I want to fuck my girlfriend, to please Jane how she needs and deserves to be pleased, but it doesn't feel right to be *happy* or satiated after everything I've done and everything he said.

I untie my boots while Jane lights candles around the room, a tartan blanket warming her shoulders like a shawl, and we sneak these smoldering glances that burn my soul into blistered pieces—and I've craved to tear off her jeans, her shirt, her bra.

To hoist her in my arms and kiss the nape of her neck. For her fingers to claw at my hair. To hear her hungered moans against my ear.

I've never been with a woman who loves sex like I do. With an animal-istic ferocity. Who needs carnal touch like water, quenching a desperate thirst. Jane is my match, my mate, and I swear to all that's holy, I'd give her my breath, my body—but guilt is slowly destroying me.

I set my boots against the nightstand, and I rise.

She shakes out a match, waxy candles lit on an antique dresser. I near Jane, my muscles contracting and my blood pumping into my cock, and I watch her breasts push out with shallow, wanting breath. She eases back into the wall, waiting for the inevitable moment where we collide.

I place a strong hand on the burgundy wallpaper. High above her head, and before she speaks, I have to lay down ground rules. "We're doing things a bit different tonight."

Her brows quirk. "Are we?"

I slip the button through her jeans. "You ready to go for hours and be spent in my arms?"

She almost moans. "Yes." Her hands clutch my ass, her hips bowed towards me. "But that's not so different from most nights." Curiosity sparkles her blue eyes.

She's flat-out beautiful.

Gently, I peel her fingers off my body, and her lips part in confusion. I clarify. "You can't touch my ass, my cock—I'm not getting off, only you are."

Jane frowns. "I don't like this." She searches my hardened gaze. "What's going on, Thatcher?"

I tell her everything about my conversation with Akara and finish with, "I've disrespected him enough, and having sex is another bullet in a gun I'm firing."

She catches my wrist before I unzip her jeans. "We don't have to have sex." We're breathing like we're already making love against the wall.

My gaze slips down my girlfriend in a sensual stroke, her wide hips still arched towards me. Her freckled cheeks are flushed and eyes big.

She needs more. I need more. My dick twitches, and I expel another hot breath through my nose.

"Okay?" she breathes, her fingers hooking my belt loop. Tension snakes around us, threatening to choke us to fucking death, and the cold house suddenly blazes at a million degrees.

"No." I brace my forearm to the wall, only a sliver of space separating our bodies.

Jane melts. "Thatcher." It's a wanting, needing, *pleading* Thatcher, but she adds fast, "If you plan to punish yourself, then you better include me. We're in this together. So if you can't come, then I can't either."

My jaw tenses. *That* will kill me.

She tries to read my features. "Frankly..." Her voice softens. "I'd much rather you not punish yourself at all because it won't make you feel any better."

I know she's right.

But I've never known how to let myself off the hook that easily.

I shake my head. "I deserve hell."

"You deserve to be happy," Jane combats with so much conviction, and I hear my grandma's soulful voice—*be happy.*

It's not a single step into happiness. Not for me. To let myself have that is five-hundred klicks away, and my trek only just began when I chose something happy in my life, for once.

When I chose Jane.

I cup her cheek. The plaid blanket slips off her shoulder, heat brewing between us.

I put words into the quiet. "I can be happy without sex for a night." Really, I might be fooling myself this one particular night.

She lifts her chin. "So can I." She puts her hands on my flexed abs in attempt to shove me back, but she applies no force.

We stare into each other.

We breathe heavier.

"I don't need you," Jane suddenly whispers.

Something sharp impales my chest. "Say again?"

"I don't *need* you." In the candlelight, I can see her eyes reddening. "I can get myself off."

I go rigid. "I don't doubt that, but would you rather have your fingers or my cock, honey?"

She intakes a staggered breath. "My fingers."

I squint at her, my pulse on a seasick free-fall. "You'd rather have yourself than have me?" I'm confused as all hell.

Jane blinks rapidly, shaking cobwebs out of her head. "Your cock is just an appendage. It's a fact." She's trying to isolate feelings from sex.

I glare at the window, then try to soften my eyes when I set them back on her. "My cock is attached to my body, and trust me when I tell you that every time I'm inside your pussy, it's never some vapid, emotionless thing."

She opens her mouth, but words are stuck on her tongue. "I…"

"My cock is yours, but I'm not a sex toy. I'm better because I love you, and I will fuck you with nothing less than *love*, Jane."

She holds onto my waist like her knees are about to buckle. "I… yes—*no*. No." She inhales. "I'm fine with my fingers."

"You are?" I think she's conning herself.

Jane blows out a measured breath. "I don't *need* your love."

It sucker-punches me.

"I want it," she clarifies quickly. "But like in this instance, I don't need it. I can survive on my own." She looks pained, and she holds my hand that encases her cheek. Like she doesn't want me to let go, but her palm still rests on my abs, a millisecond from shoving me back.

We're both at war with ourselves.

I force down a raw emotion that I've never felt before, not like this. I'm realizing in my attempt to punish myself, I'm pushing her away from me and towards whatever's been pressing her lately. I'm going to lose Jane if I keep this same masochistic course.

It's all or nothing.

And I want all of her. I always have.

I dip my head and whisper against her ear, "What if I don't want to survive without you?"

An aching noise expels from her lips, and I release my hold of her cheek and fist the back of my shirt, pulling the fabric over my head. Bare-chested, I undo the buckle of my belt.

She fixates on my movements that write a story of devotion. I step out of my slacks. I take off my boxer-briefs.

Naked.

Erect, and I slowly sink down to my knees, my hand running along the curve of her hip and thigh before I kneel on the floorboards.

Jane grasps my hair, her throat bobbing in arousal. "Thatcher."

I roll down her pastel jeans, revealing her velvet blue panties, and I hike her soft leg over my shoulder.

She whimpers. "*God.*"

Fire blazes in my veins, and my nerves light with kerosene. I kiss the inside of her thigh, watching her eyes drink me in and cling to me and beg me—and love me.

I pull aside her panties.

"Wait, wait," she pants.

I go still. "Jane—"

"Am I allowed to touch you? I have to be certain because you can't get me off if I can't get you off. Together, remember?"

I hold her gaze in a vice. "You can touch me all you want." She might think I'm choosing sex over celibacy, but I'm choosing *us* tonight and every fucking night hereafter.

I kiss her pussy, and her back arches in a soft cry.

Fuck. My cock stirs more. Hardens more. Pre-cum glistens on the swollen head. I pull her closer, my hand stroking her ass while I taste the most sensitive part of Jane.

She's sweet, and her thighs vibrate as I lap my tongue over her clit.

"Thatcher," she moans under her hitched breath. "*God, yes.* Please... *more.*"

My pulse sky-rockets, and skin-pricked heat builds sweat along my whole body. I watch her mouth break open with heady gasps.

The only time I pause is to reach over and grab a condom out of my bag. I tear the foil with my teeth and slide one on over my shaft.

"Yes, *yes.*" Her fingers tighten in my hair, and her head hits the wall. Eyes rolling back already. I could watch her come every minute, and I waste no time.

I kiss her heat before I rip her panties completely off, and she nods rapidly, hand to her forehead like her brain is spinning. I drop her leg and stand, and she claws hungrily at my body while our lips crash together.

I'm in another world with Jane.

And I never want to leave.

We devour one another, and I tear off her blouse, snap off her bra and throw it aside. Not a second after she's bare, I clasp the backs of her thighs and hoist her up my body.

She gasps against my mouth, her legs weaving tightly and readily around my waist, and I can feel her heart *pounding* like we're banging a drum together.

Candlelight flickers along her flushed face, and I bring her higher so our lips align. We share each inhale. Each exhale. Her body thrums against me.

Alive with ferocious energy.

"Please," she breathes. "*Thatcher.*"

"Jane," I groan.

We kiss in aggressive passion, our tongues tangled and lips stinging. Like we can't be close enough, and deep isn't *deep* enough. I have her ass in my hands, and her palms track burning lines along my biceps.

I lower her just slightly down my body, until her hips are in line with mine. It breaks our mouths apart.

She tries to catch her breath, but she watches my erection push against her wet folds.

"Look at me," I whisper.

Jane lifts her gaze, and as soon as she sees the affection in mine, tears crease the corners of her eyes.

"I love you. I love you. *I love you,*" I emphasize as I bridge us together, carefully and slowly fitting inside her pussy.

She wraps her arms around my shoulders and moans my name into the crook of my arm. High-pitched and staggered.

Fuck, the pressure of Jane around me is mind-numbing. She squeezes and clenches, and I move her body up and down on my shaft.

She gasps, almost choking.

"Breathe, honey."

Jane puts a hand to her heart like it's beating out of her chest, involuntary tears soaking her cheeks. My eyes are raw with emotion, and I hold her against me with one hand and use the other to clasp her face. "Breathe."

I pause and let her gulp air.

She tries to grind on me.

Christ. I grit down, my nerves snapping in pleasure.

"I don't want to stop," she says in a single breath. "Keep going. *Keep going.* Please."

I rock my hips into her. Gently.

Slowly.

Almost teasingly, and she gasps again, our eyes locked.

I sink deeper. "Would you rather survive with me or without me?"

She clutches my biceps tighter. "With you."

My muscles sear in magma. "Would you rather live with me or without me?"

"With you."

Then what are you so afraid of, Jane?

I brace her shoulders to the wall and fuck her harder. Deeper and longer strokes, and I hit a spot that drives her over the edge. Right when she bucks into me, her legs shaking, I press her closer to my chest and I carry her to a twin bed.

Her pussy contracts in pulsating waves around my cock, and I flex my abs to stop from coming.

But I'm throbbing inside Jane, craving a release. I move her off my shaft, and I set her knees on the mattress. She practically collapses on her stomach, melting into a post-climax, and I let her stay in this position and tuck a pillow beneath her hips.

"Mmm," she says, the cooing noise familiar and approving of my hands and actions.

I kneel behind her, spreading her legs wider, and I pull her ass back and drive into her heat. She tightens and pleasure builds at the new position.

Another high-pitched sound pitches its way out of Jane.

"Fuck," I grunt. *Fuck.*

She glances back over her shoulder, lips split apart with each gasp as I ram into her, and I lean forward and kiss the hell out of my girlfriend. She has to arch back, causing me to slide deeper.

"Thatcher," she gasps against my mouth.

I knead her breast, and once she's back on her forearms, I'm all the way inside, touching a sensitive place that causes Jane to cry in soft breaths. Sweat caked on our skin, hair damp, and blood on fire.

"*Deeper, deeper,*" she moans.

I'm deeper than any man has ever been in this girl, and I'm not letting up. Not as her legs throttle. Not as I ascend a peak. Not as her fingers clench the blankets.

We come together in a spine-tingling, head-whirling, body-transporting climax, and I milk the sensation in a few more pumps while she searches for lost breath.

When we're done, I pull Jane in my arms, and she splays on my chest like she's lounging belly-down on a pool floatie. I make sure she's under the blankets, as the night grows cold, and our eyes stay on each other for minutes upon minutes.

She's lost energy to speak.

I'm not sure if I can say what needs to be said, and in time, we both drift to sleep.

19

Jane Cobalt

"IT WAS SOME OF the best sex I've ever experienced, by far," I whisper quietly to Moffy. Not that many people are in earshot. The tiny pub is nearly empty as the sun drops. One local drinks hard cider at the bar, and the bearded bartender chats leisurely with him.

We relax on the small sofa section, nestled around a fireplace and mounted TV. I love the old charm of northern Scotland. Coat of arms decorates wooden-paneled walls, and the oaky aroma of Scotch permeates around us.

"Even though you started out pushing him away?" Maximoff asks under his breath.

I press my knuckles to my lips. "I hate myself for that." It pains me to admit. "I'm not even certain how it derailed there." I stare at my lap. "But then again, I can't see myself just…letting him take complete fault for *everything* and I'm trying not to be guarded about my feelings."

We glance over at the bar as Thatcher, Tony, Donnelly, and Farrow order drinks. Oscar and Charlie are talking at a high-top table near the fogged window, and I hope my brother plans to stay longer. Most everyone will be here soon, and all of us only arrived earlier for a meeting with a local chef.

Charlie even asked genuine questions about catering, and I thought Maximoff's smile would shatter the window. It's almost like high school again, the three of us on good terms.

Wedding business is actually fun to discuss, but Moffy changed the subject to my relationship before we dove too deep into his nuptials.

"Janie." Moffy scoots closer on the tufted leather sofa. "It's pretty much normal to need the person you love."

I slip my frilly pen in a binder pocket. "Do you feel as though you need Farrow?"

"Yeah." He nods a few times. "Christ, I think I needed him before he even joined security." He makes a face. "Don't tell Farrow that."

"Cross my heart," I smile, but my lips fall quickly. I place my binder on the cushion beside me. "But regardless, you can still survive on your own without Farrow. Correct?"

He cracks a knuckle, lost in thought. "Maybe, but it'd be…" Grief clouds his eyes. "I don't know. It feels like death."

"God," I murmur. "I don't want to feel like I'm *dying* if my boyfriend isn't with me." Sudden panic scorches me, and I waft my sequined pink sweater. "I think I lied to him last night."

"Wait, what?"

"I told Thatcher that I'd rather survive with him than without him, and sitting here, talking to you, I know that I'd rather be able to survive on my own more than *anything* else." Yet, my throat closes like that's not entirely truthful either, and my cheeks crinkle in a wince. "I'm not being logical, am I?"

He hugs my shoulders with a tough arm. "I don't know if there's a lot of logic in love."

That frightens me.

I lean into my best friend and stare off at the wall.

He can tell I'm strangely quiet. "Maybe you should talk out your feelings with Thatcher and see what he says."

"I've tried, and I set myself up for failure every time." Being around him tends to tongue-tie me, and whenever I delve into emotions and fears, I feel like a panicked, spinning and wobbling coin. And I'm always scared I'll land on the wrong side.

"He said he'd go at whatever pace you set," Moffy reminds me. "He's here for the long haul, so if it takes you a millennium to blurt out what you need to, he might still be around."

"I know." *Thatcher is too good for me and my insecurities.* I'm not so sure I deserve to have a man who's sacrificed everything for me and who also has to wait *forever* for me. Sadly, I mutter, "He deserves better."

"No," Maximoff snaps. He touches my forehead like I'm running a fever.

"Moffy." I start to smile.

He drops his hand. "Tu es *la meilleure*. Il a même de la chance de respirer le même air que tu respires." *You're* the best. *He's lucky to even breathe the same air you breathe.*

"It's hard to feel that way when he just had to announce how many times he thinks about *fucking* me in a single day." Charlie made us flip a card an hour ago, and it's not like either of us has kept a count of our impure thoughts. So we did our best to estimate an average.

"Last I checked, we're not normal, everyday people," Moffy tells me. "Unless we've left this universe and entered one where our faces *aren't* plastered on every *amazing* tabloid that I just love reading front to damn back."

I tip my head. "We are excruciatingly abnormal."

"And your boyfriend has to do abnormal things to be with you," Maximoff says. "And I saw you smiling when he answered *102 times a day*."

I did.

And Thatcher looked enamored by me when I answered, *81 times.*

I breathe in more, and I rest my hands on his shoulder, my chin on my knuckles. Feeling better. "Did you ever imagine our first time in Scotland would be with your fiancé and my boyfriend and we'd be preparing for your wedding?" It bursts love into my heart just thinking this.

Maximoff tries to restrain an uncontrollable smile. "No." He licks his lips. "Because I never thought I'd get married. If anything, I thought it'd be *your* wedding, and I'd be over here a forever bachelor."

"I like this better—and I'm not hijacking your wedding," I note. "Don't fret."

Media and tabloids keep speculating that Thatcher and I will marry first. Based off a complicated history where my mom and dad sort of commandeered Aunt Lily and Uncle Lo's wedding.

Their past choices keep affecting us in strange ways.

"I'm not worried about that," Moffy says with a weird look.

"What is it?"

"You know if you want to marry Thatcher before I walk down the aisle, I get it. It's not like I'm planning on marrying Farrow tomorrow. It'll be a couple years."

My eyes bug. "I just started calling him a boyfriend, and he just moved in. I'm not ready, and I doubt he'd want to put a ring on a girl who can barely utter *I love you*."

"Okay, okay," Maximoff nods. "I just don't want to be the reason you're holding back."

I give him a weird look now. "Would you really want Thatcher to be the man I'm with forever?" Thatcher has been Farrow's least favorite person, and Maximoff hasn't been too fond of him in the past either.

"*Weirdly*, yeah. He's good to you, and he makes you happy." He nods. "But if he hurts you, I'll slit his throat with a hacksaw—a *rusted* hacksaw."

I laugh at his amendment.

Maximoff smiles. "This is surreal—you and me in serious relationships and traveling with our men." He shakes his head in disbelief, and I feel that same overwhelming feeling breach the surface inside me. "I'm glad you're here, Janie." His chest rises. "I couldn't do this without you."

Emotion wells my eyes. "I wouldn't want to be anywhere else."

I'M DRUNK.

Scottish whiskey is delightful, and I nurse my third glass. Or is this my fourth? My head floats, and the noisy pub sounds melodic to Feel-Good Drunk Jane. Seventeen bodies pack in, our group overrunning the establishment.

A glittery sequin on my sweater snags my blue tutu. I rip them apart with one hand, and the tulle tears.

Oh well. Torn skirt, missing sequin—life could be so much worse. A rumor could hit the internet that I'm fucking my cousin.

I sip my whiskey with a smile. I never thought I could even *mentally* joke about the incest rumor, and one year later…

I smile more, huddled around the warm fireplace with my two female cousins. The sofa and bar area are crowded with bodyguards who stay on-duty, unable to drink alcohol. But they mingle with each other.

"I really fucking *love* that he never put pressure on me to kiss him." Sulli bites her lip, as though she can feel Will Rochester on them. "I was so comfortable with him last night. It was perfect."

My little sister would've swooned for eternity just hearing Sulli describe her make-out session with Will. How he brought extra blankets to the living room of Mackintosh House. How they cuddled by the fire and he caressed her cheek and drew her in slowly.

I wrap an arm around her waist. "That might be one of the most romantic first kisses I've ever heard."

"Uh-huh," Luna nods, popping the tab to an energy drink. "Fan-fiction worthy."

"Really?" Sulli grins, gripping the neck of a beer. She hasn't loved the taste, but she's still been timid to sip mixed drinks after passing out so quickly. Sulli feels comfortable enough here, surrounded by family and SFO, to drink though. "I bet your first kisses were fucking rad."

Luna bobs her head to the top-hits channel that plays throughout the pub and smiles into her sip of energy drink. "He made me a sandwich afterwards."

"Is that a euphemism?" I wonder.

"Nope. A real peanut butter and banana sandwich. Eliot, Tom and I crashed some senior's party, and I hung out in the kitchen with this guy named Mike…or maybe it was Rogan." She shrugs, unconcerned. "Never saw him again."

"You're a badass." Sulli fist-bumps Luna, then asks me, "What was your first kiss like—oh fuck…" She reddens in embarrassment, hand to her mouth. "I forgot. I'm so fucking sorry."

My first kiss was with *Wesley* Rochester, Will's younger brother. "It was a kindergarten kiss. It meant very little." I squeeze her in another side-hug before letting go, and I accidentally slosh whiskey out of my glass.

Merde.

The Four Drunk Stages of Jane Eleanor Cobalt are as follows:

Feel-Good Drunk Jane

Flirty Drunk Jane

Sloppy Drunk Jane

Black-Out (SOS) Jane

My sloppy-drunk-self can't come out. I haven't reached Flirty Drunk Jane yet. Skipping from one to three is like sipping the milk froth of a cappuccino and dumping out the coffee.

The actual coffee is undoubtedly the best part.

"Is it weird that we both kissed brothers?" Sulli asks me.

I'm about to mention how Uncle Loren and Uncle Ryke are brothers and their wives are sisters, but Luna already sing-songs to Sulli, "Our moms married brothers."

"Fuck, *duh.*" Sulli shakes her head and swallows more beer.

I pet her long brown hair. "She's lovesick; she's not thinking straight."

"She's infected." Luna sticks out her tongue, neon-green piercing in the center. "Should we amputate?"

Sulli elbows us with a giddy smile. "I seriously think I could lose my virginity to him."

My eyes brighten. "In Scotland."

"I don't know." She shrugs, unable to stop smiling. "Maybe. I'm comfortable with him." Her smile gradually fades at another thought.

"Uh-oh," Luna says. "She's losing the love vibe."

I sip my whiskey, my lips down-turning too. I wonder if it's possible to make yourself fall out of love with someone, as a precautionary measure. Like a button you can press to evacuate in case love goes too far, and I find myself sweeping the pub for him.

Tony, O'Malley, and Will have staked claim to the bar, but I easily spot my towering boyfriend. He stands near the sofa where SFO has congregated.

His eyes are already on me.

My body floods, and I lift my whiskey to him, a polite gesture. One that I could make to Banks without any romantic inclination.

Thatcher raises his glass of water back in response.

My stomach flutters.

"I guess it puts me on edge that *all* the guys don't like Will," Sulli confesses. "I can't tell if they're just being overprotective or if they know something about him that I don't."

"If Beckett or Moffy knew something bad about Will, they'd tell you," I say to Sulli. "Just trust your judgment. You have good intuition." She's not naïve, and she's cautious when confronted with real life dangers.

She nods. "You're the best, Jane." Sulli hugs me, and we bring in Luna for a three-way hug.

We all sway, laughing, and I try not to spill my drink on my cousins. When we part, Moffy slips into our huddle with a mug of tea. He doesn't ask for a recap, but we all quickly provide one.

"Just be careful," Maximoff tells her.

"You know I will be," Sulli nods into a smile. "He's sexy, right?"

Maximoff glances over at the bar and checks out Will, who resembles a preppy Ken Doll. "Yeah, he's pretty hot."

"Who's hot?" Farrow slides in, very casual and cool as he chews gum. He gives Moffy a once-over.

"Me," Maximoff quips, stretching his arm across Farrow's shoulders.

Farrow rolls his eyes. "You're definitely cocky." He has trouble taking his gaze off his fiancé. "I didn't come over here for you, smartass."

"But you're staying here for me," Maximoff rebuts.

Luna looks between them with such happiness.

Farrow sucks in a breath. "Technically, you can't read the future to know if I'm staying." And then he looks to me. "I don't love being the errand boy, but Omega wants me to tell you to stop giving your boyfriend 'googly eyes'." He uses air-quotes.

I bristle. "I haven't been giving him *googly* anything. He's been giving *me* some sort of eyes." I sip my whiskey, burning up from the alcohol and other carnal things. I brave a glance at Thatcher.

He's now seated on the sofa with quiet confidence that hooks me tenfold. I could so easily walk over to him.

Kiss him.

Straddle him.

"Janie." Moffy draws my attention back.

Farrow raises his brows at me. "You were saying?"

"Merde," I curse. *I'm making googly eyes.*

"Is Flirty Drunk Jane here?" Moffy asks me.

"Almost," I warn and pinch my fingers together.

He laughs, but concern also rests behind his forest-green eyes. He's been watching over my brothers tonight since I've been drinking, and I can't thank him enough for keeping an eye on Charlie and Beckett.

I notice how Sulli and Luna share a growing smile, and Sulli motions to Farrow. "Hey, is there a way to ask Tony to GTFO so he won't follow Jane and Thatcher outside?"

Luna rocks on her feet. "So she can make out with her boyfriend."

I love them.

Farrow pops a bubblegum bubble in his mouth. "You're asking the wrong bodyguard. You need to talk to the one in charge."

Sulli whips around. "Kits, can you come here for a sec?"

Akara stands off the sofa and pushes back his black hair as he nears his client.

Moffy takes his arm off Farrow and dances with his sister. Luna and Maximoff do the running man move together, and then he twirls her in a circle.

I sway to the beat, and I notice how Farrow looks absolutely and without a shadow of a doubt in *love* with his future husband. I've been a spectator to their love for so long, and now that mine is in reach, I'm scared to embrace every little part until it consumes me.

Being a voyeur to love is easier than being in love, I think.

We all look up as multi-colored Christmas lights switch on, brightening the pub in an array of colors. My head keeps whirling, and whiskey scalds my esophagus, a good sting.

"I can try to shift Tony to Moffy's detail, but I can't promise he'll respond, Sul," Akara tells her. "Jane is his client. He's allowed to protect her first."

"Fuck," Sulli curses in a sigh. "Thanks anyway." She slugs his shoulder. He just nods.

Strange. I squint at their interaction and taste more whiskey. Usually Akara would fling a strand of hair in her face or slug her back just as playfully.

Sullivan puts two fingers to her lips. "What's wrong?"

Farrow, Moffy, and Luna watch too.

"I'm just doing my job." Akara fixes his earpiece. "Is that it?"

Her squared jaw tenses. "Yeah…"

Akara nods, then he returns to the couch beside Quinn.

"What the fuck was that?" Sulli whispers to me, but she's already distracted. Will is waving her over to the bar, and a smile spreads across her face.

"Go get him, tiger." I cheer her on.

Sulli strides over to her boyfriend, and I cement to this very spot. Hardly budging. *Smart, Jane. You know if you go great and terrible distances, you will face-plant.*

Different people approach me at different intervals.

"Do you have dirt on Will?" I ask outright to Charlie and Beckett, Moffy and Farrow also in our new fireside chat. Luna dances by herself in the corner of the pub.

"No." Charlie tugs at his hair, possibly irritated that I'm even asking the important questions that he believes are obvious.

Feel-Good Drunk Jane doesn't care if they're *obvious* or not.

Beckett lights a cigarette between his lips. "Are we just going to forget his younger brother is a dick?"

"Really?" I say. "Wesley wasn't *that* awful." I tuck my hair behind my ear—no, never mind, I catch air. My hair is in a low pony. I smile at myself.

Charlie taps his finger against a glass of Scotch. "You think he wasn't awful because you didn't hear the shit he said about you."

Maximoff glares at the wall. This must have been in high school, and I don't ask what rumors Wesley spread or what terrible things he said because I don't want to award him any space in my brain.

I try to send my brothers a pointed look, but I'm sure the alcohol has dulled its effect. "Will Rochester isn't *Wesley*. The sins of his brother aren't his own."

Charlie takes a hot sip of Scotch. "We all bear the sins of our parents every day we breathe, and so why aren't the sins of a brother or sister or cousin the same?"

"Because," Maximoff says, "being a dick isn't hereditary."

We reach no real conclusion on the subject, and I'm not sure that Charlie or Beckett will ever accept Will, the older brother of someone who has wronged me. Maximoff is far more forgiving, and I see that in how he's let Thatcher back into his life and my life and his fiancé's life.

My brothers go to the bar for new drinks, and like the seas have parted, I have a clear and direct line to the sofa.

To Thatcher.

I sip my drink.

He tries to scout the pub, but his narrowed gaze returns to me in a flash. I'm drawn to him, and I practically float towards my boyfriend.

"Jane," he greets deeply. I'm only a few feet away.

My bones ache for him. I want to feel him inside me. I want the emotion, and I barely see concern tighten his eyes.

Climb him, Jane. "I want you," I whisper.

"Jane."

"Thatcher." I'm a drunken fool, but Flirty Jane doesn't give a damn. I'm one second from straddling Thatcher when hands clasp my waist.

Farrow pulls me back, and Thatcher shoots to a stance, his concern still on me. But the world rotates and blurs, and I try to cling to all the voices that pitch around me.

"Did she just call you Thatcher?" O'Malley asks.

Tony laughs. "She's just drunk. Aren't you, Jane?" He thinks he's being *cute* teasing me, but he's nothing more than a patronizing prick. And I hope I'm glaring at him, but the pub is a smear of multi-colored twinkling Christmas lights. Farrow is still behind me, I think. Thatcher in front. Isn't he? *I hope.*

Voices pile on each other. I blink for focus.

"How am I an asshole?" Tony rebuts. "I don't care that she mixed 'em up. It doesn't even matter what anyone calls them. Banks responds to both names."

I wish I could defend my boyfriend, but I'm fighting to grasp my bearings.

My cheeks roast, uncomfortable that I'm too uninhibited and not put-together among people who should meet my iron walls. I'm lost, but I feel hands on me and voices in my ear. "Thatcher?" I trip over my feet and try to right myself.

I touch something hard. A chest?

I haven't been this drunk in a long, long while.

"Thatcher?" I'm scared. "*Thatcher?*"

"*Jane*—I'm right here." He cups my cheeks.

It alarms me, more than anything, that I didn't call for Maximoff. I called for him.

For a man I...

I love him.

I hold onto his biceps, unsure of where my whiskey glass even went. "I'm fine." I speak, not even sure what he asked me. I try to strong-arm my drunken-self and not slur. "I think it's just hitting me...harder all of a sudden." *Because I moved.* I walked and now I'm speeding rapidly through Sloppy Drunk Jane to Black-Out (SOS) territory.

God, help me.

A translation comes through my brain: *Thatcher, help me.*

20

Thatcher Moretti

SWIFTLY AND EASILY, I lift Jane off the glass-shattered ground and into a front-piggyback. She just dropped her drink, whiskey soaking the floorboards, and she almost went down with the liquor. She can't stand on her own, and right when the glass broke, the team stopped yelling over each other.

I've never seen her this plastered, not even through the six-and-a-half years I've been a bodyguard. Jane Cobalt is notoriously *composed* when she's drunk. She'll do cute things like trip over her own feet and call me *Mr. Moretti*—but she'll right herself up with some type of poise. When the matchup is Jane vs. Whiskey, I'd put my money on my girlfriend every time.

And I'd lose that bet tonight.

She blinks a hell of a lot, panic behind her blue eyes.

I tuck her to my sturdy chest. Protective. One of my hands is lost in her blue skirt. Really, I'm cupping her ass, an effortless hold, and I press my other palm to the back of her head, whispering against her ear, "I have you, honey."

She eases into me.

"Here." Farrow passes me a glass of water.

"Is she pale?" Maximoff asks, voice hard-edged but he looks concerned. He's probably seen her this wasted. Hell, I know he's held her hair back while she's puked.

Before I came along, he'd be the one holding Jane, and the fact that he's not upset that I've taken over—it means we're making *good* strides.

For once I'm not trekking twenty klicks in the wrong fucking direction.

Is she pale?

"No," I answer him.

Her cheeks are somewhat ashen, but she's breathing normal and the longer she realizes I have her, the more she smiles and smooths her lips together.

Blushing.

I've been around harder, more shit-faced partying and seen a fellow infantryman wake up buck-ass naked in his own piss and vomit. She's nowhere near that level of fucked, but if you saw her best friend, you'd think she's a foot in the grave.

"She's not dying, wolf scout," Farrow says matter-of-factly. "She just needs fluids."

Maximoff nods, then slides off her feather purse that slips down her arm. I nod to him in thanks, and he tells us, "She doesn't usually go down this hard, this fast."

I try to catch her drifting gaze. "She probably didn't eat enough today. Food should sober her up."

Maximoff is already moving out. "I'll go find some at the bar." He leaves while Farrow stays to help me.

"Jane," I say, seizing her gaze. "Water."

"Mmm." She smiles up at me.

My lip almost rises. "Drink this."

She bats her lashes dazedly.

"Copy?"

"Mmhmm." She nods firmly. "Yes."

I put the glass to her mouth and tilt. Her big blue eyes planted on mine, she takes small, slurping sips like a fucking kitten. Even hammered, she's an adorable drunk.

While she contemplates taking another sip, I assess the perimeter on instinct. Christmas lights blink in the darkened pub, and ear-splitting chatter and music meld together.

Omega tends to integrate with the older famous ones like friends—especially after the FanCon tour—but we're all on.

Alert.

Always.

No bodyguards are posted at the entrance or exits, so we've all been scouting the pub at various intervals. We're in a town with a population of 50. I hate to think it, let alone believe it, but the bigger threat to Jane is another bodyguard.

In my peripheral I see Tony scrutinizing me. He stews behind the sofa and sports an insulted expression. Like him and I are white-collared-wearing, cubicle-sitting employees and I stole his coveted office project.

My jaw hardens, and I lock eyes with Farrow.

He exchanges a strong look with me. One that we used to never share, but it comes naturally tonight and says, *we're on the same side and I've got you.* There's a chance that Tony will insert himself in this situation.

And I need someone to have my six so I can have hers.

I'm not as territorial as Farrow, but when it comes to my girlfriend being scared or panicked, my spine would have to be obliterated in a hundred places before I let another man carry her to safety. Especially *Tony.*

"Done?" I ask Jane after she takes another sip.

She nods. "You're…" She hiccups.

I almost smile, and I hand the glass to Farrow.

Oscar uses comms, his voice in my ear. "I'm taking a piss. Don't let Beckett hang around my baby sister." He stands off the sofa where Quinn and Joana laugh at something. The Oliveira family has been together most of the night, and we've all been intersecting Beckett's path to Jo.

I don't know if he's bored or if he has a fucking death wish.

Farrow clicks his mic. "Can't hold your bladder, Oliveira?"

"I'm trying to save all the adult diapers for Donnelly," Oscar quips.

Donnelly laughs on comms. "Appreciation and all that."

I tune them out as Jane perches two hands on my shoulders. She tries to straighten up and compose herself, drawing out one blink. "I'm…"

"I have you," I say strongly. "You don't need to do anything tonight." She can be a drunk mess.

She hiccups into a smile. "You're…"

"Moretti!" Tony calls, approaching us. "She's not your responsibility. Take your hands off my client."

Like hell.

I grit my teeth.

Stay professional. I need to stay fucking professional on-duty. In Tony's mind, I'm Banks, and my brother doesn't deserve a tarnished reputation because of my bad calls.

Don't punch him.

She's in your arms.

Don't punch him.

I repeat all the reasons why I shouldn't launch verbal grenades or fists.

Farrow pops a piece of gum in his mouth. Casual as all hell, and as soon as Tony is in distance, Farrow puts a hand to his chest, stopping him in place. "Man, just let Banks take care of her. She's comfortable with him."

Tony sizes him up. "So you'd rather I switch details with Banks then?" He jabs a thumb to the bar. "I can go look after Maximoff for you."

Farrow glares.

"Yeah, didn't think so."

He rolls his eyes. "You talk like you're twenty-feet tall, but you look microscopic. Just back up and leave Banks alone. Jane is safe."

Tony is about to speak, but Jane brushes her nose against mine, romantically. I try to shift my gaze and shove down any visible affection. *I'm Banks.*

I'm my brother.

…and she's gorgeous.

I keep a *platonic* hand on her head. "She's comfortable here," I tell Tony.

"She'd be more comfortable with me." He starts to fucking *smile.*

I'm gonna kill him. "We're not testing that."

"Afraid she'd like me more than your brother?" He tries to shove forward, but Farrow stops him with another hand-to-chest.

"I'm so sick of listening to your shit," Farrow sneers. "Back the fuck off."

Tony is about to go in on Farrow, but Maximoff approaches just in time.

Tony falls back. "I'm carrying her out of the pub when we leave."

No way in hell.

But I'd rather fight him later.

"What was that?" Maximoff watches Tony trudge heatedly towards the bar. He also eyes Farrow's lips, and I'm eyeing the plate of food he just brought.

Looks like a traditional Scottish dish. Nothing I've eaten before.

Farrow cups Maximoff's head and kisses him. "I'll tell you later."

I scrutinize the plate of brown…balls?

"Haggis?" Farrow raises his brows. "You do realize the goal is to sober her up, not make her puke?"

"Thank you for reminding me." Hale sarcasm is thick. "Let me just swing over to McDonald's down the street. Order a Big Mac, some fries, a goddamn milkshake."

Jane rests her cheek on my chest and toys drunkenly with my mic cord. I have a hard time not watching her. I can't drown in greed and wish upon every star to kiss her like Farrow did Maximoff. Because I'm here.

Easily, I could be back in Philly.

"What else did they have?" I hear Farrow ask.

"Nothing. The kitchen closed an hour ago, and they ran out of chips. This was it."

I cut in, "I'll try it first." I take a haggis ball and pop it in my mouth. *Cold.* It'd be better nuked in a microwave. *Grisly.* While I chew, I sweep the pub—and I almost choke.

Unholy...

Fuck.

In the darkened corner of the pub, Luna Hale is dirty-dancing with Donnelly. The kind of sloppy dancing you'd see at closing times from trashed guys and girls.

But her and him—they're completely sober.

He cups her ass with two hands, holding her like I'm holding Jane, only she bounces on his lap to the beat of the music, and he sings the blaring song with Luna.

If Maximoff sees this, he might flip his shit.

I don't stare long, and I force a strict, stoic face and wipe away shock. I'm hoping *no one* notices them. Especially Epsilon.

"You okay?" Maximoff asks me.

I swallow the haggis down. "Yeah." It tastes fine to me, but I doubt Jane will like this meat. "We can see." I grab more haggis. "Jane."

"Mmmh?" She lifts her head.

I hold the meat to her lips. "Take a bite."

She chomps like a tiny animal, then crinkles her nose and spits it off her tongue.

We laugh.

"Did you pack any lunchmeat on you?" Farrow asks me seriously. Which surprises me because Farrow and SFO have been ribbing me about the ham and turkey I bought when we landed.

I'm six-seven.

I'm fucking hungry during long travels, and yeah, I stuffed a package of lunchmeat in my winter jacket and kept pulling out slices to eat.

Which is why they were losing their shit in laughter. And I caught my lip rising a few times. Receiving the wise-cracks and light-hearted jabs with no malice attached—it feels unreal, and I'm not sure I deserve the brotherhood that I hurt. But every day I plan to prove them, and myself, that I do.

The only bad thing: it dawned on me too late that Banks would never carry lunchmeat in his jacket.

And now Tony thinks he does.

I hate that.

"I brought some on the drive here," I confirm. "It's in my jacket."

After Maximoff finds a pack of turkey in the pocket, I roll a slice and feed my girlfriend. She takes tiny nibbles and chews with a smile.

The pub suddenly quiets.

Everyone stares at the television that sits above the fireplace.

Jack Highland raises the volume, and a haunting cover of the song "What A Wonderful World" plays over a montage of clips.

Ryke Meadows and Loren Hale are running at dusk.

Lily Calloway stares strong but tear-streaked in the camera.

Rose Calloway's iconic black heels clap along a sterile hallway, and the image pans back to show another pair of feet. Sandals. Daisy Calloway walks with Rose, the sisters holding hands.

It cuts to Connor Cobalt in a crisp expensive suit. He opens a door, and on the other side are flashes of images that I remember.

Some, I was a witness to. Some, I'm in as background. As a bodyguard.

Charlie stands on the orchestra stage during the celebrity auction. Back in May.

Sullivan peels off swim goggles in a pool.

Eliot falls to his knees at a theater performance, pain in his face.

"No, no, no." Lily's voice, lurched with fear, bleeds over the images.

My chest tightens.

They show a shot of Farrow as he runs his tattooed fingers through his hair, and his eyes hit the camera. We all tense because this is the *first* time in history a bodyguard is close-up in the docuseries and not just nameless background.

Luna is buried in her shirt.

"It shouldn't have happened like this," Rose Calloway says emotionally, angrily, gut-wrenchingly as they show Jane screaming into a sob outside the hospital after the car crash.

I have my hand in Jane's, leading her to a vehicle.

Professional.

I was just her bodyguard back then. But what I felt for her...

I see my narrowed gaze. I'm glaring at the off-screen paparazzi and yelling at them to get the fuck out of her way, but my words are muted as the music intensifies.

Jane's sob is silent on-screen, but I can still hear the pained sound in my ear. I can still feel the forceful push to bring her to safety.

"Just when you think you know what's coming," Daisy Calloway says, "life drags you back."

Rain beats asphalt, littered with car pieces.

The crash.

And then they zoom in on Maximoff diving off the bow of a yacht. Picturesque clips from the summer trip to Greece start playing. Gradually leading into a brighter tone as they linger on Farrow and Maximoff embracing in an intimate hug.

Title font appears.

We Are Calloway
Returns in April

A car commercial cuts on after the docuseries trailer. How did the production team land footage from the crash? It's less of a question. More of a disturbing *fact.*

Paparazzi.

It reminds me that fucking cameramen were on-site filming the event.

Footage in *We Are Calloway* mostly comes from the production team, but they also use videos from the media, paparazzi, and fans who posted shit online.

And that emotional trailer just sobered the pub. Maximoff has his arms crossed, and Farrow has a comforting hand on the back of his neck.

I hadn't thought much about what it must be like for Jane, her cousins, and siblings to watch the docuseries. But it must be hard to see their parents so emotionally raw about situations that involve *them*.

This season will be difficult for most of the team. The car crash was one of the worst events we've all been through together.

In my arms, Jane is blissfully unaware. Half the pub would love to be as drunk as her right now. She chews turkey slowly with a soft smile.

"You could've made that a little happier, Jack," Farrow teases.

"Yeah." Akara smiles. "Way to go, Jack."

"What were you thinkin', Jack," Donnelly pipes in.

"Dammit, Jack," Quinn sighs.

"Yeah, fuck you, Highland," Oscar cuts in playfully.

Jack is smiling a hundred-watt smile. "I'll take those as compliments, and honestly, this is one of the best seasons we've ever produced. And the longest. The studio gave us twice as many episodes."

I heard that from Jane. She said the season is airing later than expected because they needed more time to edit the footage, and they were given a new air date.

April.

"Have all our clients signed off on the footage already?" Quinn asks.

Affirmative.

He's been in security for over a year, not fresh blood anymore, but he hasn't been a bodyguard while the docuseries is airing. It's good that he asks questions. I've led men who try to act cool, pretending they know shit when they know nothing.

Jack explains, "Everyone shown on-screen has okayed the footage in the trailer. For the actual episodes, we still have to go through the rough edit with some family members."

Jane pinches her eyes closed. *She's dizzy.*

I brush a strand of hair off her cheek. "Need the bathroom?"

"Mmmhhmm." She shakes her head but slumps more against me. I need to take her back to Mackintosh House.

Gradually, we all start exiting the pub into the frostbitten cold. I ditch Tony with a longer, stricter stride. I'm so far ahead of that shitbag, he'd have to run to catch me.

Breath smokes the frozen night, and I wrap my jacket over Jane's shoulders while she burrows her body against my warm chest.

Bodyguards crack caked ice off the windshields, turn ignitions, and I slide the door open to a compact black van.

"*Banks.*" Tony bombards me, a furious beat from fisting the back of my shirt—and I can't let him touch me while I'm holding *her.*

"Don't," I warn and face his blood-boiling anger. My veins sear just as blistering hot right now.

Jane stirs, probably sensing my tension, and she cranes her neck over her shoulder.

Drama is shooting off in multiple directions.

"Were we not just having a good time?" Oscar asks in genuine concern. He opposes his little brother on the stoop of the pub, a twinkling holiday wreath hung on the shut door.

Quinn glares. "Bro, just drop it. We're on-duty." He tries to walk off, but Oscar grabs his arm, and Quinn rotates and *swings.*

"Quinn!" Joana clutches his waist and drags him back, but his knuckles already met Oscar's jaw.

That's Fight 1 at my twelve o'clock.

I can't watch long because of Fight 2 on my three.

"You *forced* me here," Beckett sneers at his twin brother. "You want the truth? I expected this from Moffy and Jane, but not from *you.*"

"Are you done?" Charlie glares.

Beckett laughs with hurt, breath visible in the cold. "Get me out of here, Charlie."

"No."

Fight 3 is on my ten. Behind the gurgling exhaust pipes of a blue car, O'Malley confronts Donnelly.

"Hey, I heard your dad is being let of prison this week."

I've seen this happen before. With Farrow not in earshot or view, O'Malley is less afraid to go for Donnelly's jugular. Fight 3 is about to be a knockout bloodbath.

Alarm triggers my instincts, and I reach for my mic to alert Akara, but I realize that the cord is yanked from the radio.

Shit. I scan the gravel parking lot for the Omega lead.

"Banks," Tony snaps. "You're *not* riding home with my client."

Fuck off. I spot Akara at the furthest car, popping the hood. "Akara!" I yell and point in the direction of Fight 3.

He might hate me right now, but we're still teammates and willing to die for the same cause.

"Yeah, he's getting let out," Donnelly answers O'Malley.

Akara sees and sprints after them.

"Yeah? Looks like you're missing your *meth-head* family reunio—" He grunts as Donnelly tackles him, and Akara wrenches him off O'Malley before either guy can throw a punch.

"Jane is drunk," Tony snaps at me. "*Incapacitated.* She can't consent to jack shit right now, which is why protocol dictates that her bodyguard take care of her—you aren't her bodyguard, Moretti."

I'm about to ignite Fight 4.

My nose flares, rage a flaming ball in my lungs. "I'm not just a fucking bodyguard to Jane."

I'm her boyfriend.

Tony laughs. "Right, you're her boyfriend's brother. Great." He claps mockingly. "Just because there are *two* of you doesn't mean you get double-dibs on the same girl. Unless you two are with her in some kind of weird twincest threesome thing. Which, really, isn't that shocking considering you both stuck it in the same chick in high school."

Fucking lies.

"Shut...up," Jane says drunkenly and tries to swat him but she pats the air, and then whacks my cheek. I clasp her hand, almost smiling.

In a split-second, she somehow just smothered a raging fire in my body.

I don't lay into him.

He hates that.

Tony rubs the corner of his lip. "Let me give you some advice, Moretti. You should never let girls speak for you and definitely not fight your battles for you. Man the fuck up."

Anger. I'm burning alive in pure fury. "Women are better than men. Better fighters, better lovers—and the fact that you come from where I do and can say and believe shit that *demeans* women makes me sick."

I know his grandma.

I know his aunts.

I think of my mom, my mom's wife, *my* aunts, *my* grandma, and I wouldn't exist if it weren't for a twelve-year-old *girl* who left Italy with no one and came to America with nothing.

Brave. Bold. Strong women rule my world, and I love them.

Tony cringes, hurt flaring. "Don't turn this into some sexist shit. You know that's not what I meant." His voice is softer.

"Hey." Maximoff strides over with knotted brows. "Is there a problem?"

Tony repeats the same shit about needing to "take care" of his client, and I realize the best route for Jane is her best friend.

Family outranks bodyguards, and if Maximoff wants to carry her, protocol says, *don't get in his fucking way.* After a short conversation, Tony follows protocol and lets her cousin help.

I hate passing my drunk girlfriend over to anyone, but she won't be afraid in his arms.

Maximoff cradles Jane while he climbs into the van, and she hangs onto his shoulders and murmurs, "Thatcher?"

"It's me, Janie," he whispers.

Tony tries to shove in front of me to claim the last open seat, and I block him from entering, about to take that one.

"Banks." O'Malley wipes dirt off his forearms. "One of the cars won't start up. We need your help."

Fuck.

My brother is a mechanic.

While he tinkered under cars, I was a thirteen-year-old busboy and line cook. I lied about my age to land a job, and making chicken parm isn't a skill my brother will need in Philly.

I know basics for car repairs, and I can feel my way through this. But I hate that I have to ease out of the van and drop my boot to the ground.

Leaving Jane.

Two words I hate thinking. Two words I never want to hear.

21

Thatcher Moretti

JANE CLINGS TO THE toilet bowl, and I press a cold washcloth to her clammy forehead. She hasn't puked yet, but she's been toying with the idea for fifteen minutes. Quiet in a mental battle.

Everyone else must be asleep after the pub clusterfuck, chatter nonexistent, but I hear the loud wind skating across the Scottish Highlands and slapping against the stone house. Floorboards and walls creak around me, and my ears pick up the tiniest of noises in vigilance that I don't need tonight.

Zero threats.

Zero targets.

I'm just her boyfriend. She's just my girlfriend. It makes me feel seventeen again. Before the Marine Corps, before I went to war—back when I'd hang out at the Quickie-Mart with Banks. Smoking cheap cigarettes and drinking slushies.

"I owe you one," I tell my brother, my phone resting on the floral tile. Near a brass claw-foot tub. I was on a video call, but with bad reception, the screen went black.

"I've owed you way more and you never collected." His voice crackles with static. "We're always even, you know that." He curses in Italian.

"What?" I stare hard at the phone, wishing the picture would return.

"I can't find the fucking car keys." I imagine him running around the townhouse. It's late in Philly, and he should be leaving for the Hale's mansion soon. He's on night-duty for Xander.

"Check your pockets." I gently comb Jane's hair back, and she blows out a controlled breath.

"Nothing there."

If I cemented shoes to his feet, Banks would still find a way to lose them. "I have a spare set in Jane's nightstand."

"Thanks, Cinderella."

I almost roll my eyes. "You still have my *cornic'*?" I gave him my gold necklace before I left.

The line deadens.

"Banks?"

"Yeah. It's around my neck."

Jane sits up a bit in slight alarm. "Is your brother...?"

"He's okay." I take off the washcloth and study her glazed eyes.

"Hey, Jane," Banks says. "You feelin' any better?"

"I suppose...a little." She presses her fingers to her lips. "I think I'm going to...?"

I guide Jane back to the toilet, running my hand up and down her back while she dry heaves.

Banks tells me, "I talked to ma on the phone. She called your number." Static breaks apart my brother's voice. "She could tell I wasn't you within the first three seconds."

My lip rises. "What'd she say?" I'm assuming he explained the twin switch.

"She said, *you're a buncha dumbasses, but I love you both the most.*"

I laugh, and the sound pulls Jane's attention onto me. She smiles through the queasy-drunk-feeling. And very definitively, she says, "I love your mom." The words almost slur together.

"Yeah?"

"Mmhmm." She nods.

I don't say much else to Banks before we lose service completely, but I warned him it'd probably happen.

After a few minutes, Jane stops dry heaving and breathes easier, and while she leans into my chest, I unlace her heeled fuzzy boots.

She attempts to undress. "I'm...stuck," she mumbles, her elbows jammed into the fabric of her blouse.

I tug the thing off her head, my mouth curved up in a permanent smile. "How's that?"

"Mmmmhmm." She smooths her lips, staring up at me like I'm a midnight snack. "You were twenty-two...when I met you."

I hold her gaze and pull off her right boot. "I was."

"I'm seventeen."

My mouth hikes in a larger smile. Clearly, she means she *was* seventeen back then, but she's too drunk to catch the slip. "You were," I nod and remove her left boot, setting both aside.

"What did you think?" Jane whispers.

My brows draw together. "What do you mean?"

She shivers, the house chilly but I run hot. And she's only in a blue bra and a skirt that she slowly tries to crawl out of. I help her pull the tutu down her hips and legs, and then I hoist my girlfriend up in my arms.

Cradling Jane, I walk back into the cold bedroom.

She hangs onto my neck and cuddles up against my body. "I mean," she says slowly, "what was your first impression of me? Whatwereyouthinking?" The last part slurs together, but I pick apart her question: *what were you thinking?*

I stare at her in my arms with her freckled cheeks and curious eyes, and I can almost see her six years ago.

Just seventeen.

How she'd been at the Hale house on my first day meeting Xander, and she ran hurriedly into the living room, frizzed hair stuck to her lips, out of breath, and mind racing faster than her feet would move. Confidence boosted this girl a million feet high.

She was trying to wrangle her cat on a leash to leave. I was trying not to stare too intensely.

"I thought you were smarter than me," I say deeply, carrying her to bed.

She blushes, trying to suppress a smile. "How so?"

"You knew words I didn't." I can't remember the exact word. It's been too long, and she mulls this over while I gently place her on a twin bed.

I sift through her suitcase and find her favorite flannel pajamas, and I amble over, my knee on the mattress. Easily, I slide her legs into the pants and then arms into the top. She does her best to help, but she whacks herself in the face.

"I have you," I whisper.

She lets me dress her, and when she's warm and clothed, she plops back down with a content smile.

Before I pull up the covers, she rolls over and clutches my leg. "Stay." Her body shakes as a chill ripples through the room.

"Okay." I crouch down, unlacing my boots, slipping them off, and then I stand and unbutton my slacks. Surprisingly, she's able to keep eye contact, but I can tell she's still under the influence of whiskey.

She shifts her legs more than usual and her arms hang lifelessly on her hips.

"Is that all you thought about me?" she asks softly.

"No." I shake my head.

There is a great chance she'll never remember what I say now, but the truth isn't hard to share with Jane drunk or sober.

"I thought you were young."

Too young for me.

Too rich for me.

Too much of a Cobalt for me.

I was starting a career that would include protecting *her* and the people she loved, and I didn't want to fuck it. I wanted to respect the fact that she was underage and the only thing that mattered was her safety.

Jane actually smiles. "I'm not that much younger than you… yourealize." She slurs again.

"Five years?" I climb onto the small bed, and she rolls onto her back, spreading open her thighs. *Fuck.* My hands press on either side of her head on the mattress, and I keep my body weight off Jane. "You were only seventeen."

Our eyes latch tightly as she whispers, "You were only twenty-two."

I nod a few times.

I was only twenty-two. I was younger than she is now, and I hadn't been out of the military for long. "Now I'm twenty-eight," I say strongly, "and I'm doing what I should've done on day one."

"What's that?" She blinks hard, fighting a heavy sleep.

I dip my head and whisper against her ear, "Let myself love you."

Jane grips my hair, as though to say, *stay.* Her breath comes out in a sharp wave, swelling my chest, and I slip under the covers, my legs hanging off the bed. I tuck her trembling body against my chest.

She burrows into me for warmth and security.

Moments pass, her eyes closed, and right before she drifts off, she murmurs, "Thatcher?"

"Yeah?"

She seems to hold tighter.

I cup her cheek. "I have you. You're safe, honey." I repeat the sentiments, and her body loosens.

And into the silence, she breathes, "I love you."

It jolts me, and I hang onto those words, my veins pulsing. She's only ever said *I'm falling in love with you.* It could just be a drunken slip, but it's like a drug.

And I fall to sleep with in an indescribable high.

22

Jane Cobalt

MY HEART IS RACING. "About the other night…" I speak quietly to Thatcher, as though my voice will carry across the endless rolling mountains.

Chilly wind whips my wavy hair as I try to catch my breath. We just completed a climb to the top of a beautiful plateau, the flat grassland stretching left and right while sheep roam leisurely around us.

"Yeah?" Thatcher takes a quick glance down the steep rock-littered grass: what we just trekked up, where we left Tony at the bottom, my bodyguard a speck in the distance as he waits with the cars.

I was surprised when Tony listened to my request to stay there.

Even more shocked that he didn't argue about "Banks" accompanying me. Though he made *comments*.

He said, "Take the killjoy. See how much fun you'll have without me." He leaned on the car like he was the smoothest sex god worthy of my lust, and then he flashed a flirty smile that made my ovaries shrivel.

"I don't love being around you," I snapped. "And if you believe you'll be my bodyguard for long, you're mistaken."

His smile fell. "Come on." He sounded hurt. "Whatever Moretti has said about me, it's not true."

"I can make up my own mind," I rebutted, just as Thatcher approached us.

He assessed the uneasiness and the tension that wound between me and my bodyguard. His gaze narrowed on Tony. "What'd you say to her?"

"Nothing that everyone doesn't know already." Tony tried to raise his chin to appear taller than Thatcher. "I was just telling Jane that I'm more fun than you."

To which I snapped back, "And your unsolicited opinion on Banks or Thatcher or a combination of the two is deeply *unwelcome.*" I glared.

Hotly.

I caught Thatcher smiling down at me. Maybe just the corner of his lip slightly rose, but that means more coming from a man who's stern exterior rarely crumbles. And I could practically see the light pooling inside him.

Now that we've left Tony behind and it's just my boyfriend and me, nerves flap in my stomach. Butterfly-nerves—I have them tenfold around Thatcher and his commanding presence and his hard-to-read features that I canvass eagerly.

He has his arms crossed, radio mic attached to a blue outdoorsy jacket that reminds me of Banks. And his eyes have returned to me with such raw intensity.

I squish my binder tighter against my puffy jacket.

Last night, Jane. We're discussing last night, and I shake the cobwebs from my head. "…I appreciate, more than anything, you taking care of me when I was…"

Sloppy drunk.

A sloshed fool.

Just plain messy Jane.

"Indisposed," I say aloud.

He almost smiles again. "You were cute *indisposed.*"

I brighten. "You mean I was a hot mess?"

Thatcher looks me over. "I've seen hot messes before, and you're your own thing."

"Cute indisposed," I muse.

"Cute indisposed," he confirms with a nod.

We stare deeper, and emotion tries to burrow further into me. I try to stay on track. "I meant to say more."

He nods me on.

"About last night…" I add again.

I feel and see Thatcher hanging onto my every word. Like I'm building towards a climax and it could be disastrous or the most glorious extreme we've ever reached.

It's up to me where I take us, I realize. Which is so different from when we were fake-dating; our fate was in his hands back then.

"I had less control of my body," I mention, "and I felt really quite safe with you." My pulse is strangely on an ascent, as though I'm still climbing up the steep hill. "And not because you're a bodyguard but because you're *you.*"

His chest rises.

"Someone I trust. Someone I…" I falter, burning up from nerves. "And…and I very much liked this morning." Why am I so abysmally *frightened* admitting this to him?

I adored how he doted on me the second I woke up. How he asked me how I felt, gave me Advil, made me breakfast and slyly brought the poached eggs and waffle to my bed. All without the Epsilon bodyguards noticing, he took these risks just to help me fight a hangover.

It made me feel…loved.

Yet, my emotions pull and push in a tug-of-war with my head. Logically, I know that I'm taking far too much.

I tilt my head up to meet his eyes. "And if you ever need a sober-someone to take care of you, then I'm more than willing to return the favor. It's what I'm most used to, you know. Taking care of my family."

Thatcher never looks away. "You don't need to give me what you give your siblings. I'm not your little brother, honey."

Flush ascends my cheeks as I picture his dick inside me. "You're definitely not my brother, I agree completely." Sweating, I unzip my jacket. "But if I could give you something in return for last night, what would you want?"

He runs a hand over his unshaven jaw, staring stronger into me as though he's trying to figure out the depth of what I'm saying. "There's no *cost* to being with me, Jane. I don't want to be reimbursed for cooking you breakfast or holding your hair back."

My neck flames. "But I don't want to be your burden. I want to be your equal."

Realization slams at him, and I swear he careens back from the force. He inhales, then breathes strongly out. He dips his head to be nearer, his hand teasingly close to my hand. "You're not my burden." He hardly blinks. "And you already are my equal. I hate that I've given you an impression that you're not."

I believe him, but I can't quite grasp what I've done for Thatcher in the same regard as to what he's done for me.

It still feels awfully lopsided, especially after the boozy pub night.

I'm quiet.

Thatcher rubs his mouth with a look of concern. Dare I say, he even appears *nervous*. He drops his hand to his side.

I murmur, "I'm sorry—"

"No," he interjects. "You never need to apologize to me for expressing what you feel."

I exhale a pained breath. "One part of me hates that I even apologized to begin with. I feel like I'm losing sense of what I've learned from the women before me. From Aunt Daisy, from my mom." My eyes burn. "But I also love that you reminded me that it's okay to feel what I feel, even if it's terribly confusing."

He shakes his head, a thought pinching his brows and tightening his eyes. He shifts his visceral intensity off me.

"What is it?" I whisper, aching to hear everything that rattles his brain.

He softens his eyes before placing them on me. "You're so fucking hard on yourself." In a silent beat, deep understanding passes between us because he's also tough on himself with most everything. "You're just twenty-three, Jane. You don't have to be perfect versions of the women who raised you."

My heart swells. "Women," I repeat the word. "You included my aunts?"

He nods once. "I know what they all mean to you."

If my mom were here, Thatcher Moretti would be her favorite almost instantaneously. She loves her sisters like they're a part of her soul, and I love that he understands how much I look up to all the women in my life.

Aunt Daisy has taught me to use my voice, even if the world says *stay quiet.* Aunt Lily has taught me fierce courage, even on days when you feel lesser than. And Rose Calloway Cobalt, my mom—she's taught me how to walk into a room full of men and never back down.

She's taught me familial love. And loyalty.

She's taught me how femininity is everything and anything. Harsh and icy. Soft and stiff. Boisterous and unruly. Timid and unrelenting. Oxymorons and complements and conundrums that no one needs to understand.

We're women because we say so. We feel so. And that realization freed me.

Very deeply, Thatcher tells me, "When they were your age, they were figuring out being in their twenties and in love—you're allowed this part."

I cage breath. "This part?"

"Of life," he clarifies. "The stomach-flipping, head-scratching moments where you feel like everything is going off the tracks."

Curiosity ignites me. "You've been here before?"

He lifts his shoulders. "You're the only woman I've ever loved," he reminds me. "But I've had to right a lot of wrong-tracked trains in my early twenties."

I remember that we're in this together, and I can't imagine experiencing this part of life with another man. His patience and respect constantly boosts me into another stratosphere.

He deserves better than me.

I push down that hurtful voice in my ear.

I'm amazing too. I'm triumphant and beautiful, and I deserve his love.

I have so much to offer him. Love (that I'm withholding), Strength (that keeps vacillating), Great Sex (sure, there's that).

Slapping aside my insecurities, I tell him the good I feel. "I'm really glad it's you who's experiencing this part with me." I smile at a thought. "If I had a glass slipper, I'd put it on your foot right about now."

His mouth curves upward. "You choose me?"

"Oui." I breathe. "Toujours." *Always.*

Fear tries to stab me. My shoulders bind and my back arches a little. We look into one another, and though his eyes never stray from mine, I can feel him studying my stiff posture. He's a perceptive man, which I love.

Wind whistles, and our fingers nearly brush. A strand of hair slips out from behind his ear and caresses his cheek. He tucks back the brown tendril, then swivels a knob on the radio. He straightens some and speaks hushed in the mic.

"Is everything okay?" I ask.

He nods, muscles flexed. "Tony thinks we're standing too close."

My brows jump. "Do we need to back away?"

"No." His eyes devour me. "I told him that you're cold."

I begin to smile. "Thank God for the weather."

His lips lift, then lower, and lines crease his forehead. "I just need confirmation about something."

"Of course." I inhale, more on edge.

"Did you like that I took care of you last night?"

"Yes," I say so suddenly and from deep in my core. "So much so. More than just *like*, even."

He nods a few times, his shoulders relaxing, and then asks, "How much do you remember?"

I file through my hazy memories. "Most everything in the pub. Very little afterwards." I squint. "I think the last moment I can picture is you pressing a washcloth on my forehead." What I'd give to be a fly on the wall to Black-Out (SOS) Jane.

He stares off for a moment.

I peel a flyaway hair off my wind-chapped lips. "Did I do or say anything mortifying last night?"

He shakes his head, about to speak but his phone rings. Checking the Caller ID, his expression hardens. "It's Banks."

I hug my binder closer. "Shouldn't he be on-duty?"

He tenses. "Yeah."

We share a look of apprehension. *Something's not right in Philly.* It's our greatest worry, and before he answers his twin brother, Jack Highland approaches us, strapping his Canon camera across his toned chest.

"You go talk to your brother. I'll talk to Jack," I tell my boyfriend. "Diviser et conquérir." *Divide and conquer.*

"Sounds good." Thatcher glances at my lips, a volcanic swelter bubbling around us, and we have a difficult time separating.

"See you in a bit," I whisper.

He breathes harder, and I wish he could kiss me but Tony is obviously hawk-eyeing us from down below.

Thatcher glares in that direction and then moves. "I'll be right back." He leaves just as Jack arrives, his smile radiant.

Jack is by far the happiest person I've ever met in the best and worst times. "Any footage will be gorgeous here, especially when the light hits the horizon." He points to where the sun will set.

I open my binder and click my fuzzy pen. "I'll mark that down." I write under the *pros* section of *Possible Wedding Location #6.* "Anything that could cause an issue?"

He motions to the rocky incline we climbed. "Crew is going to struggle up that hill, and so will guests."

I jot down more notes. Besides Maximoff and Farrow, Jack is the most important person on the location-scouting trip. Whatever outdoor venue they choose has to work for production—in the event that my best friend and his soon-to-be husband want to film their wedding.

They haven't fully committed, but Jack thought it'd be a good idea to tag along in case they do want the world to see their ceremony.

"Logistically, I can find a way around the hill," I tell Jack. "I can have temporary stairs placed that won't hurt the terrain." I've already made a few calls when we first arrived.

"Perfect." He grips his camera and clicks through photos. "Look." He shows me a picture of Maximoff and Farrow as they stroll across the plateau hand-in-hand, and Maximoff is sweeping the lush landscape in silent awe. All the while, Farrow is staring deeply at him with a cheek-to-cheek smile.

Happiness pours through me. "Moffy is glowing." I turn my head. Off in the distance, I see them both chatting and in a position reminiscent of a slow-dance. Hands on shoulders and the back of the neck. Taking a romantic moment for themselves, as they should.

Jack smiles brightly. "This place seems like their favorite so far."

"A top contender," I agree, making a few more notes. I wish the others could have seen this spot.

Most of the group accompanied us to Possible Wedding Locations #1 and #2: a bridge over a brook, and then a garden—but hunger struck and they all caravanned back to the house about an hour ago.

I peek up from my binder to check on Thatcher.

He has a boot on a boulder and speaks sternly into the phone. Eyes narrowed, body flexed. His voice is inaudible from here. But a sheep literally creeps away from him.

Thatcher is scaring the animals.

I want to be at his side, but while I have Jack's attention, I decide to pry just a little.

Out of cousin duties.

Specifically my loyalties to Sullivan Meadows.

"Jack." I slip my pen in a binder pocket. "You're friends with Akara." It's not so much a question, but a building block to my next point.

"Yeah." He lets go of his camera and it hangs at his side. "We're good friends."

I'd say so, considering I heard they've double-dated girls that Jack knew from college.

"Then you must have some idea why Akara is acting standoffish around Sulli. Usually he's friendly and more of a buddy-guard towards her."

Jack laughs with the shake of his head. "*That*, I wouldn't know."

I zip my puffy jacket back up as wind accelerates. "You don't talk about Sulli?"

"Not if it's about protecting her."

I tip my head. "How come?"

"Security and production don't always see eye-to-eye when it comes to you and your family. Honestly, my friendship with Akara has stayed intact because we don't constantly bring up his client and my time filming you all."

Merde.

I already asked Thatcher for answers, and he said Akara wouldn't tell him anything since they're on the outs. Farrow also has no clue what's changed. He explained, "*See, Akara will rarely vent or complain to us. He's our lead.*"

I'll have to report back the *no new* news to Sulli.

Gusts of wind blow harshly through. Jack shivers, zipping a lightweight jacket up to his neck, his skin a tanned blend of red-gold and light brown hues. He's biracial: his dad is white and his mom is Filipina.

Since he's born-and-raised in sunny Southern California, he claims he didn't come prepared for the brutal cold.

Another large gust.

"Fuck," Jack curses under his breath. Strands of his dark brown hair are airborne—cut short but long enough to take flight and block his eyes.

Mine flaps wildly at my face, and we laugh.

"If only I had one of Oscar's bandanas," Jack smiles, trying to push his hair back to no avail.

I set my binder down and retie my hair. "I actually think Oscar may've left one in the car."

"Really?" He tucks his camera more protectively, about to leave.

"I'm almost certain I saw one in the front seat."

He heads to the descent and smiles back. He makes the *hang loose* hand gesture. "Shaka brah."

I wave goodbye, collect my things, and rejoin my boyfriend.

Sheep have given Thatcher and his lasered gaze a wide, *wide* berth. One is practically cowering behind a rock.

He shoves his phone in his pocket. "We have a problem."

Before I can ask, *my* phone rings. He holds my binder for me, and with a gloved hand, I procure my cell from my sequined purse and read the screen.

My brows bunch. "It's my dad."

"That's the problem." Thatcher gestures to the phone with my binder. "He tried to call Banks *three* times."

"And Banks has your phone," I realize. Meaning, my dad has been trying to reach my boyfriend. "Okay, I can fix this." I stare wide-eyed at my ringing phone. "I just have to speak to my dad, who is scarily good at catching onto deceit. Though, we've tricked him once." I talk quickly. Nervously. "He didn't know that you actually had feelings for me. But I suppose that means *you* were better at pulling the wool over his eyes. Not necessarily me."

"Jane—"

"Yes?"

"It's going to ring out." He nods to my phone.

Oh. "Right."

"You don't have to lie to your parents," Thatcher says strongly. "I know you don't want to, and I don't want you to go there."

"Okay." I take a single breath in preparation. "I'll find a non-deceptive avenue if I can." I answer on the last ring. "Dad?"

He greets, "Mon coeur." *My heart.* Hearing his voice causes a small wave of homesickness. There's no one like my dad, and I love him very much so.

"How's everything back home?" I hope I sound 0% fretful. Thatcher edges nearer, nodding in encouragement. His towering build is like a stone wall, shielding the raucous wind from me.

"We're all doing well here." His voice is smooth and untroubled. "I'm just wondering why your boyfriend is screening my calls."

Thatcher fixates on the phone like I'm clutching a weapon, and if he blinks, it'll detonate in my palm.

I lift the speakers closer to my lips. "Do you have the right number?"

I picture my dad arching a single brow. "Phone numbers aren't that difficult to memorize, especially ones that matter."

I touch my smile with my fingertips. *Thatcher matters to him.* I take a breath and turn the tables. "Why are you trying to reach him?"

"I wanted to invite him to lunch tomorrow."

My eyes bug. *Oh my God.* This is very, *very* bad. He can't have a face-to-face with Banks.

Thatcher's biceps look like they're going to explode in his cross-armed state. He nods to me and mouths, *deflect.*

Right.

Deflection. "Are you rescinding the invitation?"

"No. But the more he avoids my calls, the more he reminds me of the only person who consistently hangs up on me—and I never imagined my firstborn daughter would date a man like Ryke Meadows." He sounds a little bothered by this fact, though I know he cares deeply for Uncle Ryke.

"Date is a weak word," I correct. "What we are to each other is very serious, him and I." I'm less nervous to admit this to my dad, strangely. I'm more nervous when I meet Thatcher's strong eyes.

My stomach backflips.

"Have you two talked about marriage?"

"No," I squeak out. "No, *no.*" My face is red-hot. "Dad, that's far too soon." I step around Thatcher to welcome the aggressive breeze, hitting me in a cold wave.

Thatcher uncrosses his arms, his gaze tracking my movement. The lack of holster on his waistband reminds me that security has no firearms on this trip, due to gun laws. All are armed with legal tactical knives.

Facts.

Facts are easy. Simple. Emotionless at times. And distracting.

"And you'll be happy to know," I tell him, "that the probability of someone marrying their first boyfriend or girlfriend is statistically low." My pulse skips. "Maximoff is an outlier." *Stop talking.* "So there's that piece of helpful data."

Thatcher is staring at my back.

I hang my head, my heart in my throat with a looming sadness that I push aside. I'm not sad. *I'm not sad.* I can live without him.

"Where are you pulling your data from?" my dad asks, voice calm.

"Places," I say, being as cagey as him. I'm the first of his children in a serious relationship. Guessing his motives concerning my boyfriend will be as accurate as shaking a Magic 8 Ball. I have no idea what my dad is truly thinking. "Are you inviting Thatcher to lunch out of kindness or to interrogate him?"

"That depends if we agree on the definition of interrogate," he says smoothly like he, himself, is the arbiter of definitions. I once believed he wrote the dictionary under the pseudonym Merriam-Webster. I was five. And clearly deluded.

"Dad," I say in warning.

"It'll be a civil conversation, I promise." I can feel his billion-dollar grin.

"I think you should wait for me to be there. I'll be back in three days. *Please.*"

"If that's what you want." He pauses. "But sooner or later, I'm going to get to know him on my own. You're not just seriously dating him, Jane. You're bringing him into our world, and there's only so much a background check covers."

All bodyguards go through background checks, but my dad makes it seem like he pried right after Thatcher and I became a couple.

I'm frozen, but somehow I thaw, just to glance over my shoulder. At him.

Thatcher looks anything but surprised.

He knew that my family would take a bulldozer to his history and excavate any dead, decaying skeletons he buried away.

Of course he did. He's a bodyguard. He's probably helped do the digging in the past.

I raise my phone again, my eyes locked on Thatcher. "I understand," I tell my dad.

My world—it's barricaded and protected by a thousand force fields. Us, Cobalts—we have traditions that my cousins don't even share. Letting an outsider into our well-guarded fortress is frightening and new, and I wouldn't want or trust anyone to enter except for Thatcher.

I emphasize, "Just, *please* wait until I come home."

"Pour toi n'importe quoi." *For you, anything.*

After a quick goodbye, we hang up, but relief doesn't exactly strike. Not after the awkward "marriage" moment and me mentioning *statistics* and our low probability of lasting.

Maybe it's not even on Thatcher's mind.

Maybe he's forgotten my word vomit already.

He scans our surroundings, then me. "I'm not trying to kill your dreams, Jane, but your probabilities seem off."

"How so?" I hug my arms around my body.

"You said it's statistically low that someone marries their first boyfriend or girlfriend. How does that work between you and me?"

I'm confused until he adds, "You're not my first girlfriend."

"Oh." I flush.

He nears. "I'm not as good at math as you, but in my head, it doesn't make sense that our odds are different when we'd be marrying each other." He blinks back something raw. "Hypothetically."

"Hypothetically." I nod in agreement. Emotion bubbles to the surface, and I've never experienced this strong swell surging and surging and breathing life and sentiments so unwieldy inside of me. I tuck my hair behind my ear. "I'll have…have to recalculate." I sound breathless.

Our hands toy with touching again, and then the sky cracks.

We look up. Dark clouds gather and rumble violently.

Maximoff and Farrow sprint over to us as rain suddenly descends in heavy sheets. Thatcher draws me to his chest to keep me semi-dry, and I spin to face him.

Rain soaks our hair and shoulders, and he fits my binder beneath his jacket. Protecting the pages and ink.

I love him.

Moffy shouts over the storm, "We need to leave before the weather gets worse!"

It's already freezing, and we have a slippery, dangerous descent.

"Hold onto me," Thatcher says with severity.

I ache and desire and want to say, *always.* But the word is stuck. And all I manage to get out is, "Okay."

23

Thatcher Moretti

IT ALL HAPPENS IN a fucking blink. As we descend the hill, Jane slips on the slick grass.

Her hand slips out of mine, and she slides and slides. Too rapidly to catch, and Maximoff loses his footing. He falls next.

Farrow and I rush after them, but both land in the knee-deep, bone-chilling *rocky* stream. I've never moved this fast. I've never picked Jane up this quickly, and I've never felt her arms wrap around me this tight.

How the fuck did this happen?

It plays over and fucking over in my head when we reach the car, and I slam the door shut. Rain beats against the vehicle. Dry cover as Farrow and I move with severe urgency inside.

I'm in the backseat, and I slide Jane's soaked and torn jeans down her thighs, down her ankles. Crimson bleeds into the mint-green fabric, and I throw aside the bloodied jeans. Her trembling fingers struggle to grip the zipper of her wet jacket.

I take over and skate the zipper down.

How the fuck did this happen? It rings in my ears. Slams at my chest. Jane being hurt is a thousand jackknives to the head and heart, and my feelings for her are bursting at me like blazing fireworks in my face. My greatest duty in this lifetime is to protect the woman I love.

She's the only one, and this singular purpose pushes me to stay focused, gliding her jacket sleeves off her arms. Her brown hair sopping her shoulders as she shudders.

I tie her hair into a high messy bun, and in the front seats, Farrow is helping the man he loves remove his jacket and drenched shirt beneath. Maximoff tries to peel the crew-neck off his vibrating body, but Farrow does the job for him.

Shaking uncontrollably, Maximoff glances back at Jane. He looks how I feel. "Her lips...are blue," he chatters.

Jane stares petrified at him. Because his lips are blue too.

Their panic just *tanks* the air, and I understand the bond she shares with Maximoff because I share the same one with my twin brother. But I'm also connected to her, and the love I wield for Jane and the love Farrow carries for Maximoff—it drives two more sets of pain.

Two more weights *tanking* us.

We're three-ways in hell, and the only good thing is that all four of us are built to withstand the fire.

I draw her on my lap, careful with her leg, where a rock cut her from knee to shin. "He's okay," I assure Jane.

"She'll be fine, Maximoff," Farrow says with certainty.

My muscles are taut. Searing.

"I can't..." Jane takes sharp breaths like her lungs are ice. Her wet blue-feathered blouse makes her look like a trembling bluebird caught in a rainstorm. *I have to get her out of these clothes.*

"I have you." I cup her cheek—her skin is freezing. Blood is also dripping down her leg, and I have to prioritize one. I make the call and choose her leg. Farrow is already reaching back and handing me a first-aid kit and water bottle.

I pop the kit's plastic lid.

"Is the cut deeper than a quarter of an inch?" Farrow asks while he helps Maximoff pull off his soaked jeans.

I examine the cut. "Almost."

She squeezes her eyes closed, fighting for fuller breath.

Heat expels from the car's A/C, and Maximoff ensures the vents are open and directs them towards Jane.

"Okay, you need to wash the cut and apply pressure." Farrow stretches between the driver and passenger seat, closer to the backseat to get a better assessment. He's calm but looks serious. "If it doesn't stop bleeding after fifteen minutes, I'll suture her."

I nod.

Thank the Lord he's a fucking doctor. It's not the first time I've thought that. Wasting no time, I splash water on Jane's shin, washing off some dirt, and I expect her to *wince*. But she shakes.

Shivers.

Shudders forward, too cold to feel the pain—and alarm quickens my actions.

Swiftly, I bite open a packet of gauze and press down on the wound. I fist the hem of her blouse and tug the drenched fabric off her head. Her nipples prod against her soaked, see-through pink bra, and her cat-printed panties aren't dry either.

She quakes. Her arms hug her belly—and I'm about to draw her onto my lap. I'm about to rub her skin for hot friction and cradle my girlfriend as close as I fucking can.

But I catch movement outside.

I narrow my eyes on the blurry windshield, rain slithering down the glass—and I see her bodyguard.

God-fucking-dammit.

My veins pulse with anger. Tony exits a car that's parked in front of ours. His stride is arrogant, like he's about to turn the rain into wine.

"Fuck that guy," Maximoff says shakily. "I'm going—"

"No." Farrow tugs him away from the door. "Let us worry about that dipshit. You and Jane need to get warm."

I click my mic. "Banks to Tony, return to your vehicle. We have enough hands here."

He smiles at our car like I'm bullshitting him. Like he's the best bodyguard on the team and there's no way he's *not* needed.

I'm about to pop off. Badly. I wrench open the door and tell Jane, "I'll be fast." If she weren't frozen, she'd probably pass me an umbrella or hand me another knife.

I shut the door.

Rain pelts my shoulders with harsher impact, and I realize…it's sleeting. Tony spreads his arms wide, approaching, only a meter away. "I'm here to help."

"You're not needed!" I yell between my teeth. "Get the fuck back in your Victor." *Fuck me*—I meant *vehicle* not *Victor*, but military slang spills out of my mouth.

He cocks his head, eyes flashing hot. "Why don't you? That's *my* client. You and your fucking brother are always stepping on my territory. First with Xander, now with Jane—and you think *I'm* the one with the problem? You want what I have, and it kills you—"

"Tony," I growl, time slipping. "Back off or I swear to fucking God I will throw you against your car." My hand is a white-knuckled fist. If he protests, I'm swinging.

His brows pinch, something flickering in his eyes. He's studying my features. "Banks?"

I stiffen.

I forgot that I'm my brother, and I didn't think, out of everything, that my shorter fuse and blistering wrath would cause suspicion.

Nothing else has.

I breathe harsh breaths through my nose. Controlling my anger, and I force out, "Back off."

Tony gives me another once-over, then raises his hands. "It's her loss. She could use another pair of hands, and you're just hurting her."

He knows where to stab me. His words fester under my skin as I return to the car, and I wonder if he's right and I'm wrong.

Can't do anything about it. I already made the call.

I open the car door.

Farrow is in the back with Jane, putting pressure on her leg, and he switches with me and takes the driver's seat again. We work in unison, seamless, without much verbal communication, and I shut out the sleet and strip off my wet jacket.

I draw Jane onto my lap and collect her trembling hands in mine. She watches me blow hot breath on her palms.

Her shaking slows and slows, less violent than before.

"Christ." Maximoff makes a strange noise in the passenger seat. Like he's frustrated from not being able to control his body and eliminate the cold.

Farrow whispers in his ear, his tattooed hands moving over Maximoff.

"I can't…" Jane inhales, and when I clasp her cheek, she nuzzles into my palm, bathing in my warmth. Our eyes lock, and I run my hand back-and-forth over each arm, each leg, the curve of her hip—my touch burning a fire across the planes and valleys of her beautiful body.

She burrows into my hard chest. "Don't…stop."

"I won't," I whisper, my large palm gliding up and down the length of her back, along the line of her smooth shoulders and her soft thighs.

She reaches back to her spine and tries to snap off her wet bra.

I unclasp it, slipping the straps down her bare shoulders. I watch her eyes follow my fingertips that track scalding trails as I remove her clothing.

And I glance at the windshield. To see if Tony has a visual inside our car. With our body temperature and the heaters on full-blast, we've created a sauna, the windows completely fogged.

Farrow makes sure Maximoff doesn't look back and see his cousin topless.

All clear.

I warm her cold skin, kneading her breasts and puckered nipples, and Jane melts into me. My pulse pounds.

She rests her chin on my chest, just to look up at me. Her breath becomes shallow…then deeper.

Finally.

I clasp her cheek, our lips brushing before I press mine to hers in raw, deep passion. Breathing life into Jane, and she careens into the sweltering kiss. Her fingers gripping stronger on my biceps. My muscles contract and I pull her against me.

When our mouths break apart, I make sure my girlfriend doesn't look forward and see Maximoff stripping off his wet boxer-briefs.

Farrow undoes his own belt—about to give his fiancé his dry clothes.

I do the same. My white tee off, I pull the soft fabric over Jane's head, which hangs down to her thighs. The car is heavy breath and blood-scalding heat.

Jane wraps up in my shirt and lets out a soft noise, more content. But then she shifts slightly and winces.

Her leg. I check the cut. *Bleeding has stopped.* While I apply a bandage, I ask, "How bad does it hurt?"

"It stings," she whispers. "But I don't want to move."

I weave my arm around her hips and shoulders. Tucking her against me. I look at the front seat. "Farrow, you good to drive with the rain?" In the past, storms have triggered certain memories for him.

"Yeah. It's not affecting me." Farrow pulls off his dry black V-neck and passes the fabric to Maximoff.

"No, man." Maximoff shoves the shirt back to Farrow. "You need that more than I do." A shiver runs through him.

His brows spike with a barbell piercing. "I'm sweating, so no, I really don't." He snaps in his seatbelt.

Maximoff relents, already tugging on Farrow's black pants over his waist. He kisses Farrow, then focuses on his cousin. "You okay, Janie?" He restrains himself from glancing back.

"Yes." She buries her cheek in the crook of my arm. "Are you?"

"Yeah."

I speak into my mic. "Banks to Tony, we're Oscar Mike in three."

Comms crackle. "Roger."

While Farrow puts the car in gear, I detect this sadness in Jane, her lips downturned and eyes on the passenger seat. Where her best friend sits.

"What's wrong, honey?" I whisper so they can't hear.

She has a pained face. "Moffy won't pick this location for the ceremony. I know how much he loved it, but we all know it's not safe, especially if it rains."

I skim her and can't help but think that she's the most loving person I've ever met. She just fell in freezing water, and instead of being concerned about her leg, she's here empathizing with Maximoff.

Still, she's so afraid to love me.

I don't know why. Not completely.

I just don't.

And a part of me is scared of the full-blown answer. Maybe that's why I haven't pressed her hard enough to give me one.

24

Jane Cobalt

AN OUTING *ALONE* WITH my boyfriend should have been a recipe for a wonderful, epic day. It's why I jumped at the chance to go grocery shopping for seventeen people.

No one wanted the task of driving an hour in sleet and rain to the nearest food market. Especially after being caught in a storm after location-scouting yesterday.

Maximoff already promised Farrow he'd spend today *indoors* by the fire, and Tony was all too happy to relinquish his duties as my bodyguard to "Banks" when I asked.

For Tony, I think the drudgery of having to watch me shop for green beans was the least appealing. Or maybe he's finally conceding in this strange bodyguard cock-fight. I can only hope.

Biscuits and jams line wooden shelves in the small Scottish shop, and it's just Thatcher and me. No cousins, no siblings, no other bodyguards. A dream-like scenario. Only this isn't the epic, wonderful day I imagined.

We're currently at a standstill in the pasta aisle, a shopping cart wedged between us, a literal and metaphorical barrier.

This isn't our first argument, but this one feels different.

More intense.

Like the billowing steam of a geyser right before the eruption.

I clutch a grocery list, torn apart in two equal halves. Ten different handwritings are scrawled on the paper after being passed around the house.

"We can't split up, Jane," Thatcher tells me for the second time. His tone is definitive. No room for compromise.

"We can actually." My fingers curl around the list. "I'll take the dairy and produce. You stick to the middle aisles. We'll cover more ground that way. It's more efficient than wandering around the store together." I check my pink wristwatch. "We've already wasted ten minutes trying to locate the ketchup." All the brands are different than the ones I'm used to in the States.

His frown deepens. "I understand that. But you know how this works. I'm on-duty, which means you have to be in my sight at all times."

I draw in a heady breath.

My first reaction: utter, unequivocal *attraction*. Dear God, I'm attracted to how much he's around me. Always present like an ever-consuming forest fire.

My second reaction: *shame*. Guilt. Horrible feelings that compound on each other.

My head is telling me that I shouldn't want these things. I shouldn't want him around me all the time. I should be able to walk around a food market without my boyfriend.

Pressure assembles on my chest, and I follow my head. "We're the only customers." I stick to facts about *safety*. "The one employee is up at the front register, and she looks like she was alive during the Fall of Constantinople. She's hardly a threat. This market might as well have been bought out and shut down for us."

"But it wasn't. And I usually don't have to explain my job to you—"

"You don't now," I say stiffly. My chest is on fire. I waft my sweater for more air circulation. I drop my gaze for a fraction of a second.

Thatcher watches me with intense scrutiny, his eyes an extra furnace engulfing me whole. "Is this really about groceries? Or is something else goin' on?" His South Philly accent comes through. Dog tags rest against his blue jacket.

He looks like Banks, but he couldn't be more Thatcher Moretti. Stern and bold and commanding.

I lick my wind-chapped lips, air barely passing between them. Oxygen is dead-bolted inside my lungs. "I…" Words fail me. This is so new and different and I'm battling with too many warring emotions.

Head vs. Heart. I'm a Cobalt. My head should always win.

Concern ripens in his eyes. "If something is wrong, you can tell me." He's like iron and wine. Sturdy, unfailing, intoxicating, and mind-altering. Willing to banish my insecurities but jumbling my senses.

"I don't know how," I admit. My palms are so clammy—ink from the paper smudges on my fingers. I fold the list and slip it in my purse.

He hasn't shifted an inch, his grip cemented on the handlebar of the cart. I think he might be afraid that one small movement could scare me off. I *feel* skittish, at least.

He sweeps me over one more time. "When I don't know what to say—or if I think I might fuck it, if I do speak—I just try and take a couple breaths first."

My mouth dries, and I attempt to inhale, but air crushes more pressure on my sternum. I'm going to have to just expel as much as I can, hopefully as bluntly as I can. He deserves the words I struggle to find.

"It *is* about the groceries," I tell him. "At least, that's a part of it."

He nods me on.

"The other part," I continue, throat swollen but words gush out harder and faster, "is the fact that the public learned I'm planning Maximoff's wedding. All today I've been confronted with horrible opinions about my life." I take out my cell and pop up screenshots of blog post comments.

Thatcher animates and raises a hand towards me. "You don't have to read them to me, honey."

"I want to," I say. "They don't hurt me." I begin. "*Jane Cobalt, the coattail rider. Never doing something for herself. If she's not working for her cousin, it'd probably be her mother, father, or siblings.*" My hand gripping my phone starts to tremble. I squeeze tighter. "'*She's such a disappointment. Imagine being the daughter of Rose Calloway Cobalt and choosing to follow Maximoff Hale around like a lost puppy.*'" I blink back a sliver of pain. "'*Jane Cobalt could have been our queen. Instead we got a weak imposter who can't do anything on her own.*'"

Thatcher takes a stringent, urgent step around the cart.

My pulse spikes and I shuffle back.

He holds up his hands like he comes in peace. "Jane." He says my name with concern and severity. "You can stop reading that horseshit."

They don't hurt me, I want to repeat. But they have to some degree. I always prided myself on rising above hatred and not letting the world's ridicule affect me. I feel small when I let them in and they tear a chunk out of me.

"I used to think it was *horseshit* too," I say into a nod. "I did. I read the same garbage when I worked at H.M.C. Philanthropies, and I truly believed that they were wrong. Because at the end of the day, my job doesn't define me." I point at my chest. "I'm more independent, self-sufficient than anyone on the other side of a screen even knows. Sure, I can work for Moffy. I can work for my mom or dad or siblings. But I don't *need* someone in my life. I don't want for anything or anyone. The love I carry for myself is enough. It's *always* been enough." Tears my burn eyes. "Until I met you."

I expect him to look like I took a sword and shoved it through his ribcage, but he stands before me like a soldier wearing Kevlar, used to taking bullets.

He doesn't even flinch.

"Keep going," he demands.

So I do.

"It's about the groceries." I reroute to the beginning. "Because I *want* you around me every hour of every day. Not just as a bodyguard but as a boyfriend. In these small moments, I feel it tenfold. And I shouldn't want it. I just shouldn't. It makes me some co-dependent, weak-willed girl like all these people have theorized for *years*. I'm proving them right—and…and…" I can't breathe.

I tug at the collar of my sweater.

Thatcher rushes forward and tries to touch me.

But I keep him back and press my hand to his chest. Applying little force.

His palms hover over my shoulders. "Stop for a second, honey. Just take a breath." He gently cradles my elbows while I push a little harder. Uncertainly.

Fumbling, my hands *fumble* against his body.

"Just get away," I say half-heartedly. My head wants him gone. My heart is telling me to fold into him. Let him wrap me up. *Help me.* God, I want that. But that's the problem, I should be able to help myself.

"*Please,*" I plead.

He steps back, just one foot, and his hands drop off me.

"This is all wrong," I tell him through frustrated, helpless tears. I wipe at my eyes. "I shouldn't be treating you like this. I'm not capable of having a boyfriend." *At least, not him. Not someone I want* this *much.*

"Jane, it's fine—"

"It's not," I say, adamant. "We're done. I'm done." *Oh God.*

He grinds down on his teeth. "What are you saying?"

I'm wide-eyed.

"You're breaking up with me?"

"I am." The words release quicker than I realize.

He's quiet, and I gather enough strength to meet his gaze head-on. He wears the same concern and intensity that he started this conversation with.

"Are you going to say anything else?" I wonder. My body is still on fire. My heart in vicious knots. I've just broken up with my boyfriend. My first boyfriend. I feel no better than I did five seconds ago. I feel worse even, but I can't take it back.

Thatcher adjusts his mic in his ear. "I meant what I said in the limo before this trip. I'm going to match whatever pace you set. If you want to break up with me, fine. We're broken up." I can't read him. His tone is more authoritative and impassive than angry.

"So that's it?" I ask, hurt suddenly pinching me. I didn't purposefully break up with him so he'd fight for me, but I also never thought he'd give me up so easily.

"No," Thatcher replies, seriousness pushing forth. "We're going to talk more tonight. You're overwhelmed right now, and I don't want to push you. But if you think this discussion is over, it's not."

Oh…

He glances past my shoulder, and his brows furrow. He clicks his mic at his collar. "Banks to SFO, what's the word on the weather?" Him referring to himself as Banks throws me off for a second. I follow his gaze. Flurries stick to the windowpanes of the market.

The sleet has officially turned to snow.

Security checked the weather before we left, so I'm aware of the incoming storm, but it wasn't supposed to arrive until later tonight. We should have plenty of time, yet the heavy snowfall outside doesn't look promising.

I take a tight breath and rub the tear tracks off my cheeks.

His attention is on me, watching every little movement. I feel like I'm unraveling, and I don't know how to stop.

He clicks his mic once more. "Say again."

He waits and lines crease his forehead. Something's happening.

"What's wrong?"

"Comms are fucked." He takes out his cell, and I fish mine from my purse. I lost signal twenty miles from the market, so I'm not even surprised when I see *No Service* in the top corner.

"No signal," I tell him. "We can ask the woman up front about the weather."

He tilts his head towards that direction. "Let's move out."

We abandon our shopping cart in the aisle, for now, and Thatcher walks ahead of me like he does when we're on a crowded street. Uncomfortable tension winds between us. *We're not together anymore.* It hasn't fully hit me yet, and I think when it does, I'll be throttled completely.

Right now I'm just numb.

We find the elderly gray-haired woman knitting behind the register. She drops her large needles when she sees us approaching.

"Ready then?" Her Scottish accent is thick, and she searches for our items.

"Not yet, ma'am," Thatcher says. "We're wondering if you heard anything about the weather."

She peers towards the window. "Aye, looks a bit brisk. Be careful on your way home. I should be locking up soon too."

He sweeps the rustic check-out counter, possibly looking for a computer, but she only has an old manual register. I'd bet that she's never been on the internet before, let alone Google-searched weather reports.

Thatcher must sense the same because he gives up with a polite, "Thank you, ma'am." He turns to me. "We need to finish shopping in under five minutes, or else we could get stuck in the storm."

I open my mouth, but he's unusually quicker than me.

"If you're going to say splitting up will be faster, I'm going to remind you *again* that it's not an option." He seems stricter. More adamant. Maybe he's pissed we're no longer dating. Maybe he's just more serious now that the storm is looming and his comms are down.

Either way, he's radiating the *I'm in charge of you* energy that draws me in, and at the same time makes me want to push him away.

It's spinning my head.

"I was going to mention it, yes," I reply. "But I won't anymore. Let's just find the essentials and get this over with." I reach for the list in my pocket and try to focus on the task at hand. Not on the fact that I'm standing next to my ex-boyfriend. Not the fact that strain still stretches between us.

No, definitely don't think about any of that, Jane.

Definitely not.

25

Thatcher Moretti

WE'RE DONE. I'M DONE.

Her words rush through my head as we make the drive back to Mackintosh House. We're alone in a cramped rental car, and there are so many things I want to say. But I'm fighting between keeping focus on the snowy road and trying to formulate words that won't push her further away.

Unfuck this.

I want to.

I'm going to.

We just left the food market five minutes ago, and the wind has escalated substantially. Snow sticks to the ground, and my windshield freezes in the corners, the shitty defroster not working that great.

I steal a glance at Jane. She's staring out her window, fist to her chin like she's deep in thought.

One hour.

That's how long it's gonna take to get home.

Maybe even longer if the ice slows me down.

Suddenly, the car radio switches on as if it has a life of its own. Static and incoherent voices pour through. We both reach for the knobs at the same time.

Our fingers brush, skin-to-skin. My muscles tense. Images of her naked, sprawling across our bed flash before my eyes like some erotic movie. Heat blazes everywhere.

She inhales a shuddered breath and retracts as if she's been electrocuted.

Goddammit.

Quickly, I shut off the radio and decrease the heat in the car. I'm sweating through my jacket and there's a fucking snowstorm outside.

"My mom would say that's a bad omen." Jane breaks the uncomfortable silence.

She's lost me. So I ask, "The radio turning on or us touching?"

"The radio." She fidgets in her seat. I can tell she wants to say more, but she goes quiet again.

I keep one tensed hand on the steering wheel and shrug off my jacket with the other. I'm quick enough that she doesn't have time to help me, and then I throw the fabric in the backseat.

My eyes never leave the road. The snow grows heavier, obstructing the streets and my line of sight. It's my responsibility to bring her home safely.

Whatever discussion we need to have, it has to wait.

I'm just not used to this unbearable silence with her. It weighs on me the longer we're stuck together in the sedan. Sun sets behind rolling hills, the Highlands breathtaking but more ominous in the dark. Wind howls outside, trembling the car. I've been in plenty of snowstorms in Philly, but this is incomparable. In a blink, the entire road is gone.

Lost to a sea of white.

We're in a fucking blizzard.

"Thatcher." She tries to peer through the whiteout, but I hear worry on the tail end of my name.

I force myself not to look fully in her direction. *Stay frosty.* But in my peripheral, I can tell she has a hand firm on the dashboard, bracing herself.

She asks, "Can you see anything?"

"Less than a meter." I decelerate to a crawl and turn on the fog lights. "We're fine. I'm taking it slow."

No other cars are on the road. Darkness creates a tunnel-like feeling as snow piles on the car. *She's safe.* It's the only thing on my mind.

I lose track of time in the quiet, and I don't want to look down at the clock. My deltoids ache from sitting upright and tensed. I try to roll out my neck and crack some strain—

Tires skate and the car drifts to the right.

My jaw locks. Correcting immediately, I lift my foot off the gas and strengthen my grip on the wheel. My pulse hammers in my ears.

"What was that?" Jane asks.

"We hit a small patch of ice." Black ice will ruin us, and if we slide on a larger spot, I won't be able to course correct.

I weigh the risks.

Without cell service and internet and with no clear view of road signs, I'm not 100% certain of our distance to the house. All I know is that it's a direct shot. One road. One long stretch. Nothing but land.

I ask Jane for the time.

She tells me and then says, "Why?"

"I'm trying to calculate our distance to the house."

She does the mental math in one second flat. "Based on our speed and current time, we should have about thirty miles left to go."

Roughly fifty klicks away. Maybe more. Too far from the house to park on a bank and wait out the storm. If snow buries our car, we'll need to hike thirty-miles in the morning—which means we're fucked. We're not prepared for an eight-hour trek on foot...but we could manage a three-hour walk to the house tomorrow if the weather lets up.

"Here's the plan." I speed up the wipers. "We're going make it as close to the house as possible, and then I'm going to pull off and we'll wait it out in the car."

She inhales deeply. "You don't think we can reach the house tonight?"

"Not with black ic—" I lose control of the car again. *Goddammit.* Front wheels skid to the left for a full second. Quickly, I counter and right us onto the road.

"Merde," she curses.

I rip my eyes off the windshield for a split-second, just to check on Jane. She has a hand posted on the door, but her blue eyes are focused pinpoints.

I think she might be scanning for road signs.

Returning my concentration to the street, I exhale through my nose. "If we can make thirty more klicks, we'll be fine."

"I'm trying to keep track of our distance," she tells me. "But it's quite difficult." Even now she wants to be my right-hand. I swallow back emotion that surges, constricting my lungs.

And then, just like that, we're spinning.

It happens faster and swifter than the first two times, and I have zero control over the wheels. Nothing I do will stop tires from skating like four hockey pucks on ice, but I try to right us without causing more problems.

Disorientation kicks in for a split-second before we stop. I assess our surroundings with almost no visibility, but two tires dip a bit. Which means we're probably on the bank of the road.

I turn to her. "Jane, are you okay?" I reach for her before I remember we're not together, and she might not want me to touch her.

I pull back.

She blinks hard. Her chest rises and falls heavily and she sweeps my frame just as much as I sweep her. Confusion pinches the creases of her eyes. "Why don't you look like we just went through a rollercoaster?"

"Because I've spun out on black ice before," I tell her. "It's nothing new." It's not as violent as a car crash, but the shock is the same. "You didn't answer me. Are you okay?"

She nods, gulping a bigger breath. "I think so. I just kept thinking we were going to flip like Maximoff and…" *And Farrow and her brothers and little cousin.*

"We didn't," I say strongly. We're just fucked. We're nowhere near the house.

"So now we wait in the car, and tomorrow we hike." Confidence blazes her words. She pulls her shoulders back like she's preparing for every war to come.

"No, there's not going to be a hike."

Her brows bunch. "Then what?"

"We have to wait for help." She can't walk eight-hours in the snow without the right gear. I can't put her in that situation, and unfortunately, I also can't radio the team. Comms are still down.

"You think we're too far away." Jane realizes into a slow nod. "Alright then." She unlocks the glove compartment and grabs a flashlight. "We should gather provisions from the trunk and make sure the exhaust pipe isn't blocked." Goddamn, she's smart.

My lips almost lift.

Bottom line, she's one of the best people to have in this situation. I'm sure of that. Desire pumps through my body without much warning. *Bottle that shit.* I hate right now how much I'm enticed by each and every part of her.

"That was my plan," I tell her stiffly. "Except you're not a part of it." I hold out my hand for the flashlight.

She doesn't move.

"Jane, your shoes."

She glances at her leopard-print ballet flats. Our boots are back at the house, still drying from yesterday's thunderstorm. Only difference is that I had an extra pair.

Jane sighs at the sight of her shoes. "And here I thought you were being over-prepared by bringing two pairs of the same boots to a week-long trip." She brushes a strand away from her eyes. "My mom would call you intuitive."

I shake my head. "It's just a habit. I'm a size 15 shoe. I can't run to the store if anything happens to my boots." I stop and then push myself to say more. "As soon as I started making good money in security, the first thing I bought was an extra set of shoes for each that I own."

"I love how practical you are." She flushes immediately. "Sorry, I didn't mean to say that. It just slipped." Her eyes are reddened from crying earlier. "Which, I suppose, is why they call it a slip of the tongue. And I'll just stop talking…"

I want to tell her to never stop.

I want to tell her that I could listen to her forever.

We're broken up.

I fight between being a pushy asshole and giving her space that she needs—and I land over on respectful ground.

Give her space.

I keep my mouth closed.

She passes me the flashlight, the plastic thudding into my palm.

"You're okay staying here?" I ask, just to confirm

She nods. "We don't need to have another problem to deal with, and me getting frostbite on my toes would surely fall into that category."

I take a good look at her—head to toe—one last time before I grab my jacket from the backseat and leave.

Brittle air and freezing winds bite my exposed skin and burn my eyes. I tug on my gloves. No time to waste, I bend down and clear snow off the exhaust pipe.

And then I stand and try to wrench open the iced trunk. *I forgot to unlock it.*

I step back, wind whipping my hair and snowflakes wetting my cheeks. My lungs burn from the cold, breath visible in the dark, and I pull my jacket higher, covering my mouth.

The trunk pops.

Suddenly. Without me doing jack shit.

Jane.

I almost smile again.

And then I remember we're not dating anymore. *Don't think about it.* I reach into the trunk and fumble through the bags and consolidate some of the items into two.

When I shut the trunk, my stomach sinks at what I see.

Jane is outside of the car. Or at least *half* of her is. She leans out the driver's side window and ties her purple scarf to the side-mirror.

In case we get buried under snow.

Her body is exposed to the elements, flurries kissing her brown hair and wetting the strands.

I'm about to help, but she's so quick. In a blink, she's back inside the car, window rolling up. *Good job, honey.* I want to tell her those words, but somehow I know that staying in the blistering cold might be more comfortable than sharing a cramped car with her all night long.

We're not together anymore.

She made that clear.

I double-check the exhaust pipe one more time before climbing into the backseat. Some food and supplies now accessible, I tear off my gloves and stick them in a seat pocket.

Jane is still in the driver's side, reading the time off her wristwatch. "We should turn off the car in a couple minutes to preserve battery. And only turn it back on every two or four hours after that. I've also cracked this window about a half-inch to avoid carbon monoxide poisoning. Just in case snow covers the exhaust pipe while we're asleep."

I won't be going to sleep tonight, but I don't tell her that. "Looks like we're all squared away." I lean back, but my body is a cement block. "We should do four-hour increments, not every two-hours." I'm not taking any chances.

If we can dig the car out tomorrow morning, we might be able to drive. But if the car dies because we fucked the battery, then we've lost that opportunity. Suffering the cold tonight in favor of better odds tomorrow—that's the plan.

She inhales a deeper breath and angles her head, watching me unlace my boots and take my feet out of them. Her eyes feel like hot lasers on me, scorching each inch of flesh. I shrug off my jacket, damp from the snow, and I stuff it behind my head in the gap between the back window and seat.

Silence.

It eats around us. Painfully, uncomfortably. She's the only person who could make me despise the quiet. Before her, it never really bothered me. I craved it. Pined for it. Now silence is too loud, too blistering, and I'm begging for her voice to deaden it.

I rub at my lips, frustration building. Not at Jane, but at this situation. I didn't want to do this here where there's not an exit for her. Where she can't run away into another room if she wants.

But I can't wait.

I can't spend the next however-long in this fucking cramped car with nothing but the sound of pelting snow and howling winds.

I just fucking can't.

"Jane," I say her name a little too loud. My ears ring. "We should talk."

She hesitates for a long moment like she's trapped in her brain. And then she says, "I agree." She ties her frizzed hair to the side. "Give me a moment." She shuts off the car and drops the keys in the cup holder. I watch as she crawls over the middle console.

I shift towards the door, giving her room.

Now in the backseat with me, we're staring at each other head-on.

"Ready?" I ask.

Her gaze dips down to my crotch. She blushes and raises her blues back to my face. "I didn't mean to look at your dick. It was involuntary. You usually ask that during sex. And I shouldn't even be thinking about us having sex right now." Her words come out rushed and she touches her temple, eyes squeezed closed. "I am *so* incredibly sorry. I don't know how to do this."

"Do what?" I wonder because she's losing me. I've been lost by her verbal derailments before, but this is different. It feels heavier.

"Talk to an ex-boyfriend."

I don't blink.

This is worse than I thought. She's already filed me under the ex-boyfriend category. I should have prepared for this. She's the type of person that will slice you open but immediately cauterize the wound.

By breaking up with me, she thinks she's protecting me from herself. But I don't want her protection.

"I'm your ex-boyfriend," I say bluntly, gauging her reaction.

Jane swallows hard, eyes bloodshot, and she opens her mouth but closes it quickly. Even lost for words, she doesn't break my gaze. We hold it, and somehow the contact feels even more powerful than a single, brief touch.

I continue, my voice never wavering. "To be clear, you broke up with me because you feel like you're not treating me well."

"Precisely." She places her hands on her knees, gripping them tight. "You don't deserve to be pulled in and then pushed away by anyone. And I can't promise I won't keep doing it. My head is a jumbled mess."

I run a rough hand through my hair. "Most people don't have thousands of strangers bearing down on them with their shit opinions. Acting like they have a say in your life and know who you are—I understand if that's fucking with your head. It'd drive anyone insane."

She breathes in sharply. "Just…wait for a second. It's…" She shakes her head, blinking. "It's far too hot in here."

It's not that hot.

Really, with no heat in the car, the chill starts to creep in. The window next to me is like a block of ice.

She hurriedly tugs off her fuzzy sweater, her elbow catching the sleeve. I'm about to help, out of instinct, but she frees herself. Brown hair strewn in every direction, the elastic tie lost, she straightens her pink-and-yellow striped blouse. Her freckled cheeks are rosy-red, maybe partly from the cold.

She's beautiful.

One readying breath later, her eyes land back on mine. "What you just said—it's the problem."

I don't get it. "Why?" I ask. "Because I'm wrong?"

"Because you're right." She fists her crumpled sweater, balled in her hands. "Because you're making me feel better, and that's the issue, Thatcher. *You* are helping me when everyone says I should be helping myself. These aren't horrible comments about my weight or appearance or upbringing. They're attacking my independence…and for me, that's…" Tears well up in her eyes.

"It's your identity," I finish for her, understanding fully now. Complete realization washes over me like a tidal wave. "And you feel like you're losing it to me."

Which is why she's been pushing me away.

Pain twists her face as she nods. "I've never had to rely on a man for emotional support…I've never wanted that. But I find myself wanting your reassurance, your help, your everything. It *terrifies* me to know that *want* inside of me could turn to *need*, and there are moments I feel myself suffocating under the weight of that fear."

My chest constricts.

I won't lie to Jane. "I can't promise that your fear won't come true," I tell her.

A tear rolls down her cheek.

I force myself not to touch her. "I can't promise that if you let yourself love me *completely* that you won't want me or need me."

She holds her body.

My eyes scald. "Because I love you *completely*, Jane, and I want and need you during the worst and best moments of my life."

Her voice is a whisper. "You don't have to placate me."

"What I said is true." I fight emotion that fists my lungs. "I fucking *need* you, honey. I'd be going out of my mind with guilt if I couldn't turn to you. So many times I've thought about you, and you've made me feel good about myself." I stop there, a rock lodged in my throat.

She has a hand to her mouth, overwhelmed.

Processing.

"I…" She swallows. "I'm still scared."

I nod.

I gave her no reason not to be. Because I can't fix this. A quiet moment passes. I'm unsure of where she's mentally at.

"Can I touch you?" I ask.

"Yes." She doesn't hesitate.

I bridge the distance, my knee on the seat between her split thighs, and my other foot on the ground. I brace my hand to the door behind her shoulder.

Her breastbone rises and falls while I hover over her body. My right hand encases her face, my lips ghosting her lips as I whisper, "All I can promise is that I will love you and respect you, Jane. And I will *never* abuse your love or take advantage of what you offer me."

Her tears wet my hand, and my eyes sear raw. She clutches my shirt with two fists. Slowly drawing me closer. We stare into each other. Frostbitten air trying to seep into the backseat, but together, we're too volcanic to turn cold.

And we erupt.

Our lips meld in sensual, emotional force, and I hold her against my body while we dive deeper. My tongue slides against hers, warmth blazing me from inside out. She clenches her thighs around my waist, her fingers curling strands of my hair.

We're tethered by something unexplainable, and I can't let go.

Muscles coiled in taut bands, I'm on fire. I suck the nape of her neck, and her head tilts back, a high-pitched noise breaching her lips. She returns to kiss me like she can't consume me fast enough, and we slow in heady, mind-spinning strokes. Our touch drawn out.

Magma.

I guide her back to the seat so she's lying down beneath me, and we kiss and grind and with my forehead pressed to hers, she chokes out, "I want you back."

Light explodes inside my chest. Fucking disorienting me, and with no doubt, I say, "You have me."

Our hands touch every single inch of each other, eradicating the cold, and we live inside a fire-born passion that grows and grows.

The next minutes are things made of soul and carnal flesh. Stripped naked, my erection is swollen, veins protruding and aching in primal need for Jane.

I slide two fingers against her pussy—*God, she's soaked.* And she writhes and whimpers, "Please, now. *Now.*"

She clutches my waist while I cover my shaft with a condom, and I push into her heat that wraps tight around me.

Fucking. My head spins, and I thrust and lift her by the hips so we're at a perfect angle with my height—and she pulses.

"Thatcher," Jane cries. "*Thatcher,* harder. *Harder, please.*"

Sweat glistens our skin, and I rock at a rougher, deeper pace that pushes me to a sensitive spot in her body. *Holy.*

Fuck. I grip the door handle, then her thigh, keeping her leg higher on my waist. "Jane," I grunt. "*Fuck*fuck."

Her mouth is broken open in overflowing arousal, and her soft, aching noises prick my veins and twitch my cock inside her.

"*Yes,*" she moans. "*Yesyesyes.*" Tears crease her eyes.

My muscles flex with each thrust. A gnarled groan scratches my throat. I knead her breast, her perked nipple, my hand skating down her wide hip and soft thigh, and she tries to hang on.

"More," she cries. "*More.*"

I'm deep in the woman I love. My cock filling her pussy to the brim, and my abs contract with another push in. "I could fuck you all night."

"*Yes.*" She clutches tighter. "Fuck me all night."

Your wish is my command, honey.

My nerves pinch like something unholy, and she bucks her hips, her thighs spasm, back arching. Jane lets out an overcome cry, and that sound and her clenching shoots white light in my vision.

I slow, flexing to keep from joining her climax, and I fuck her softly. Gently. Eking out every second I'm inside Jane.

"All night?" she asks eagerly, catching her breath with heavy pants.

"All night," I confirm. Staring down at her beneath me while I move.

Her lips part in another soft moan, but I can see an apology in her eyes. For breaking up with me, and I shake my head. I almost stop rocking, but she whispers, "Keep going."

I push deeper.

Truth is, I'd rather Jane break up with me than be some kind of unfeeling robot. I'm with a human being, and we might not deal with our emotions well. But we're both trying to deal with them together.

"You did what you felt," I remind her. "You don't have to be sorry for that, not with me."

She opens her mouth to reply, but my erection knows her well and finds that sensitive spot again. Her lips split apart and eyes roll back. Body quivering, and my muscles tighten, about to release.

26

Thatcher Moretti

MORNING LIGHT PIERCES PACKED snow on the windshield. Sun beginning to ascend. I hold a sleeping Jane in my arms, angled on our sides so I've cocooned her between my chest and the seat.

Cold bites my shoulders and triceps, my back exposed to the front of the car. I ensure she's fully covered, tucking my jacket snugger around her hips.

She stirs a little, nestling her cheek into my warm chest. I don't take for granted the mornings I have with Jane. Even if this one is really fucking different.

I assess our surroundings. Awake. Alert—I never shut my eyes. About an hour ago, I started seeing my breath smoke the air, but I welcome the chill after running hot all night. We're both still naked under jackets and her sweater. Cum-filled condoms litter the area beneath the seats.

I fucked Jane until her intense orgasms forced her asleep, and upon her request, I stayed inside of her for an extended time, while she slept.

It was…unlike anything. She's always been the best sex I've ever had, but in Scotland, the intimacy is on another level. We're surviving together, withstanding the cold, and those notions were like pulsing heartbeats fastening us at the fucking soul.

I glance at my watch. *Ten minutes.* Then I'll go outside to see how deep we're packed in, and I'll start the car.

Jane rustles against me again, and this time her eyelids gradually open.

"Are you cold?" I ask.

"Warm," she murmurs, and our eyes latch in a strong beat. Both of us recollecting last night, and I press my lips to her temple.

"You sore?" I whisper.

She shifts her knees. "A little."

I cup her pussy, protectively, and her smile dimples her rosy cheeks. She breathes, "I love you there, very…very much." Her eyes soften. "I love you other places too."

"Where?"

Jane rests her elbow on my muscular side, sitting up some. She takes my other hand, and our breaths shallow as she places my palm on the top of her soft breast.

To her heart.

I inhale deeply. "You trust me here?"

"Yes," she says without pause.

Her heart thumps faster beneath my palm, and I glide my hand up higher, tracking across her collarbone in a sensual stroke. Ascending to the nape of her neck. She shudders with a desirous ache against me, and nestling closer, she peers over my side. Eyeing my bare ass.

"Are *you* cold?" she whispers, a second from shifting the sweater off her legs, but I stop her.

"No."

Jane nods, and in the quiet, she smiles at the inked writing across my ass cheek—she's already traced the letters a thousand times in bed.

Her big blue eyes are poised on me. "You're my Cinderella, you realize."

"I know." My mouth curves upward. "I'm happy to be." *I'm living the fairytale.* And this moment feels like one giant escape from reality. We're stowing away from the bleak situation, where snow could still be falling. Where a *long* journey on foot could be ahead of us.

She's more fixated on my rising lips than my words. Her smile brightens my whole world, and as she drops back in the cocoon of warmth I create, she whispers, "One more time, before we have to leave the car...can you...?" Flush stains her neck, but she never wavers. "Mr. Moretti—Thatcher." She blushes more.

"Jane."

She tilts her chin. "Would you be so kind to spread my legs and fill me?"

I harden, and my blood cranks to a swelter. "Anything you want, honey." With one swift movement, I pull her further down between us, so she's in line with my cock, and a noise ejects from her mouth along with, "*God.*"

I sheath my long shaft with the last condom, and I stretch her leg higher over my waist. She extends her other leg as well as she can, holding steady beneath her knee.

Still on our sides, I cup her face, which is down at my chest, and the swollen head of my erection nudges against her glistening folds. I flex my hips forward, edging inside Jane, and she gasps, pleasure washing over her features.

I grit my teeth, jaw locking. Blistering sensations escalate towards a peak. *Overwhelming.* Sweat builds again as I rock against my girlfriend, her soft breathy gasps warming my chest.

This position is fucking *tight* as all hell, and her calf spasms. I gather her in my arms and seamlessly shift us upright, her back to the seat like she's sitting.

My head almost touches the roof. With my knee on the cushion, my other foot on the floor of the car, I have two perfect handfuls of her ass and I thrust with a deep, annihilating pace. Jane watches my cock sliding in and out of her pussy.

"Thatcher*ThatcherThatcher,*" she cries, fingers gripping my shoulder. "Yesyes, *oh God.*"

"*Fuck,*" I groan between clenched teeth, my muscles flaming in primal hunger.

She's gone, just completely engulfed by our passion, and I love her—I *love* her.

I clasp her cheek again, and she looks up at me. I stare down while I pound into her pulsating heat, and she chokes on a gasp, then a sharp sound that rattles my core.

"You okay?" I breathe.

She nods. "Don't…stop."

I'm not. Warmth wraps around my cock, the friction skin-pricking, mind-numbing—and Jane rakes her nails down my back.

"*Jane,*" I groan, fucking her harder.

Her spine arches, and I have her in my arms. I'm not letting go, and we climb towards a soul-fucking climax that shakes her whole body. I tighten up, muscles flexed, and I come with a heavy grunt.

Fuuucking…

I start to milk the unbelievable feeling, pumping slowly inside her swollen pussy—but then, my ears pick up noise from outside.

Snow crunching. Like footsteps.

Shit.

Carefully, I pull out of Jane. She blinks through the fog of sex, questions surfacing in her big blues, and I tell her, "Someone's here."

Probably a local who spotted our car. Fog and morning mist coat the windows, so it's not like they can see inside.

Jane and I dress fast. Pants on, jackets on, and I jam my feet into my boots before wrenching open the door—*dammit.*

It's stuck.

Snow has barricaded us. If we were alone, we're resourceful enough that we'd find a way out ourselves. But thankfully we have help now—and we don't need to break a door or bust a window.

We share a look, light in our eyes. It'd be easy to be upset that reality has caught up. To wish away whatever person is here to help us.

But I think we're both grateful for our fairytale and our reality—because we're together in each one. We're leaving this car as a couple when we entered it broken up.

"Jane?! Thatcher?!" Maximoff's voice is unmistakable.

"Moffy!" Jane shouts. "We're here!"

Not locals, then.

Surprise barely touches me. Because Maximoff Hale searching for a lost family member is in his nature the same way Jane hanging outside a window to tie a scarf to the car—in a fucking blizzard—is in hers.

Relief surges through me. Just knowing the help that's arrived is *capable* and prepared for a rescue.

I try to force open the jammed door, budging a little bit more. Farrow and Maximoff dig us out in a matter of minutes.

Wind whips my hair, the sun hiding behind thicker, darker clouds. Hefty hiking packs lie next to the buried tires. I know they belong to Maximoff and Farrow. Both are dressed in full winter gear, their noses and cheeks reddened. Like they trekked here on foot through hellish weather. With a quick glance, I assess the car.

Fucking dammit. Deep in the snow, every door is obstructed, and the windshield is caked with ice. It's not just that. The road is gone.

Just a valley of snow.

Even if we unburied the car, we wouldn't be able to drive home.

While I attach my radio to my waistband and fit in my earpiece, Jane hops out behind me. Her ballet flats sink in the snow. "Sorry I didn't come home, old chap—"

Maximoff rushes to his best friend and wraps her up in his arms. Picking her off the ground in a hug and saving her feet from the cold. "You're okay?"

"I'm okay." She clings tighter to him.

Farrow comes to my side, and we both watch the people we love embrace. They whisper to each other, and Maximoff keeps sweeping her from head to toe. Making sure she's in one piece.

"I never want to see him like that again," Farrow tells me, his voice low. My chest tightens. "That bad?"

"Man, you have no idea." His brown eyes almost glass, carrying the hours where he watched Maximoff fear the death of his best friend.

I think of the car crash last May. "I have some idea." I watched Jane face the possibility that Maximoff was dead on-site.

Farrow remembers and nods. We need to catch up, and I skim him: a black beanie covering his hair, one earring dangling, and a black snow jacket with black snow pants on. I don't care if he came in looking like Captain Jack Sparrow.

His comms should be accessible. "Where's your earpiece?"

He rolls his eyes. "I don't know, Mom, where's yours?"

"In my ear," I snap.

"That you just put in," he says, irritated. Comms are a hot button issue between us because this is the one thing that *really* grates on me after a while. I need him.

The team needs him.

I know he's pretty much always accessible, but still, it'd be *easier* if I didn't have to fucking badger him to get there.

I narrow my gaze. "The team could be trying to reach you."

"They can't be." Farrow lifts the hem of his jacket, showing me his radio on his waistband. "I turned off comms an hour ago."

I glare. "You what?"

"I turned off comms," Farrow repeats. "To preserve battery. I lost signal thirty minutes after we left the house and static was draining the thing."

I run my hand across my jaw. Irritable tension building between us for a second.

Maximoff tells Jane, "Wait a second, I brought your boots." He unzips his hiking pack, and she digs inside.

Farrow angles more towards the car. Head tilted, peering inside just slightly, then eyeing me with raised brows. "Have fun?" Humor is in his rising smile.

He literally encapsulates the saying: *don't sweat the small shit.* Letting go of insignificant rifts with the snap of a finger.

I rub my mouth, feeling my lips lifting some at the memory of Jane. "It was a good night." *Not denying that.* "I have to clean the car before we leave. Her brother will fucking kill me."

Farrow frowns, leaning casually on the car. "Who? Charlie?"

I nod strictly. "He's not a fan of people fucking in communal places." I change frequencies on comms, hoping to find a working signal. "He basically eviscerated Maximoff for hooking up with you on the tour bus shower, and I'm trying to avoid a war with my girlfriend's brothers. Not start one."

Farrow nods. "You have nothing to worry about, Moretti."

My brows knot. "What do you mean?"

"Charlie doesn't give a flying shit about people fucking in communal places. If he did, he would've called out Beckett for screwing in the bus's lounge. He just wanted to hurt and provoke Maximoff."

That doesn't make me feel any better. "I thought that was more likely." I adjust my earpiece. "But I just want to cover my bases where her brothers are concerned."

"You should worry more about Tony seeing the condom graveyard—and I'm going to be honest here: it's not that you look like the aftermath of a hetero porn. You smell like one."

Noted. "I'll take a shower before I see Tony." I hold out my hand for his radio. "Let me check the battery."

"Sure, Mom." He slaps it in my palm.

I almost roll my eyes now. "How long did it take you and Maximoff to get here?" I look up, just to check on Jane.

She's lacing one boot, and her best friend ties the other for her. Both chatting and catching up like we are.

"At his pace, three hours. We would've been earlier, but we couldn't leave the house until the wind died down." Our eyes lift as snow flurries turn thick, sticking to the ground.

The sun is gone. *Not good.*

Farrow stands off the car. "The others wanted to come too."

"Her brothers?"

"No. They just wanted Maximoff to go."

That's how much the families trust him as their leader. Charlie probably didn't see a purpose in going if Maximoff was there.

"I meant Oscar, Donnelly, Quinn...Akara," Farrow tells me.

"Omega."

I freeze, hand on my mic cord, then surprise leaves me in a breeze. "For Jane," I realize.

Farrow nods. "And you."

It slams me back. Almost hard to believe. Hard to accept. "You're bullshitting me."

He laughs. "Fuck, I'd come up with better bullshit." He reaches into his pocket and pulls out a stick of gum. "Sulli was dying to go to, and the only reason they're all not here is Tony." He pops the gum in his mouth. "That dipshit was determined to rescue Jane. And most of us were concerned he'd walk into this."

This.

He's referring to me and Jane sleeping together. The twin switch could've been blown, and the consequences are heavy if Tony finds out and tells the Alpha lead. Banks could lose his job.

I could lose my job.

Tomorrow is December 20th and we're flying back to Philly. I barely have a day left pretending to be Banks. I can't fuck this up, especially this close to the end.

"So Akara told everyone to stay back and Tony listened?"

"Basically." Farrow chews gum. "Tony was fine with Maximoff and me going." He doesn't add why Tony would be okay with just them, but I already know the reason.

Farrow is essential. A doctor. And Maximoff is resilient enough that most of the team believes he could protect himself and then some.

As the weather worsens, we wrap this up and get what we need. They brought two extra packs, and we stuff some groceries in them. It should be a six-hour hike back, but that's not even what's bearing on our minds.

We all look up at the angry sky.

"Do we think this'll let up by tomorrow?" Maximoff asks.

Jane inhales, normally in preparation for a battle but none of us expected to face Mother Nature over and over again. "God, I hope so."

27

Jane Cobalt

"WHAT DO YOU MEAN we can't leave?" Beckett stops at the bottom step of the wooden staircase. Luggage is piled near the door of Mackintosh House, overloaded with backpacks, suitcases, and duffels. Our flight leaves tonight, but we're supposed to make the long car ride to the airport this afternoon.

Delayed is a kind word for what's happening here.

And unfortunately, Beckett—of all people—has risen early enough that he's stepped into an informal meeting about the situation.

My palms warm around a mug of steaming coffee, and I stand uneasily in the foyer where wet jackets hang on a coat rack and frost resembles spider-web cracks on the door's windowpanes. I'm the only female at this tense gathering, and Maximoff is the only family member of mine. Until Beckett arrives.

The other six men here are Security Force Omega: Thatcher, Akara, Farrow, Oscar, Donnelly, and Quinn.

And I wish I had better news for Beckett. He already has on a blue snow coat, Ray Bans on his head, and a duffel bag strapped across his chest.

Beckett gestures to the door, his arm gliding with more poise than hostility—even his voice is even-tempered. "The exit is right there."

I step forward. He's my brother after all, and I put him in this mess. "We're snowbound, Beckett." I explain how temperatures have fallen to the negatives, and snow and ice dominate the remote village with no reprieve just yet.

His face contorts like he can't believe what I'm saying.

Seeing my naturally calm brother look so pained drives a wedge in my ribs.

"Wait, wait." He squeezes his eyes shut, then opens them. "But we can leave in a few hours?" His chest rises and falls harder.

I open my mouth, but I struggle to say the truth that we both know exists.

Thankfully, the Omega lead steps in. "You can physically leave," Akara explains, "but you won't make it far. Every car is packed beneath snow."

"We can shovel them out," Beckett says like this is just another thick snowfall in Philly. He looks to Moffy. "You've shoveled out two-feet of snow before. This is easy for you, and I'll help."

SFO goes more rigid.

Maximoff cracks a knuckle. "It's not just the cars, Beck."

"Roads aren't plowed," I tell my brother.

Akara nods. "We have no way to reach the airport, and even if we do, the planes are probably grounded."

"*Probably*." Beckett blinks a terrible ton. "So no one knows for sure?"

I step closer, only a couple feet from him. "The phone lines are down. No one has service, not even to check the internet. But before we lost cable, Akara saw local news. They're calling this a *big freeze*, and they suggest residents and winter visitors wait out the cold front and ration provisions."

As soon as I say the word "ration," his entire face falls. Beckett steeples his fingers on the bridge of his nose and the corners of his tightened eyes.

I wince just seeing him wince. "I'm so sorry," I breathe softly. "But we'll make the best out of this…" I trail off as he shakes his head once.

Silently and kindly telling me to shut up.

I do.

Akara pushes his hair back, and the black strands fall back forward. "Look, I don't want to be the bad guy here, but no one can leave the house until the roads clear. It's just too dangerous."

Beckett drops his fingers and his pain is on me. "You told me *one* week."

I take a tight breath, the heat of eight pairs of eyes bearing down on me. Most of them are consoling, the only ones that pierce and shred are my brother's.

Suddenly, Thatcher comes up to my side, and I stare up at him like my archangel has swooped in to defend me. "Respectfully, Jane didn't know we would be snowed-in."

Beckett pinches his eyes, as though that'll change our fate. "She knew there could be a chance."

"A slim possibility," I say quietly. "If we could foresee the future, we wouldn't have brought you here."

"Bullshit," Beckett says smoothly and takes his duffel off his shoulder. "I'd *still* be here, sis. I have a hard time believing you wouldn't love a week to turn into two weeks, three weeks—however long you think it'll take for me to kick a problem that I don't have."

Thatcher almost touches me. His fingers lightly brush against mine, and I ache for his comfort. A hand in my hand.

He can't.

Not while he's pretending to be Banks. Tony or O'Malley could walk in, and the thought of the twin switch extending beyond the one-week plan...is harrowing.

My body ices over. I want to tell my brother, *I wouldn't love a week to be longer*, but possibly, he's right. Of course I'm glad he won't touch cocaine for another day.

"Janie isn't the only one that dragged you here," Maximoff says as he comes closer. "Don't just blame her for that."

Beckett rubs a hand down his face. "Trust me, I'm not feeling that kind towards you either. She's just in my line of sight." He shakes his head, upset. Frustrated. Rightfully angry. "I'm leaving in three hours."

I wince. "Beckett, you can't. We've just discussed this. The roads—"

"I don't care." He massages his tensed hands. "I'm leaving."

"Don't freak. We'll figure this out, man," Donnelly says consolingly while seated on a hard-shell suitcase.

Beckett glances at his ex-bodyguard, then cuts his yellow-green eyes to the scuffed floorboards. Their exchange only seems to flood more grief into my brother. He straps his duffel back to his chest. "Three hours, and I'm gone."

"How do you plan on going home?" Oscar wonders. "This isn't Oz. You can't click your heels."

"Helicopter," Beckett says tightly.

I gape. "That is outlandish." I'd expect that more from Charlie, but Beckett's desperation starts to cling to the air like fog.

His joints lock up. "You don't understand. None of you understand. Your jobs are here right now while mine is in another country. I can't miss any more performances." He blinks rapidly, on the verge of tears, and he keeps smearing a hand over his face. "My career is going to go to shit."

I inhale an agonizing breath, practically sucking in glass shards. *I did this.* I fucked up his life. "I'm sorry."

Maximoff gestures to my brother. "When we go home, we'll do what we can so you won't lose out on anything."

I nod. "We'll make this right."

"I don't want you two to pull strings." He takes his Ray Bans off his wavy brown hair. "I earned my spot in the company, and the only way for me to keep it is if I'm there. So I'm leaving." He glances at the grandfather clock near the staircase. "Three hours from now."

Dear God. He's still stuck to that. "Did you just pick an arbitrary time frame?" I ask. "Why not seven or eight hours from now?"

"Because I think it'll take about three hours for a helicopter to arrive."

Beckett. He's not thinking this through. We have no access to a phone or internet, and before I say so, Akara chimes in, "None of us can call for a helicopter."

Thatcher nods. "We don't have the resources right now."

My brother doesn't seem deterred. So either he's fooling himself or he has an ace in his sleeve. With a lithe movement, he spins towards the banister. "Charlie!"

Oscar shakes his head and then turns into Farrow to say, "That kid's got every helicopter and private plane service on speed dial."

Farrow whispers something back that I can't hear.

And it's not Charlie who descends the staircase into the foyer.

Joana Oliveira tosses her backpack on the growing pile. "Why does everyone look like they just got their asses kicked by me?"

Everyone is ominously silent.

"What they're not telling you," Beckett suddenly says, "is that we're stuck here."

Her face plummets. "What?" She whips to Oscar with wide, horrified eyes. "*Bro.*"

Oscar holds up a comforting hand. "I know—"

"My fight is in *two* days." Joana shakes her head in distress.

Quinn motions to his sister. "We'll get you there, Jo."

Oscar rubs his forehead, not as assured or willing to promise their sister. This has now turned into a royal *dilemma* and not how I saw this informal meeting going.

I haven't even taken a sip of coffee.

Really, I like Jo. From our short time together, I've found her put-up-or-shut-up energy very refreshing and rather amusing when directed towards SFO, who see her as a little sister. But right now, the air is very strained.

"I *can't* miss this fight," Joana emphasizes to her brothers.

Beckett tips his head to her. "Welcome to the Screwed Club."

Oscar's eyes flash with protective heat. "Beckett, watch yoursel—"

"We're not in the same situation." Joana cuts off her brother and spins on Beckett with angry brown eyes. "You're a ballerina. I have a televised fight, and if I'm not there, I have to *forfeit*. I don't have an understudy."

Beckett restrains a soft smile.

She cringes. "Are you grinning?"

"Yes," he says honestly. "Look, I don't have an understudy." He stiffens more. "I have a douchebag, asshole who's vying for my spot. If I'm not there, he'll replace me, and I'm out of work for an entire season." He inhales a sharper breath, and then he rotates to the staircase. "CHARLIE!"

Jo storms through the foyer with a blistering stride and cracks the door open. She rocks back. "Holy shit."

Cold sweeps inside like a mad, furious rage, and I block the slapping wind with a hand to my face. Until Thatcher steps in front of me and shields me from the freeze.

My pulse skips.

I've already peered outside. Where the view is an endless sea of glaring white.

"What do you want?" Charlie climbs down the stairs in nothing but a pair of boxer-briefs. He rubs at his eyes, sandy-brown hair matted from sleep.

Beckett looks over his shoulder. "Can a helicopter fly through that?" He nods his chin towards the door that Oscar begins to shut.

Charlie barely glances at it. "Not unless you want to die."

"No one leaves the house," Akara declares, speaking to his men and to my family. "I don't care where you have to be. Or how important the shit is that you're missing. No one goes anywhere until the storm ends." He stomps off, leaving uncomfortable silence in his wake.

28

Jane Cobalt

ONLY 2 DAYS AWAY from Christmas Eve, an anxious urgency permeates through Mackintosh House like an inescapable toxin. The need to be home for the holidays is a ticking clock we all hear and feel.

I speak quietly. "Charlie said he's sick of everyone. Beckett won't look at me, but Sullivan and Luna seem to be faring well. For now at least." I sit on the washer/dryer combo, a plaid tartan blanket snug around my shoulders. And I have a rare high-up view of Thatcher as he's seated on the cold tile.

Since early this morning, I've taken inventory of food, firewood, and other necessities like medicine. Thatcher and I split up most of the day to lessen Tony's suspicions about the twin swap.

I've only been in the laundry room for a couple minutes, and already, Thatcher is looking up at me with heady, concerned eyes.

"How are you doing?" he asks, his voice so very deep.

His question blooms inside me, a budding rose through the thick impenetrable ice.

I must've forgotten *myself* in the equation.

"I'm about as well as Moffy." My ribcage feels like a painful corset cinching my lungs. "Possibly better considering I'm sleeping more than he is. I love him dearly, but he's going to drive himself over an edge." My throat tightens. "It's easier knowing he has Farrow now." He's the only person who can help Moffy relax.

Thatcher assesses me. "You feel responsible for your family's well-being too." It's not a question, yet I feel the need to explain.

I shrug, tensed. "In a lot of ways, yes. But Maximoff feels more responsible since he invited everyone to Scotland, and they all believe he'll fix this more than they think I will."

His frown is a dark scowl. "You help out just as much as him."

"He's the leader. I'm just the second-in-command, and really, I'm lucky. I don't envy his position, and I definitely don't *want* that pressure." I quickly add, "How's SFO doing?" I don't know why I'm so uncomfortable talking about myself right now.

He skims me, the scrutiny scalding me in the chilly laundry room. It's the second coldest place in the house, the first being the cellar. "Most of the team hasn't racked out in over 24-hours either."

Our bodyguards bear a great responsibility for my family's welfare too. And there's strange comfort in knowing it isn't just Moffy and me holding down the fort.

Two men who we desperately love and trust are helping us. Plus, the rest of Omega.

I try to take a breath.

Skin pleats between his focused eyes. "You look scared."

I attempt to swallow *fear*, but it fists me. And I realize he captured the emotion that has me deflecting. How smart he is—this man of mine.

I inhale. "I am."

He starts to stand—and quickly, I hold out a hand. "Please, don't. You're busy." He has a laptop on his muscular legs, and the laundry room had the best reception before we lost all signal from the storm.

Thatcher's been tasked with pressing *refresh* on a webpage. SFO has taken turns trying to send an email to our families. A futile effort really, considering we don't have internet. But he's not a man who'd disobey these kind of orders, and I don't want him to start for me.

Thatcher reluctantly stays seated. "Talk to me then."

I blow out a loud breath, puffing my cheeks. "I'm afraid what happens *after*."

"After?"

"After my brothers and cousins realize that we're most likely going to be stuck in Scotland for Christmas. After we actually are. Because it means this is the second Christmas we're not in Philly."

Last year, we were all on a tour bus.

I continue, "The second Christmas we miss Xander's birthday, the second Christmas I've taken from *you*."

Thatcher sends me a stern look. "You've taken nothing from me, Jane."

"Christmas Eve is your grandma's favorite holiday, and who knows how many you'll have left with her—and yes, I didn't know how she fawns over Christmas while we were on tour." I speak hastily. "But I know that now, and I know how much she wants you there, and now you won't be. Not alone or with me." I do the best I can to keep eye-contact.

His intense gaze isn't defeating me.

It wraps me.

Tightly.

Protectively, and oh God, I wish I never told him to sit back down. Because I also love that he's willing to break orders for me.

Constantly.

Even now.

He nods a few times. "I won't lie to you."

"Good," I say pointedly.

"Good," he repeats, "because you need to hear that you're right. We're probably not making it home for Christmas, but you didn't take *time* away from me or anyone else. We're just spending a holiday with other people. And if my grandma doesn't make the next Christmas…" He pauses, his jaw muscle twitching. "I have enough memories of us together to last a lifetime." He softens his gaze. "I could just as likely die tomorrow. And I'd want to spend my final moments next to you."

My body caves, then rises. His declaration pricks tears, but the thought of him dying nearly doubles me over. I straighten up. "If I were to die, I'd want you beside me too. And also Banks."

"Banks?" His furrow-browed confusion is cute.

"You'd need your brother after I died, and I'd want someone there for you."

His affection for me flows out so apparently. He padlocks nothing, and his *love*, so powerful and frightening, begins to eliminate the anxious toxins around us.

Thatcher glances briefly at the laptop, then me. "I'm revising what I said."

A smile spreads across my face. "Let's hear it, then."

"If I were to die tomorrow, I'd also want Maximoff there."

For me.

If a heart could sigh happily, mine just did. The pressure that's taken residence on my body begins to gradually subside.

I smile more and quirk a brow. "Are you copying me, Mr. Moretti?"

He is all masculinity and confidence. "Just following your lead, honey."

My boyfriend has never been sexier. His gray sweatpants draw my eyes downward, molding his muscles and well-endowed assets. And ladies and gentlemen, he's not wearing underwear.

Evidence: *the defined outline of his incredibly large cock.*

Carnal desire flames my skin, but I banish any and all *want* from my face. I respect his job, and I'd rather not tempt him.

I tuck a flyaway hair behind my ear, my fingers skimming my *hot* cheek. *You're too flushed, Jane.* "So…" I smooth my lips.

"So…" He almost smiles and presses a key on the laptop. "You okay?"

"Yes." *Touch me.* My heartbeat dips between my legs. I cross my thighs and accidentally tangle up in the tulle of my purple skirt. *Course correct.* "I think my brothers and Sulli are hopeful that we'll be home soon because of the satellite phone." I stop fighting with my skirt. "Though, Akara hasn't found a spot outside that won't block the signal yet. But I still can't believe Oscar brought one."

Thatcher looks unsurprised. "He started packing a sat-phone when Charlie spent a week in a dead zone in Mongolia."

"I had no idea Charlie traveled there." I'm not shocked that this is new information for me.

My curiosity piques. "How much more do you know?"

"About Charlie?"

"Oui."

Thatcher stretches out his bent leg. "Not a lot. Mostly his location while I was a lead, and even that didn't always come in…" He trails off a little, watching me unearth a bottle of whiskey from beneath my blanket. "Where'd you get that?"

"I swiped it from the cellar. Second to last bottle." I swish the liquid, then uncap it and put the rim to my lips. Warm liquid runs down my throat, and I wipe my mouth with the back of my hand.

Thatcher stares at me like the clouds have parted and I've descended from the sky.

I blush under his heated stare. "What?"

"You're the hottest woman I've ever been with," he says like a fact. *Point-blank*, as he sometimes adds.

I pulse. "I'm learning new things about you every day." My lips rise. "Thatcher Moretti finds whiskey-drinking hot." I take another sip.

"*You* drinking whiskey from a bottle is hot," he clarifies. "And you just existing is fucking hot."

"Likewise," I murmur, sweating beneath my blanket. "Did you know arousal increases body temperature?" I blurt out like a helpful but embarrassing factoid. "Of course you do," I quickly add and roast thinking about our nightlong sex in the car. "It's an obvious…" I watch his eyes dip down the length of me. "…fact."

I stop breathing.

He stands.

"Thatcher—" I cut myself off as he grips the opened laptop. Not letting go of his orders, his duty. But he locks the door to the laundry room. His strides are confident and purposeful, and I'm like a cat clawing onto every inch he moves.

He comes up to the washer/dyer and grabs the whiskey bottle from my hand. And he sets the laptop on a pile of folded bath towels. In distance to refresh the webpage.

He swigs the whiskey, then places the bottle aside.

Now he's so near. I clutch his muscular shoulders while his arms wrap around my waist.

His scent dizzies me: wood smoke and cinnamon. He usually doesn't smell like the latter, and I take a deep sniff of his white tee.

Our eyes suddenly meet mid-sniff, and it's not the first time I've been caught inhaling his scent. Still, I flush like I'm baking under the sun.

"You smell different—not in a bad way," I clarify quickly. "Just different. You have notes of cinnamon, which isn't your typical scent. I don't think…is it?"

Thatcher doesn't answer immediately. Instead, he's quiet as he leans past me, his arm brushing my shoulder as he flicks on the washer/dryer.

It rumbles to life beneath my ass.

Dear God.

My body shakes with the vibration.

Arousal builds, and I inhale another lungful of his scent. "It's more of a feminine fragrance than what you wear…" I freeze.

All rational thinking vacates my brain. Because *rationally*, I trust Thatcher and know he'd never cheat on me. *Rationally*, there are only three other girls in this house, and two are my cousins.

There has to be another reason.

Yet, my mind places him in this moment with other girls. Where he's loving, sexy, and assured, all for them. My stomach overturns and clenches.

I could never share him with another woman, I realize.

"Luna was spraying her body mist in the living room." He seizes my gaze with a look of unadulterated fealty. He must know what I was concluding, and instead of being hurt at the unwarranted assumption, he just wants to reassure me.

I love him.

I expect fear to be exterminated at the thought of love and Thatcher, but a bit lingers. Like a thorny vine ensnared around my heart, one my head refuses to snip.

Give yourself to him.

He can't promise that I won't lose my agency. It's something that I have to work through on my own, and what if it takes years?

At least I understand the fear. I suppose that's the first step in learning to let go and move forward. I just hope I can.

I nod, easing some. "It does smell like Luna."

"She said she was winterizing the house, and I got hit with it." He grips the back of his white tee, pulling the fabric off over his head. His sculpted abs come into view, dog tags lying against natural hair on his chest.

He spreads my thighs in one swift movement, my dangling legs no longer obstructing the washer door. My lungs expand and contract in heavy waves.

His hand brushes away my blanket and tulle skirt—to plant on my bare thigh like it has found a home, a resting place, a heaven and hell and will not move unless some exorcist performs a ritual.

If eyes could be lip-locked, ours are attached in desirous, soul-bound fashion, and I'm not ready to look to the left or right.

I just want him.

His fingers press into my soft flesh as he tosses the shirt in the washer/dryer, and then he knees the door shut. "I don't want to smell like Luna's body mist."

"Fair point," I breathe.

My eyes glide down his chest, and a thousand animalistic thoughts stampede in my head. There are risks involved with having sex in the laundry room with Thatcher who's pretending to be Banks.

Yet...

"Thatcher." His name is throaty and desperate off my lips, and my arms swoop back around his neck. He shoves into the embrace. Until our lips unite in a blistering, soul-bodied kiss. His fingers on top of my panties, massaging me above the fabric.

A moan strangles our kiss.

My moan.

His free hand cups the back of my head, strong and controlled. He deepens the intensity of the kiss like he can put my noises to bed.

The muscles in my belly tighten. Nerves firing in too many places to make sense. The friction on my clit, the vibration under my bottom, the taste of him on my lips—it's a full-body sensation and I'm being submerged under it all.

Between our kisses, I remind him, "Your laptop."

He reaches out and sightlessly refreshes the page.

I scoot closer into his hand between my legs. But also so I can clutch his ass. I dive my hands beneath his sweatpants and bite his bicep.

"*Fuck*," he grunts and his eyes make love to me a thousand different ways.

He tears off my peach-hued blouse, then pulls up my bra to my collarbones. In one swoop, my breasts are exposed to the chilly air, and I'm grinding into his hand. "*Please.*"

He holds the back of my head like I'm his to protect. And to love and to supply *many* earth-shattering orgasms.

He curls the crotch of my panties aside, his large fingers pulsing in me, and I let out a whimper, my limbs trembling. His other thumb feels feather-light over my hardened nipple.

"*Jane.*" He says my name like he's already fucking it.

Wetness pools between my thighs, and I see the sheer length of his hardness against his sweatpants.

Oh…

My.

His lips crash against mine again. Hands begin exploring. I move away from his ass to take hold of his cock, his waistband falling low past his muscular hips.

I rub him in deep long strokes. He curses under his breath, and I want him in me too fiercely. Our bodies are reacting in hungered need for closer contact. *In me.*

Please.

I pull his fingers out.

Scooting forward, my ass is near the edge of the washer, and with my other hand around his shaft, I begin to lead his tip into me.

Thatcher takes hold of his cock, quickly stopping me. His strict eyes bear down on me. "Jane." He grinds down his teeth, forcing back arousal. He takes a giant breath through his nose. "I'm not wearing a condom."

My lower abdomen contracts. "Merde."

We've never had sex without a condom, and I'm not buying into the theory that it'll feel miraculously better without one. I'd rather be safe, most especially since I'm not on birth control.

But in this very moment, I can't fathom him moving away from me. I'm willing to leap off a deep-end with Thatcher, no matter how terrifying.

"You can pull out." My body is on fire as the words leave my lips.

He's already shaking his head, and he squats down where I left my purse. He knows I keep condoms there, and his hand—his hand glides down with him. He holds my ankle like he refuses to let go of me.

Seconds later, he stands upright, all six-foot-seven of him, and he tears the foil packet with his teeth. He stops suddenly. Concern piercing his eyes. "What's wrong?"

I realize I'm wincing. "I offered the pull-out method. Statistically speaking, one in five people who do pull-out get pregnant." I know those facts by heart because I looked them up when I was fifteen and it's been drilled in my head ever since. "But I offered it like it was nothing." I shiver.

He rubs my shoulders for heat. "Because you trust me, Jane. You don't need to feel guilty."

I trust him. With my life.

With my *body*.

I'm so willing to just lay down on a freeway for him, and maybe it is trust because I'm certain he'll stand in front of traffic protecting me. But it's something else too. Because smart people don't choose to lie down on busy roads.

An overwhelmed feeling avalanches suddenly and brims water in my eyes. "I don't...know what this is..." I touch my chest, pressure mounting. But I do.

I know exactly what it is.

I'm just terrified that I've already given my entire self to him. And what if I'm half of what I was? What if...what if I'm not ready?

Thatcher keeps his hand on my thigh. "Take a breath. *Jane*. Look at me." My eyes cement on him and he inhales deeply. His chest rising.

I follow him and do the same. My head feels light as air. I wipe my cheeks. He probably thought this insecurity was resolved. "I'm being unfair—"

"No."

"You don't deserve—"

"Jane." His eyes redden. "I love you. I'm here for these moments. Every fucking one. We're going through fear, shame, guilt, back to fear *together*. A hundred, million times if we need to."

I feel like my ribcage is cracking in two.

We stare at one another for a long moment, just timing our breaths. The washing machine thunders below me.

"What if love makes me do stupid things?" I mumble. "Like almost having sex with you without a condom."

"That wasn't stupid." His features harden. "It was in the heat of the moment, and I would try to stop you if I knew you were doing something you wouldn't normally do, just because of love." He presses his lips to mine, slow and sensual. Our kiss igniting a smothered flame. He breaks apart just to whisper, "I'm going to protect you. Sempre toujours."

I breathe in, shock and something stronger crashing into me.

Sempre toujours.

The first word is Italian, the second French.

It means, *always always.*

"Sempre toujours," I repeat, letting the combination of the two sink in deeply.

His reassurance shouldn't be so comforting. Shouldn't fill me up. But it's the perfect remedy, and I'm ready once more.

"I still want to." I nod to the condom. "If you do."

Headiness coats his gaze, and the washing machine stops suddenly, the cycle finished.

I freeze.

He checks the door and simultaneously refreshes the webpage. *No internet.*

My ears catch muffled voices, but they seem rather far away. Thatcher reaches around my body to switch the dial again. Vibrations crawl through me like they live inside my limbs and veins.

I hold onto his carved biceps. "I've never really craved anal," I admit. "But this is…it feels really good and kind of makes me more curious."

The corner of his lip rises, a shadow of smile. "I've been waiting for you to ask me."

Now I'm truly intrigued. "You think I'd like it?"

"No idea." He sheaths his length. "But I know you're too curious not to try." He must see the deep *interest* in me. "Just tell me how soon."

"Today," I say without pause. "After one vaginal orgasm." I'm so eager and invested in this adventure that he lets out a laugh.

"I'll fuck you better than just *one.*" He fits between my legs, his erection pressing against my inner-thigh. He sweeps me in a quick once-over. "You're gonna need to hold onto something."

I look around. Nothing really to grip. Not even above me. "I'll be fine." I'm confident about this.

Thatcher stares at me with a hard look.

"I'm not a porcelain doll—"

He pounds into me, and I immediately reach behind my back, planting a hand on the washer. "Ahh," I choke on a cry, trying to be quiet. Pure pleasure rattles my senses.

His jaw tightens, gritting back a groan.

My thighs are in his strong grasp, and he thrusts in hard, quick movements. Bursting the nerves along my skin like cracking embers.

Slowly each one catches fire to my body, and an orgasm already rips through me.

My spine arches, and I shudder. *God.*

Fuck.

Ahhh… "*Ahh.*" I can't capture that noise, and he covers my mouth.

Sure enough, he was right: I don't have a good grip. I fall back onto my elbows. Breasts exposed, skirt still on. Panties not even stripped off but pushed aside. It's the raunchy sex I lust for, and I have the best view. He crashes into me with primal need, his jaw tensed and nose flared, breath mixing with curses.

His cock slides past my cervix—*oh God.* Lights dance in my vision as he finds *the* spot of my dreams. And he repeatedly pushes against the nerve-spindling place in rhythmic bliss and skill.

He annihilates me. Body and soul.

I lose time to pleasure. Pleasure to flesh. Until I'm melting under carnal sensations. All sweat and skin and pressured points.

After another wave of euphoria, I can't hold myself up on my elbows any longer. I collapse to my back, and Thatcher slows, eking out the movement while I climax *again.*

He kisses the inside of my thigh, and still hard, he pulls out. I try to catch my breath.

"Too spent?" he asks.

"Not at…" I pant. "All." I stare at his erection. He puts on a new condom and finds lube packets in my purse and warms them between his hands. "Ready?"

"Yes." Curiosity returns tenfold. I wonder how different it'll feel to have him inside my ass.

He hooks his ankle around a wooden stepstool and slides it over.

"How does this work?" I wonder. "Not the mechanisms of anal, just the position I need to be in."

"Come here." He holds my waist, and gently, he brings me down the washer/dyer. My feet touch the stepstool, and I feel so safe here. With him.

Thatcher bites open the packet. "I'll bend you over, and you'll brace yourself on the washer. We're at a good height. Copy?"

"Oui." I smile, excitement flip-flopping my nerves, and he turns me around. So I face the washer/dryer, and I grab hold to the machine.

With his ankle, he pulls the stepstool back just slightly. I'm sufficiently bent over for him, and I crane my neck over my shoulder. Watching very keenly as he lubes himself, then teases open my hole with his finger. His grip on my ass is protective, caring, and cautious.

He eases his cock in, not far at all, and I don't have the best view, but it can't be more than a half an inch. And then he pulls out. Breath caged, I continue to watch. Slowly, he slides in a bit deeper, gradually and carefully expanding me. And with his size, the pressure is…

I wince into my arm.

Excruciating. Like a hammer is being jammed into me.

He stops suddenly, pulled fully out.

"Keep going," I urge. "I want to feel more."

"It's not going to hurt any less."

I cringe at the idea. Pain doesn't bring me pleasure, but my fascination isn't exactly quenched. "Just a few more inches." I haven't even taken half of him.

"Hell no." He snaps off his condom. "This isn't *curiosity fucked the cat.* If it hurts, I stop."

"Wise words." I face him, and he's already lifting me up. My back on the washer, legs over his shoulders as he bends in a lunge—he eats me out with such skill, and I turn my head, seeing him jack himself off.

Yes.

This is better.

I would give him a world-class hand-job, but I'm not in reach. And I think he'd rather make my eyes roll back. Which they do.

Again.

We're well and good. He reaches a peak, coming in his palm, and in the next few minutes, he has time to wash his hands and we clean up and begin to dress.

Bang!

I jump.

His head turns to the door. The bang is just a knock.

"Oh my God." I touch my heart to see if it's still inside me. *Still beating.* We finish putting on clothes at rapid-speed.

Just please don't be Tony.

Please.

29

Jane Cobalt

AFTER THATCHER UNLOCKS the door, Akara enters, his red jacket wet. Snowflakes melt in his black hair, and ice crystalizes on his eyelashes.

Just seeing him makes me shiver. I pull my blanket back on my shoulders and clutch the whiskey.

Akara glances from Thatcher to me, back to Thatcher.

"We're not staying alone together for that long," Thatcher tells his lead. "I have a timer set on my watch."

One hour.

We both agreed on the timeframe, and I bet we only have minutes left.

Akara shrugs off his jacket. "I wouldn't push it any longer than that. Tony has already asked some of the guys if they thought you were acting weird."

Thatcher nods and looks him over. "You found signal?"

"Yep. On the east end of the property."

"How deep?"

"A hundred feet from the bird feeder."

My mouth drops. "That far?"

"Yeah." He throws his jacket in the hamper and blows on his palms. "Without walls blocking the spot, it's freezing. I couldn't spend more than five minutes there. But I spoke to Connor."

I sway back. "You called my dad?" Out of all people, Akara chose to reach out to him.

Thatcher frowns. "You didn't call Price or Sinclair?" *The Alpha and Epsilon leads.*

"I could only stand out there long enough to make two calls, and they were my third and fourth." He speaks too urgently for me to interject. "Connor is going to relay our status to the families. I explained that we're fine and waiting out the storm. On his end, he's going to try and have people come up here and clear the roads...but this storm is *bad.*"

"How bad?" I swallow whiskey as tension mounts.

"Last time the snow fell this hard here, residents were stuck indoors for months."

My jaw is on the floor. "Months?"

"Until March."

"March?" My eyes have now joined my jaw. They live on the ground. I thought the only true fight we'd have is against boredom, but if we're here past the New Year...

I picture my brothers going mad.

I picture Sulli terribly homesick.

And my cats...

They're with Audrey. My sister is taking good care of them, but I worry. It's not like I can easily call her and ask how they're doing. What if one is sick? What if something happens while I'm away?

My maternal concern to six furry children escalates to new heights. Worse even: we don't have enough food for seventeen people for *that* long.

I find my voice. "How did we not prepare for this?"

"We couldn't have known," Thatcher says strongly.

"I feel like a straight-A student who forgot to do her homework for an entire year," I say aloud. "There's precedent for snowstorms in this area, apparently."

"This isn't an annual occurrence here," Akara tells me. "It's only happened twice in the last thirty years." He grabs the doorknob, about to leave. "One more thing." His eyes are on mine. "I had to tell your dad about Beckett."

My stomach somersaults, and I down another gulp of sharp whiskey. "Which part?" I lick the liquor off my lips. "That he wants a helicopter to fly him out of here? Or that we forced him on this trip because of his cocaine use?"

Akara gives me an apologetic wince. "Both."

Merde. I fist the neck of the bottle.

"He didn't seem surprised about either," Akara says. "But with your dad…"

"It's hard to tell," I nod.

My incredibly intelligent father vaults his emotions like secrets inside Fort Knox. If he were shocked, he most likely wouldn't let Akara know. It's entirely possible that my dad and mom sniffed out the situation since Beckett took off dance for Scotland.

Which is a rarity in itself.

I can't predict what they'll do once Beckett goes home, but I feel like I've thrown him in boiling hot water when I only intended a light simmer to start.

Akara continues, "Connor said if things get serious, they can send a rescue team. But it's not advisable unless someone's safety is at risk. Other people need those resources, and I consulted with Jack. He said a helicopter picking up rich white kids stuck in a million-dollar house would be bad publicity."

Those headlines and the fallout could destroy Beckett's career more than a couple absent weeks from ballet. My brother has been banking on the skies to clear, not wanting to wait for road transportation. But the helicopter scenario is solidly down the drain.

"You have to tell Beckett," I say. "I can't do it. He won't want to hear it from me."

Akara agrees and then turns to Thatcher. "The snow is accumulating, and today might be the only time we can exit the door without having to shovel our way out. Anyone who needs to use the sat-phone, needs to use it *today*."

Thatcher glances at the door.

Akara adds, "I've already spoken to your brother."

"What?"

"He was my second call." Akara pushes back his wet hair, visibly shivering. I lean towards him and outstretch the bottle of whiskey. He's not exactly on-duty while we're in a secure house, so he takes the bottle with a quick, "Thanks." And downs a large gulp. "Banks is fine. He doesn't want either of you to go call him."

Thatcher glares at the ceiling, then rolls his eyes.

"He's more concerned about you." Akara passes back the whiskey. "Said to tell you not to be a dumbass or a jackass. But we both know it's too late for that." He steps out of his wet snow pants, sweats underneath, and the door to the laundry room creaks open wider.

My pulse thumps in my throat. If Tony just overheard us...

"Hey."

I calm as soon as I see the chestnut hair and tattoos of Paul Donnelly.

"Any of you know how to sew?" He raises a sweater, and I recognize the orange and green stitching as Luna's handiwork. One she knitted for him in exchange for a tattoo design. "I pulled out a thread and now there's a hole." He seems laidback about the whole ordeal.

"No," Thatcher answers him.

Donnelly looks to me.

"Unfortunately, I can barely thread a needle. Luna and Beckett are the only ones I know who could fix it."

His face saddens at the mention of Beckett, and then he nods to Akara. "Got any thrifty nifty skills, boss?"

Akara cracks a crooked smile. "Not at sewing."

Donnelly throws up a hand gesture that means *love*, like he didn't just meet bad news, and he struts out of the room, as unconcerned as he came.

Akara nods to Thatcher. "You're relieved of your duties. With the sat-phone working, we don't need to worry about emails." He leaves, not giving Thatcher a chance to reply.

Their friendship is still on shaky ground, and I wish I could help, but their issues seem too deep and personal.

With Akara's abrupt exit, the laundry room becomes eerily quiet, and then feet pound above us, dust billowing off ceiling rafters. Voices heighten in chaotic madness.

"Something's wrong." Thatcher finds his radio. Comms work only inside the house, and he fits in his earpiece.

I climb off the washer/dryer and pick up my purse. Readying. I wait for his response, my pulse gaining speed.

His eyes land on me. "Pipe burst."

I wonder if this is an omen of what's to come. Broken pipes, interpersonal fights, and all of us just trying to hang on...till March?

"We shouldn't tell my brothers that we could be here for months."

"Agreed."

30

Thatcher Moretti

"'TELL US IF YOU'VE ever paid for sex.'" I read a lion-decaled card out loud and gnaw harder on a fucking toothpick. Which I'm *only* chewing because Tony keeps walking past the parlor. He thinks my brother is standing in for me with the Truth or Dare game.

Oscar and Farrow lean on the doorframe, deterring Tony from entering to bug the holy hell out of me. And the dwindling deck of cards is spread over a baby grand piano, where Jane and I stand close (but not too close).

Charlie sits at the piano and slides his fingers over the keys. "And?"

I focus back on the card. And the girl beside me. Jane perches her hands on her hips, sweater pink and fuzzy, and a 50s checkered scarf is tied around her neck.

I'd give her a Best Dressed award every day, every time. No contest.

She smiles up at me. "You first?"

Easy. "I've never paid for sex."

She tells me, "Neither have I." Her whole face brightens, treasuring a common fact that we share, and I try to force my affection in a cramped box.

Don't go there.

Being stoic used to be too easy, but I have a serious problem now. I can't look at Jane Cobalt with a blank expression—not when I'm engulfed with affection that ranges from innocent *my-heart-is-yours* to sensual *I-want-to-fuck-you-on-this-piano*.

Counteract this shit.

I stare at the window. Where heavy drapes frame a snow-piled landscape, so glaringly white that it practically sears the eye.

Christmas Eve is tomorrow, and as we all take breaks from executing "escape plans"—Jane's cousins and siblings have slowly started to realize we can't defeat Mother Nature. We have to wait, and the team now has a new objective.

Keep morale high.

Not just among bodyguards.

No one wants their client to be sad or moping during the holiday, and if we can make this snowed-in catastrophe easy for them, we'll try.

Charlie plucks the card from my fingers. He burns it in a glass cup.

Arms crossed, I glance to my three o'clock. Sensing Tony's presence, and sure enough, he lingers near the doorframe. His arrogant smirk on me.

I glare.

Oscar chats with him.

"Ignore Tony," Jane whispers. "He's bored and looking for entertainment."

I nod once and bite harder on the toothpick. I hate the taste. I hate how my jaw aches, but I could hug Banks for his obsession with these motherfuckers because it's a shield that could help me through the extended snowstorm. How is Banks doing pretending to be *me* in Philly? ...I can't know.

Hopefully he's kept his head up. It's hard not to worry about him.

Jane starts to gather the deck off the piano.

"We're not done," Charlie declares and bangs a high-pitched key. "Leave them there. Choose another."

I eye Tony. He's out of earshot, but he gesticulates towards us and speaks to Oscar. My best guess: he's asking what Banks (aka *me*) and Jane are doing over here. You know, just playing with Truth or Dare cards.

Talking about sex.

A weird thing for my brother to be doing alone with my girlfriend.

Clear-cut, the risk has just heightened, and we've been toying with trouble enough.

"Later," I tell Charlie.

"No. Now."

"Charlie," Jane says hotly. "This is serious."

"So is this." His left hand presses keys, playing a melodic classical tune. "You should *thank me*, I'm giving you ample time to spend with your—"

"*Charlie*," she hisses, wide-eyed.

"He can't hear us over the music."

Maybe, and that's a weak *maybe*.

"And anyway, he already thinks you're sleeping with both Moretti brothers. This won't make a difference."

"God," she winces and sends me an apologetic look.

I'm used to it, and I just make a fast decision. "Let's do it."

"Really?" Her eyes bug more.

"Yeah." Through all this Tony horseshit, these cards have strangely brought Jane and I closer—and I want to flip another.

She pulls back her shoulders. "We'll carry on then—" Her voice cuts off, and our heads turn at the thundering sound of indoor *jogging*.

Five people pass the doorway in workout gear. Sulli, Maximoff, Will, Quinn, and Joana.

While Maximoff jogs past, Farrow gives him a blatant once-over, and we all watch Maximoff trip on a rug.

Everyone laughs, and my lip begins to lift.

"Jesus Christ," Maximoff curses. "You didn't see that."

"I definitely did," Farrow teases.

I stare down at Jane. She's radiant seeing their love, and the only reprieve I can give myself is this: I didn't ruin Maximoff and Farrow. I would've *never* forgiven myself if I had been a cause to rip them apart, but those two—they're unshakable.

I'm jealous of how good Farrow is at navigating rough terrain in relationships. I feel about as graceful as an ox on a ship.

Those five start to jog away. Footsteps trailing in the distance.

Luna Hale nicknamed that group "House Fit" since they've been running through hallways and up and down stairs. Sulli invited me, but I have little patience for group workouts unless a punching bag or gloves are involved.

Normally Akara would join the runners, and I'm not sure why he declined. Beckett is also noticeably missing from House Fit. His absence isn't a mystery.

Sulli invited everyone *but* him.

I hear piano music, and I focus back on Charlie. I want to be there for Jane's brothers, so I leap over a professional line and ask, "How's Beckett?"

Charlie blinks for a long second and then motions to the spread cards. "Pick one."

Jane glares on my behalf. "He asked you a question."

"And I chose not to answer it." Charlie breathes into a tired sigh. "As is my right to choose."

"Well, I'd also like to know how Beckett is doing," Jane snaps. "He won't talk to anyone but you."

Charlie plays an angrier melody with one hand. "Let's be thankful he's talking to me then. Because if he were smarter, he wouldn't be. I'm just as complicit in bringing him here." He looks to me. "Put me out of my fucking misery and pick."

I tried.

I peel a card off the piano and hand it to Jane.

She reads, "'Tell us if you believe in love at first sight. Explain.'" Her eyes are like saucers, and my pulse pounds in my ears.

"We don't have to agree here," I remind Jane before either of us answer. "It doesn't mean we're incompatible."

"Right." She nods, more confidently. "It just means we view love differently, and two adults can have different opinions on love and still have feelings for each other."

"Right," I confirm, feeling Tony watching us from the door.

Charlie hits louder keys on the piano.

"Right." She wafts her sweater. "My answer is *no*. I don't believe in love at first sight, not as much as I believe in fascination at first sight. Which I felt with you—which, you must know." She blushes. "Right?"

I shake my head. "I didn't know."

Don't stare below her neck. Don't look at her like that. I narrow my eyes on the window, and I revisit our first encounter at the Hale house. How she was frazzled but poised, how she tried to capture and harness her black cat. Did I think that someone like me—poor Italian-American trash, too serious, too stern, fresh out of war—would interest an American princess?

No.

Before I start reevaluating our first encounter, I remind myself that she was *seventeen*. For fuck's sake.

"You helped me with my cat," she says like a fact, cheeks beet-red as I look back down at her.

"I did," I say. "She's a cute cat."

Jane can't holster a smile.

I ask straight out, "I fascinated you from the beginning?"

She nods. "You very much did."

This is when I'd pick her up and carry her towards heaven, but we're still living inside my hell. Where I can't touch the woman I love.

Charlie drills his eyes into me. "It's your turn."

I tell her the answer. "I don't believe in love at first sight either." But I also can't imagine a time where I wouldn't love Jane.

Her brows crinkle. "Why not?"

"I can't love someone until I know them. Attraction—that's not love."

She smiles. "I concur."

I stop short from adding more. I might if her brother weren't here. I'd say how attraction is just my cock wanting pussy. It's my hands wanting her body. It's my ears wanting her voice and to be drowned out by her. It's lust.

Love is more.

It's the days I wake up, feeling a need, an urgency to protect her. Not just her body but her spirit—her entire soul. It's the days I imagine losing her, and I'm met with a bottomless empty, nothing there but hollow numbness.

Worse than death.

It's the days I yearn for her laugh, for her companionship, and thoughts. It's every day she makes me feel worthy of her and this life. All of it and more.

Charlie rubs at the edges of his eyes, almost irritably. "Pick another."

"We can break," Jane suggests for him.

"No." He points at the deck.

She draws a card and passes it to me. I glance at the words.

Fuck.

No.

My jaw hardens.

"It's that bad?" Jane wonders.

I rake a hand over my mouth before reading, "'Tell us if you've seen a Rose Calloway and Connor Cobalt sex tape.'" I solidify.

Worry cinches my girlfriend's eyes.

Shit.

Is this a deal-breaker question? Will my answer put a chink in our relationship? And I wonder if that's the purpose of these cards: to make sure I'm the perfect man for Jane.

I go cold. Colder than the already frigid-ass room.

Jane shifts her weight uneasily.

She can't read me. I'm suddenly a fortress unwilling to be unlocked, and I'm aware that's the opposite intent of Truth or Dare.

Jane addresses her brother, "I haven't seen any of the tapes. Nor do I ever want to."

Charlie cocks his head. "You never stumbled on one?"

She gapes. "Have *you?*"

"A thumbnail," Charlie admits. "I didn't click into it. I'm not that much of a fucking masochist."

I'm not either, but things were different when I was a teenager.

I didn't know the Hales, Meadows, and Cobalts.

I didn't know *her*.

Charlie sizes me up. "And?"

Jane frowns. "Thatcher?"

"I didn't go looking for it," I explain, my voice void of emotion. "Guys in my unit were playing a clip. I saw maybe three minutes." I can barely even remember the images in my head. It was just another porno that my platoon laughed at or jerked off to. It didn't mean anything then.

Her jaw is unhinged. Completely fucking *shocked*. "You didn't…"

"I did," I say again.

"Oh my God." She cringes, fingers steepled to her lips. "You've seen my parents having sex."

I grimace. "Yeah."

I think she already believed I'd *never* watch one of their porn tapes. Because the man I am now would *never*. But I was eighteen. I was just a kid, and I didn't know then what I know now.

"You didn't look away?" she asks, confusion and hurt cinching her eyes.

I'm hurting her, and it's like stepping across broken glass, rolling around in it, willfully slicing and tearing apart my flesh.

"I didn't look away," I confirm. "I was eighteen. Back then, it was just porn to me."

Deep wrinkles crease her forehead in a frown, and she shakes her head. "But you knew how their sex tapes came about. They didn't consent to have them taken. They were illegally filmed and *leaked* online."

My throat feels like sandpaper. "I didn't know that until I started working for your families. Honestly, I didn't know much about your parents except the basics."

She's quiet, and I think she's just in her head.

But goddammit, I feel like I'm fucking this up. So I fight to say more. "It probably seems like common sense—that if someone knows about those sex tapes, they must know how they originated. But the un-fucking-fortunate truth is, people didn't care about those details enough to share them."

Charlie plays a dramatic song on the piano while eyeing me. Having a third-party witnessing my inability to speak is just the cherry on top of this shit pie.

Jane lets out a breath, shoulders dropping. "I understand." She nods. "It'd be wildly self-absorbed to think that everyone knows every little thing about my family. Most people aren't doing deep-dive wiki searches on Rose and Connor Cobalt." She nods again, certain about this.

"Did you get off on it?" Charlie suddenly asks.

Jane chokes on a noise. "Charlie!"

"It's porn, Jane. It's there to arouse. I'm just asking what our brothers would want to know for the sake of this game."

"For the sake of your own curiosity," Jane counters.

"That too." Charlie is unabashed.

I run my fingers through my hair. "No, I didn't jerk off to it."

"Because there were other people in the room?" Charlie asks.

Jane groans and flashes me an apologetic look.

I'm fine, honey. "Because I didn't. It was ten years ago. If you want to know if I was hard, I don't remember. Is that good enough?"

"I'm satisfied with your answer, if Jane is."

"I'm highly satisfied, thank you," she says without hesitation. She's what I care most about, and she gives me an assured nod.

I didn't completely fuck this into the ground. That's something.

"One more." Charlie nods towards the cards.

I pick the last one and I silently read the words.

Take three nudes and send them to Jane.

Unholy fucking *shit*.

"Charlie, he can't do this," Jane says after reading the card in my grip.

I can.

I will.

I'm not worried about me. I'm concerned about *her*. She can't join me in this. Not a fucking chance. Her brothers might have thought twice about this card, had they known she'd be a part of the game.

Charlie's shoulders rise in an apathetic shrug. "Then he loses."

"I'm doing it." Resoluteness bleeds from every word.

"What?" Her lips part, eyes widening tenfold. "You want to?"

"I'm happy to send you nudes of myself. It's not a problem."

"You're certain?" She's in a daze, disbelieving.

"Yeah." It's easy for me. I meant what I told her on tour—when my bare ass and the nickname *jockstrap* circulated online and on entertainment TV. I didn't care.

I was just glad it didn't happen to her.

She smiles but as her turn to make a decision approaches, her lips falter and flat-line.

I wait for Jane to tell me that this is something she absolutely *can't* do. Can't fathom. We just went through a whole discussion about her parent's sex tapes, ones that were *leaked* online. I know Jane's feelings about nudes.

I know she wouldn't dare. Not for a second. Because as soon as there are naked photos of her on any device, she's created a probability where they could be leaked. No matter how small that probability, it's always been too great a risk for her.

I know that.

I've heard those words verbatim from her lips to my ears.

She was my client.

She *is* my girlfriend.

So right now, Jane lifts her chin and eyes on my eyes, she tells me, "I'll do it, too."

I bite down too hard and break the toothpick in half.

31

Jane Cobalt

3 DAYS SNOWED-IN

THATCHER SPITS OUT his broken toothpick.

If he's willing to shed his clothes and take nudes, then I surely can do the same. We're equals.

Right?

I'm frozen. Collarbones jutted out, eyes perilously big. I imagine bracing the weather outside would feel better than my iced-over bewilderment.

Thatcher is looking at me like I'm a book he can no longer read. Missing pages and smudged font. His own confusion draws his brows together. "I must not have heard you right."

I word-vomit. "I'm going to do it too." Every syllable is a stab to my own heart.

"Jane—"

"I understand the consequences." *We're equals.* I can do this for him. For us. I clear my swollen throat.

Charlie has been playing obscure piano pieces, until now. He switches to Chopin, the romantic melody often accompanied with waltzes. He's poking fun since Thatcher and I are more at odds with each other.

I want to be unconcerned about my brother, but he'll voice his opinion—whether on my side or not. He's just biding his time.

Thatcher never breaks my gaze. "I'd like to go over the consequences one more time before you make this decision."

"That's fair." I face him more, but I'm careful of our distance. Tony is still loitering outside the parlor door. "And it's simple really. If we both take nudes, then there's a fraction of a chance they could be leaked online." *Easy enough, Jane.*

Right?

Right.

His forehead wrinkles in heavier concern. "And…" He waits for me to keep going.

"And we'll both have nudes online. Simply that." I weave my arms over my body.

Confidence. I scrounge for more.

"You're not that daft," Charlie butts in.

"What do you want me to say, Charlie?" I question. "That men will masturbate to naked pictures of me? That people will jeer? That I will be critiqued and criticized from my areola size down to my pubic hair. I *understand.* All of it." Tears threaten to rise and knives wedge between my ribs. Every breath tight.

I can do this.

I can.

I can.

Can I?

Charlie bangs keys with twice as much agitation.

I spin back to my boyfriend.

He's locked down, walled up. He's now the book *I* can no longer read.

"Why don't you care about those consequences for yourself?" I question. "Fans are just as likely to spread your dick over the internet and jack off to the photos."

"It doesn't bother me." He sighs out frustration. "Except…"

Banks. They're identical twins. They look so similar. "Your brother."

He nods slowly. "He'd be okay." He pins his focus to me. "It's also easier for me than you. I'm not a girl. I'm not born into fame. I'm not Jane Eleanor Cobalt. These consequences don't hold the same severity for me." He pauses. "If I give up here, will you?"

And ruin this game for him?

I feel awful just at the thought. So I shake my head and say, "Let's continue this together."

Thatcher doesn't hesitate. "No."

"No?" I blink, my eyes burning.

He glares, and the intensity is like the hottest heat wave. He quickly diverts his eyes to the ceiling. "You don't want to do this, honey."

"I just said I did."

He dips his head down, his brown eyes hitting mine again. Glare softened just a fraction. "And you've said the opposite up until now, so the only fucking thing that's changed here is me. Tell me you're not doing it for me."

I can't deny the truth. "If you're taking a risk, I have to, too. There's no way around that." I add quickly, "And you *want* to do this, so I won't stop you. I just don't want you to stop me from doing it too."

"Fuck that," Thatcher says. "If you think, for a second, I'm going to stand around with my dick in my hand and watch you do something that could harm you—all just for me—then you don't realize what I'd do to protect you."

I'm on the edge of a cliff. I've always loved how he's my safety net. But… "I have to try."

His narrowed eyes are bloodshot. "I'm sorry, but I can't let you."

I fight for deeper breath, and I hate that this has all spiraled here. The threads of this relationship have tangled, untwisted, and slipped between my fingers.

How can I be in a relationship where I let my number one, my life and soul run through fires without me?

Thatcher turns to my brother. "Throw this card out."

He won't.

"No," Charlie says. "You quit, you lose. You finish, you win."

We are given hard choices, and I feel this one barreling down. "I can take a few nudes." My voice has risen, confident and blazoned. *I can do this.*

I can do anything.

Thatcher stares at me deeply, and I realize the chess game is now between him and me. We're in a standoff. Rook to rook, and I make the next move.

"You can't physically stop me." The words come out fast, and immediately, I feel like a brat. *Dear God, just bring in the shovel.* Bury this whole thing into a thousand-foot grave. I'm waiting for someone to cover the dirt on top of me, suffocating me. I hate what I said. I hate how this is going. I want to eject from all of it. "I'm sorry, I just...this is wrong...and what if we're just not right for each other?"

My breathing does a weird dive.

His nose flares. "I promise you we are." He checks on Tony over at the door, then back to me.

"I don't know how to do this..." I drop my gaze. "I don't want to break up with you again, but I just..."

Thatcher is about to speak, but Charlie's brows jump sky-high. "*Again?*"

I ignore that to ask, "How do we even send nudes with no cell service?"

"Swap phones." Charlie plays a new classical piano piece. "Take your nudes on each other's. It'll be like you sent them." He zeroes in on me. "I'm curious though. Breaking up with your boyfriend, is this some strange ploy to have makeup sex, or are you just copying Mom and Dad?"

With those words, he obliterates the oxygen from the room. "What?"

"Mom and Dad," Charlie repeats, the music shrill. "You do know Mom used to break up with Dad before they were married. All the fucking time. But she would do it because she was pissed at him. Not at herself." He waves a hand at me. "There's a lot of self-loathing coming from this corner."

I can't breathe.

"Stop," Thatcher says.

Lightheaded, I don't know if he's talking to me or my brother. But his hands are on my cheeks, and I turn to my left and right.

Tony isn't at the door. Neither is Oscar nor Farrow. They must've pulled my bodyguard out of view, and Thatcher speaks to me. "Jane, take a breath."

"I'm not…I'm…"

I love myself.

I do.

I do. But I hate who I am right now. Simpering mess of a fool. One who can't make decisions, or choose to have a relationship that might not be what she envisioned. But one she loves.

One she can't live without.

One she desires so deeply, so fully, and so dramatically.

Charlie's voice rips through my head. "Jane, come on."

He's never seen me this way. I don't want him to. I gather leftover confidence, and air reaches my lungs while I push Thatcher off me.

"I'm sorry." We apologize at the same time.

We're both hurting.

"I quit," I announce. "I won't take nudes. You go ahead. I'll cheer for you on the sidelines." An involuntary tear slips out, and I angrily wipe it away.

"I'm not playing this game anymore either."

"I won't let you quit because of me. And that's what you'd be doing, isn't it?"

Thatcher nods once. I won't let him sacrifice the *one* chance to be accepted in my family. He won't let me sacrifice my body. It feels as though we both lost here because we're no longer in this together, and I hate that too.

32

Thatcher Moretti

CHRISTMAS EVE IS HERE, and I wish I could've gifted Jane the ability to rejoin me in *Cobalt Truth or Dare from Hell*. Without her having to send nudes. I even tried to barter with Charlie.

That kid—sorry, *that guy* runs on 100% emotions. I'm a practical, logic-based man, and I can't follow Charlie's line of thinking or motives if my brain were screwed to the fucking thing. So either he's emotion-fueled, or his IQ is just beyond me.

Whatever the case, he shut me down.

I can't unfuck this, but I wish I could. Partly so we could continue the game together. Mostly because Jane wouldn't feel like she failed.

I focus on something I can do.

A box of dead radios sits at my ankles, and I work on changing out the batteries. Chatter escalates around me, along with laughter. Flames crack in the fireplace.

Last night, the heaters broke again, and everyone congregates in the living room so they don't freeze their asses off. Holiday classics play from Quinn's phone, but no lights are strung. No eggnog to drink. No tree. No presents.

The gift that I planned to give Jane, I left at the townhouse.

Really, we just have each other, and that almost kills the homesickness. Bodyguards and clients play poker with cash, others talk quietly on couches or keep to themselves.

Like me.

I sit alone on a long bench near the doorway, where cool air flows in from the kitchen.

My eyes linger on the other side of the room, near a deep mahogany bookcase. Filled with dusty encyclopedias and almanacs. Jane and Maximoff huddle close together, alone, whispering in a heavy conversation with coffee and hot tea.

They've been like that for the past ten minutes, and every now and then Maximoff will pass Jane a box of shortbread cookies.

Can't change the past. My inaction eats every part of me. So I just unclip the back of a radio and ditch out the dead battery.

Farrow exits the kitchen and stops next to my bench. "Here." He taps a beer bottle to my shoulder, holding another in his right hand

I frown. "I thought we were out of beer."

"Oscar hid a couple bottles."

I'm not about to decline the offer. And a beer sounds good right now. I nod in thanks, untwisting the twist-off cap. "Does he know you're giving me this?"

Farrow nods. "Yeah. We all agreed you need a beer more than any fucker here."

I take a stiff swig. It's been less than 24-hours and everyone who knows that I'm Thatcher is aware of the argument Jane and I had.

Over nudes.

The level of awkward has reached middle school dance territory. No one on the team has ribbed me, but I can tell they want to but aren't sure how serious the fallout is. So every time I walk into a room, I'm met with silent stares and cagey glances.

I lower the bottle. "Me and Jane—we're good." I'm not sure Farrow cares to know my relationship status, but I tell him anyway since he's here. I don't go in-depth about how Jane and I talked all last night or that we're on the same page, same understanding again.

We're good sums it up.

Farrow isn't petty, I realize. If he were, he'd steal my beer back.

To my surprise, he takes a seat beside me and leans against the paisley green wallpaper. "That's one of my favorite things about being with someone." He sips his beer.

"What is?" I pop in a battery with one hand.

"Going through shit together. Growing with the person you love." He smiles into his next swig, his gaze on Maximoff Hale.

I swallow more beer, eyes latched to Jane Cobalt.

She sits pin straight, ankles crossed, and brushes cookie crumbs off her sweater.

My chest rises.

I'm more used to imploding relationships when shit happens, but with Jane, I never want to give up on us. It'd be a sucker-punch to the gut if she decided we weren't worth the hard parts. We can come out on top together, and the time we're taking to pick each other up has only made us stronger.

I talk to Farrow. "Difference between us, the shit you had to go through wasn't orchestrated by your boyfriend's family." I place the powered radio on a side table. "The Hales gave you water wings."

"More like one water wing." He lifts a foot on the bench, knee bent. "The Cobalts are definitely too much; the second those cards came out, I would've trashed them."

Farrow might be used to going rogue, but I'm more battle-tested to withstand fucked-up rules. To push through them rather than go around.

I grab another fucked radio from the box. "That's why I'm dating a Cobalt and you aren't."

"No shit." He smiles.

The corner of my mouth upturns, and we swig beer at the same time. When we look over at Jane and Maximoff, we notice they're already watching us, their expressions thunderstruck and curious: mouths gaping, eyes cinched, question marks dangling over their heads.

It's fucking comical.

"He's too precious." Farrow grins at him.

Maximoff scowls and flips him off.

It's strange that my brother is thousands of miles away, Akara is icing me out, and the bodyguard I'm closest to in Scotland is Farrow Redford Keene.

That isn't lost on me.

But I'm nowhere as shocked as Jane or Maximoff. I almost forget they're five years younger than us and *famous* and not trusting of most people. Other friendships outside their families, especially bodyguards and our rifts, are uncharted lands—and it sparks Jane's curiosity like ten thousand Roman candles.

She bows forward, knuckles to chin, and eyes shimmering.

I swig my beer. I could be in South Philly this Christmas, left to wonder what the fuck is happening to my girlfriend. Instead I'm here. Knowing Jane is safe.

Keeping her safe.

Sharing in this experience with *her*.

Can't ask for more.

As the poker game dies down, Oscar and Donnelly come over and test the waters with me.

Oscar upnods. "If you need pointers, Moretti, we have a professional dick pic photographer on the team." He squeezes Donnelly's shoulder.

"Straight up." Donnelly slips a ballpoint pen behind his ear. "I can make your five-inch wiener look like a foot-long."

I've seen every dick on SFO. Just like they have. Comes with quick-changes on-duty. But this, right here, is the first instance they've felt comfortable enough to rib me about my nine-inch cock.

Maybe they realize I won't reprimand them.

Oscar grins. "Donnelly, if he's five-inches, you're a centimeter."

"Give me a tape measure, man."

Farrow swallows beer and stands. "I was trying to get away from you fuckers." He always acts like the three of them aren't tight, but they spent *years* at an Ivy League together.

The Yale boys are about as solid a friendship as lifelong ride-or-dies.

Donnelly takes his seat next to me, and Farrow ends up staying, his boot on the bench and forearm to his thigh.

I hand Oscar my beer, giving him the rest, and I dispose the dead battery out of a radio. My voice is low as I say, "Jane already took the dick pics."

Oscar chokes on beer. "Jane took them? So you two are…"

I nod.

Farrow translates. "They're good."

"You pose for her?" Donnelly banters.

"Close-ups?" Oscar chimes in.

"Girls love that anus shot, you get that one?"

Farrow laughs hard, and fuck it, I laugh too. I wish my brother were here. He'd be rolling over in laughter just knowing my girlfriend is three dick pics richer. And how she tucked the phone to her chest like she was guarding the Hope Diamond.

I test the radio. "What I do for love and pussy."

Amen, Banks would say. Not hearing it just makes me miss him more.

Quinn Oliveira joins us right after the words leave my mouth, and the air strains. Oscar assesses his little brother, to see if he's okay. Last I heard, they weren't talking since Quinn punched him.

Oscar nods. "I'm cool if you are, bro."

Quinn nods back. "Yeah, I'm cool."

Tension gone, Oscar picks up the conversation. "I could cheers to that: love, pussy, and add in *good dick*."

Farrow quips, "What's bad dick feel like, Oliveira?"

"I don't know, Redford, you tell me. You're the one who slept with that redheaded witch." He brings up *Rowin Hart*, his ex-boyfriend, who almost assaulted Maximoff in Greece.

Farrow cringes into a sip of beer. "He's worse than a witch, but nice try."

Quinn interjects, "Why's Akara hanging out with the Epsilon douche-bros?"

Our heads turn.

Akara is in a conversation with O'Malley, more than Tony, but they're all on the red-green plaid couch, the SFE guards pocketing wads of bills they won.

I shut off the powered radio. "Recon."

Quinn scrunches his face. "What?"

"Keep your enemies close, Quinnie," Donnelly says.

"But not too close," Farrow advises.

My jaw hardens as I suddenly zone in on a target. Tony is smiling over at Jane like she's a chick in a bar he wants to fuck-and-chuck, and my blood is boiling. Muscles flexed, and I barely hear the guys talking about a game of charades tonight. To lighten the mood for Christmas Eve.

If Tony stands up, I'm Oscar Mike.

I will shove off and shove him back from her before his eye twitches in a fucking wink.

He folds his hands behind his head, then looks at me.

Good.

Stay the hell away from her. Tony thinks I'm Banks, but my brother would be just as protective of Jane as I would of his girlfriend (if he had one).

I glare, and the more I stab him between the eyes, the more he grins. He smacks O'Malley's chest, stealing his attention, and very loudly, he says, "You know that Banks' brother does butt stuff?" He laughs.

That affects me about as much as chugging water, but it shoots a bullet through multiple people.

"Excuse me?" Jane springs to her feet, and Maximoff stands at her side.

Farrow and Oscar are glaring at Tony.

I carefully watch Jane as she marches to the couch and confronts him. She can handle her own, but it fucking kills me knowing he won't respect a word she says.

"What?" Tony playfully crosses his arms, still seated.

"I want to know why you laughed like that was an insult," Jane demands. "Please, share with us."

Tony lets out another laugh and raises a patronizing hand. "Hey, Jane, it's okay if your boyfriend wants you to play with his asshole. It just makes him a little less, you know...manly."

You could hear a pin drop.

I don't blink. More focused on her anger than anything.

"Someone educate this motherfucker," Oscar says under his breath.

Farrow catches Maximoff's wrist before he storms Tony, and he brings his fiancé's shoulders and back into his chest. "He's not worth it, wolf scout."

"First of all—" Jane raises a pointer finger "—men are not less masculine for having anything in their ass—"

"But it makes them gay," Tony cuts her off with a smirk.

Jane steeples her hands. "No, it doesn't. You see, every man has a prostate gland, and prostate stimulation is not an indication of sexual orientation. It feels immensely good to some, and you can enjoy this very much and prefer any gender."

"There we go," Farrow says quietly.

Tony leans comfortably back and smiles up at Jane. "If that's what you need to tell yourself."

Jane stews. "I feel sorry for you, that you can't see how insecure you are and how secure he is. He's a better man than you'll ever be."

I hit the jackpot with this girl, and holy hell, I'm smiling.

Until I see a switch in Tony.

His eyes go dark.

It kicks my ass to a stance.

"You don't know what you're talking about, Jane." He stands, puffing out his chest. "Go sit down—"

"Hey," I cut in, my stride severe. Urgent. "What the fuck are you doing?!"

Tony uses his height to loom over Jane. To physically intimidate her—and I bolt, fury blasting in my veins, and I draw her behind me in an instant, and I confront him full-force.

I'm not shoving him back.

I'm *done* with that shit.

I fist his shirt and pull him up, his feet off the ground.

He curses me out in Italian and swings. Knuckles bash my jaw, pain lost under adrenaline and rage, and I head-butt the fuckbag and throw him on the floor.

Yells pitch the air. But no one stops us. No one comes to his defense. I'm *done* going easy on him.

Because he's family.

Because I know better.

Because I'm too strong and I should use my strength to defend.

Tony scrambles to his feet with a wince. I knock his ass back on the floor, and we're in a brawl. Fists flying, knees in ribs, and my pulse is ringing in my ear.

Blood in my mouth, I spit to the side, and we're on our feet. I outsize Tony, and I pin him against the wall, a framed picture of Loch Ness crashing down. This isn't even a fair fight. I could drag him halfway around the house, and the fire in my lungs starts to die.

He's weaker.

I don't hurt weak things. I protect them.

He tries to head-butt me.

I fake left, then slam a fist in his gut, and he chokes out, "Outside." He coughs. "Let's go outside…and finish this."

I narrow the hottest glare on him and I'm thinking, *how stupid can this shitbag be?* If the cold doesn't kill him, I will.

"Scared, Banks?" He tries to slam me back. I don't budge, and I twist his shirt more around my fist and hoist him higher up the wall.

He writhes.

"I'll kill you," I warn him.

Fear strikes his eyes for a fleeting second, then arrogance causes his lips to rise, and he shakes his head strongly. "I have you beat."

My eyeballs sear, unblinking, and my chest is on fire—and if I take him up on his offer, if we go "fight it out" in frostbitten temperature and waist-deep snow, I won't be fighting Tony.

I'll be fighting *myself.* To stop from killing him, and I want to be a man that Jane deserves.

Not a killer.

My hands are soaked in blood from war, and I haven't taken a soul since.

"For a second, I thought you were Thatcher…"

I stiffen.

"But he'd never hesitate like you." Tony laughs into a slight cough. "Looks like we know which one has the bigger balls."

"*Fuck you*," I growl between gritted teeth.

He tries to pry my hands off his shirt. "Let's do this."

My neck is tensed, and I release my grip. Breathing coarse breath through my nose.

Tony slides down, and he takes one step towards the front door— and I cold-cock him. Fist to jaw, and the blow is lights out.

He thumps to the floorboards.

Unconscious.

33

Banks Moretti

WHAT A FUCKIN' DAY to have a killer migraine. I can count on my hand the number of times Xander leaves the house and greets daylight in a given week. And of course today—the day I have a blistering, thunder-fucking headache—I'm outside.

My aviators need three times the tint to combat the sun because Lord knows sunlight and I are old enemies. That billion-years-old burning ball of roid-raging fire likes to ramp up my headache by a thousand degrees.

Good thing Xander has no clue I'm in pain, or he probably would've insisted we return home. The last course of action I want is for that kid to change his plans for my ass.

I scratch the scuff along my jaw, grown out more than usual. Gold horns rest against my black button-down, the sleeves rolled as heat radiates from an outdoor fireplace.

The patio to Easton Mulligan's house—excuse me, *mansion*—is as bougie as every other landscaped backyard on this street: sheared hedges, stone-rimmed pools, lounge chairs worthy of grape-eating narcissists. Pretty sure some teenager around here has fallen into the deep-end staring at their own reflection.

Or snapping a selfie.

Easton's mansion also includes heated *patio stones*. The Hale house in this same gated neighborhood doesn't even have that. Snow soaks the grass, but the sitting area around the fireplace is dry.

Seated on the warm stone, Xander faces Easton around a glass coffee table, a board game and colorful pieces scattered between them.

But this isn't Candy Land (unfortunately for me), it's a three-person strategy game, and I was recruited as the "third" player.

We're four hours in, and I'm still confused as hell.

Xander rolls the dice that has twelve sides and symbols and shit. "I'll trade you a musket for a fire spell." He's looking at me.

"Sure, yeah." I hand him a card.

"That's a rocket flare," Easton says.

Shit.

I shuffle through my thick deck and find another. "Here."

Xander nods, then frowns, catching sight of another card in my hand. "Wait, you have the Empress of Tomorrow?"

"No fucking way." Easton leans forward, elbows on the table. He's a lanky, pale, dark-haired sixteen-year-old—no kidding, he looks like a vampire. Thing is, I bet he gets *more* sun and Vitamin C than Xander.

I scrunch my brows. "What's the Empress of Tomorrow mean?"

Xander grins after a sip of Fizz. "With your position on the board and your two blocking spells, you just won the game, man."

"Well, damn," I say into a satisfied nod. Forget it, I fucking rock, and just then, a hammer pounds inside my temple. I bite down while Xander and Easton gather cards and game pieces.

I'd give my left testicle for a cigarette, or at least a toothpick that I'm not allowed to grind on.

'Cause I'm Thatcher Alessio Moretti. He already fucked up, and now I'm gonna be known as the guy who stuffs lunchmeat in his jacket.

It's kinda funny. I'll take it. But I'd rather all of them come home. It's December 27th. They're a whole week late, and it's killing more than just me.

Xander checks his cellphone, waiting for a text that says *they're back*. His sixteenth birthday at Superheroes & Scones was quiet and somber without his older brother and sister there.

The parents even cancelled Christmas at the lake house this year. They wanted to stay in Philly, so they'd be here for when their children return home.

Easton slowly straightens the cards and eyes Xander. "Is everything okay?"

"Uh, yeah. Sorry." Xander overturns his phone. He hasn't mentioned that his older siblings and cousins are stuck in Scotland, but it's all over the news.

So Easton *knows*. He's just waiting for his friend to share with the class.

He won't. Xander keeps personal shit vaulted about as much as every other famous one.

Awkward silence hangs as they *slowly*—ever so fucking slowly— shift game pieces. Unsure if the other person wants to play another round. It's clear they both do.

I'm just a third-wheel.

I'm not supposed to *nudge* them. So I just lean back and watch the teenage soap opera.

Easton taps a silver wizard piece to the board. "Good game, man."

"Yeah, definitely." Xander crunches his soda can and flips a dice, staring at Easton, then the snow, then back to Easton. "So…?"

"You want another Fizz?" Easton rises.

"Uh, that's okay." He pushes his hair out of his eyes. "I mean, yeah…that'd be good. You want to play again?"

"For sure." Easton smiles more. "I'll be right back." He goes to retrieve a soda, and Xander watches him in deep thought before his head whips to me.

"I suck at this." His eyes darken. "Like literally, *suck*."

My lip curves up. "You're doing fine, kid."

He exhales a heavy breath. "Sometimes I think it's better for everyone if I just stayed in my room and never came out."

"It'd be worse," I remind him. "Everyone would be sad."

He lets this sink in, massaging his sore knuckles from a boxing session.

When Easton returns, we play another round of the geekiest stuff I've ever seen. Besides LARPing.

I'd enjoy this more if my migraine weren't about to blow a hole through my temple. During an intense battle, I slyly pop some Advil.

The pills go down rough without water. It'll be worth it later.

Once Xander wins, they pack up the board game. And then, we get ready to shove off.

"Hey, Thatcher, thanks for being our third," Easton tells me, reminding me I'm my brother and wearing these stupid aviators that have no tint. Spoiler alert: they're not mine. "We'll probably need you if we play again. Not many people appreciate nerdy shit around here."

"Only the 'popular' nerdy shit," Xander adds, and these two linger at the back gate. He awkwardly waves Easton goodbye. "Later...or whatever." He sucks in a tight breath.

Easton stuffs his hands in his preppy khakis. "If you ever want to play again, just text me. I'm free a lot, so..."

"Yeah. Okay. Cool." Xander nods.

Easton nods. "Cool."

I suppress a smile and adjust my earpiece. Not interfering, but man, I feel like a proud Mother Goose who sent her little chickadee out into the world.

But you better believe I'm still a bodyguard. I hawk-eye their hand movements, not about to let Xander pass off antidepressants to this kid.

Back in Greece, Thatcher and I (along with most everyone else) found out Xander had been giving away his extra meds to Easton, and the fact that Xander had also been doing it with other kids back when he was thirteen—on *our* watch—still puts a rock between my ribcage.

Missed it.

Not that I can really shackle too much blame on me and my brother. Xander is a teenager. If he wants to hide something from us, he'll find a way. I'm not a motherfucking spy. And he may trust us with serious shit, but he also knows where our trust would end. Had I seen him willfully giving his meds away to gain popularity, I would have called his parents in a heartbeat.

He knew that.

Still, I'm not missing the same thing twice, so I laser focus on their hands.

We're all good.

They depart, and I walk on the freshly plowed road beside Xander. Constantly surveying the mansions. Christmas lights, wreaths and bows are still up. No threats in sight. Most bodyguards go off-duty in the gated neighborhood—but extra vigilance makes Xander feel safe.

And I like living life on my toes.

Semper Gumby.

"He's pretty cool, right?" Xander asks, popping a Sprite.

I stare straight ahead. "He's only cool when he's not taking your meds."

Xander sighs. "How long are you and Thatcher going to give me shit for that?"

"Until we forget it happened."

Xander mumbles something about that being *never*.

Static from SFE comms is in my ear, and I pick up a couple bodyguards discussing New Year's Eve plans. My muscles tense, just thinking about my brother stuck in the middle of bum-fuck nowhere Scotland past January 1st.

With the weather reports I keep checking, I doubt he'll be back before then. And the longer we keep up this charade, the more I have to *lie* to people like Easton. But I convinced Thatcher to swap places, and I'm chugging my share of salt.

"Moffy and Farrow will get everyone home. Thatcher will too," Xander tells me, like I need the confidence boost. Seeing this kid dish out encouragements almost makes me smile.

"Amen." I bounce my head. "Your big brother can do anything." I stoke that belief that'll keep him afloat, especially when Thatcher and I leave.

Xander begins to smile. "Yeah, he can."

"So can you," I add.

He lets out a short laugh into a sip of Sprite. "Sure." He believes this more when Maximoff tells him, and I don't blame him. I'd believe the ground was *gold* if my big brother said so.

Agitation festers at the thought of Skylar.

Hate-plus-love is a cruel asshole.

I stare straight and suddenly spot a limo in the distance. It's headed this way.

"Mother of Christ," I say under my breath, and I push my aviators up the bridge of my nose. *I'm not fucked yet.*

Xander must've heard me. "Maybe that's not my uncle's limo."

"There's only one other house in this neighborhood that has a limo, and it's on a different street." *Ready or not, Connor Cobalt, here I am.*

Because what I know: Connor won't ignore his sixteen-year-old nephew and drive right on by. And sure enough, the limo slows.

Forcing us to stop.

Don't talk to me, Connor. I stronghold and rattle the hope and dream like it'll fall out of a piggybank and into my possession. Talking to Jane's dad is a worst-case scenario and I wouldn't be here if Thatcher and Jane hadn't been snowed-in.

But I'd do just about anything for those two.

There's never been a woman so good for my brother, and I'd like to think he's good for her too. Thatcher and I—we don't need much in life and we haven't had much until security work. To know that the Morettis could somehow be linked to the Cobalts (the bougiest family of all three) is fucking weird and unreal.

And now that quirky, cat-obsessed Jane is my twin brother's girlfriend—I instinctively will always look out for her like she's my flesh and blood.

"Maybe we can run?" Xander whispers.

"No, I'm gonna handle this." I'm not digging Xander's grave beside me and my brother.

He nods a few times.

The window rolls completely down. "Do you want a ride?" Connor asks Xander, snow flurries beginning to sweep the brittle air.

"No, I need the exercise." He scratches his cheek. "But thanks."

Connor nods, then zeroes in on me. My arms are crossed, shoulders squared and features stoic. *I'm Thatcher Moretti, bitch.*

I'm a fucking dumbass—because I almost, *almost* crack a smile at my idiotic thought.

His forehead twitches slightly before his expression flat-lines. Unreadable. "You do know how a phone works?"

"Yes, sir."

"You know how to accept a call?"

I nod. "I must've just missed yours. Sorry." *Don't talk a lot.*

"Will you have dinner with me and Jane's mom tomorrow night?"

"Can't, sir." I stiffen. "I have plans with my grandma. She's expecting me." My voice sounds stilted, but what can I do? I'm not an actor or trying to win a fucking Academy Award.

I relax when I realize Connor looks understanding.

He even offers me a friendly smile. "Another time. If you can't answer a call, I'll text."

"Sounds good."

He says goodbye to Xander, and the window rolls back up. That went about as poorly as expected, and not even Xander could tell if Connor saw through me.

That's the thing about the Cobalt Empire; they don't show you their cards until the very end. And I just hope and dream up one more thing.

That I haven't completely screwed Thatcher and Jane's ending.

34

Jane Cobalt

A LITTLE PIECE OF me thought that possibly, just *possibly*, the fistfight between my boyfriend and my bodyguard would diffuse tension, eradicate bad blood, and cause them to come together—the way that families sometimes do.

I was wrong.

They stand more divided than ever.

Tony keeps egging on my boyfriend, who he still believes is Banks. He's been asking for a round two, even though he lost *miserably* the first time. And I'm proud of Thatcher for not taking the bait. Once was enough. A second physical altercation won't heal the wound.

It is vitally clear that Tony has become an insufferable disease-ridden sore in Mackintosh House. His only redeeming quality is that he's not a terrible bodyguard.

But the longer we're all trapped here with him, the less "bodyguard duties" he has and the more his ugly personality shows.

New Year's Eve should be a celebratory occasion with glitz and glam, but Tony has soul-sucked the house. And serious matters are still at the forefront.

Like the freezing cold and the depletion of *certain* supplies. Which has brought us to an Emergency House Meeting and split the living room: Omega on one side, Epsilon on the other, and my family strewn in between.

Jack Highland and surprisingly Will Rochester have chosen to sit with my family.

I clap my hands together. "Thank you all for coming to this meeting. We appreciate having your undivided attention."

4 girls to 13 guys.

The ratio is very apparent as I stand with Sullivan, Luna, and Joana near the fireplace hearth. We take center stage and capture the attention of all thirteen men. Most of them seem readied—despite not knowing the issues we're about to drudge up—but I suppose that's what happens when you face a room full of bodyguards.

They're prepared for anything.

But I highly doubt they've guessed *this*.

I take a breath, and my gaze drifts to the back wall. Where Thatcher stands stoically next to an old record player. Arms crossed, he nods me on encouragingly, even though he's in the dark like the other men.

More breath fills my lungs, and I continue on with a rising smile, "As you all know, there are some things that the four of us experience that none of you do."

Bodyguards shift, realization striking some.

"This meeting is about menstruation," I announce.

Silence.

Dead.

Utter. *Silence.*

Concern is the prominent emotion from Omega's corner. From Maximoff and my brothers as well.

Epsilon's side is another story. O'Malley is leaning back in a rocking chair and suddenly enamored with the ceiling. And Tony looks far too amused.

Joana threads her arms. "Menstruation is a *period.*"

"Shark week," Sulli adds, drawing a grin from all the girls, and she whispers to us, "It's what my sister and I call it."

Oscar bows forward on the couch. "We know what menstruation is, Jo."

She nods to her twenty-one-year-old brother. "Quinn looked confused."

His brows are rather scrunched.

Tony interjects, "Wait." He licks his lips, a laugh on them, and he talks directly to me. "You came here to discuss being on the rag?"

I cringe.

On the rag might be my all-time least favorite phrase, and before SFO, Maximoff, or my brothers jump down his throat, I answer quickly—and hotly, "Yes, we did, Tony, and we've called this meeting to let you all know that we're running out of feminine products."

Thatcher stares off a little, and I bet he's mentally counting to determine my next period. He can easily keep track of my cycle since we have sex so often.

Quinn scratches his unshaven jaw. "Shouldn't you have planned for that?"

We've discovered the source of his confusion, ladies and gentlemen.

"Like we all planned to be stuck in this house?" Joana says, hurt in her voice. "Like I planned to miss my fight in London?"

Quinn grimaces. "Sorry, Jo." His apology to his little sister sounds sincere.

"We'll fix this," Oscar says to his sister. "What do you girls need?"

I interlace my fingers. "Well, this trip was supposed to be *one* week. And the only person who packed tampons was the girl who knew she'd have a period here. The rest of us brought one emergency item."

I purposefully omit names. Even if Sulli wouldn't mind, the men don't need to know she started her period at the beginning of the trip.

I continue, "And since we've been in Scotland for almost three weeks, some of us are now having periods that we didn't anticipate—"

"If I were a girl, I'd just bring a box of tampons everywhere with me." Tony is the loudest, most obnoxious man I've ever had the misfortune of meeting. At least it feels this way stuck here with him. I'm sure once I return to strangers heckling me in Philly, I'll feel differently.

Thatcher glowers at Tony. "Cut her off one more time, and—"

"And what?" He chuckles. "You're gonna hit me again, Banks? Let's do it. Right now—"

"Do you ever shut the fuck up?" Farrow glares.

Tony smiles more. "You think you're such hot shit, Farrow, why don't you go outside with me then? I'll show you and Moretti who's the better fighter."

Farrow raises his brows. "You were literally knocked out unconscious seven days ago."

"It won't happen twice."

Joana steps forward. "How about I kick your ass instead?"

Beckett has been sullen all day, but I catch my brother beginning to smile.

Tony flashes a dry look at Jo. "I don't punch girls. Sorry."

Akara interjects fast. "We're getting off track, guys."

Tony gesticulates towards me and the girls. "If they didn't bring enough tampons, then at least one of them should be on the pill. That stops a period, right?"

"Thank you for bringing up the pill, Tony," I say between gritted teeth. "That's my second point. Some of us have run out and are now spotting. Which has created a greater *need* for feminine products."

"We can snowshoe to the supermarket," Donnelly suggests like that is reasonable. It'd be an eight-hour hike for tampons.

Thatcher checks his watch. "We'll have to leave tomorrow at first light."

A smile tugs my cheeks, and I do my best not to smile *at* him in front of Tony. Thatcher being in his element always attracts me.

Akara nods. "We'll send a team of four. Briefing is in five…" He catches me shaking my head.

"There's no need," I announce. "The girls and I have already devised a strategy. It involves toilet paper and hand towels."

I feel badly that I'm not the one suffering. My period shouldn't come for another week. Luna is spotting, and Jo started yesterday. But they agreed to a makeshift pad plan.

Luna pulls the ties of her *Thrasher* hoodie—and the hood squeezes around her face, only her nose poking out. "We just need you to conserve the toilet paper."

"One fucking square when you shit," Sulli adds crudely.

Akara breaks into a smile, but it fades when Will jokes with Sulli, "Just one square?"

Sulli bites her lip. "Yeah, just one." She hasn't slept with her boyfriend. Yesterday, she confessed that she was feeling more insecure than usual. He touched her prickly leg and jerked away a little.

She told me, *"He's been so sweet. Maybe this is all in my head. Him, thinking I'm too hairy. It's just made me feel weird, and I don't know how to fucking get over it."*

I suggested she talk to Will and ask him about the moment, but she's nervous to broach the topic.

"Are you sure you don't want us to snowshoe?" Donnelly wonders with a frown.

"Positive," Luna nods. "Don't sacrifice your life for a tampon."

"More like your comfort, you know?" Donnelly shrugs.

"We're fine," I chime in. "We'd rather not send anyone out into a blizzard." Conditions have only worsened lately, and this fact sinks a weight into the room that no one can lift.

We're quiet.

Only the crackle of fire heard above the mad, angry wind.

THE REST OF THE DAY, I'M PRACTICALLY BURSTING

at the seams—my thoughts churning, my emotions rattling. And as midnight hurriedly approaches, only a few hours from the New Year, I know what I must do.

I need to word-vomit all over someone.

I must talk and talk and purge every last thing that throttles my senses, and there is only *one* person I desire to be on the receiving end.

But unfortunately, survival takes precedent.

I carry a clipboard and walk along the upstairs hallway. With freezing temperatures and broken heaters, we're all camping around the living room fireplace tonight, and every door must be shut to combat drafts.

I check each tightly closed door and cross rooms off my list. I've also been reminding everyone to gather their belongings for the night and head downstairs. All the while, my body hums in anticipation of seeing Thatcher.

I blow out a measured breath. Nerves swarming me, but I refuse to be too nervous to speak this time.

I peek into a cracked bedroom. *Empty.* Just as I shut the door, Luna waddles past me, dressed in so many layers of clothing that her oversized galactic sweatshirt looks like a crop top.

She throws up a Spock sign. "Beware of the frostbite."

I smile. "Do you need any extra blankets?"

"Nope. I should be good." She waves, descending the staircase. "Thanks though." Once she disappears, Thatcher suddenly ascends the same steps.

I press my clipboard to my swelling body.

He locks onto my eyes with this primitive look, as though we're two lions protecting the pride. Without saying a word, he stops a foot away and plucks the clipboard from my arms. He scans the list swiftly. "The third floor still needs cleared."

"Oui." I almost forget what pushes at my soul.

"I'll take it." He passes back the clipboard, his assertiveness melting me. *Come on, Jane.*

"We have to talk." I clasp his wrist in haste and open the nearest door.

I pull him into the *tiny* broom closet. His head almost collides with the low bulb, and I can feel his uncertainty swallow up the air.

He tugs the string light while I shut the door, and a warm glow bathes the dusty space. Cobwebs in corners of wooden shelves, which contains random items like wax paper rolls, a mop bucket, and a broken bagpipe.

"Ever since the house meeting, I can't stop thinking." I start gushing. "Maybe it's because of Tony, because his opinions are so gross and ridiculous, and how he views women is absolutely *appalling*. And I'm not so sure if he'll understand *why* what he says hurts people and how what he thinks is wrong." I barely take a breath. "Or maybe it's because we're stuck here without internet, and I can't let callous things said about me seep too deep if I'm not able to see them."

I pause.

Dear Diary, he looks tragically *confused*.

I inhale. "If you need me to shut up—"

"Never," he says deeply, and I'm glad he cut me off there. "Never stop talking, Jane."

He's my everything and more.

I lift my chin to meet his serious brown eyes. "I've been thinking," I continue, "about how I've been so insecure about my worth if I don't find a passion, even more so now that I'm tied to you." Emotion burns my eyes.

His chest tightens. He's barely breathing too, but he nods me on.

I'd be pacing back and forth if the closet were bigger. I'm happy to be forced to stand perilously still in front of him. His comfort blanketing me.

"If I knew at seventeen what my future held, that I'd be passionless, ambitionless, and the world would attach my value to a man, I would've screamed at the top of my lungs. The realization—to *think*—that all I could be good for is to be your girlfriend, to be a sister, a cousin, best friend, daughter, and nothing else, it's terrifying. It's scared me to know that my purpose in life is just love." I wipe a hot, escaped tear. "*Love.*" I repeat the cofounding word. "When this is all said and done, where am I supposed to end up? Married? With children? Giving love to you and them?"

"We don't have to get married, Jane," Thatcher says suddenly, seriously—staring down at me while I look right up at him. "I'll never make you do anything you don't want to do."

My heart thumps strangely. "You wouldn't want to be married one day?"

His jaw tics. "I would want that, but if the choice were marriage or you, I'd rather just be with you." He holds my waist, his hand sliding around my hip to the small of my back. He's not letting go of *us*, and I don't want to either.

I know, deep in my heart, that we're already bound together. And maybe our story won't end like a Shakespearian comedy. No wedding in our future.

No marriage.

Possibly, that'll do.

I nod and breathe and say, "I'm absolutely positive about one thing. I don't need a passion."

Thatcher Moretti is smiling. "You don't." He agrees.

I smile into a flood of tears. "I've never needed to have ambition, and it's taken me *so long* to reach this place. Years. And you're the first person I wanted to tell."

He sways at that realization, then cups my face, brushing away the wet streaks. "What else?"

It bursts my heart.

How well this man knows me.

How he *knows* when I have more to say.

"I don't need a career to be a smart woman." I go on. "I don't need a job to be talented. I am both smart and possess talent, and the love that I give is just as important as the fashion empire my mom built. I am *enough* just as I am."

It is so freeing, and I soar. He hoists me in his arms, my legs wrapping around him. My hands threaded behind his neck, and our foreheads nearly press together as we stare into each other.

Very deeply, he tells me, "I am in awe of you."

Tears spill, and our breaths come fuller, timed together. "The feeling is mutual," I whisper, thinking of his self-restraint with Tony. "You're a good man."

"You're a better woman."

I choke on emotion, and he cups my cheek and whispers, "Jane."

Thatcher.

His name is inside a kiss, our lips colliding with slow-burning affection that floats me up another thousand feet high.

We can't stay hidden in the broom closet for long. To be frank, we could easily be carried away and seal this moment with glorious sex. As we often do, but we've accepted house duties. Thatcher takes the third floor, as promised.

He pats my ass and moves past me.

I flush, my lips rising with my heart, and I continue on the second floor, clipboard in hand. Perhaps the year won't end so sadly after all, and excitement carries me like a gust of wind. I'm dying to share my epiphany with my best friend now.

Like perfect happenstance, his bedroom is the next stop on my checklist. I can't quell my smile. The door is shut, so I turn the knob and breeze inside.

"Moff—" My feet brake, body frozen in alarm.

Farrow is on top of Moffy, sheets unfortunately bunched at the foot of the bed, and his tattooed body bears down and welds against Maximoff's back and…bottom, while Moffy sinks into the mattress. I can also unfortunately tell that they're nearing the *end* of an intimate moment that I'm not supposed to see, one that I've so mortifyingly interrupted.

I'm too distraught and scarred to describe *why* I can tell.

Farrow immediately stops moving. He swings his head to me, breathing hard like he's…well he is having sex, so… "*Shit,*" he curses.

He is very quick to toss a pillow at Moffy, blocking my cousin's view of me, and then he whips up the green sheets. Covering themselves.

"I'm so…so sorry," I squeak out.

Move, Jane.

I still have a massive flaw called the inability to divert from embarrassing situations. My eyes are popped and unable to close.

Please close.

"I thought you locked the door?" Maximoff speaks to Farrow, shifting out from under his fiancé.

"I did," Farrow says, sounding truly certain.

I roast head-to-toe and force my feet to back up. *Go to the door.* I'm a voyeur here, and I don't particularly love *seeing* a family member hot and heavy. "I'm so, so, *so* sorry." I ramble out more deep apologies, and I reanimate more and lift my clipboard to my face.

Perfect.

I can't see them.

I do my best to tune out their private conversation too, but I pick up a bit of the exchange.

"Are you okay?" Farrow whispers. "Wolf scout, hey, look at me."

"Are you alright?" Maximoff replies with total concern. "You're okay?"

Finally, I spin around and reach the door, and I've never been happier to clasp a knob. I tug and—*oh God.*

It breaks off the wood. Dislodging right from the door.

I gape wide-eyed at the brass knob in my hand. "No."

No, no, no.

Frantic, I try to open the door without the knob, but it's jammed into the frame. I rattle the wood, realizing that Farrow most likely *did* lock it earlier. But the door is old and worn and revolting on us all.

"Come on," I say in distress, my pulse reeling. I pound a fist on the wood. "BANKS! Banks!" *Please save me from embarrassment. Merci beaucoup.*

Footsteps sound.

My archangel. He's arrived.

"Jane, what's wrong?" Shadows flit beneath the door. He must be right outside the room. "Talk to me, honey."

Shock has my tongue, but I breathe out. "I accidentally walked in on Maximoff and Farrow, and I'm trying to leave and the knob broke, and now I'm trapped in this room."

"Hold on. I'll get you out of there." He works on wedging open the door from his side.

My panic begins to recede. I think of the time I saw Donnelly giving Luna head, and I wince. "I can't believe this is happening again."

"Again?" Farrow repeats, coming up beside me to check the door. His barbell piercing ratchets up with his brows.

Thank God he's dressed. Drawstring pants hang low on his waist, inked sparrows in view on his hips.

I'm so discombobulated about this entire situation that I don't even realize what I said or what he's questioning. Not until he asks, "Isn't this the only time you've walked in on us?" He combs back his sweaty platinum hair.

Oh.

Oh.

"*Yes,*" I emphasize. "Yes. I've prided myself on *never* seeing you two... like that. And now that streak has ended." My entire face radiates heat.

I glance over at Moffy.

He's in gray sweatpants, and he pulls a Harvard shirt over his head. He looks as mortified as me, but neither of us shies away—and I try to make light of the awkward run-in.

"You looked very comfortable," I note. "And very pleased by what Farrow was doing, which is to say that you must really trust him..." I'm on fire.

Maximoff smiles a little bit.

Possibly I haven't made this worse.

I nod repeatedly. "I'm so, *so* sorry." It wells up inside of me.

"It's okay, Janie." He licks his lips, then gestures to his head. "I'm just processing...it's a lot."

"I know." I wince. "And Thatcher and I will absolutely let you two walk in on us to even the playing field."

"*Jane,*" Thatcher says strongly on the other side of the door.

He's not thrilled at that idea.

I waft my sweater.

"I'll pass on that," Farrow says easily. He tries to figure out the door situation, communicating with Thatcher for a minute. They work together, but the door isn't unsticking.

Thatcher finally says, "It's not coming down without removing the hinges. I'll need tools or I can kick it in."

As much as I'd rather flee quickly, I don't want to destroy the owner's house. "Don't break it. I think there's a toolkit in the laundry room."

"I'll be right back." He pauses. "Jane?"

"Yes?"

"You'll be okay?" He must know the ditch I've dug, and I'd want him to stay but I want to be in his arms more.

"Oui."

I can feel his towering presence leave, and I look over my shoulder.

Maximoff stands off the bed, confusion in his green eyes. "I still don't get why you said this has happened *again*."

I turn, facing him fully, my clipboard pressed to my lips. I can't lie to Moffy. Our friendship is one of complete transparency. We tell each other everything.

We often share secrets quickly. Almost immediately. Guilt overturns my stomach because I've kept one from him for weeks on end.

For Luna's sake.

I think he'll understand why I did, but his reaction to this news is what Luna feared. He will go 3/4ths Uncle Loren, and Luna doesn't want to know how their overprotective dad might respond to her hookup.

But I'm about to see.

I lower the clipboard to my belly. "You should take a seat."

He goes rigid. "What happened?"

Farrow leaves the door and joins Maximoff. He clasps his hand.

Moffy lets out a breath, but his shoulders never loosen. His attention is on me, waiting.

"It's not so terrible," I tell him. "Really, it's not."

He blinks. "Is it about your brothers?"

"No."

"My brother?" He points to his chest.

I pause. "Not quite."

He stiffens. "My sisters?"

"Sister," I correct.

"Luna?"

I nod.

Farrow runs his thumb over his lip piercing. "You said this happened *again*, so that means you walked in on Luna having sex?"

Maximoff cringes. "Christ."

"Yes." I hug my clipboard. "It was as unlucky and unfortunate as walking in on you two."

"But you didn't tell me when it happened," Maximoff realizes. "Why?"

"Luna asked me not to, and I promised her."

Farrow processes fast and tells Moffy, "Your sister thought you'd be pissed."

"Oui."

Maximoff fixates on the wall in deep contemplation. "I already know she's having sex, and I'd *never* shame her for that. I just want her to be safe, so I really don't get why she thinks I'd overreact." His eyes hit mine with pure brotherly protectiveness. "Did the guy hurt her? Is she okay?" He's already storming towards the door.

I'm suddenly very thankful we're locked in this room.

Farrow sprints in front and blocks him, a hand to his chest. "Wolf scout, let's hear Jane out before we go on a fictional manhunt."

He glares. "If someone hurt my little sister, it's not going to be a fucking *fictional* manhunt. I'm going to kill him with a switchblade laced in arsenic."

I try not to smile. My best friend has murderous hyperboles that my mom would applaud in a heartbeat.

"You don't even know why you'd be committing murder," Farrow says matter-of-factly. "Or who you're supposed to be killing."

"She's fine. Really, *really* fine," I emphasize. "She enjoyed the moment greatly. It was completely consensual."

Maximoff tries to relax, his hand sliding back in Farrow's hand. "Who was it? What'd they do?" His tone is sharp, so it sounds like he's asking for a culprit and a motive.

I take one breath.

And I say just it. "I walked in on Paul Donnelly giving Luna great head—the *great* was her assessment, though from my vantage it did look very pleasing…" I trail off, so sweltering hot that I can barely think straight.

Farrow's jaw has dropped. Shock slowly washes over his face, and he swings his head to me. "Donnelly?"

"Yes."

Maximoff lets go of his hand, just to set his palms on his head. Like he's winded and attempting to catch his breath. He spins to Farrow. "You told me not to worry about him."

"It was consensual," I remind them. "Luna asked Donnelly to go down on her."

They're both staring at me like I'm speaking an entirely different language.

"It was for science," I add, unhelpfully. "She *enjoyed* it." *Yes, stick to this point.*

Maximoff's glower intensifies.

I give him a disapproving look. "Not that it matters. At all apparently."

He groans, frustrated. "That matters. That's not why I'm glaring." He rakes his hands through his thick dark-brown hair, then lowers his arms to his side. "Are you sure it was Donnelly?"

"Positive."

"You're sure it was consensual?"

"*Yes.* No doubt."

Farrow leans casually on the antique dresser. "Shit, how much did you see?"

"Far too much."

"When?" Maximoff asks.

I explain the entire ordeal. Every little detail of how I went to find a condom and instead walked in on Luna and Donnelly, and somehow this explanation is the easiest and breeziest compared to everything else tonight.

By the end, Thatcher has returned and begun unscrewing the hinges. I've expected Maximoff to be upset, so I'm not surprised when he charges for the door.

Farrow catches his arm. "Where are you going?"

"To have a tea party with a bodyguard, who apparently decided to play Bill Nye the fucking Science Guy with my sister."

I whisper to the door. "Thatcher?"

"Yeah?"

"Work slowly."

"Copy that." He understands that it's better if Maximoff does *not* confront Donnelly right now.

"The door is jammed," Farrow tells him. "You're not going anywhere, so just relax, *relax*." He cups his jaw.

His eyes are reddened. "I'm totally relaxed." His Adam's apple bobs. "More relaxed than you."

"Keep trying because you're not even close yet."

"Yeah?" He holds onto Farrow's waist. "I feel pretty goddamn *Zen*."

I smile, but my lips fall as Maximoff hangs his head and pinches his raw eyes.

"Donnelly was doing what Luna asked," I remind him.

He winces, looking up again. "Are we really going to justify this?" He turns to me. "She was *eighteen*."

Farrow tosses his head from side to side. "Technically, she was about to be nineteen in a couple weeks."

Maximoff glares. "Donnelly could've said *no*. You told me I could trust him with her."

"And you still can—"

"He went down on her!" Maximoff yells and looks between us. "Am I living in the Twilight Zone? Why are you two okay with this?" Hurt pulses in his eyes, and he puts his hands on top of his head again, distressed.

I step forward. "Because Luna is an adult and she asked him."

Maximoff is stone, staring painfully at the ceiling.

Farrow stands off the dresser and nears him. "Donnelly is good people. I know he has some rough edges, but he'd never hurt Luna. I'd swear on my life to that."

"Would you swear on mine?" Maximoff asks.

He runs his tongue over his molars. "No. But not because I don't trust Donnelly." He loves Moffy terribly so, and he's the type of person who'd never put his love in harm's way, even at the sake of making a point.

Maximoff crouches, forearms on his knees. His adrenaline must be pumping. He looks up at me. "He's *eight* years older than her, Janie."

"I know," I say softly. "But Aunt Daisy and Uncle Ryke have a seven-year age difference. It's not so different."

His gaze darkens at the floor. "Do you know how much shit they got for that? The media eviscerated them. My little sister gets piled on every damn day, and I keep thinking about how more people are going to shit on her. She just left high school bullies behind." He slowly rises to try to be at height with Farrow. He rotates to him. "I know I sound like a fucking hypocrite. This is exactly why my dad didn't want me to date you. He wanted *easy* for me, and dating a bodyguard was light-years from that."

My eyes soften. "Relationships were never going to be easy," I remind him. "For any of us."

Maximoff ponders this.

"Also to note," I say aloud. "Media has been speculating that she's with Quinn." They've paired all of SFO with their clients. "So it's not as though they'll shit on her for dating a bodyguard."

"Quinn is around her age," Maximoff rebuts. "Donnelly isn't."

Farrow says, "Luna is strong as hell."

Maximoff almost eases. "Yeah. I know she is. But I'm not the brother I want to be if I don't give the third-degree to every guy that wants in her pants."

"Every guy?" Farrow whistles. "Man, you have some catching up to do."

"Pretty sure only one guy wants in her pants and he's downstairs."

"You're definitely off."

"No."

He raises his brows. "Pretty sure thousands of guys want in Luna Hale's pants."

He blinks slowly into a glare. "Thank you for that visual."

His lips rise. "Happy to provide."

Maximoff growls away an emerging smile and looks to the locked door. "Is that open yet? Donnelly is due for a third-degree."

"Soon," I tell him.

"He can handle whatever you give him," Farrow says. "I'm more concerned about what happens when your dad finds out."

Maximoff shakes his head. "That can't happen."

Oh thank God.

I expel a huge breath and tap the door. "You can work faster."

"Already there," Thatcher confirms.

Maximoff cracks his knuckles. "You said this was a one-time thing, right? Because Luna told me she's the one who ran out of birth control."

"A one-time thing, yes." I nod. "At least, that's what they said."

Farrow makes a face like he's slightly disbelieving. I don't buy it either, but that's only because Thatcher divulged to me what he witnessed on the dance floor at the pub. Lots of pelvic grinding.

"To be on the safe side," Farrow says. "I'm going to let Donnelly know Luna's not on birth control—or we should tell Luna to tell him. In case they are still having sex."

Maximoff's face turns to fire again. "I'm going to ki—lightly murder him. No arsenic."

"Still murder, wolf scout."

"New plan," I say. "For the sake of your sister, let's not confront either of them about this while we're all stuck in a house. Blasting her sex life to sixteen people would be a terrible embarrassment that might scar her for life." I've already endured enough mortifying moments to last everyone a lifetime.

Farrow grabs a black V-neck off the ground. "Smart." While he dresses, he zeroes in on Maximoff. As do I. We wait for him.

He's in deep thought again.

"Moffy," I say. "Let's not make this worse for her."

He instantly nods. "Alright. We'll wait." We only want the best for our siblings, and he has to be hard on them to help them. I have to be hard on Beckett too, but being a hardass isn't in my arsenal like it's in his.

I feel like I'm failing Beckett every single day.

And I'm worried Plan Z might be implemented while we're here.

Our heads turn as Thatcher removes the entire door, and I walk into his arms. He constantly checks the hall to make sure Tony or O'Malley don't appear and witness our embrace.

Behind us, Maximoff and Farrow are chest-to-chest in a long hug. I can't really tell who is holding who.

"You're burning up." Thatcher has my cheeks in his hands.

"Embarrassment is a very hot and mighty thing," I say softly. "Is midnight here yet?"

He checks his watch. "An hour till." His eyes flit to my best friend. "You should tell him what you told me. He'll be happy for you."

"I will." I smile, emotion building because this man wants me to share my life with my best friend too. No jealousy. No hurt. Just understanding.

I love him.

Fear pinches at the feeling, just slightly, but I slip my hand in his back pocket. Not wanting him to go.

I'd like to spend midnight in his arms, but we can't if Tony is in view. "Will the others notice if we stay up here for a little while longer?"

"No."

So we do. And we hide from the harsher realities that will come all too soon.

35

Jane Cobalt

"IF WE DO THIS, there is no return," I tell Charlie.

I want to ensure this is the right choice and he's not just zipping down to the last resort plan because he's been cooped up in Mackintosh House.

And the last resort is also known as *Plan Z*.

Charlie has fingers to his lips, gazing out the window. The tower room is the highest point in the house with panoramic views of the highlands. Snow drifts softly from the sky, the storm letting up today. Hopefully tomorrow. Hopefully it will all just melt and we can finally leave.

But until then, we have graver issues.

Thatcher stands stoically against green wallpaper. An old black-and-white sketch of the Holyrood Palace is framed in gold and hangs near his broad shoulder. We share a serious look off my brother's silence.

Charlie is usually confident about whichever road he drives down. Even if that street is riddled with regrets and hatred, he will meet all at full speed.

A moment passes.

Just one more, and his yellow-green eyes land on me. Assuredness etched in his irises. "We're doing this." He seizes his cane that leans up against the windowsill. "Beckett still hasn't made up with Sulli, and he's made *no* promises not to use coke." He lets out a dry laugh. "What's even the point of bringing him here if he's going to keep using drugs the second he returns to ballet?"

No point.

Not really.

We just delayed the inevitable.

It's why Plan Z always existed from the start, but it's one Thatcher, Charlie, and I didn't want to have to execute.

Maximoff can't even be here because if he's in the room, we all worry that Beckett will try to incite Charlie and Maximoff's feud to redirect the attention off himself.

I try reverting to a different option. "Mom and Dad know. Akara told them about Beckett, and they've most likely had suspicions long before. We could wait and see their point of attack. I'm sure they've been planning one."

Charlie rolls his eyes, frustrated. "We know what they'll do, Jane. They'll find a way to take *ballet* from him. Just like we've done during this trip. Only it'll be permanent, and he'll be a fucking shell after it happens."

My blood chills.

Beckett needs ballet.

It's his soul.

His passion.

"Mom and Dad taught us to be self-reliant, did they not?" Charlie questions. "We're working together and solving this *now*. We've dragged our feet for too many weeks."

Thatcher adjusts his earpiece. "What happens if this doesn't work?" His voice is deep and serious.

"It's going to work," Charlie says, confidence emblazoning him. He wraps himself in it like a cloak. I wonder if the sentiment conceals something else underneath or if his core is just as certain.

I trust him with everything I have. And so I take a deeper breath and say, "Go get him."

Charlie braces some of his weight on his cane and passes me for the door. He pauses just to whisper, "Que l'audace soit mon amie." And then he leaves.

His words ring my head. It's one of our family's favorite Shakespeare quotes, and in French, it's become one of our many mottos.

Boldness be my friend.

I meet Thatcher's gaze. "Do you think we're making the wrong choice?"

"No." Zero hesitation in his voice. "Any choice you both agree on, together, is going to be the right one." His jaw hardens and he blinks. "But I can't lie to you—it's gonna be hard for me to just stand here and watch you do this. It's going against every fucking instinct I have."

I know.

"Do you want to leave?" Even offering him that option nearly steals my breath. I want him here. I *need* him here.

That need nearly pummels me, but I welcome the strong feeling in this second. I could shout from the rooftops of the world.

I need him!

I need him!

I need Thatcher Moretti, the love of my life, my boyfriend and safety and comfort and armor!

"I'm not leaving." He's as confident as my brother, and I'm quite certain that I'm the one floundering.

I'm the one flopping around in this room. In less than sixty-seconds, I'm going to need to pack on every piece of battle gear I have.

Charlie isn't the one directing this plan.

I am.

"You're not leaving me," I repeat, letting this lift my chin and pull back my shoulders.

"I'm staying here," Thatcher adds. "Even if it fucking kills me. I'm not moving a muscle."

Emotions tunnel through me. I've never had fealty from someone who isn't family, and this isn't the fealty of a bodyguard. Because if he were, he'd stop me. He'd walk out of the room.

He's here as someone else.

My confidante in life. My right-hand. My wingman.

My hope and future.

I blink back *the* feeling, the surge, the swell that causes my breath to stagger.

"What do you need to tell me?" Beckett questions, just having stepped inside the tower room. Floral tattoos spindle down his arm, only in a black muscle tee. Beads of sweat are built on his forehead, and damp pieces of his dark hair hang over a rolled bandana.

Like he just finished a workout.

He must not be cold because he glides across the room and leans against the windowsill. The chilliest area.

Charlie closes the door and flips the lock, but Beckett doesn't notice or doesn't care. He just crosses his arms, calm but not content.

He looks anxious these extra days here and without contact back home. "What is it?"

"Do you plan to use drugs when we return home?" I ask.

Beckett lets out an aggravated breath and looks from me, to Charlie, then to Thatcher, realizing that this is about *cocaine*. "I've been in Scotland for almost three weeks—have you seen withdrawal symptoms from me even once?"

Stay strong. I don't cower. I take three steps, closing the gap between us. "No, but that doesn't change the facts. You're using coke *every* day you have a performance. That's six times a week." My eyes widen. "That's not healthy. You could have a heart attack, a stroke, and you're destroying your nasal lining from snorting it."

"I don't need a Web M.D. side effect rundown, sis. And if you want to give me one, you better tell him too." He nods towards his twin brother.

Charlie rolls his eyes. "Please." The *please* is a bitter one.

"No." Beckett stands up to his full height, two inches shorter than Charlie. "You act like I'm the addict because I'm doing coke. But you're taking God-knows-what from God-knows-who. I mean, peyote? Really?"

Charlie blinks. "You're twisting this. You know I don't take drugs regularly."

"So just because I'm careful with coke every day, I'm the addict." He nods. "Okay, sure, I think Mom and Dad will buy that logic. How about we have a meeting when we're home? They can hear what you've been up to." He counts on his fingers. "LSD, ecstasy—"

"You wouldn't," Charlie interjects, casual and unconcerned. "I'll call your bluff every time, *brother*."

I jump in. "It's every day, Beckett. But what happens when you grow a tolerance and you have to start using it twice a day just to achieve the same high? Then three times. Four. Then you're doing meth—"

"*No.*" He rubs his temples with both hands. "Why aren't you listening to me? Hear what I'm saying. I'm not using any more than *once* a day."

"Did it start out like that?" I counter.

He goes quiet, but his glare intensifies. It burns me up. I feel Thatcher's presence behind me, silently telling me he's here. And *I'm* strong. I can do this.

Plan Z.

"Substance addiction runs in the Hale and Meadows families, Beckett," I say, fighting back tears. "You say you're not an addict. Fine. But I can't just sleep soundly knowing you're in New York using cocaine every night just because you believe it helps you dance better. I *won't* do that."

He shakes his head, pained.

My throat swells but I keep talking. "I've imagined what happens in a year or two or three. I'm going to receive a phone call from Charlie or god-forbid Eliot or Tom. And they're going to tell me that it was an accident. That maybe it was laced with something or you just took too much that night. And you'll just be another rich kid killed too early from a drug that caters to the wealthy and bored. A sad statistic marked in your Wikipedia page. While our family has to mourn you every day for the rest of our lives. Because you will leave a gaping, miserable hollow hole. *Toujours.*" Forever.

Tears roll down his cheeks, matching mine.

With reddened eyes, he says, "You can't make me stop." It's the truest thing he's ever said. Addiction is a wretched monster, and the only one who can truly defeat addiction is the addict.

We've learned well enough from our family. We can do everything in our power to help Beckett, but at the very end, he has to want to help himself.

And he's not even close to that point yet. So we are fighting the greatest losing battle with our brother.

But we'll still fight for him.

"I know," I breathe. Admitting that is a pain to my heart. *I know.*
I know.

I know. And even with that knowledge, I'm going to try anyway. Because I've failed far too many times in my life to be terrified of failure now.

"So here's what's going to happen." I wipe the rest of my tears from my cheeks. *No return, no going back.* "If you don't promise me here, today, that you're going to stop using, then I'm moving to New York. I'm going to live in an apartment on the same hall, and every day that you snort coke, I'm going to do the same."

His eyes flash hot. "*Jane—*"

"If you're going to destroy your life, your body, then I'm going to destroy mine." I add in French, "Ton destin est mon destin." *Your fate is my fate.*

Charlie steps forward. "Ton destin est mon destin."

"You're insane." He rubs away his tear tracks with the heel of his palm. "You're both insane."

"We're Cobalts," Charlie declares.

Beckett extends an arm. "So being a Cobalt is now synonymous with insanity? That's great." He plants a look on me. "You're not taking coke. You freaked out when you ate a pot cookie. I call your bluff."

Charlie reaches into his back pocket. "We thought you'd say that." He procures a small baggie. Filled with white powder.

36

Thatcher Moretti

CHARLIE WAVES THE SMALL baggie of coke. Which he bought in town before we were snowed-in. I knew—*I fucking knew* this part would be like a swift kick to the gut.

It'd throttle me to move. To come to her aid. To sweep Jane protectively in my arms and pull her from immediate danger. I watch this play out in real-time, and it's fucking unbearable. Tendons in my neck pull taut, searing inside out. I grit down on my teeth and stay frosty.

Focused on *her*.

Back when I first heard the plan, my immediate reaction was to say no.

Fuck no.

Hell no.

Anyway you want to say it—*no*.

But Jane loves her family, and she'd do just about anything to protect them. Even put herself at risk. Being the barrier between her and *that* is like telling her not to be all of who she is.

So I said yes.

But seeing the events unfold, I'm questioning my judgment seven ways to hell.

Beckett has a *what the fuck* expression as he stares at the baggie. "Where did you get that? How...?"

Charlie arches a brow.

"Right. You've been to Scotland before," Beckett remembers. "I'm guessing you knew someone here who could sell to you?"

"Maybe."

"Fantastic," he mutters.

Among the security team, Beckett is known to be somewhat reasonable, mostly calm and dedicated to his craft—but I'm staring at a twenty-one-year-old who's so fucking frayed at the seams. I question how many times a day he spends ensuring every thread is hidden, every fucking stitch sewn.

I want to protect him.

I want to protect her.

He glances at Jane. "Sis, you're not really going to go through with this?"

"I am."

Sickness burns my throat. I blink infrequently, almost not at all.

Charlie sits on the edge of a red floral couch. He pours cocaine on a glass coffee table and uses a black credit card to separate the powder in lines.

Beckett looks haunted. He pushes away from the windowsill but he stops short of the table. He turns on me. "You're really going to let Jane snort cocaine?"

I don't answer. My pulse is in my ears. Ever since my PTSD crept outside of a nightmare, I worry I might meet it again.

Not today, I pray.

"Seriously?" Beckett shakes his head. "What kind of boyfriend are you?"

"One who knows how important this is," I say with severity. "You're the *only one* in this room who can stop her."

"Bullshit."

I glare, and my anger bursts. "If you want her to stop, just fucking tell her!"

Tell her, goddammit.

"You tell her!" Beckett points at Jane.

"I can't!" I shout. "You're the *only one.*"

His face contorts. "No. I'm getting Moffy." He heads to the door.

I side-step to block his exit, and I stare down at him. "Maximoff already knows."

His eyes darken. "There's no way."

Jane sinks down to her knees in front of the table. "Well, technically Moffy thinks you'd never let me do this."

Maximoff believes in him.

Farrow doesn't. I don't, and I feel like 9 out of 10 outcomes involve Jane using drugs in this room. If we repeated this ten times, I only see Beckett choosing his sister and brother *once.*

Is this that one time?

I doubt it.

Charlie went a darker route when we planned this, and he said, *"We might need to call in Moffy to join us."*

"No," Farrow and Jane said.

But the reality is that Maximoff is sober. He has the family history of addiction, and Charlie thinks that forcing Maximoff to use drugs could push Beckett to quit more than them.

Maximoff agreed.

He's waiting in the hall.

If Charlie gives me a signal, I'm supposed to radio Farrow, who'll tell Maximoff to come inside. But I can't put Farrow in the position I'm in.

I can't put Maximoff in the position Jane is in.

Beckett has to choose his sister.

He stares past me and out the many windows. Confliction tearing up his face—and I just tell him, "Choose her."

His eyes redden.

It's the easiest call in the book. *"Choose her.* She's right there." I point at his sister, knelt in front of his vice. "Choose your twin brother."

Charlie meets Beckett's eyes, both the same yellow-green.

He slowly, almost involuntarily, shakes his head. He faces the door. "Let me out."

"No." Acid drips down my throat.

I've never been addicted to anything in my life—not like my twin brother who's been trying to kick his own habits for years. I understand it can't be that simple for him. Something in his head is telling him it's the hardest call of his life.

So difficult he's standing here wrestling with himself.

Jane frowns, then asks Charlie, "So how do I do this?"

Beckett is turned towards me. Only me. And when he hears that, his face begins to crack, a fissure running through his features.

Charlie instructs, "Press your finger to one nostril—"

"Stop," Beckett says in a whisper that I can only hear.

Charlie keeps talking, and I nod Beckett towards his siblings.

"No." He battles emotion. "You have to stop her. If my parents hear that you let her do this, they'll *never* accept you. Do you want that?"

I narrow my eyes on him. All I've wanted is for her family to fully accept me. Beckett knows that, and I realize what has to be done.

I click my mic on my collar. "Banks to Farrow, barricade the door. Don't let Beckett out."

"Done," Farrow responds.

I leave my post with a determined, assured stride, and I lower next to Jane on the floor. "Make me a line," I tell Charlie.

He frowns for a millisecond before smiling.

I finally look to Jane.

Her lips are parted, eyes wide. "Thatcher?"

"We do this together," I say. "You and me."

Tears gather in her eyes. I brush them away.

"People do stupid things when they're in love," Charlie says, but it's not in disdain. It's warm, heartfelt and he looks at me like he's acknowledging that I am stupid-in-love with his sister. And fuck it, that's the best outcome there is.

Three lines streak the table. I've never done cocaine, but I can't think of a better reason to. My mind is right. That's all that matters.

"You ready?" Jane asks.

"I'm good to go."

She smiles.

I hold her hand, and we dip our heads down to the table with Charlie.

"Stop!" Beckett shouts. "Wait, just stop!" He storms over and places a hardback book on top of the cocaine lines. "*Don't* ever." He's speaking to his sister and brother. "Not for me."

Jane tenses. "Only if—"

"Yes, okay. *Yes.* I'm going to stop. I won't use anymore. Not for performances or rehearsals."

"Or anything," Charlie says.

"Or anything," he promises.

"Because if you do, I'll be your roommate," Jane reminds him. "Thatcher, Charlie, and I will be using every *single* day—"

"I know. The threat still stands, I heard you," Beckett nods. "I know, sis."

We all are on our feet.

"It's not just a threat," Charlie says. "It's an oath."

Beckett surprisingly nods. "Okay. Let's spit on it."

"No." Jane begins to smile. "This one has to be done with blood." She turns to me, and I unsheathe my knife, the kind every bodyguard here is armed with, instead of guns.

The four of us make a blood pact in the tower room. Jane glances at me while Charlie cuts his palm, and we share an acknowledgement that Beckett's promise could be temporary. The only thing stopping him from using isn't a pact. It's not Jane. Or me. Or Charlie.

It's himself.

And the moment he decides this isn't worth it, he'll start again. But for now, we all settle with taking his word. Hopefully it means something.

37

Thatcher Moretti

20 DAYS SNOWED-IN

AKARA HAS CALLED AN emergency security meeting, Epsilon bodyguards included—and no one is throwing jabs or backhanded horseshit. We gather around the circular breakfast table in the cold kitchen and carry complete focus and intensity. Committed to the same purpose, the same reason we're here.

Our clients.

These families come *first*.

We've sworn to put them before our feuds, before our personal problems, before our hunger and aches and pains and needs.

Akara unzips his wet jacket, the sat-phone on the table. "Here's the deal, guys. The village's inn is a ten-hour hike on foot, and the owner said she has enough provisions to house six people if we can make it there."

"Scots are dope," Donnelly says.

Residents here have been more than friendly. Over a few days ago, a Scottish local trekked here to check up on us. Just in time too. He helped us fix another burst pipe. Without the generosity and kindness of the Scottish residents, we couldn't stay here long in these conditions.

"We have two problems," Akara announces. "1. We can't leave until the winds die down—and from what she said, it didn't sound like anytime soon, and 2. Only six people can go." The change of scenery, getting out of this house—it'll be like a life raft for some.

The priority list is unspoken.

Six clients are in Scotland: Jane, Maximoff, Charlie, Beckett, Sullivan, and Luna. *They come first.* Along with the little sister of two bodyguards. We take care of our own.

Joana Oliveira is high-priority.

Which makes seven. But we all know Maximoff will volunteer to stay behind.

"You only want six people to go on the ten-hour hike?" Oscar asks for clarification.

Akara nods. "Just six."

Quinn frowns. "Why not send bodyguards as escorts? We can go with the clients, drop them off, then hike back here."

"We can't risk it," Akara explains. "If the weather changes, you won't be able to return to Mackintosh House, and we have to respect the fact that they're letting six stay. It needs to be a group of two bodyguards and four clients."

Tension stretches in the brief pause.

Akara peels off his gloves. "Most of them are nearing breaking points. It's not a secret."

Chairs creak as men lean back or shift.

I cross my arms, my jaw hardened. Bodyguards—we're used to the grind. Being snowed-in for almost three-weeks with little communication back home is more or less a cakewalk, but it's not as easy for these families.

Being useless to the people we protect, especially as they unravel—that's a hundred times harder than splitting a bowl of oatmeal eight ways.

Which we did this morning.

"We have to priority-rank them," Akara says. "High is critical, medium is urgent, and low is fine to stay. I want an evaluation of your client and a rank. We'll go around the table, and if anyone has information about the client being discussed, you need to share."

Going counter-clockwise, we start with O'Malley. Beckett's bodyguard.

"His hands are raw," O'Malley tells us. "He's been washing them too many times a day. He needs to go back to PA more than anything."

"It's not an option," Akara reminds him. "How would you rank him?"

"Critical."

Everyone is nodding.

Quinn scoots forward, elbows on the table. He brushes a knuckle over the scar under his eye. "Okay, so Luna has been pretty emotional…" He stops himself short. "I'd say she's critical." He's being tight-lipped on his client's behalf.

He picked this shit up from *Farrow.* Who gives half-answers and vague responses during debriefings. The bare minimum.

Flat-out, it's annoying.

Akara gives him a look. "How does that make her critical?"

"She's been crying." Quinn tries to clarify.

Oscar pulls on a Yale sweatshirt. "Is she homesick?"

"No, that's not really it."

My eyes narrow on Quinn. I understand it's uncomfortable to unleash private information about the clients we're closest to—but Akara needs this intel in order to make a call.

I glance at the Omega lead. "She's the one who ran out of birth control." This might be affecting her hormones on some level.

Quinn shoots me a glare. "What if Luna didn't want everyone to know?"

"We're fucking past that, Quinn," I say seriously.

Akara nods. "We could be here for another *three months*, guys. This isn't the time to censor any shit. You know something, *say it.*"

Donnelly smacks a pack of cigarettes on his palm. "She's been having bad cramps too."

"There's no more pain meds," Farrow reminds everyone.

"She's critical," Akara agrees with Quinn, and we move on.

To me.

But at this meeting with Epsilon, I'm Banks Moretti. Which means that my client is Maximoff Hale, shared with Farrow.

So I turn to him beside me. "You go ahead."

Farrow balances back on his chair legs. "Maximoff isn't sleeping. He's probably clocked in two hours in three days, and that's being extremely fucking generous."

"Is he taking Ripped Fuel?" O'Malley asks, actually being cordial.

"No." Farrow shakes his head. "He's just stubborn as fuck, and he feels responsible to help get everyone home."

Akara nods. "Where would you rank him?"

"Urgent, but he's going to place himself as *fine*."

Maximoff won't take up a spot that his cousin or sister could fill.

We continue, jumping over Donnelly who has no client here.

Oscar sounds deadly serious as he says, "Charlie can't be here. I've never seen him locked in *one* place for this long. He can't handle it, and I'll tell you right now, he's critical and he's number one on the priority list."

Akara nods. "And Joana?"

"Other than being pissed she missed her fight, she's fine." Oscar shifts forward. "But she's attached to me, so if you send me with the four clients, Jo has to be one of them. I love most of you motherfuckers and I trust you all, but I'm not leaving her."

"Can she stay with Quinn?" Akara asks.

"No." Oscar looks to his brother. "Sorry, little bro."

"She's my sister too," Quinn retorts.

"I'm ten years older than you and *twelve* years older than her—so let's not fucking start this. Okay?"

Quinn nods tensely.

We have two clients left to discuss. *Jane is last.* I wait in anticipation, my chest tightening, and Akara brings up his girl.

"Sulli is homesick." Akara rubs his chilled hands. "She can't call her dad or mom here, and it's been getting to her."

He's my closest friend, and I hate that he hasn't talked to me about this. I can see that Sulli's pain is tearing at him.

"She's urgent." Akara ranks her.

"What about the Rooster?" Donnelly asks. "Won't he wanna be with his girlfriend if she leaves?"

Akara restrains an eye roll at the mention of Will Rochester. "He can't go. If he wants to complain, he can complain to the nearest wall."

Farrow and Oscar are grinning.

Yeah, Akara sounds jealous. But he nods to Tony, keeping the show on the fucking road, and my senses sharpen as her name reaches the air.

"Jane is fine," Tony says easily. "She's just been keeping to herself."

I swallow a rock. I want to say how last night she almost had a panic attack. How I held her in my arms and I practically rocked her to sleep while she cried in my chest.

But I can't.

They can't know that I spent the night in her bedroom. Or that we've run out of condoms days ago and have resorted to going down on each other, hand jobs, and fingering. We're both too sexually frustrated, and that's on top of the power flickering out randomly. Sporadically. At the worst possible times.

But that's not what has built her emotions to a cliff.

Luckily, I can say what has out loud. "She's been missing her cats."

Tony zones in on me. "How can you tell?"

"She's told me. Not being able to call home and know they're safe is hard on her. She's used to being sent videos and pictures when she's traveling."

"She's urgent?" Akara asks me.

"I just said she's *fine*," Tony cuts in.

Oscar gives him a look. "It's not a knock on you, bro. Banks spends time with Jane off-duty. He knows her personally."

When Tony calms down, I confirm, "She's urgent, but she won't want to go."

I can already picture my girlfriend prioritizing Sulli and Joana over herself.

With all the intel on the table, Akara has a hard choice. Oscar should be going if Charlie is going. He's one of the only men capable of keeping Charlie safe.

But that means Joana is onboard over Sulli.

He makes a decision. "The clients going are Charlie, Luna, Beckett, and Sulli. As for the two bodyguards, I have to stay here." He's the lead and needs to be with the core group. "So I'm sending Farrow and Banks."

Goddammit.

No one complains or backtalks or second-guesses, but I'm not happy to be split from Jane—if or when that time comes. Leaving her back here with that shitbag...

I shove down my feelings.

And I focus on my duty. If something happens to one of them, the world will mourn. So many people idolize these famous families. They represent something bigger than themselves. They are hope and inspiration and light in dark times, and inadvertently, by protecting them, we're protecting that essence too.

Once the meeting ends, we disperse.

Most men head into the living room, and Jack Highland sees the trail of incoming bodyguards. He stands off the fireplace hearth, freeing his spot for us to get warm.

"Where are you going, Long Beach?" Oscar asks in passing. "You move one muscle from that fire, you're going to turn into an icicle." He flashes a grin. "I already see your weak California blood crystallizing as I speak."

Jack smiles as he lowers back down. "Not all of us have warm sweatshirts like you." He looks him over. "You willing to part with it?"

I'm not sure if he's flirting. All I know is that Jack has said he's straight.

Oscar pulls off his Yale sweatshirt and lightly chucks the clothing to Jack.

"You sure?" Jack asks, about to pull his arms through the holes.

"For sure. It's already in your hands, Long Beach," Oscar says with a laugh, and I leave that interaction behind when I find Jane on a chair scribbling math equations in her notebook.

I can't comfort her here. But I walk over anyway, cautious of Tony in sight. He plucks an almanac off the shelf and sprawls on a couch.

Her blue eyes lift off the notebook. "I'm better, really. Did the meeting go well?"

"Menzamenz." *Half and half.*

She smiles at my use of Italian, and the rest of the morning, we play *Clue* with Maximoff and Farrow, the board game worn and dusty from being crammed in a cupboard.

I stretch out my legs under the coffee table, and while Maximoff fights exhaustion beside Farrow on the couch, Jane and I sit side by side on the floor. Pillows beneath us.

Don't touch her.

I hammer the thought in my brain.

Don't touch her.

The shitbag is looking.

"It was professor plum, with a revolver, in the library," Jane guesses.

Slyly, I reveal the revolver card in my hand to Jane, and she scratches the weapon off her list. Maximoff should be taking his turn.

I look across the table.

Exhaustion has won out. His eyes are shut, head on Farrow's shoulder. Body slumped against him too.

Farrow holds him pretty tenderly. They've been on the edge of the seat together, and without waking him, he carefully draws Maximoff and himself further back against the couch.

He doesn't stir. Still sleeping.

Jane has a pained expression, just seeing his sleep deprivation. "I'm afraid if we wake him, he'll be upset he fell asleep and try harder not to."

Farrow whispers back, "Which is why he's staying like this."

Their closeness makes me wish I could bridge the small gap between me and Jane. Just for a moment. A second.

Don't touch her.

We're about to scrap *Clue* and play a round of poker. And then Charlie Cobalt walks past our table, favoring his right leg, a book in his grip. He looks disturbed, like a ghost trapped inside a haunted house.

Jane watches her younger brother carefully and whispers to me, "He's bored and irritable."

Charlie slows when he sees Maximoff sleeping against Farrow.

This isn't good.

"Shh, Charlie." Jane puts a finger to her lips. "We're trying not to wake him." She's warning her brother.

Farrow is glaring at him to back off.

I'm about to stand up and guide him away.

"I can help with that." Charlie pats the hardback on his palm, and then he *hurls* the book at Maximoff's head.

Farrow catches the book midair, but the action jostles Maximoff. And his eyes snap open.

All hell breaks loose.

Farrow is on his feet, heat in his eyes, and I tower and have a hand on his chest so he won't near Charlie. Because in my head, Charlie isn't just a client. He's Jane's brother.

Protect him too, but he makes it hard.

"He's been a saint to you," Farrow sneers. "You couldn't let him have one fucking second of peace—"

"He's had a million seconds," Charlie retorts. He leans on the antique TV hutch.

"Stop, Charlie," Jane says hotly, standing off the floor-pillows. I leave Farrow to come to her side, and she looks up at me with a jolt of fear.

Don't touch her.

Fuck me.

Fuck Tony, who's still watching. Hell, a lot of people are. This is the biggest show we've had since my knockout fistfight.

Charlie rolls his eyes, irritated. "For fuck's sake, you're acting like I put a gun to his head. I simply threw a book at him."

Maximoff rubs his tired eyes and slowly stands up.

"Maybe I should've thrown it harder so he could read me better."

"I'll read you," Farrow says. "I'll read you to fucking hell and back, and you couldn't take one minute of it."

Charlie's eyes burn. "I'm waiting."

"No," Maximoff cuts in and sweeps an arm around Farrow's shoulders, affectionately. "Don't, Farrow." He glances at Charlie. "No one is lashing back at you."

"Who made you king?"

"No one," Maximoff growls. "Christ, Charlie, just take a breath."

"I'm breathing," he snaps, then veers to Jane.

No.

He's picking tender, vulnerable flesh to attack, and I've been in fucked positions before—but I'm at a loss of what to do to protect Jane from her own brother.

"I'm dying on the side of the road," Charlie says. "So is Thatcher. Choose who to save."

She blinks back tears, a sharp breath escaping. "I'm not playing this game."

I will.

"She'd choose you," I tell him strongly. "My brother, Thatcher—he'd want her to choose you."

Jane's face twists.

Charlie doesn't even pause. "I'm dying on the side of the road. So is Moffy. Choose—"

"Charlie!" Maximoff yells.

Jane is winded, and I place a hand on her back. My stomach knots a thousand different ways.

"Yes?" Charlie arches a brow.

Maximoff growls, "You're being a sadistic asshole."

"I'm fine. I'm fine," Jane mutters repeatedly, a hand to her face. This is a combination of emotional hell she's felt.

They're all breaking, and my instinct is to carry her out of here.

One more minute of this shit, and I will.

"Sadistic." Charlie nods slowly. "You want to see sadistic?" He addresses the room. "Just so *everyone* is aware—this isn't Banks Moretti." He points at me.

I'm rigid.

"NO!" Jane screams bloody murder. "Charlie!"

I come up behind and hold her around the waist.

It's over.

Charlie wipes away a quick, fallen tear off his cheek. He broke her fucking heart, and I think he broke his own too.

Her legs buckle and she falls in my arms. "Jane, Jane," I whisper in her ear. "It's okay."

She shakes her head. *Guilt*—God, I understand her guilt.

But I won't let it drag her down. "It was gonna happen," I whisper. "Sooner or later." We can't blame him.

We can't blame anyone but ourselves, and then, at the end of day— I'm good at carrying the blame.

She takes a strong breath and straightens up in my hold around her waist. Her hands sliding along my arms.

Charlie leaves for the kitchen, and his twin brother sprints after him. Beckett glances back at me before he disappears, an apology in his eyes. And I know he's trying to give one *for* Charlie.

I'd do the same for Banks.

I recognize that Charlie didn't announce that I'm Thatcher, but the damage is done. He said enough, and Tony knows.

He's staring haunted at me. He deduces after some muttering with others that he was one of the few people to *not* know.

And then he lets out a breath of disbelief and rises off the rear couch. "You've got to be shitting me—all this time…" He shakes his head, emotion in his eyes that I didn't expect to meet.

I thought he'd threaten my job. My brother's job.

First.

Foremost.

He rubs his mouth and spits out, "The good sons. You know that's what everyone calls you two in the family—the fucking *good* sons." He laughs. "What a crock of fucking *shit*. If only they knew…maybe then I wouldn't have to hear from my grandma 'why can't you be more like those twos, huh?'—or from *my* uncles, askin' why I didn't go to war like the Moretti brothers. Tellin' me I should be a soldier, a leader like Thatcher. Tellin' me to go play football like you. And then my sister Nicola, tellin' me to be *good* like you."

I fixate on his jealousy.

I thought he was just insecure and punched down on me to make himself feel better. I didn't know…

Honestly, I didn't think anyone *could* be jealous of me. I was poor. I was an identical twin who got mixed up with another fucking person constantly. I wasn't popular in the traditional sense.

I felt like no one knew me.

No one saw me.

Except my brothers. My family.

My family.

Realization sinks deep. His family is my family. Ramellas, Morettis, Piscitellis.

He gestures to me. "How is it that you could lie to me for weeks about who you are?"

"You made it too easy," I say honestly.

I must be the worst son on the planet, because I can't apologize to him.

Tony sees my hate for him. More clearly than I think he ever has. He hangs his head, looks from side to side before looking at me. His eyes more reddened. "You really thought you could get away with it?"

"Yeah."

For one week.

Tony just keeps shaking his head. He exits into the parlor, not giving me the satisfaction of knowing what the hell he plans to do. But I can't see an outcome where he doesn't rat me out to the Alpha lead.

It's over.

Banks and I—we're fucked.

38

Banks Moretti

SECURITY'S TOWNHOUSE is empty at oh-two-hundred—a rare thing and this beauty belongs solely to me. Really though, I fucking hate being alone.

So being the only SFO bodyguard in Philly sucks major ass. I miss my brother, and I'm waiting for those unlucky souls to make it back home.

Until then, I lounge on the leather couch, feet kicked up on the coffee table. Cold beer in one hand, my cell balances on my knee. Set to speakerphone.

"Am I...in clear?" Akara's voice fractures over the line.

"Negative. You're breaking up." I swallow more beer.

He hasn't been able to call in weeks because of the wind chill. It's finally died down this morning. Enough for Akara to stand in the blistering cold with a sat-phone. Static cracks against the line.

I've already been informed of the two shit pies.

Tony knows about the twin switch. Yippee-ki-ya, *motherfucker*—I'm not excited, but I take the bad and just keep going. We'll see what happens.

I also just heard about the plan—a ten-hour hike to the village's inn—and how Thatcher is set to go. If the weather stays like it is, the group of six might be able to move out tomorrow. Apparently a storm has delayed the journey for seven days.

I wish I could be there to stay back with Jane. My brother must be losing his fucking mind to have to leave her behind with Tony.

"How about now?" Akara asks.

"You're clear."

He starts venting about the Rooster, and I think I mishear Akara.

My feet drop to floor, blown forward. Glaring at my phone. "He what?"

"He jerked away after touching the hair on her leg."

I hold the phone to my mouth. "*Fuuuuck* this knuckle-fuckbag." My blood is boiling.

Akara laughs. "Shit. I needed that." He means the laugh.

"What's he looking for, a two-holed plastic doll?" I shake my head. "He made her feel like shit, didn't he?" I take a harsher swig of beer.

I can't stand men like that.

"Sulli said Jane made her feel better about it." He lets out a rougher breath. "He's getting on my last nerve."

Akara has insane self-restraint, which makes him a great lead. He knows the Rooster is untouchable. As the boyfriend to a client, we're not allowed to glare at him.

Can't air our opinions about him.

Can't punch him—which I'd love to do—sorry, Mom.

Unless he's abusive or a threat to her safety in some other way, we're supposed to be impartial. I'd like to impartially declare that I'm *not* a fan.

"Are you gonna tell Sulli what he said to you?" Right before they boarded the plane, this Richie Rich had words with my best friend.

"I can't. He came to me in confidence. As her bodyguard, I have to respect a request from her boyfriend." Tension ekes on the line. "She *really* likes him—and I'm not sabotaging this. He's her first kiss."

From what Akara told me, their first kiss was a good moment. Good experiences are hard to come by. My first kiss was shit on wheels. We wouldn't want to morph the good thing into something bad.

I tuck hair behind my ear. "You think she'll be that mad at him if she hears his request?"

"She'll break up with him." He's that assured.

I don't tell him to go and do it.

Selfishly, we'd both love for them to break up, but our opinions on the guy don't hold weight to hers, and that's how it should be. We're not the ones making out with him.

Akara sighs out his frustration. "I can't fucking believe he told me to stop being her friend."

That wasn't exactly the request.

I smile into a swig of beer. "He told you to stop *flirting*." I can feel Akara's glare all the way from Scotland.

"Sul and I have *never* flirted."

They've flirted.

Hell, I've flirted with the girl. She's funny, competitive, a fucking smokeshow, and also very, very virginal but I wouldn't call her naïve. I'm just not sure she understands when men are hitting on her versus when they're just being *friendly*.

Akara's denial has probably confused the shit out of her.

"You're really gonna keep telling me you're not attracted to Sulli?"

He curses me out. "She's like my…*sister*."

"Your dick gets hard for your sister?"

He laughs lightly, the line cracking. "Always with the one-liners."

"You're the one freezing your nuts off for sister-fucking jokes."

"Yeah, my bad." Akara sounds less stressed. "Hey, at least she's not fucking the Rooster." He pauses. "If that's who she loses her virginity to…"

"I'd lose my shit."

"Not before me."

"Amen." I finish off my eighth beer, and then stretch my legs back out. "Are you—" I cut myself off at the sound of shattering glass.

Distant.

Coming from the famous one's townhouse.

"What was that?" Akara asks.

He could hear it over the fucking phone. "I don't know." The noise alerts my dulled senses. No security alarm is triggered, but I stay deathly still and pick up the squeak of floorboards.

I whisper, "An intruder." I grip my cell, shoot to my feet, and smack my toe into the coffee table. I catch a falling beer bottle before it crashes to the ground and causes more commotion.

Jesus fucking—I swear under my breath. What I hate, more than anything, is that I've been drinking. If my brother were here, he'd be dead sober.

For this reason.

To catch this fucking intruder.

God-fucking-damn. With that final curse, I leave my frustration behind. Already moving into action.

I skulk more soundlessly into the kitchen and grab my gun from a drawer. I pull the slide back to load a round in the chamber.

"Someone's in their townhouse," I whisper more clearly to Akara.

"Mute the phone, put it in your pocket."

I do as told, cell in my back pocket, and I attach my radio as fast and *quietly* as I can. Adrenaline sobers me more, my blood super-charged.

The thought of some piece of shit in *their* house. In *their* space. It makes me want to pop a bullet between eyes.

Jane's cats.

4 out of 6 cats are at the Cobalt Estate. Audrey is watching them, thank the fucking Lord. But there are still two left in the other townhouse.

The squirrelly little ones that dart every place—they were too hyper to corral in a cat carrier, so I told Audrey I'd take care of them while I'm here.

She wanted me to spit on her hand to promise. What the hell—I did it.

I switch comms frequencies. I can't let anything happen to those cats. "Thatcher to Price," I whisper to the Alpha lead. "I have movement and noise in the townhouse. Is anyone supposed to be there?"

"Not that I'm aware. Check it out and report back."

"Roger copy," I mutter in the mic, then *gently*—ever so gently—I push into the townhouse through the adjoining door.

I step on a cat toy, and the foil crinkles beneath the weight of my foot.

My pulse pounds.

Eyes narrowed.

I grip my gun with two hands, and I assess the first floor, the pink loveseat empty. Rocking chair is completely still. Pictures are upright on the mantel, and what little visual I have into the kitchen—it looks and sounds empty.

I peek into the kitchen archway. Glass litters the sink, window busted out. Enough space for a man to crawl through. How the hell did they cut the security alarm?

I shelve that.

First floor clear. I move forward to the staircase.

The ceiling creaks.

These stairs are the only entrance and exit, and so I *run*. Bolting up the second floor, skipping steps with my lengthy stride, and I'm fast.

Quick.

I'm on the landing, and I swing open Jane's door first.

Thoughts eject.

I'm on automatic, all action as I see a middle-aged white man with his dick out. He stands at the foot of the bed and strokes his erection, thrusting towards her mattress.

Two calico cats—Walrus and Carpenter—skirt around his ankles, biting his sneaker laces.

Right when he sees me enter the room, my gun raised, he freezes with big wide, bug eyes.

I recognize the target.

Greasy hair, thin lips. We called him *Sneakers*. Back in October, we caught him masturbating in his car outside this house.

He tries to lift up his blue jeans, dick dangling. "I didn't do anything wrong." He deserts the struggle with his jeans and charges for the window against the bed.

I'm faster.

Closing the distance, I seize his shoulder before his knee touches the mattress. I wrench him backwards, and I slam the butt of the gun against his head. Light force. The harder hit is my knee in his dick. And he crumples like a rag doll with a guttural noise.

Walrus and Carpenter dart under the bed.

He groans, still conscious but too disoriented to do much of anything. I squat down and roll him on his stomach.

Sick fuck. I fight back the heat that brews in my body and do my damn job. I should touch my mic and call this into the Alpha lead. Price is the one who'll send backup.

But first instinct takes hold, and I pull out my phone. Unmuting my best friend, I tell him the target, and Akara asks, "Is he responsive?"

"Barely." I sift through his pockets. Wallet, keys...*condom*. I go cold.

Thank God my brother didn't see this. He would have committed murder.

Thank God Jane wasn't here. She would have been scarred for fucking life.

I'll carry this.

"Are you good?" Akara asks.

"Yeah. He's down." I explain everything else that happened and then end with, "Don't tell my brother there was a break-in. Let me do it when he's back."

"That means I'll have to keep it from Jane, Maximoff...everyone."

"*Please*," I breathe. My hand shakes a little, and I close my fingers into a fist, then open them to touch my mic. I think Farrow might have some cigarettes in his bedroom...

"I'll let you do it," Akara agrees. "Radio Price. I'm hanging up."

"Stay frosty." I pin Sneakers down with my knee and speak on comms. I'm hawk-eyed, eyes never leaving the target.

He had a restraining order and broke the thing like it was nothing. This shouldn't be the price of fame, and now my brother—my *family* is under that spotlight.

Fuck anyone who thinks they can hurt the people I love.

Fuck them all.

39

Thatcher Moretti

WE HAVEN'T TAKEN THE ten-hour hike to the inn. But weather calms at dawn, and we thought this morning, again, we'd gear up for the trek.

Turns out, we don't have to.

Roads are being plowed and salted. Which means after over a month in this house, we're all finally leaving Scotland. *Together.* No chance in hell any of us are staying a second longer. We were supposed to be home December 20th.

Today is January 23rd.

Most of us are just thankful this didn't last until March. We got lucky.

Everyone is worn out. Emotionally. Mentally. But the mood is lighter, at least with the famous ones.

While Jane and her family are already in the cars, ready to move out, security crams in the foyer. We've been finishing a house-sweep for belongings, and tension is at a high between Omega and Epsilon.

Tony knows who I am.

He's known for two weeks. And he's been making off-handed comments about telling the Tri-Force that I pretended to be Banks.

I don't doubt he'll radio the Alpha lead the moment we land in Philly. He's been working himself up to that point.

Tony leans on a wall beside an empty coat rack. He has a pompous grin. He thinks he has me cornered, and I can't help but feel *sorry* for him.

I thought nothing could hurt him—because he couldn't see past his own inflated head. That his gold-shitting arrogance made him an *invincible* toolbag. But more than ever, I see through his annoying fucking bravado.

He's just...sad.

And bitter.

Jealous. Always feeling like he has to prove that he's *better* than me—when here I am willingly admitting to *every* mistake I've made. I'm a low bar for perfection.

Fucking over me and Banks won't make him feel better tomorrow. Our family will give him hell for this, and he'll never hear the end of it.

I glare at him from across the foyer and adjust the wire to my earpiece. I'm not cornered. I thought long and hard about what Akara said to me at the beginning of this trip.

"There's always a way out. You don't have to fall on a sword because it's sitting in front of you, waiting. You put together the team that's going to find the right exit. You sidelined me. That's on you."

This time, I tapped him in.

I asked for his help. And the takes-no-shit Omega lead is standing beside me, his eyes also locked on Tony.

A second later, O'Malley climbs down the staircase and throws his duffel near the front door.

"Ramella, O'Malley, I need a word with you both," Akara says in a way that makes it clear this isn't a request.

The Epsilon guards amble over, and the rest of Omega lingers in the foyer, eavesdropping.

O'Malley's head is somewhere else because the first thing he says is, "I know everyone says I'm a shit driver, but I think I should at least be in a front passenger seat to navigate."

"Sure, that's fine." Akara nods. "But we need to talk about what you two are planning to tell Price and Sinclair when we're home."

Tony extends an arm. "I'm not about to lie to my superiors. Sorry not sorry, but I have a good reputation with the old guard."

Surprisingly, that's a fucking understatement coming from Tony. The old guard treats him like Jesus Christ.

I understand that asking Tony and O'Malley to lie is asking them to break protocol. *They won't.* I wouldn't for them.

I deserve this. A punishment, a suspension—being fired, maybe, but I love her too much and I want to protect her too badly to accept that.

O'Malley looks from me to Akara. "I'd rather not rock the boat. It was fucked up, Thatcher, that you told everyone the truth and then lied to me, Tony, and Will—but at this point, you're still Jane's boyfriend. I'm Beckett's bodyguard. It's a conflict of interest, so I'd consider keeping my mouth shut."

"You're not lying," Akara says to them. "You're just not going to say anything about this. Price and Sinclair won't ask you straight out if a twin switch transpired. Keep quiet, and in return, I'll make any transfers happen that you want."

Tony rocks back with a laugh. "For real?"

"For real."

My muscles contract. Akara is offering *power* to Tony. I wouldn't give him a socket wrench, and he's handing him a fucking jackhammer.

"I want to be the Omega lead," Tony says without pause.

I glare. Give the guy a rope and he'll take the entire fucking ship. "No," I say severely. "You can't be a lead."

"Then no deal. Take it or leave it."

O'Malley sends him a hesitant look. "Way to shoot for the stars, man." He shakes his head. "Akara, I like where I'm at. I don't want a transfer."

Back to being fucked. I expel a breath through my nose.

He looks to me. "But I'd like a promise from you."

My brows draw together, and I think of Jane. What would I do to stay in security, to work near her, to protect her day in and day out?

I tell O'Malley, "Anything."

"I've only ever been on Epsilon. Before Jane, you had too, and I always considered you one of us. Even after you transferred to Omega.

Even after our fight. I guess the moment I realized you weren't was when *I* was the one being kept in the dark about the twin swap." He lets out a laugh. "Shit, I should've known it was you, Thatcher. It sucked that I didn't figure it out. It sucked being blindsided again by a guy I'd die for." His forehead wrinkles in a deeper frown. "I just want honesty. Just promise me *that* going forward."

My men.

It's been a while since Epsilon was my responsibility. Since he was, and like O'Malley, I feel that loss. I'm Omega.

My loyalty is with those men first. But I won't give my word flippantly. I have to mean what I say or else I've lost all fucking sense of integrity, and I can't live with that.

"I promise," I say seriously, deeply. "I'll be honest with you going forward."

O'Malley gauges my sincerity and then nods. "Thank you."

I nod back.

Genuine feelings exchanged, he grabs the duffel strap and pats Tony's shoulder. "Good luck swinging lead." He leaves out the front door.

I cross my arms and nod to Tony. "You're not getting lead."

"At least not immediately," Akara says, deadening the air.

Muttering and whispering and *what the fuck is he doing* comes from the foyer, but none of the men interject or approach.

Tony smiles. "When? Because I'm not waiting around a year."

The bottom of my stomach drops out. "Akara, you can't." *Not for me.* This is exactly what I feared the first time—back when I was sleeping with a client. I didn't want him to bear the repercussions for my actions.

"I'm the Omega lead. I can do whatever the fuck I want." Akara says this while staring at Tony, and he tells him, "Price and Sinclair love you. They'll be fine with the promotion as long as the recommendation comes from me. Short term: you should stay on Jane's detail until I have the transfer approved. It'll probably take a couple months."

I grit down so hard my jaw feels like it's splitting in two. I could fucking *scream* at the top of my lungs—but I stay quiet. I scowl and glare—and *this can't be right.*

We're losing everything.

Akara as SFO lead.

And Tony was supposed to be off Jane's detail *weeks* ago. His probationary period has been over, and all the confetti-popping parties I planned to have just fade away.

I turn my head. "Akara—"

"It's two months." He pulls a beanie over his head. "You and Jane can handle it." To Tony, he says, "Long term: you can't stay on her detail. So pick someone else."

"Charlie," he says. "You all say he's the most difficult client, but he just hasn't had me on his detail yet." *Fuck.*

"Done," Akara says. "We good?"

"All good." Tony nods. "And Akara, if this doesn't happen in two months, I'm going to tell Price and Sinclair what I know."

"That's fair." Akara slings his backpack over his shoulder. "Everyone move out. We need to get on the road." He leaves out the front door, a gust of snow flying in before it shuts.

Tony trailing right after.

The rest of SFO come up from behind me and stand on either side.

Farrow.

Oscar.

Donnelly.

And Quinn.

We watch Akara leave, and Oscar says, "Either Kitsuwon is the smartest motherfucker here or we've all just been fucked raw."

"Tony as our lead," Farrow says the unbelievable reality. "Count me out, boys."

"You're quitting?" Quinn asks.

"No." Farrow slings his duffel across his chest, and walking backwards, he says, "I'm just not listening to a thing that fucker says." He spins around, raises his fingers in goodbye, and exits into the cold.

Quinn grabs his backpack. "Me too." Strap on one shoulder, he heads out.

Donnelly stuffs his hands into his pockets and saunters out next.

It's just me and Oscar left.

I take fault for the cards he's been dealt. "I'm sorry."

"Don't be." Oscar ties a bandana around his forehead, curly pieces falling over. "We're all glad that you and Banks switched."

Confusion hardens my face.

Oscar is already telling me, "She needed you here." He clasps his duffel by the short handles and follows the SFO bodyguards.

I'm last.

I stare around the quiet Mackintosh House that isolated our frustration, anger, feuds, fistfights, hurt, and rage—but I'm going to remember the good.

The laughter, the love.

Growing closer to Jane. Growing closer to her family, to Farrow and this brotherhood of men.

I smile.

And I lock the doors on my way out.

Right now, I want to see one person. Rental cars are lined up in a row, and I spot Jane in the first one. She sits in the backseat, Maximoff already in the front.

Swiftly, I slide in beside her and shut the door before cold air blows inside.

"How'd it go?" She takes my gloveless hands, rubbing my palms to warm them.

I'm entranced by Jane for a second. Her wavy hair flows out of a cat-eared beanie, a purple puffy jacket zipped up, even in the heated car. Cheeks rosy, she looks warmed. I wrap my arms around her shoulders, and she leans her weight into me.

I find the words to explain everything.

When I finish, she takes a sharp breath. "Akara said not to worry?"

"Yeah, pretty much."

"Then we shouldn't worry." Her confidence is palpable.

But unsaid sentiments still claw at the fucking air. Two more months of Tony Ramella is sixty days too long.

40

Thatcher Moretti

THE TOWNHOUSE SMELLS OF garlic and tomato sauce, a familiar aroma that should be comforting. On any other night—maybe.

But it's the first night we've been home.

Hours ago, I learned about the break-in from my brother. I just stared at him for a long…long time, and I shook my head. I should've been here in Philly.

He should've been in Scotland. But I remember what Oscar said—and I know we were right where we were supposed to be. If I confronted the target, he'd be dead.

"You pistol-whipped him?" I asked for confirmation.

"Lightly," he clarified and saw my concern. "I'm fine." He'd been alone and had to wait for half the team to arrive.

That's what gnaws at me.

I moved in closer, and we brought each other in a hug. My brother will always have my soul. Twenty-eight-years together does that.

A tough part came next.

I had to deliver the gut-wrenching news to Jane and Maximoff. After I finished, I thought it would have dissuaded them from staying in the townhouse. Hell, I'd grab a one-way ticket to anywhere but here.

Instead, they feel *safer*.

The intruder has been caught. He admitted to breaking in once prior and paying some tech friend to disable our security alarms. He was charged with a slew of crimes including two-counts of trespassing and violating his restraining order. So now he's in jail, awaiting sentencing from a judge, but there's not a chance he'll skate by without at least a year.

Target *officially* neutralized.

It's nice being back in my own clothes: red flannel over a gray tee, gold horns around my neck. But too much barbed wire lies ahead to relax.

And I have to let Jane crawl through and be torn up. I can't move aside the painful parts anymore.

My muscles tense as I use a wooden spoon to stir thick, red sauce in a decent-sized pot, where meat has been simmering for hours. Cooking dinner for Jane is just one of the many things I love doing for her—but tonight's dinner is going to have a side dish of hard truths.

She has a vague concept of what happened. She has no fucking clue that Banks caught a middle-aged man with his dick exposed, jacking off over her bed—or even that this bastard masturbated in his car right outside the house.

Providing the briefest, nondescript image and skimming over the full picture—that has always been our dynamic. I've been saving Jane from visualizing the disturbing realities of her fame.

I hate that I need to do this. I hate painting *graphic* pictures of what sick fuckbags say and do. But she can't make an informed decision about living here without *all* of the details.

Still, this'll hurt her.

I'm going to hurt her.

I strain pasta, steam billowing, and by the time I have food set on the iron café table, Jane climbs down the stairs and twists her damp hair in a bun. Just coming from the shower.

She sniffs the air and smiles brightly. "It smells like heaven."

"You hungry?"

"Mmhmm," Jane nods. "I'm mortadafam'."

I didn't teach her that word. "Where'd you hear that?"

"Banks." She trots down the stairs, six cats almost tripping Jane, jumping at her calves and springing down the steps. Starving for attention from their mom. "He said it means you're really hungry. Famished, even." She reaches the first floor. "Did I say it well?"

"Perfect." My feelings for Jane balls up in my ribcage and tries to crack the bones a million and one times.

And then my stomach tanks.

I fixate on the calico cat she picks off the floorboards. Carpenter nuzzles his furry head against her cheek.

She smiles and scratches behind his ears. "I missed you too, my love."

Carpenter—*that cat*, he'd been in the bedroom with a fucking pervert, and that fact might kill her more than the other. It's staking me in the chest.

"Can I do anything to help?" she asks while kissing Carpenter on the head.

"It's all done."

She frowns at my expression. "What's wrong?" She sees me eyeing the calico cat. "Thatcher?"

"We need to talk, honey."

Jane swallows. "Okay." She gently sets Carpenter down, and then she assesses the glassware and food set on the table before disappearing into the kitchen.

She returns with parmesan cheese, which I forgot.

My lip lifts slightly, and the pressure in my chest *almost* relents. Ophelia and Licorice are rubbing up against my ankles, purring. Normally I'd pet the white and gray cats, but I crouch down and toss them a catnip-laced Darth Vader mouse.

They chase after the toy.

I stand back up and notice Jane frozen with a hand on an iron chair.

She's zeroed in on the pasta in meat sauce. "I thought you said you wouldn't cook me your grandma's braggiol' because you can't do it like her?"

I did say that.

"It's comfort food."

Worry widens her gaze, but she takes a readying breath and lowers on the seat. "You think I need comforting?"

I sit across from my girlfriend. "Not just you. This won't be easy for me either." I nod to the soup in the small bowls. "I didn't cook the pasta vasul'. My brother said our stepmom brought a container over yesterday for you and me."

My family had been worried about us being snowed-in, and coming home to familiar food, made out of love, is simply *pure love.*

Family constantly makes me feel like the wealthiest man in the world. There's not a day I'd ever take them for granted.

I look at Jane more. "I just heated it on the stove."

She tries to smile, but her lips fall. "That was awfully sweet of Nicola." She inspects the soup. "Pasta and beans?"

I nod, just once.

Say more. I'm naturally quiet, but in this setting, my conciseness and brevity packs on tension like ten tons of weight.

Jane pours wine, a dark Cab, in our glasses. Strain stretches between us. "I'm guessing this is about the culprit, but you should know that I feel *extraordinarily* safe here. I can already sense the warmest, most relaxing sleep tonight. Better than in a long while."

Whatever great sleep she thinks she'll have, I'm about to fuck it all.

She studies me and places the wine bottle aside. "Do you feel safe?" She looks pained. "I'm so sorry, I should've asked you sooner."

I hold her gaze. "You don't need to apologize. I feel safe, but I feel safe most places."

Jane nods once, like I did, and cups wine between tense hands.

My ears ring in her silence. And I focus on my talk with Farrow hours ago. He said he was going to take Maximoff out to dinner and lay down every single *horrific* detail that occurred in this house.

I agreed to do the same for Jane.

We're both just praying they'll consider moving.

"I have to tell you what happened here," I explain.

She inhales a sharp breath. "Must you?"

I nod. "You have to know."

She takes a dainty sip of wine, then places the glass down. "Okay." She folds her arms on the table. "I'm ready."

With steaming pasta between me and my girlfriend, I have visions of *Lady and the Tramp*—but this is a fucked-up version of a Disney movie. Especially with the next words out of my mouth.

"He masturbated on your bed, Jane." Direct. To-the-point.

She blinks a few times.

I'm more specific. "The police found his semen on your bed." My muscles are flexed, just seeing her cage breath.

She reaches for her wine, thinks against it, and bends over to the floor. I watch Jane hoist Lady Macbeth, and her childhood black cat curls up on her lap. I realize, pasta is my comfort.

Her cats are hers.

Jane strokes her fur. "I thought…perhaps, the culprit just touched my bed, and that's why you changed the duvet."

"I threw away everything: the sheets, the blankets." I pause. "The mattress is new too."

She fights a swell of emotion. "Thank you." Her eyes redden, hand staying still on her cat's belly.

I want to hold Jane. Cup her cheeks in my hands and tell her that I have her six. That for as long as I live, no one on this earth will touch her with ill intent or hatred or harm.

I can't.

I can't give her a false sense of security. And I don't want her to normalize what stalkers and *revolting* pricks do. We can avoid them better in a gated location.

"Security called him *Sneakers*," I explain. "Because he always wore these dated white-scuffed sneakers whenever he stopped by the house."

She blows out a short, controlled breath. "Is he a heckler?"

"A fan, or really, a suitor from your grandmother's newspaper ad."

"Oh." Her chin trembles a little and she breathes in, the deepest breath she can.

"He was allowed to walk past the house. As much as he wanted."
Jane nods.

"He was allowed to park outside the house. It's public property." I take a beat. "He was in his mid-forties, almost your dad's age. And the first time he was caught, he was masturbating in his car outside this townhouse."

Her lips slowly part. "Oh God...he's done it before?"

I nod. "A restraining order was filed, which he broke. He's not the first, second, third, or last fuckbag that I've slapped with a restraining order. He won't be the last man to break into this townhouse either." I grip her gaze with severity. "I feel safe. You feel safe, but the truth is, you aren't safe here. Maximoff isn't safe here. Neither are Luna and Sulli."

Her blue eyes are glassy with tears that won't fall.

My words—*mine*, are pushing Jane to this place, and chewing broken glass would feel better. I continue fast. "I'm not saying any of this to hurt you. I just need you to understand what's happening and why I can't protect you here."

She buries her face in Lady Macbeth's fur for a moment.

Her silence is a toxin dripping in my veins. I can't stand it. "Please say something."

Brushing tears away with the heels of her palms, she glances up. "I have an overactive imagination, you see, and I just keep picturing some gross old man in our room with his cum on our bed..." She perches her elbows on the table, palms covering her face, agonized. "They saw, didn't they?"

My brows knit, and I shake my head. "Who?"

"The way you were staring at Carpenter." She lets out a guttural noise that wrenches me to my feet. Lady Macbeth springs off her lap.

"Jane." I crouch down beside her chair.

"Walrus and Carpenter were in the room with him." She won't uncover her face. "I thought he could be worse than a burglar. I thought he could do something as sickening and heinous as what he did—but *knowing* for certain feels..." She chokes on a sob. "It feels like...my skin is crawling and it will never stop." Her hands fall, and I kneel and pull her into my chest.

She wraps her arms around my shoulders. I hold the back of her head, and she cries into the crook of my neck.

"It will stop," I whisper, deeply. "There are places where they can't reach."

A minute passes before she lifts her chin, her tearful gaze meeting my hard eyes. "I feel as though…I'm letting them win by moving away. Like they've taken my home from me."

I brush the wet lines off her freckled cheeks. "Back in Scotland, you missed your sister, your parents, your brothers, cousins and your cats." I take another beat. "A home isn't a house, Jane. It's the people you love, and by moving, you're protecting them and you're protecting yourself."

She wipes her face, easing more. "I know we have to move."

My chest rises.

"But it's such a drastic change, and I don't just want to snap my fingers and be done here."

"I understand," I say deeply. "This doesn't have to be a fire drill. You can take your time looking for a new place."

"We," she corrects.

I nod, "You and Maximoff."

She frowns and clutches my shoulder stronger. "You and me."

We.

My lips lift into a heartfelt smile, one I didn't think would come at the end of this conversation.

41

Jane Cobalt

"NO BOY'S ALLOWED!" my mom screams from the treehouse window. "Go away, Loren!"

Uncle Loren glares up at her from the foot of the tree. "Fine, Cruella, I was just asking if you needed more blankets. Freeze your titanium pussy off for all I care!"

"Go fuck a cactus!" My mom gets the last word in before returning to the mound of blankets. With stiff grace, she sinks onto her butt pillow like a beautiful ice queen. Black silk nightgown, royally expensive diamond necklace and earrings to match—she appears fit to sleep on a throne.

Instead, she's lounging in a homemade treehouse. Her silky, lush brown hair flies as wind blows through the wooden structure.

I stare fondly. I revere every little bit of my mom, and lately, I haven't needed to remind myself that I'm just as worthy and beautiful.

I just feel that I am, and I've been more content with myself these days.

Her piercing yellow-green eyes ping between me and her two sisters. She's a fire-breather of epic proportions, one encased with love. "Where were we?"

A smile spreads across my face.

Boozy PJ night in the Meadows treehouse is forever a top-tier favorite occasion. My mom, aunts, and I try to have them a couple times a month, and after I returned from Scotland, they announced an *emergency* PJ night.

One week into February and the winter chill still nips my skin—but the weather feels brisk and cool compared to the frostbitten temperatures in the Highlands. Portable heaters keep us toasty enough that no one wears coats.

I'm quite warm in a pastel pink and orange heart pajama set, topped with a cat-eared beanie.

Aunt Daisy digs into a bag of chocolate chips. "We were talking about the great and *glorious* house hunting adventures." She spreads her hand in the air, miming a rainbow.

We laugh.

After I sip my beer, they look more serious, awaiting my response.

They were all too happy when Moffy and I announced that we planned to move. Our parents have expressed *firm* disapproval of us living in the townhouse after the first break-in. But we're adults, and they try to respect our choices.

To be frank, I think they softened their worry so we wouldn't clash. Some of the worst, most strained days between our parents and us were after the incest rumor. No one wishes to have a repeat.

But with the most recent break-in, I know they wouldn't be able to restrain the brunt-force of their feelings. And they would've gone absolutely mad if we decided to stay.

"At the moment, we're only certain about one thing."

"What?" Aunt Lily asks.

"We all still want to live together." I nod with each name. "Luna, Sulli, Moffy, Farrow, Thatcher, and me."

They're beaming and looking proudly to one another. And I'm positive it's because their three oldest daughters are staying roommates.

"Don't smile just yet," I warn with a slight wince. "You'll be displeased to know that we're in no rush to leave the townhouse this week or even next month."

My mom shoots me an icy look and snaps her fingers. "Timeline."

"Post-summer, we'll be gone."

She scoffs. "*God*, that is too slow. Do you need help? I can find you a place tomorrow."

"We have this handled," I assure. "We just want to spend one more summer there. Sulli is the exception, of course."

Aunt Daisy nods. Her daughter has already moved completely out of the townhouse. As soon as Sullivan heard that a pervert "busted a nut" on my bed, she told me, "I'm GTFO-ing really the fuck fast."

She's staying with her parents and little sister until we find a new place.

I rest my chin on my knuckles. "Plus, this gives us plenty of time to choose a location."

It reminds me of Charlie.

We'd been on shaky ground after he blew up Thatcher's cover. I forgave him. He's my *brother*, and he just needed out of Mackintosh House to cool down.

When Charlie heard we planned to move, he welcomed all of us to plant roots in New York. He said, "To be closer." He even included Moffy.

It feels like a peace offering. All things mended.

But I know it's very possible that Charlie just wishes to shirk responsibility onto Maximoff and me. He's had to look after our brothers in Hell's Kitchen, and it's a role he's never filled to this degree before.

With us closer, he'd be free to leave more often.

"Philly or NYC?" Aunt Daisy wags her brows. "I wager fifty chocolate chips on *Philly*."

"New York," my mom rebuts.

We look to Aunt Lily. Her eyes are drawn to the cutout window in the treehouse. "Did he look cold?"

My mom glares. "No. Your husband wasn't even *carrying* blankets. He just wanted to worm his way up here like he always does."

Truth: 9 times out of 10, Uncle Loren will find a way to either pull Lily away or become a part of the PJ party. He might also be the biggest gossip queen of us all, so I don't even mind the addition.

"Maybe he misses me," Lily says pensively, tugging her long gray tee over her gangly knees.

"You saw him five minutes ago," my mom retorts like her younger sister is losing her mind. She glances at Aunt Daisy. "What are you doing? No phones." She steals her cell.

Daisy just shrugs, not minding. Blonde hair and arresting green eyes, her cotton shirt has a graphic of two hugging avocados, and she wears a pair of matching boxers. "Ryke wants us to let him know when we leave, so that we don't have another...situation."

Situation is a kind word for all of us getting plastered last November and Aunt Lily falling down the third step of the ladder.

She face-planted in a pile of leaves and sprained her wrist.

"We don't need his help," my mom snaps. "We are perfectly capable of leaving this treehouse on our own." She refills glasses of wine, set on an overturned box, and she checks the amount of beer left in my bottle.

I'm nursing the same one.

The wedding binder weighs on my lap, and I flip through a couple pages. I've already exhaustively talked their ear off about the event planning. So I just silently skim the pages and smile, beyond excited to talk to more vendors tomorrow.

With Maximoff and Farrow's happiness attached to this event, I find each minute spent crunching numbers and making calls that much more rewarding.

I turn to the *location* page, and my lips downturn. "The saddest part of being trapped in Scotland is that Maximoff and Farrow will never choose it as their wedding location. It's cursed. So now we're back to ground zero."

Daisy raises her brows. "Your binder is overflowing. That doesn't look like ground zero."

Lily nods. "You've got a lot of stuff going on there." She scoops a handful of M&Ms from the snack bowl.

My mom has a coy smile as she passes around full wine glasses to her sisters. "You've enjoyed planning their wedding." She doesn't phrase this like a question.

"Of course." I run a finger over the possible guest list (still to be refined). "Must be the Rose Calloway Cobalt gene in me. Planning and organizing."

She sends me a pointed look like I am so wrong. "You do know that I planned Lily's wedding, and I despised every second of it."

My mouth falls.

I knew she organized Lily's wedding, which eventually became her own wedding to my dad when Aunt Lily and Uncle Loren decided not to marry that soon. But I always thought my mom loved the planning process.

"But...you're..." *You.*

"My gremlin." She gives me a look. "Do you really believe I'd have a good time calling florists, venues, and delegating out every last inch of a party? No, that you got from your father."

I'm intrigued. "I guess I shouldn't be surprised that I'm more like him and a little less like you."

"You're not more like him." She sounds resolute. Definitive. "He's hardly the type to celebrate *love*, let alone organize a party around the concept—unless it involves the very few people he does love."

Lily nods in agreement. "Your big, overwhelming heart comes from your mom."

Into a sip of wine, my mom says, "Even though mine is hidden behind a layer of ice."

So I'm a bit of both. My mom and my dad.

The knowledge warms me like the feeling you receive when you finish a very good book. I flip another page and skim my fingertips over tablecloth samples, stapled in the binder.

My mom watches me. "Have you given thought to your passion?"

I look up with a bright smile. "Yes. I've realized I don't need one." I explain my epiphany that I had in Scotland, and they all seem happy until I add, "Once the holidays are over, I'm going to ask Dad to work at Cobalt Inc. in the finance department. I'll enjoy it there for a while, then I'll bounce around to another place to help the family."

Daisy chugs her wine.

"You don't need a passion," my mom agrees. "You never have, but Jane…" Her yellow-greens drill into me like I'm missing a glaring sign smack-dab in front of my nose.

"I don't…understand." I frown.

"Tu as déjà trouvé ta passion. Regarde." *You've already found your passion. Look.*

I follow her eyes to the binder on my lap.

My pulse is on an immediate ascent. "No, no…this is just a project for Maximoff and Farrow. It's not…" I stop myself because my aunts and my mom wear these loving smiles.

My mom deserts her wine glass on the crate. "You just spent thirty minutes telling us everything from food options to table arrangements. And I wish we had a mirror, Jane, because if you saw yourself, you wouldn't be questioning anything."

Everything slows around me.

The air whistles and my skin chills. Is it possible for a love of something so deep to creep up on you without even knowing? Without even searching?

How long have I explored far and wide for a passion that I could turn into a career? And here it found me…triggering a yearning that I haven't felt before.

My heart opens completely. To possibility. A future. Where I smooth chaos and solve puzzles and juggle madness all at once. And seeing, *feeling* the spellbinding happiness of loving partners on their special day.

The image…it fills me.

"I could plan other weddings besides Maximoff and Farrow's," I say, hopeful, letting that reality into the air.

My mom looks at me like I'm her daughter. Flesh and blood come to life. "You can do anything, gremlin."

Anything.

I choose this.

"Thank you," I breathe.

I'm not sure I would have been able to see what was in front of me without them. I touch my watering eyes. Lily is sniffling, already crying. Daisy passes her a tissue.

My mom wafts a hand at her face, drying her eyes before they well up. "I hate you *all*. I'm wearing fresh mascara."

We laugh.

"Speaking of Scotland." Daisy tosses a chocolate chip in her mouth. "Tell us everything that happened with you and the spritely hunk."

Spritely hunk.

I love my family dearly.

How do I describe Thatcher? I've tried to before, but this is different. We've spent over thirty days stuck in a house together. We spent a night trapped in a car. I've broken up with him, made up with him, and he's still embraced me fully, without compromise.

I love him.

I smile into a soft breath. That much has been clear. *But…* "I shouldn't need him so much, and I find myself aching to be swallowed whole too often to be healthy." Setting the beer aside, I hug the binder to my chest and bend my knees. "I'm scared to love him, but God, I do. So *infinitely* and terribly."

It's a truth I've never shared with them. One I've become much better at expressing aloud.

My mom leans forward and takes my hand in hers. Our eyes close, noses near, and I hang onto every word as she says, "You're not two halves, Jane. You don't *lose* when you love. You gain." She draws closer to whisper, "You have all of him."

And he has all of me.

Not yet.

I consistently pull back on Thatcher.

Realizations wash over me coolly. "All this time, I thought love is a compromise of equals. 50-50. But it's not…is it?"

She leans back and gives me another pointed look. "With the right person, they'll ensure you're always whole."

A dam bursts inside of me. Freeing all restraints, and a feeling flutters so wildly. I rise quickly. Hurried. "I have to go. I have to…" I can hardly release the words into the air.

"Go." Her eyes twinkle and she waves towards the hatch.

My pulse beats and beats, and I scale down the ladder. Cold air nipping my neck and bare feet.

"Where is she going?" Aunt Lily asks, her voice carrying behind me.

"To make a grand gesture." My mom has to be smiling. I hear it beneath her words.

"We're following her, right?" Aunt Daisy asks, hopeful.

"Grab your coats," my mom tells them as I drop down to the soft grass. Snow melted a few days ago, and I sprint.

Really, it's a light jog.

I head down the driveway into the cul-de-sac and race up the neighborhood street. Gated and safe, no irksome bodyguard named *Tony* needed.

Cold slices my lungs, and I keep pace, reaching the long, winding driveway of the Cobalt Estate. My childhood home.

Naked tulip trees frame the driveway, and I take a single breath before ascending the path. Thatcher was invited to an *Outlander* marathon with Eliot and Audrey. Since he was off-duty tonight, he agreed to go. I love that he's spending time with my siblings like they're his own.

Sentiments whirl around me. Fuel me.

I run harder.

I'm out of breath as I reach the ornate fountain that guards a castle-like mansion. Icicles drip off the stone fountain, but its not frozen solid. The sound of rushing water calms my spinning brain, and I text Thatcher to meet me outside.

Fifteen seconds later, the door swings open, and Thatcher emerges, all six-foot-seven of him. Bold and quiet and assertive.

"Thatcher," I greet deeply.

"Jane," he says just as fully. He assesses me in a sweep. Lingering on my bare feet, pajamas, and lack of coat in the winter. He's already removing his brown leather jacket while he closes the door behind him.

I can barely contain what aches and pleads to *explode* out of me. My breath smokes the air as he approaches. Towering above.

I crane my neck to look up.

He stares down and places his warm jacket on my shoulders.

"Thank you," I breathe, slipping my arms through the big sleeves that engulf my frame. I hug the jacket around me, his scent dizzying. "I just..." I inhale. "There's so much I want to tell you."

A sliver of space separates him from me. Tension beckoning us to draw skin-to-skin. Neither crosses the distance, because once we do this will turn into raw, desperate passion. Our lips together, bodies fused—and right now, words must come first.

He seizes my gaze, with me to the end. Ready for whatever grenade I toss, but this one won't blow us to pieces.

And I gush, "I need you. I need you like the air I breathe, and I want you like ground beneath my feet. I'm not afraid—I'm *not* afraid, not even a little. You are the man who has respected all of who I am and protected every little piece of me."

His chest lifts in a strong breath. We stare powerfully, not wasting a moment to blink.

"You keep me whole," I profess. "And *love*—that dreaded, beautiful word—*love*." I breathe, "Love is two wholes. We are two-hundred percent—an illogical number, maddening, and I will forever embrace every illogical, *maddening* second with you." Tears threaten to surge.

We've drawn closer, touching without touching.

"I love you, I love you, I love you." It pours out of me. "Je'taime, je'taime, je'taime." He's already clasping my face, and I'm in his arms, legs wrapped around his waist. Our foreheads nearly press together, and his lips skim over my lips.

"Jane." My name is cast in love.

We kiss, so intensely that the cold breath in my lungs sparks into flames. For the longest time, out of all the March sisters in *Little Women*—I aspired to be Jo. Fiercely independent with career passions and desires far outside a household.

It turns out, all along, I resisted against being Meg. I want to be a wife and to one day raise children, a life as traditional as they come, and that ending is as worthy as any other.

We stare deeply into each other. His hands beneath the backs of my thighs, my fingers woven behind his neck.

I take a deeper, stronger breath. "Mr. Moretti, will you spend the rest of your life with me?"

His mouth breaks apart. He looks stunned.

"I'm asking you to marry me," I clarify.

He smiles. Ladies and gentlemen, a full-blown smile that overtakes his face.

My lips pull to extraordinary heights. Happiness swelling between us.

"I know what that was." He places me gently on my bare feet.

Fountain still rushing beside us.

I don't understand what he's doing until he drops down to one knee. And he unpockets a paperclip, twisting the metal between his fingers into a little ring, and I laugh, tears pricking my eyes.

My steepled fingers touch my lips.

His eyes are reddened, and he holds up the paperclip ring. "Yes. My answer will always be *yes*." He slides the ring onto my finger. "Sempre toujours."

Always always.

He stands back up and lifts me effortlessly. I'm in his arms again. Kissing, and my heart is overcome with a thousand words. Branded on his lips, on his body and soul.

Our kiss ignites fires. Melts snow and burns the grounds beneath our feet. It is filled with epic, soul-crushing love. And we're armored for whatever storm comes next.

I hope and plead that nothing will ever tear us apart.

42

Thatcher Moretti

A SINGLE BEAM OF morning light slips through blinds, through cheetah-print curtains, and glides across Jane's cheek as she sleeps soundlessly. I lean midway up the headboard, holding her against my chest while her arms curl around my bicep.

I don't move a muscle. I could stay right here all day long.

And the fact is—I can.

Nowhere else I have to be, not until tonight at least. *Wednesday.* I'm off-duty thanks to Donnelly, picking up the extra slack with Xander.

He told me, "You've got a Wednesday Night Dinner to prepare for. First non-Cobalt to walk those hallowed halls. Do us proud, man."

Her parents invited me to the mysterious and *legendary* dinner party. But only after they admitted to knowing about the twin switch…and they knew from the moment Banks dodged their calls.

And they didn't tell the Tri-Force.

Rose said to Jane and me, "We kept the secret because that's obviously what you both wanted, and it's just a *morbid* fact that you didn't trust us and decided to keep us out of the loop." She seemed hurt but layered on a cold glare.

"You're close to Price," Jane explained in a rush. "We were worried you'd tell the Alpha lead."

Rose frowned. "Of course we trust Price, but that does *not* mean we'd put him above you. I'm sorry if your dad and I made you feel like we would." She held her daughter's hands. "We will always choose you first. You're my blood and bones."

Jane hugged her mom.

I looked to Rose, then to Connor. "I'm sorry for lying. It wasn't our intention." I explained briefly how we thought it'd just be a short week.

"You're dating our daughter," Connor said like that had made all the difference during the switch. "I recognize that Jane didn't know how this would go since she's the first of my children to be in a serious relationship. But know now that there's a hierarchy." His lip rose in a grin. "Many people need me, but there are only a handful that I'd drop everything for—and you're now among them." He cocked a single brow. "Just so you understand: you rank higher than security, and I would lie for you, if needed."

He'd lie for me.

That knowledge still whirls my head.

"Lastly," Connor said, "don't apologize for trying to deceive me, but I will accept an apology for failing."

We shook hands.

He's unlike most men I meet. Which isn't surprising. We're not cut from the same cloth. He grew up affluent and went to an elite boarding school in upstate New York. He's bred for prep school games and aristocratic rules that I'm still learning.

But he treated me like I was worthy of his daughter.

That's all I could ask for.

I feel good about my standing with her parents. But with her five brothers and little sister—fuck if I know. Charlie said I haven't finished the Truth or Dare game yet. I could walk into Wednesday Night Dinner, and they could banish me for fucking eternity.

Even being engaged to Jane hasn't changed anything with her siblings. They reacted to the news like someone offering a weather report. Jane said they're keeping things close to the vest until the game ends. But I hated seeing Audrey purposefully temper her excitement.

At least I don't have to fucking guess how the rest of her family feels. Overjoyed is a soft word for their reaction. Her parents, aunts, uncles, and cousins were beyond ecstatic. Luna and Sulli shrieked and grabbed Jane's hands and the three of them started jumping up and down together.

But the biggest reaction was Maximoff's. Her best friend. He hugged Jane. Then gave me a hug. He said, "I'm proud of Jane for following her heart, and I'm glad you're the guy on the other side of it."

I'd repeat that moment a thousand times just to see the happiness on Jane's face over and over again.

Back in bed, Jane's eyes begin to flutter open. Curiosity in them as she looks up at me. "How long have you been awake?"

"Not long." I brush some frizzed hair off her cheek.

She stirs more, smiling, and then glances at her left hand splayed on my muscular bicep, the makeshift ring still on her finger.

Our engagement wasn't a dream.

It was real. It's been real since she proposed a couple weeks ago.

"I'm getting you an actual ring," I tell her straight out.

Her lips suddenly downturn and she props herself higher, her left hand sliding to my chest. "I like this one."

"You're not wearing a paperclip forever." I'm resolute and unyielding about this. I might not be able to afford a 5-carat diamond, but Jane is worth more than a two-cent piece of metal from OfficeMax.

She opens her mouth to argue, but I kiss the top of her head, then her temple.

Jane flushes and quiets at my touch, her nipples hardened against a silk blue top, and I clutch her ass that peeks out of the matching shorts. My cock twitches.

Her smile grows, and she shifts on me and straddles my waist, palms splayed on my chest. As she bows forward, dog tags suspend from her neck.

Same ones I wore during two tours overseas. They mean something to me, encapsulating a time of my life that civilians can't understand— and I always planned to give them to the woman I'd marry.

I wish I had brought them to Scotland, and I was kicking myself that I hadn't.

Because the dog tags were her Christmas gift.

She notices me staring at them and her fingers clasp the metal. She cried when I first put them around her neck, knowing what they mean to me.

Knowing what *she* means to me.

"Have you thought more about what kind of car you'd like?" Jane wonders, sitting up straighter on me. My shoulders press into the headboard, and I warm her thighs with my palms. She knows I'm practical, and she wanted to gift me a practical thing for Christmas.

A car.

Too fucking much. But then, I thought about it, and she could've easily said the dog tags were *too much.* I need to let her give me more, and I could use a car.

"Yeah." I nod once. "Surprise me."

Her eyes brighten. "That, I can do."

My lip curves upward.

And Jane struggles not to grin. "We're engaged." Her cheeks are beet-red.

"We're engaged."

Wouldn't dream of anything else than to be next to Jane forever.

Every now and then, the enormity of what this means slams at me.

The poor Italian-American boy from South Philly is marrying an American princess. I'm marrying into the Cobalt Empire. She's marrying into my rowdy, obnoxious, and loving Italian family.

When I called them, they screamed so fucking loud I thought it'd burst the speaker. My mom and her wife put as many uncles and aunts on the line as they could.

Happy. Thrilled.

Crying.

"When's the engagement party?!" they asked.

"Youse have a wedding date yet?! We gotta mark this down." Doesn't matter who the person is, if they're family they assume they're invited.

"What are you thinking?" Jane wonders, her eyes twinkling.

"That it'll have to be a big wedding." I watch her unconsciously scoot closer to my dick. My blood heats. "I have to invite everyone I know, unless I want to create about a hundred different lifelong grudges."

"No grudges will be formed," Jane says confidently, still smiling. It's fucking contagious. "Our wedding will be giant and wonderful. We'll play Italian music, most surely."

That, right there, does a number on me. "Yeah?" Emotion fists my ribcage. My family means everything to me like hers does, and she remembers. *Always remembers.*

"Your grandma told me it's the best part of Italian weddings. That and the food." She was on the phone with my grandma and mom for an hour after the proposal.

We would've told them in person, but the news was going to leak fast. Jane's blue-blooded grandmother overheard Rose talking, and no one trusted that Grandmother Calloway wouldn't spill the engagement to the press.

She did.

Media have run a variety of articles. Most fixate on the timeline of the engagement.

Too fast, they say.

Doesn't bother me. I couldn't be more certain of where I'm headed. Life is short—I've known that since I lost my older brother. And while I'm on this earth, I want to be happy.

But to the world, Jane isn't known as a spontaneous, wild Meadows girl. She's seen as a logical, rational Cobalt—and in less than five months, she's engaged to a bodyguard.

Pregnancy rumors are already circulating tabloids.

But the "Omega is fake" rumor is catching fire ten times more, ten times stronger. Entertainment *journalists* have been theorizing that Jane and I knew each other before I became a bodyguard—and that this wasn't a shotgun engagement since we've been together for years.

I'm concerned about the other men.

SFO has to deal with fans aggressively pairing them off with their client (or ex-client in Donnelly's case with Beckett). Because the media, fans, the fucking universe seriously believes they're all real couples and fake bodyguards.

I don't mention the media to Jane in bed. We've talked about tabloids enough.

As I lace her left hand in mine, we stare at one another, drinking each other in, and I say, "You're going to be my wife."

Her lips part in arousal.

I slide my large hand from her thigh up underneath her silk top, along the curve of her hip, and against her breast.

She grinds her hips.

I grit down on my teeth, blood rushing through my cock. I harden, and her fingers dig into my shoulder.

"Thatcher," she murmurs achingly.

My lips a breath from hers, I whisper, "I'm the last man that'll ever touch you here." My thumb brushes over her perked nipple.

She gasps against my mouth.

My muscles contract, and with my other hand, I cup her pussy. "I'm the last man that'll ever be inside you here."

"*Yes*," she moans the word. Temperature cranks in the room to a boiling swelter. I throb as she palms my erection that pushes against my black boxer-briefs.

I'm rock solid.

Her lips quirk. "I'm the last woman to ever touch your cock." *Fuck.* Hot breath gathers in the pit of my lungs. Jane stares at me head-on, all confidence blistering inside. I love her. Every last part down to the bottom of her soul.

"Without a fucking doubt. I'm all yours, honey." Swiftly, with both hands, I scoop Jane up by her gorgeous ass and easily flip her onto her back. Winded by the sudden movement, her chest rises and falls heavily.

I yank off her silk shorts and spread her thighs open with my knee. As I stretch her legs wider, she mutters, "Oh my God."

I bend down to her ear. Very deeply, I say, "And you're all mine."

She pushes my chin back towards her mouth—*fuck*—and just like that our lips collide. Crashing together in a hungry wave. Rocking against her pussy, friction mounts between us. I lift her ass, pushing her heat up against my hardened length.

She shudders, a high-pitched noise breaking apart her lips.

The room blazes with our knockout passion. Gripping my muscles and senses.

We devour each other. Hands not touching fast enough. Ravenous and primal like being starved for years. Seamlessly, I tuck her to my chest and toss a pillow near the side-edge of the bed.

My kneecaps dig into the mattress, and I lay her down, folding the pillow snug beneath the small of her back. At perfect alignment, I shed my boxer-briefs, and she soaks up my muscular build as I kneel between her spread legs.

"Thatcher," she whimpers, raising her hips. Bucking into me.

Sweat glistens along my abs and biceps. I clutch the soft flesh of her hips and thrust against her pussy, pink panties obstructing me from her warmth.

"*Please, please.*" She tilts her head back, hanging slightly off the bed.

"Jane," I grunt. *Fuck.* I watch her pull herself up onto her elbows. Higher. Just so her palms can explore every inch of me. Rounding up my ass cheeks.

She pants, her big blue eyes asking, *can I?*

I extend over to the nightstand in arm's reach and grab a bottle of lube. *Go ahead, honey.* I rock harder before she can even touch the lube.

"Oh…God," she gasps.

My dick bangs against her entrance, and she almost falls off her elbows.

I groan into a choked noise. *God-fucking-dammit.* I need inside her. Urgently, I pry the pink fabric to the side, exposing her soaked pussy. I don't even have to waste time to grab a condom. She's been on birth control since we got back from Scotland.

Veins pulsate in my cock.

Christ, I want in.

"Wait," she pants and sits further up. Collecting herself, she snatches the lube, and I breathe hard. As much as I love Jane playing with my ass, I crave to sink my dick *deep* in her right now.

"Be quick," I say, parting my knees more, which only opens her wider.

She gasps and touches her sensitive pussy.

I move her hand aside and thumb her bundle of nerves, then slip two fingers inside of her.

She moans, eyes almost rolling, "Wait...don't move."

I keep my fingers still inside her warmth, and she swallows a ragged breath. Collecting herself for a second time, she lubes her finger.

Jane clasps my ass with one hand and slips her other finger into my hole—*fucking*...my abs flex as she finds my prostate and makes a *come hither* motion. Rubbing the sensitive spot, full of nerve endings that shoot electric currents through my veins.

I breathe hard through my nose, tendons stretching my neck. *Fucking* fuck—I thumb her clit, and her thighs shake.

Her pleasured cry ripples down me.

"*Jane*," I say through gritted teeth. The head of my cock is swollen. Ready to fucking be inside her, and the longer she's back there, the more her hand will cramp.

So I draw her wrist out, and I reach back to the drawer. And I grab a prostate massager. She hasn't used a toy on me yet, and her eyes spark with a thousand *yeses*.

Jane removes her finger, and I push her back down. She wiggles, and I drink in her whole beautiful frame in the morning light.

Fuck. "I love your body."

Flush ascends her cheeks.

I lean closer and suck on her perked nipple, trailing hot kisses down her wide hip, belly, and soft thigh. My tongue flicks over her clit, and she squirms. "*God*, Thatcher."

Swift movements, no pauses—I sit back up and clutch her hips again. Her mouth is in a perpetual gasp as she watches me drive my erection inside her heat.

She's mine.

I rock, only about halfway in, and her legs tremble, head falling back.

She lets out a louder cry of pleasure, and I ease in and out, never deeper than four-inches. I work my thumb over her swollen bud, and every muscle in my body is fucking *burning.*

I crave to fill her up until my cock disappears completely. But the look on her face—I'm unable to stop what I'm doing.

She's lit up.

"Thatcher," she chokes, wrapped completely in spinning pleasure.

Her whole body seizes and her back arches in a beautiful, earth-shattering climax. It takes all my energy not to come right here with her.

Jane is too sensitive to touch, so I remove my thumb off her clit and keep thrusting while she pulsates around my cock. Little noises pant from her lips before she brushes hair from her eyes. Our gazes meet in a strong beat.

She sits up on her elbows, silk top twisted and hair messy. She's spent, but curiosity glimmers in her eyes and awakens her enough. "Can I?" she asks subtly while I'm fucking her—her voice raspy and fingers curling around the sheets.

She's hot as all hell.

I nod, and I pull out of Jane. She crunches up towards my chest, the prostate massager already in hand and lubed.

Still kneeling, I move closer to her body, which purposefully tugs her legs higher, the backs of her knees under the palms of my hands. She returns to a state of aching *need.*

She quivers. "And I thought…I was terrific at sex."

I almost smile. "You're the best there ever could be, Jane." I feel pressure on my asshole as she reaches under me. I breathe in, and she's careful as she inserts the toy.

Oh…fucking…Christ.

Vibrations against my prostate send extra shockwaves through my nerves—and ragged breath comes harsher through my nose.

Watching Jane—her eagerness and excitement—just throbs my cock even more. I stroke my shaft a couple times.

"How's that?" she asks after fitting the massager inside me.

"Good." Every time I clench around the thing, my nerves prick a million eye-rolling ways—and my biceps and traps flex into stretched, searing bands.

I pull her ankle, drawing her further onto the bed. She collapses off her elbows with a wanting noise, and I stretch her right leg higher, filling her back up with my length.

Carnal, visceral *need.*

I fuck her. Deep into her pussy. Over and over. Mounting towards a peak. She loses hold on my shoulders, her fingers slipping and her body trembling. She contracts around my cock, and I just rock through her orgasm without pause. No break.

Each thrust forward, my ass flexes and the massager nails my senses. Light bursts in my vision. *God-fucking-dammit*—a groan scratches my throat. "Jane."

"*Thatcher.*" Tears prick her eyes, and I brush them away with my thumb. "Deeper," she whispers as her eyes start fluttering.

My whole body thrums, blood rushing, head splitting. I'm on another level, and she's just as far gone. Wedging a second pillow under her bottom, I bend her legs more and curl my arms around them higher against my chest. Sinking in faster and *deeper.* Building and building until there's nowhere to go.

One more thrust, and a prostate orgasm rips through me. I come hard into a mind-numbing bliss. I bask in every fucking second, a few more pumps, and I ease out of my fiancée.

Jane is gathering awareness of the room and her body. Still breathing like she's racing up a hill. "That…was…" She blinks and remembers the toy. "Do you need…?"

I reach under and pull the thing out. "I'm good."

"Did it work?" she asks curiously.

"Hell yeah."

Jane smiles, looking satisfied and satiated.

We end up lying back down together. Under the sheets at the head of the bed—and I notice Ophelia perched near my ankle. Honestly, I've noticed her there for a while, watching us.

By now, I'm used to the feline audience.

Jane turns into my chest. Our lips meld together, and she rubs my dick lightly before she yawns. It's still morning, and she's about to fall right back to sleep. But she fights exhaustion.

"Go back to sleep," I whisper. "I'm not going anywhere."

She playfully pats my cheek. "Sounds like a terribly wonderful idea…but first I have to tell you something." She battles a deeper yawn. "Or rather, *two* somethings."

We just had deep sex, and I'd prefer Jane to relax and not force herself awake. But she folds her arms across my chest and rests her chin on her forearm.

And I see slight concern in her eye. Which pushes me to shut up and let her speak.

"I'm not sure how you'll take this," she starts.

I stroke sweaty pieces of hair off her face. "Try me."

"I've always dreamed to one day be there for Moffy the way that my mom was there for her sister. I plan to extend the offer now that he's with Farrow. I'd love nothing more than to do this for them…you look utterly confused."

"I'm not." I understand what she's saying, what she's referencing.

Rose Calloway was a surrogate for Daisy. She carried her sister's child, and almost fifteen years ago, Rose gave birth to Winona Meadows.

"You want to be a surrogate so you can help Maximoff have kids?" I ask if I'm right.

"Precisely." She smooths her lips. "Since you and I are building a future together, I want to make sure you're okay with this before I tell Moffy and Farrow."

She'll be pregnant with their baby… "From what I remember, Winona is still genetically Daisy and Ryke's child, right?"

"Right. My mom just carried her, but obviously Maximoff and Farrow need an egg, and I thought…well, I'd be willing to give them mine." She looks more nervous because this changes things.

She'd be the kid's biological mom. They would have Jane's DNA, her features.

"Moffy and Farrow might not even say *yes*," Jane says quickly, but I can see that she hopes they do. "Say something, please."

I realize I'm stoic, nothing passing through my hardened face, and I let go and stare deeper into Jane. In awe of her kindness and love. "You're a beautiful person. I hope you know that."

She starts crying.

I hold her, and I kiss the top of her head and whisper, "I love you, and I'm by your side in everything." After a few minutes, she dries her eyes and looks back up at me.

I nod. "The second something?"

"Yes. It's good news." Her cheeks dimple in a smile. "Remember how we agreed not to get married before Moffy and Farrow?"

"Yeah." *I remember.*

Jane doesn't want to take the spotlight from her best friend, and I can appreciate that. If roles were reversed and Banks were Maximoff, I'd want my brother to get married first.

When my mom asked me about the wedding date—I told her the truth. We didn't have one, and it probably wouldn't be for *years*.

Maximoff and Farrow have always wanted a long engagement. *Two years*, they said. Which would make our engagement even longer.

I can wait decades, but I'd love nothing more than to call Jane my wife. I'd marry her tomorrow if I could.

Her lips lift in a smile. "Maximoff said he doesn't want my engagement to last so long just because of him. Farrow agreed. They're getting married this year."

I'm blown back for a second. Emotions surging. My eyes burn, overwhelmed, and I rake a hand over my mouth. *I'm going to marry her sooner.* Maximoff and Farrow gave that to Jane because they love her.

She gives up everything for everyone, and maybe they could see that she shouldn't have to give something up for them.

"Jane," I breathe and touch the top of her head. "I don't know what to say."

"You don't have to say anything." She lightly presses her fingers to the creases beside my eye. "I see it."

We just stare at one another, love flooding us.

I wish *love* could be enough to carry me through dinner tonight. But knowing her brothers, I could strap on a million pounds of adoration for their sister, and it still wouldn't be good enough.

43

Thatcher Moretti

THE LOGISTICS OF TONIGHT can go straight to hell.

I'd have preferred driving my fiancée to her childhood home. But I'm not her bodyguard, and I'm still dealing with the fact that Tony is on her detail. He has one month left. *One month.*

After that shit, he'll be transferred to Charlie's detail—which puts Oscar in a bind.

And on top of that shit, he'll be promoted to Omega lead.

All I see is shit.

I remember Akara's words. *Don't worry about it*, he said.

I am worrying about it, but I trust him. When we were leads—when it was me and him—he'd explain more of what's happening. Now I'm just left to follow.

And that's the easier part. I'd follow Akara into darkness time and time again.

Banishing the aggravation and pure dislike I have for Tony is more difficult. It'd have been simpler, if I could've accompanied Jane to the Cobalt Estate.

But she said that she wanted to talk to her siblings before I arrive. To make sure they won't slaughter me tonight.

I feel like I need swords, axes, and a fucking trebuchet to attend this dinner.

Making it out alive without causing a Cobalt Civil War is my main goal.

To make matters more fucked, all the cars in the garage are gone. Which means I have to take one of the security SUVs on the curb.

When I step out onto the sidewalk, I'm met with a succession of flashes. Glaring in the night.

Paparazzi—their voices topple on top of each other, fighting to be heard. I raise a hand to my eyes, trying not to be completely fucking blinded on the way to my car.

"Thatcher! Thatcher!" a stocky guy with a Canon yells, short enough that his head stops well beneath my shoulders.

"Move." I'm one second from shoving. *Don't touch him.* I don't want to risk getting arrested on my way to this dinner, and if he falls on his ass and claims assault, I'm going to be met with a lawsuit.

Follow protocol.

Security rules still exist—they don't suddenly disappear because I'm off-duty or engaged to a client.

He doesn't listen and just as I come up to the black Escalade, he stops moving *right* in front of the door. Blocking me.

I glower.

He holds up his camera. "How many years have you been with Jane Cobalt?!"

His question is like a cannon blast in my ears, opening up my focus to the others that have been yelled around me for the past minute.

"When is the wedding?!"

"How did you ask her?!"

"Is she pregnant?!"

I scowl harder at that one and focus on the shitbag blocking me. "I'm not going to ask you a second time. *Move.*"

The stout guy clicks five more times and sears my corneas. White light stabs my vision and before I can grab him, he darts out of the way.

I'm quick. Inside the Escalade and shutting the door. It takes me a good twenty minutes to lose the trail of paparazzi. I glance at the clock.

On time. I planned for traffic, but I wish I were earlier. I don't have much wiggle room in case something—

You've got to be fucking with me.

My eyes are narrowed on the fuel gauge. *This can't be happening.* Someone on SFO left this SUV with a nearly empty tank. I slam a hand against the steering wheel and reroute to the nearest gas station. "Buncha fucking idiots."

We have rules.

One being to *always* leave the cars fueled up in case of an emergency.

Right now, I'm in a motherfucking dump truck level of a crisis. I'm about to show up *late* to my first Wednesday Night Dinner, and there's one thing I know about Connor Cobalt—he hates how I remind him of Ryke Meadows.

Who is perpetually fucking *late* to events. I can't even count the number of times I've heard Ryke's bodyguard on comms say something like, *"We're coming in an hour past."*

Being late might just obliterate the ground that I made with her parents.

I growl out my frustration and curse out loud for all three miles to the gas station. By the time I put the SUV in park, I'm barely accepting my fate.

Jane will vouch for me, and that's the last thing I want. Defending me shouldn't be what tonight is about. "I'm going to kill someone on Omega," I mutter under my breath. "Except my brother. If this was on him, he'll survive. Maybe."

I'm talking to myself.

My jaw clenches, and I swear in my head. *Fuck.*

Fuck.

Fuck.

I think I'm nervous.

Fuck.

I hop out of the car and slam the door closed with a loud *thump.* The noise stirs something in the space between the pump and the trashcan, the movement caught in my peripheral.

I don't have time for this.

But out of instinct, I check the shifting shadow, wanting clearer visual. Squatting down, I expect to locate a rat.

I rest my forearms on my knees and tilt my head. All I see is brown fur, a little thing curled in a ball next to the trash.

And then its head pops up, and my whole stomach drops.

What...?

Breath cages my lungs.

I'm staring at round, blue orbs for eyes. A tiny brown nose. Two perked ears. Long whiskers and dark-striped fur. I've been to enough cat shelters to know what I've found.

I'm staring at a tabby kitten. *How could this happen?* Out of all times and all days and all gas stations...

I look up at the star-blanketed sky.

I'm not as religious as others in my family, but I have faith. And call me nuts, but I feel like this kitten *is* Jane. Sent by someone who knew I'd need her. Come here to tell me that it's going to be okay. Calm down. Breathe.

Maybe I'm just losing my fucking mind.

But I can't walk away from this stray. She wouldn't.

I hold out my palm, waiting for the kitten to approach me. "Hey, girl."

She crouches on her tiny paws and tentatively creeps towards me. She barely hesitates before nudging her cheek into my knuckles. And I'm just gone. Right here. Right now. "Jane?" I ask like a fucking idiot.

Banks would be laughing his ass off if he saw me.

She keeps nuzzling my hand.

I draw in a deeper, stronger breath. It's her. No one can tell me otherwise. "Fuck it." I gently pick up the kitten. "Let's go to dinner, Little Jane."

TO PREPARE ME, JANE TOLD ME THREE THINGS

about Wednesday Night Dinner.

1. The dress code is anything and everything and nothing. Costumes are acceptable. Being buck-naked is also acceptable. *There are no rules.*

2. Conversation is not a requirement. Talk as much as you want or don't talk at all. *There are no rules.*

3. But there are rules. *Only one.* Come as you are. Be true to you. And all will fall into place.

I took everything Jane said to heart, so I'm not wearing a suit. I'm not wearing my black slacks and a black button-down like I'm on-duty.

I'm on time. Made every green light. Surprisingly, I'm here before either Connor or Rose. And I sit at her family's dining room table as *me.*

Dark denim jeans and a red flannel shirt, a kitten currently alert but tentative in the breast pocket—yeah, that's a new development.

"She's absolutely, positively the loveliest thing I've ever seen." Audrey Cobalt swoons, her gaze fixated on the tabby kitten. Jane's sister turned fourteen in January, and right now, she looks transported from one of those PBS historical shows my grandma is always watching. A bonnet with fresh roses in a ribbon plopped on her carrot-orange hair, which spills over a ruffled white dress.

I'm hawk-eyed. Attentive.

Perceptive of everyone, everything, but there is too much to absorb. My eyes are feasting on the lavish elaborate scene. This is made for the movies.

For theater.

For history.

For *The Phantom of the Opera* and ancient sword-wielding times.

Not exactly for a man like me, but I'm not turning around. I'm not back-tracking. And I'm not made to cower. Nerves retreat.

I'm steel in a room of guys and girls ironclad from birth.

Seven sets of eyes are pinned on me.

I've sat down for one minute. Just as ready for hell as the minute before, and I'll be ready a thousand minutes after.

Roasted goose and gold candlesticks line the table. I've always seen the remnants of this dinner in leftover containers. Strange, seeing the food before it's torn to pieces.

A unique aroma clings to the air: a mixture of gamey meat, rosemary, garlic, vanilla and tobacco. I do another quick sweep around the dining room. Only Jane and her siblings are here, the heads of the table empty, but I think the absence of their parents might be purposeful.

I focus on Charlie.

He's kicked back on an ornate chair, expensive shoes on a gold dish. Like he has no care in the world—but he's watching me watch him.

Fans would go ape shit if they saw Charlie Cobalt in this setting. Teenagers would sob and cry outside this house just for a *peek* of him shirtless while wearing a blue floral suit—tailor-made, probably in the high-thousands—and a black choker necklace.

Most bodyguards have seen his deep flaws, his hatred and pain.

I've seen more as I've been dating Jane. But I don't think I'll ever really know Charlie. I doubt many ever will.

He tilts his head to Audrey. "We have more pressing matters than a stupid cat."

"Excuse you," Jane snaps. "This kitten is not stupid. She is an adorable sweetheart. Do you see her just resting in his pocket? It was meant to be."

My lip almost lifts. I have an arm around my fiancée's chair. And she looks drop-dead gorgeous.

Like always.

Pastel pink breezy skirt, a cheetah-print blouse and baby blue fur coat. Cat ears studded in rhinestones are perched on her wavy brown hair.

She looks the same as usual, but also different. Jane glows. Head-to-toe effervescence. When she catches me staring, a smile spreads across her rosy cheeks—her freckles more noticeable without any makeup.

Since I arrived, she hasn't seemed nervous. Not once.

Her faith in me is like a beacon of light guiding my ship to shore.

Charlie rises and leans over the table to peer at Jane. "If it was meant to be, why have you been checking it for flees for the past three minutes?"

Jane has been doing that. Pulling back the kitten's fur just to ensure I didn't bring a flea-ridden kitten into her mom's home.

Great first dinner impression—having to make Rose Calloway flea bomb her entire house. *Didn't think about that.*

Mainly because I thought Little Jane was a sign from the Real Jane. Rational thinking was chucked out the fucking window.

"Because she doesn't want Mom to murder Thatcher." Eliot pours himself a goblet of wine, a pipe between his lips while wearing a vintage-style coat with tails. He plucks the pipe from his mouth to add more clearly, "We all want our future-brother-in-law to survive tonight."

My brows pull together. It can't be that easy. I remember every card I've drawn. Every Truth or Dare I've completed, my response pissed off at least one Cobalt.

I never pleased all six of her siblings at one time.

It felt impossible.

"Speak for yourself," Ben says to Eliot.

There it is. That was the reaction I expected.

Ben has a black eye from an ice hockey match that his team won. A blue environmental tee is tight on his toned build, with the slogan: *don't be a fossil fool.*

"Still bitter, brother?" Eliot asks.

Ben lets out a heavy breath. "He ate *rabbit hearts.*" He's talking like I'm not here. Which isn't fucking good.

Tom twirls a knife. "We're about to eat goose."

Beckett looks to Ben next to him. "And you don't hate us."

I can't tell if they're defending me or just trying to steer their brother towards a better emotion. But I know Jane has said that Ben is usually fine when other people eat meat around him.

"It's different. That situation felt *different,*" Ben emphasizes.

Jane lifts a finger. "I also ate rabbit hearts."

"You wouldn't have if Thatcher didn't. He can perish in one of Mom's great and terrible fires for all I care. Let him burn alive."

I wait for the sting, but that blow never comes. His words aren't a shot to the heart or head. I'm not even surprised that he's still upset about this.

He's sixteen. He's a Cobalt. He's dramatic, and I'm just honored to be here and understand how this family operates.

No holding back. No holding in.

Let it all out.

"Pippy," Jane starts.

"He ate some rabbit hearts," Charlie snaps. "Get the fuck over it, Ben."

Ben stands up abruptly from his chair. I follow suit, careful not to startle the kitten, and I hold out a hand. "It's fine."

But Ben is looking at his empty plate. He's grinding down on his teeth and trying to stop himself from crying.

"You can hate me," I say with severity. "I don't need you to like me right now. Or a year from now or ten years. Just when you're ready, I hope you can give me a chance."

Ben slowly takes a seat. And quietly, he says, "You're here. This is your chance."

Tonight.

Don't fucking nuke it.

I lower back down, a hand to my breast pocket (to the kitten), and Jane leans into my shoulder. "He's going to warm up to you."

It's weird to think that I know it's okay if he doesn't.

Charlie rests his ass on the edge of the table. Turned towards me, he hoists a single lion-decaled card between two fingers. "Here's your last one."

My last one.

That hits me hard. For a long time, I thought this game might be never-ending. That they'd keep filling up the deck every time it got low.

It's over.

Almost.

He stretches and passes me the card.

I take it from Charlie and flip it over. Words stare back at me. I read them.

And reread them.

Five times to make sure I'm reading it right.

Tom grins sitting on the top of his chair, his black trench coat long enough to sweep the floor—a thousand-and-fucking-one patches sewn crudely in the fabric. He opens and closes a Zippo lighter.

He knows what this says. All her brothers and her sister do.

They were all in on the game. Not just Charlie.

I read out loud, "'Tell us why you belong in the family without referencing Jane.'"

It might be the hardest thing this game has ever thrown my way.

Jane is the reason I am sitting at this table, but she's not going to be the reason I fit into this family. I have to do that on my own.

Weighing my words, I glance between each of her siblings. All six are so different from the next. Years ago, I think I would've said I fit in better with the Hales, or even the Meadows, but there's not a shred of doubt now.

I'm where I'm supposed to be. I just have to find a way to articulate it.

I'm quiet for a beat, and Beckett meets my gaze. Dark brown hair slicked back and in a casual white crewneck, he takes a drag of a cigarette between leather-gloved fingers.

"You have to answer," Beckett says kindly. No hint of animosity or resentment in his voice. Even after he came home to find his role replaced in *Cinderella* by Leo Valavanis. But according to Jane, the company is starting to audition parts for next season's production of *Romeo & Juliet*.

Beckett is in contention for Romeo. And so is Leo.

You have to answer.

I nod strongly. "I know." And I drop my arm from Jane's chair, and with zero doubt, zero hesitation, I stand.

Not afraid to tower.

Not afraid of anything.

"I belong here," I start. And then I look at her on instinct.

Jane smiles up at me with sky-high confidence.

My chest rises, and I look around at her family who I hope will one day be mine. "I belong here," I say again, "because I love deeply and I'm learning to feel deeply too, and I make no apologies for who I am."

Jane is beaming, glassy-eyed with hands to her lips.

I continue, "And at the end of the day, the people I care about are the ones I would die for. No questions asked. I'm standing at the battle line." *Say more. Say what you feel,* and I just go. "You're a family of warriors—I'm a warrior too. We just have different weapons. You use words. I use a gun. And ever since I was a young kid, I wanted to be that Spartan hero for someone. I belong here. Not anywhere else."

Not because of Jane. But because when it comes down to it, I'm a fucking lion.

I'm a shark.

For the first time, I really believe I'm the same as them.

Not saying a word, Charlie stretches forward and plucks the card from my hand. He extends his arm across the table. Passing the thing to Eliot, who holds the card over Tom's lighter.

A flame incinerates the paper.

I thought I'd want their applause or approval at the end of this. But standing here, I realize, I don't need that recognition or their validation. I feel good about who I am and what I completed.

"That's it?" I ask Charlie.

He nods. "Congratulations. Some of us still hate you. Some of us like you. Others don't give a shit. And yet, you're still here."

I'm still here.

My mouth curves upward, and I nod once. The game was never designed for me to win them over like I thought.

It was designed for them to push my limits. To tap into unapologetic confidence. To survive a battle.

I'm still here.

I'm back in my seat next to Jane, and she gathers my hand in hers. "You're amazing, you realize."

I kiss her knuckles before wrapping an arm around her shoulder, and I lean in to whisper, "I love you, Jane Eleanor Cobalt."

I hear her sharp breath. She's about to reply, but Tom points at me with a steak knife. "What's its name anyway?" He means the kitten.

I watch the tabby stretch a paw mid-sleep. "Jane usually picks the person who'll name her cats."

She rests her chin on her knuckles. "*Our* cats."

Our cats.

I hang onto that declaration.

Looks like I'm a father of six—now *seven*—cats. This is bigger than Jane asking me to marry her. These cats are her babies, and she's sharing them with me.

Happiness isn't in the same stratosphere to the raw emotion that's balled up inside my chest. I block out the mental image of my brother ribbing me about being a cat dad.

Jane rubs the top of the kitten's head with her thumb. "And you found each other. You should pick her name."

I already have a name for her, and everyone here will give me shit for it. So I just say, "LJ."

"LJ?" Jane frowns for a second.

"I love it." Audrey adjusts her bonnet.

"You don't even know what it stands for, Audrey." Eliot grins, deviously. "It could be something horrible like Lube—"

Jane cuts him off in French, and I recognize a couple words. The ones that mean *little devil*.

I make a call and decide to rip this Band-Aid fast.

"LJ is short for Little Jane."

Silence layers across the table before Tom and Eliot explode into laughter. Ben and Audrey pound the table with their fists, and almost everyone drums the ground with their feet. Charlie clinks his glass with the back of a knife.

Living breathing noise rumbling around us.

"They love it," Jane explains to me. "As do I."

I'm constantly in awe of her, and now, I'm in awe of her family. More orderly but disordered sound reverberates and floods the room when Rose and Connor arrive hand-in-hand.

What happens next is history.

My history.

Maybe they never explained these dinners because you can't. I'm twenty-eight, but here—no person is older or younger. Time is frozen, and a soul-bleeding feeling sings and screams—an experience that philosophers and mathematicians would fail to encapsulate.

I'd try.

But then again, I'd rather carry their secrets to my grave.

44

Thatcher Moretti

"SKY! *SKYLAR!*" I YELL out and drop my bike. I bolt into pitch-black water. Soaked up to my waist before I swim, and I reach the facedown floating body, turning my brother over—our gold necklaces snag. My strong pulse beats in my ears, and gripping him, I swim and pull. I drag him to the graveled shore.

My strong pulse beats.

Water drips down my eyelashes. I lie him down, chained at the necks, forced to stay close.

It beats.

I pump on his chest.

It beats.

I blow breath into his mouth and compress his chest—Skylar jolts up and grabs my arms in panic. "Thatch!"

My eyes snap open, a cold sweat coating me. *Nightmare*—just a fucking nightmare. I stay still and blink a few times, my pulse on a decent. *Fuck me.* I blink and gather spatial awareness. *I'm in Jane's bedroom.*

Our room.

She sleeps peacefully beside me, tucked under a purple blanket. Naked, both of us, except for the cornic' around my neck and my dog tags around hers. Quietly, I grab my phone off the nightstand and check the time, squinting as the screen lights up in the darkened bedroom. It's zero three hundred hours.

Early. Too early for sunlight.

I lie back, head to pillow, and I smear a hand over my eyes. My nightmares are always related to my time in the military—I can't remember ever having one about that night in the quarry.

Back when I was twelve and Sky was fifteen, my brother—he never woke up.

I try to think about other things. Like how it's nearing the end of March, and we're only three days away from Tony's transfer to Charlie's detail. And him becoming the Omega lead.

Yeah, that's not making me feel any better.

To slow my heart rate, I take a few deep, measured breaths, and I smell something...

I sniff the air.

My pulse shoots back up, and I narrow my gaze on the door.

Filmy lines of smoke billow underneath and spill into the room.

I'm on my feet in a split-second. "Jane." I tug on my drawstring pants, then I jostle my fiancée. "Jane!"

She flinches awake. "What, Thatcher?" Panic strikes her eyes as I leave the bed to cross the room and swing open the closet.

"Oh my God." She sees the smoke pooling inside, and while I grab the fire extinguisher behind a shoebox, she hurriedly puts on panties and my black crewneck. And she glances at the wall. "LUNA! WAKE UP!"

Her cats—our cats. They barrel to the front of my mind.

I sprint out. Smoke skates across the second-floor landing and narrow staircase, stinging my eyes. I cough into my bicep and yell up towards the attic, "MAXIMOFF! FARROW!"

The fire isn't coming from their room.

I slam a fist on a second-floor bedroom. "LUNA!" She's a heavy sleeper. Could take more than that to wake her—but I run downstairs to stop the fire.

Heat is pouring from the first floor. The cracking sound is as violent as the sweltering temperature, and I enter an absolute fucking *horror* scene. Fire spreads to the ceiling, eats the floorboards, attacking the wood foundation, and it tries to crawl up the brick walls.

Pink loveseat in flames, but the kitchen—the kitchen is *engulfed*, maybe in seconds. I extinguish the living room, protecting the front door exit.

"BANKS!" I yell at the adjoining door.

My brother.

SFO.

They're asleep in the other townhouse. The door opens, and Donnelly almost blows back. "Shit." He's been crashing on security's couch. I remember Akara spent the night here too. He hasn't moved back to the gated neighborhood yet.

I throw the empty extinguisher, abandoning the task.

We can't put out this fire. I spot a gray cat cowering beneath the rocking chair, tail on fire. Sweat drips off me as I run and snatch up Licorice, putting out the flames with my hand. Fur singed.

Donnelly shields his nose and races towards the staircase like he's going to find someone.

I yell back at him, "Wake Akara, Quinn, Banks, and Tony! Get them outside!" Licorice claws up my chest, and I pull the frightened cat down.

Donnelly coughs, stops, and reroutes back into security's townhouse.

Farrow runs down the stairs. "*Fuck*," he curses at the sight and winces. Cringes.

The heat is un-fucking-bearable. My eyes sear from smoke, lungs burning. "Less than two minutes before it's upstairs!" I yell. If the fire barricades Jane, Maximoff, and Luna, we'll need to exit a window. I point to the front door, the better exit.

The clock is set. *Less than two minutes.*

Farrow nods and eagle-eyes something on my six. "Go."

I trust him. I don't wait to look at what he sees. I leave Farrow and sprint back upstairs. Back to the people we'd give our lives to protect.

Jane is already on the phone with the fire department and corralling Ophelia into a cat carrier. Her eyes widen when she sees Licorice's singed tail.

"He's fine." I shove him in with Ophelia.

"I have Toodles!" Maximoff yells from the landing, a tuxedo cat tight in his arms. That cat—he never lets Maximoff hold him, except for right now. Toodles isn't fidgeting. "Luna, you ready?"

"Yeah." Her *Thrashers* sweatshirt consumes her gangly frame.

I zip up the carrier while Jane hangs up. Fire truck sirens blare in the distance.

We're missing four cats.

We have no time to search a house that's going down fast.

Jane is near tears, but she pushes through the grief and fear. "We need to leave now." She stands with the carrier.

"Where's Farrow?" Maximoff asks.

"Cover your nose." I hand Jane a shirt from the floor. Luna already buries her nose in her sweatshirt.

"Thatcher, where's Farrow?!" Maximoff screams.

"Downstairs. He's fi—"

Maximoff is already running down the steps.

I walk out in front of Luna and Jane in case the fire has swarmed the stairs. Farrow is already at the bottom, grasping the furry necks of two calico cats. One in each hand. "The door is clear!"

Two cats missing.

Maximoff sees Farrow is okay. Farrow assesses his fiancé, and we all work together to leave. I press against the brick wall, making the girls pass me, and I come up in the rear, my hand on Jane's hip.

Maximoff draws his sister closer, protecting Luna while Farrow leads them through the fast-burning, tiny living room.

One clear path.

That's all we have.

We cough, and through the thick, bright haze of smoke and fire—I stay vigilant and see a black cat in the *unlit* fireplace. On the mantel, flames eat away and consume family photographs.

I reroute.

Jane feels my hand leave her side. "No—wait, *Thatcher!*"

"Don't stop!" I yell. *Don't wait for me.*

Maximoff pulls her forward.

I barrel through fire, heat licking my chest, and I don't think. I just collect a scared Lady Macbeth, and I exit behind the four of them.

We're on the street. At a safe distance while the old Philly townhouse burns and burns. Flames lick the second-floor windows.

Our room.

I cough out a lungful of smoke, and Jane tears Lady Macbeth out of my arms. More so I can catch my breath without a cat clawing me to death.

"Thatcher?"

I nod to her that I'm fine, and I sweep her—*she's alive, safe, breathing.* And I sweep the chaotic perimeter. Fire trucks aren't here yet. Neighbors pool out onto the street. Paparazzi shout, spilling out of their cars. They toss water bottles to us, ask if we're okay, and take pictures and videos.

Banks.

I search for my brother, but he's already jogging up to me. "SFO is good. Everyone is out." He glances between me and Jane. "The cats?"

Jane looks up at me, and agony finally reaches her—she breaks down, tears pouring out. Face contorting. I hold her against my body. My stomach is in knots—*I fucking failed.* All I can do is comfort her.

"How many?" Banks asks me.

"We didn't find LJ."

"What?" Tony hears that last part, walking closer. "You left the kitten?" He combs back his hair, eyeing the opened front door.

He wouldn't.

I look back at the end of the street. For one second, and when I turn, Tony is running towards the engulfed townhouse. To save a cat that's probably already dead.

To prove something.

That he's worth more than me.

"TONY!" I growl out. "STOP!"

He doesn't stop.

"What the fuck is he doing?!" Quinn shouts.

"Saving a kitten," Banks says, his voice tight like he's caging breath. Probably hoping Tony will retreat at the foot of the door.

Farrow jogs closer. "Luna has LJ."

"What?" Jane chokes out, unburying herself from my chest.

Tony. I yell at the top of my lungs, "SHE HAS THE CAT!"

He doesn't hear and he disappears into the fucking fire. Alarm triggers a reaction in me. I touch my collar for a mic. *I'm shirtless.* And no one grabbed a radio. *There was no time.*

I have one last instinct that tries to shove me forward.

Get him.

I let the reflex take over me, and I touch the top of her head, lovingly, and I run back to the house. My strong pulse beats in my ears.

"NO!" Banks screams.

"You can't," she cries out.

If my life means anything, let it mean this: I tried with my whole soul to protect the ones who couldn't protect themselves, and I loved while I was here.

I will always love my brother.

And Jane—I will always, *always* love Jane. Death can't take that from me.

45

Banks Moretti

I RUN AFTER MY TWIN—he enters a literal burning building like he's immune to the flames. That's my brother. Six-minutes older. Entering hellfire with vigilance and confidence that'd make his men feel safe.

I follow. To stop him. Lungs fucking ablaze.

I don't even reach the curb before Akara tackles me.

My chest and knees thud to the hot cement. *No, no*—fucking *no!* "Get off!" I scream between gritted teeth, and I thrash against Akara. "Get the fuck off me!" *Someone stop my brother.* My chin digs into pavement, eyes wide-open. Super-glued to this misery.

Fire lights up the night sky, smoke mushrooming above us, and flames burst through every window on every level of that stupid fucking house.

I scream out the anger and pain and ruthless agony. I thrash and fucking thrash. Snot runs out of my nose.

My pulse is ripped out of my veins.

Akara has a knee on my spine—Donnelly and Farrow are also pinning me down. Three of them restrain me. To save me because my brother is gone.

Thatcher and I—we were never allowed in the same platoon. Because of a military rule about brothers.

They don't put them together in the unfortunate event that one dies. It ensures that the other will survive. So a parent won't lose two sons at the same time.

I never understood that.

Call me a dumbass, a stunad. But to survive my twin brother's death is worse than being six-feet under.

I fight them. It's all I have.

"You can't go in there!" Akara yells in my ear.

"He's gonna die for Tony," I choke and spit out into the pavement. But I know Thatcher.

He'd die for just about anyone.

I hear Jane behind me, crying in anguish that already slashes up my body.

"Close your eyes, Banks," Akara orders, his voice almost cracking.

I'm watching the house burn down with my twin inside. I can't feel the flames tearing at his skin—I just feel the pain of losing someone who's a part of my soul.

"Just kill me," I choke.

Akara covers my eyes with his hand.

And everything goes black.

46

Jane Cobalt

"I CAN'T..." *I CAN'T breathe.* I kneel on the street, our cats—I think Quinn and Luna took them to a car or neighboring house.

I can't...

I just...

Thatcher is gone. Our house is in flames. In a matter of *minutes.*

"Breathe, Janie." Moffy holds me from behind. His arms wrapped around me, and I clutch his biceps for dear life. I feel like I'm falling and falling into an endless abyss and I can't reach the surface. Suffocating and suffocating.

We were going to marry.

He'd be my husband, and I'd be his wife.

Breath is strangled in my windpipe. "Thatcher," I choke.

Maximoff hugs me, telling me he's here. Tears flow like broken dams down my face, and my eyes burn from worse than smoke.

I barely notice the fire truck arrive. Firefighters roll out hoses to contain the blaze—and right as they approach the townhouse, the roof collapses.

I can't even hear my own blood-curdling wail.

Maximoff picks me up. He carries me further away from the fire, but the pain follows, attached to me like a parasite. I bury my face in his shoulder, and when we're behind a parked SUV, I vomit.

Gravel digging in my knees, I puke until nothing else comes out, dry heaving, and Moffy tries to help me stop. I dazedly touch the shirt on my body. Baggy, a men's crewneck.

I'm wearing his shirt. And his dog tags.

I fall back into Moffy. He catches me, and I curl up into a ball.

"I love him," I cry. "I love him...*I love him.*"

My biggest regret is not saying it enough.

47

Jane Cobalt

IT FEELS LIKE ETERNITY that he's gone.

I can't count the seconds, the minutes. Every passing moment extends into utter oblivion, and I calm behind the SUV.

Enough to stare blankly at the road, numb and hollowed.

"Janie!" Maximoff pulls me to my feet.

"What…?" I follow his gaze to the collapsed, burning townhouse. As firefighters hose down the battered structure, the garage door slowly begins to open.

Is it…?

Thatcher emerges with an unconscious Tony. He's cradling him in his arms.

I run towards him. Air pumping into my crying lungs. I feel out-of-body, like I'm floating, and to my left, the SFO bodyguards release their weight off Banks, and he races towards his twin brother.

First Responders pry Tony out of Thatcher's clutch—taking him to an ambulance—and Thatcher nearly stumbles forward, but I come beside him.

I hold his waist.

Banks holds his other side, and we bring him to the second ambulance. Soot is smeared across his face and body. Skin eaten on his right shoulder. He's badly burned.

Thatcher coughs, "I found him like that...a rafter knocked him out." It must've taken him a while to carry Tony to the garage. He hacks up a lung. "I'm fine."

"Like hell," Banks says.

I can't be upset at Thatcher for risking his life for Tony. It's engrained in him, and to tell him to do differently would be to tell him to be less of who he is. I'm angry that it had to happen.

I'm angry at the circumstances.

I think Banks is too.

Thatcher takes a seat on the back of the ambulance. His hand— his hand is in mine. He seizes my gaze like he's implanting me in his memory.

I'm crying all over again. "I love you, I love you. Don't go anywhere. *Please.*"

"I won't." He brings me closer to hold me, but I won't let him with his third-degree burns. I don't want to hurt him.

"No. You need a hospital." I flag down a paramedic, but I keep my hand in his.

Light touches his serious eyes.

Banks huffs at him. "You're a fucking gabbadost'. I fucking wanna kick your ass right now and hug you."

"I had to," Thatcher coughs lightly. "Tony is family."

"Yeah, and we all would've mourned you more than him."

Thatcher shakes his head. "You're just making me feel badly for him, Banks." He suddenly doubles-over in a coughing fit.

We need to go.

Farrow jogs over to us, med bag slung across his chest. "Tony is alive and conscious." He sweeps Thatcher. "Get your ass in the ambulance, Moretti."

He straightens up, done coughing, and we're about to help him. But he dips his head down and kisses my cheek, his lips brush my ear as he whispers, "I love you. Always, always."

My heart swells. "I'm not leaving you."

"Good. I don't want you to."

I climb into the ambulance right behind him. We steal glances in every beat.

He's still here.

48

Thatcher Moretti

I PUT HER THROUGH hell. I put my brother through hell, and I hate that I dragged them down into that inferno. I understand too fucking well that what they endured was worse than smoke inhalation and third-degree burns.

It weighs on me at Philly General.

I'm on my feet in the hospital room, gripping my IV stand. Abandoning the bed. I can't sit. I've already had to be motionless for hours while a nurse dressed my burn, applying moist, sterile gauze on my right shoulder. I'm lucky that I don't need skin grafts.

One chest X-ray later, results normal, and I'm now on observation for damage the smoke might've caused my lungs. Farrow said, "It's extra precaution in case of delayed lung injury. I might order a second chest X-ray."

I have to stay overnight.

You put her through hell, Thatcher.

I cross the room, IV wheels screeching as they roll. Patient drawstring pants ride low on my waist.

"You look distraught," Jane says softly, an empty Styrofoam cup in hand. Banks just left to go buy more coffees from a machine down the hall. She's the only one with me, and she's still wearing my black crewneck that hangs past her thighs.

Reminding me that the fire incinerated her closet. And all of her belongings.

Gone.

I walk back towards her.

Jane stands poised in the middle of the room, like she didn't just experience one of the worst nights of her life.

My fault.

My fucking fault.

I stop in front of her.

"Do you need more pain meds?" she asks.

My throat is scratched raw, hoarse from hacking up, and my shoulder stings—but that pain is pushed so far back in my mind. Boxed and packaged away.

I shake my head. "No." I keep shaking my head, upset at what I've done. "You always say that you're being unfair to me somehow, but tonight, I feel like…" I swallow a rock, my bloodshot eyes on fire and filling. "I feel like I threw you to the fucking wolves, and you deserved better." I blink and tears track down my face, slipping off my jaw.

Jane quickly sets the cup on a tray table, and I watch her walk to the corner of the room. She drags over a stepstool and climbs up. A foot taller, she reaches my exact height.

I breathe stronger.

We're eye for eye, and her small hands brush the wet lines off my face, before staying still on my jaw. "I've fallen madly in love with *you.*" Her powerful blue eyes flood with tears, and I hold her wet cheek while she says, "And the *you* that I know is all unwavering strength and resilience and South Philly grit—and every day, you risk your life for me and for other people who need *your* strength and resilience and grit."

I almost shake my head again because I still feel like I let her down.

Gently, I place my hand on the top of her beating heart, and I stare deep into her tearful gaze. "You're my duty. My heart, and you come first."

"You think you put me second or third tonight?" She frowns. "You didn't, Thatcher. I was safe." She clutches my jaw stronger. "Your entire life is built on service to others. I don't want different. I don't need different. I need you exactly as you are, just as you've loved me as exactly as I am."

It crashes against me. There are no words.

I wipe her face; she wipes mine.

And in this moment, I let go of the seven-ton guilt I was ready to bear. Our breaths come heavy, and then I just bring her lips to mine. Her fingers coil around my hair while I deepen the kiss. Sensual and slow, eking out emotion that strings me to her and her to me.

WE BREAK APART WHEN SFO SPILLS INTO MY

hospital room. They all ask how I'm doing, and I tell them, "I'm good." Coffees are passed around.

Toothpick between his teeth, Banks comes closer, and we share a look that says, *you're my brother. I love you.* It's simple and silent.

We've never needed to say much for the other to understand.

Heaviness leaves, and as Banks passes, he yanks down my pants and spanks my bare ass. "Looking good, Cinderella."

A shadow of a smile plays at my mouth.

Half the room laughs. Flush creeps on Jane's neck, trying not to look at my dick, and after I raise my pants loosely on my waist, she smooths her lips together and braves a glance at my crotch.

Standing next to her, I whisper, "It's yours."

She heats. "Forever?"

"Forever," I confirm.

Jane sips her coffee, smiling. "I like it up here." She's still on the stepstool, surveying SFO bodyguards and Maximoff as they gather around. "You and Banks have a nice view."

My lip wants to lift.

Mood is light, but tense as the room quiets and everyone glances to each other.

We've experienced a lot of shit as a team and with our clients, but a fire that took down a whole house—that's new terrain we just crossed together.

Akara steps into the middle. He snaps his fingers to his palm. "We have a lot to cover." He's including Jane and Maximoff in this impromptu security meeting. "First, I'm opening the floor for questions."

I have one. "Any word on the cause of the fire?"

"Electrical?" Donnelly leans on the bathroom door.

"It's an old house," Oscar agrees, eating a mini-can of Pringles. "Kitchen appliance could've blown a fuse."

Quinn slouches forward on a chair. "Why didn't the fire alarm go off?"

Maximoff is rigid and stares hard at the ground, and everyone goes quiet. That question hit a nerve. I should've rechecked the alarm too.

We all lived there with people we love and take care of—but we can't go back. Pushing forward is all we have. And I'm snapped to.

Farrow has an arm around his fiancé's waist. "The batteries were fairly new."

"Fire alarms malfunction sometimes," Banks says with the lift of a shoulder. "It's not that uncommon."

"Oui." Jane nods resolutely.

I narrow my eyes on Akara.

His brows are scrunched, looking concerned. "Police are opening an investigation, guys. They're not ruling out arson."

It tanks the room like dumbbells hitting the bottom of an ocean.

I scrape my hand over my unshaven jaw, tugging my fucking IV cords. I untangle them. "Any security footage?"

"Damaged."

Jane frowns. "But it still could potentially be electrical?"

"Yeah," Akara says. "That's likely, but we won't know for sure until the police report." He looks around. "Any other questions?"

Oscar raises a hand. "Our favorite doctor over here"—he gestures to Farrow, who rolls his eyes—"told me Tony wants back on-duty tomorrow. Is that happening?"

I swallow a rough cough in the back of my throat. Truth is, I ran into Tony earlier. We were waiting for chest X-rays together.

I was quiet.

He was quiet, until he said, "Thanks." Curt. To the fucking point, and I nodded in reply.

I didn't need more. Could've been fine with less.

Before the fire, he only had three days left as Jane's bodyguard. Did I know he wanted back tomorrow so he could finish out her detail?

Hell no.

I would've said something to him. Like *fuck you.*

My hand is clamped on my mouth. I'm motionless. Waiting for the gavel to drop.

"I talked to Alpha and Epsilon," Akara says, voice tight. "And to put this *lightly*, the leads admire that Tony was willing to risk his life for a client's pet."

Half the room restrains groans, the other half are eye-rolling around the world.

I'm glaring.

"It's not ideal," Akara agrees.

Oscar swigs coffee. "We're not wishing the guy seven months in the ICU. We just want to know if he's coming back tomorrow."

"If the doctors clear Tony, he's allowed on-duty."

Donnelly spins to Farrow. "You clearing him or what?"

His jaw muscle twitches. "If he's medically fine to work, I have to, and to be honest, that's probably happening tomorrow."

Silence entombs the room. We're breathing dead air.

It's not just about me. Jane and I can survive three days with Tony. This is about the team, our careers and future. We're meeting the end of a golden era in security.

We're losing Akara as a lead.

We have zero power in the Tri-Force. Akara was all we had, and with Tony as a decision-maker, he can transfer us. He can fine us. Suspend us and fire us for minor infractions.

Akara cuts his gaze to everyone. "You have to obey Tony. You have to respect him. He's your lead."

No one says a word.

I shift my glare to the wall.

Following incompetent officers into combat, ones who make a platoon two klicks off and six hours late—I've been that infantryman grinding his teeth and shutting the fuck up. Then getting chewed out because that officer just got reamed by the Battalion Commander.

Done it.

And I'll shut the fuck up again, but there are officers you meet who are *good*. Just flat-out fucking good—and the respect comes easy. No gnawing or clenched jaw or grumbled curses.

Akara was always a better leader than me.

He still is, and to lose him is to lose the best authority the team has ever seen.

Akara runs a hand through his black hair a few times, more nervous, and we watch him grab a motorcycle backpack he threw on a chair. He unzips and pulls out folded papers. Turning back to us, he says, "You do have a choice—and I'm telling you upfront, the grass isn't greener."

I'm confused.

Jane smiles into another sip of coffee.

She knows.

Maximoff is also more relaxed than usual.

He knows.

While Akara passes stapled papers to each bodyguard, I whisper to Jane, "You going to tell me?"

"And spoil the ending?" She brightens. "Never."

Akara stops at me and hands me a thick, stapled stack. "It's you and me." Banks will tell anyone that his best friend is Akara, but he'll also say that he knows he's not Akara's best friend.

Because I'm Akara's ride-or-die.

I have trouble calling Akara anything other than my closest friend. Truth is, I don't like assuming anyone wants me to be their best friend.

But I feel like he's mine. I'd do anything for him.

I take the papers and instantly see the typed title.

Kitsuwon Securities Inc.

This is a contract. He's building his own private security firm.

"Yours is different," Akara explains. "You'd be a rank above the other men, but below me."

I flip the page. "As it should be."

He smiles, but his lips downturn fast. And before anyone can edge in another word, he addresses all of us. "This isn't a life jacket. It could be a sinking ship. Kitsuwon Securities will be completely separate from Price's Triple Shield, and all the resources that we've built are gone. Security's housing belongs to *them*. The whole temp roster we've grown—I don't have. Which means we need to train new temps. You won't have seasoned guards when you need a day off. The rumor about us being fake bodyguards and in relationships with our clients—it will definitely ramp up. Your pay will be cut, substantially, and I can't tell you where you'll be living yet." He expels a tense breath. "You'll have to bear with all the kinks of being a part of a new company."

I'm good to go.

Oscar looks around. "Who has a pen?"

We're all smiling.

Happiness doesn't encapsulate what hits the air. It's elation. Rapture.

Akara tries to restrain his smile. "Come on, guys. Think about this."

"What's there to think about?" Farrow asks, chewing gum casually.

"Yeah, boss. We heard all we needed to." Donnelly slips a pen out from behind his ear.

Jane hands me a ballpoint pen and turns, so I can splay the papers against her back for a hard surface. And I sign my name on the dotted line.

I pass my brother the pen.

We've all joined Kitsuwon Securities in a matter of minutes.

No one hesitates.

Akara nods to us, overwhelmed. He turns his head. "Alright." He takes a deeper breath, collecting his emotion. "You want to hear about what happens with your clients now?"

"Lay it on us, Kitsuwon," Oscar says.

"Clients can now choose which private security to hire. Either mine or Triple Shield. But if the client is a minor, their parents will need to hire my firm."

I process this. "What happens to Xander? He's the only minor with an Omega bodyguard."

Maximoff says, "I've already spoken to my parents, and they asked Xander which private security he'd rather use. He said Akara's team."

Banks bounces his head. "Right on."

Quinn frowns. "What happens if more than *seven* clients request this firm? There are only seven of us."

"That's not an issue yet," Akara says. "Most of the family that are protected by Alpha and Epsilon are happy with their bodyguards, and they'll stay with them."

"Which clients want to hire the new company?" Oscar asks.

Akara looks to Jane.

She perks up. "Moffy and I are objectively positive that Charlie, Sullivan, and Luna will opt in, besides us of course."

Donnelly frowns. "Not Beckett?"

Jane shakes her head. "I'm unsure. Charlie thinks he's content with O'Malley at the moment."

"He could come around, Donnelly," Akara says, "but until then, I have new details to assign." He massages his palm. "So here's the deal, since all you dumb-fucks decided to join a sinking ship, there are no Omega bodyguards over at Triple Shield. SFO is *here*." He points at the floor.

My lips rise.

The men are grinning. So is Jane next to me.

"Tony can't be a lead if there's no Force to lead."

Oscar claps loudly, and the other two Yale boys join in the applause.

Banks messes my hair next to me, and I say, more to him, "Christmas came late, gents."

He cracks a smile. "I'll take that gift."

"Tony can rat out the twin switch to the Alpha lead all he wants," Akara says, "but Price can't fire Thatcher and Banks if you two don't work for him."

I almost laugh, in shock. This was Akara's plan to pull me out of the twelve-foot ditch. And it worked.

More applause fills the room.

"I don't know where Price will put Tony," Akara continues, "but I can tell you all, here, that you're staying with your current clients. Except for you."

He's looking at me.

"You have Jane."

"I, what?" I stare hard, unblinking, not registering the fact that I could be on her detail again. I've punished myself for so long for screwing the team—it just didn't feel like a position I should be given.

But I want it.

I want *her.*

With every fiber of my being.

Jane's hands fly to her mouth, wide-eyed and stunned. *She didn't know.* Our eyes fasten together while Akara repeats, "You're Jane's bodyguard."

It slams into me.

I can protect my wife.

That's what she'll be. *My wife.*

My hand slides along her cheek, her tears falling, and our foreheads drift closer. Men chat softly behind us, giving me and her a moment, and their voices fade to the background.

"Thatcher." She inhales like we're on an ascent.

My chest caves and expands. "Jane."

"You're my bodyguard." She speaks our blissful reality into the world.

I hold her close, emotion barreling into my body. Surging and stinging my eyes, and very deeply, I say, "You're going to be my wife. I promise you that."

She cries into a tearful smile, and her lips find my ear—her cheek brushing against my hard jaw—and tenderly, Jane whispers, "I love you, I love you, I love you, and let me tell you how terribly and tremendously I do."

I listen to Jane ramble quickly and slowly about her love for me, right against my ear—and I could shut my eyes and breath in. Like it's my first breath on this earth.

I stand strong, my pulse soothed, and my hand lost in her frizzed hair. I can live inside hell, but for the first time, I've *finally* reached heaven—and I'm happy and I'm staying. *I'm staying.* To build a life and future and family. Right here, with Jane Eleanor Cobalt.

For forever.

49

Jane Cobalt

RATHER QUICKLY, I SNIP off tags hooked to store-bought cat toys: new vibrant colored mice, a few feathery stuffed balls, and a cupcake and unicorn stuffed catnip set, thanks to the Meadows family.

And I steal a glance at the sexiest, sternest, and most iron-willed man my eyes have ever loved. Thatcher slices open packaging to a new litter box, our seven cats prancing curiously around him and me.

He's careful with the knife as they nudge closer.

I smile, but then I remember where we are. Only two days have passed since the fire, and we're all still picking up the pieces.

I turn more towards him. "Are you sure you're okay to stay here until we all decide on a new place?" I add in haste, "And I know I've asked you a dozen times already, and this will be the last—I just need to be certain."

"Yeah." Thatcher rips open the cardboard box. "I'm good here."

I eye him, more intrigued. He's not even surveying his surroundings—which are *very* pastel blue. And frilly, and I suppose not entirely different to my room in the townhouse.

Except for the sheer opulence.

A diamond chandelier hangs over a four-poster princess-like bed. Set in the very center, the bed presides over a rosé-hued vanity, a handcrafted wardrobe from Florence, shelves of jeweled Parisian trinkets—and not to forget the boas and outlandish costumes strewn over a dressing curtain, which costs more than his salary.

I am obnoxiously wealthy.

I have been this entire time. But now, he's immersed in this luxury while he's staying in my teenage bedroom with me. Right where I grew up.

The Cobalt Estate is our temporary home for the time being.

Neither of us envisioned living with my parents and my youngest brother and sister—but Thatcher agreed it's safer to "post-up" in the gated neighborhood until we find a permanent place.

He glances back at me in my silence. "You're okay with this arrangement?"

"It's strange being here with you, but maybe that's because you're my future and this room is entirely nostalgic. And our present is finding its footing."

His lip almost rises. "Our present is already standing."

I smile more. "I agree, wholeheartedly. We haven't fallen over." I watch him set up the litter box with ease. My parents had a couple old ones, but we needed more for all seven cats.

If I think too hard, I can still feel the nauseous heat from the fire.

Thatcher, Farrow, Maximoff, Luna, and I—we lost everything we owned in the townhouse. Yesterday, we went to the site and walked the rubble. Soot and charred brick left behind.

I'm fortunate that I have the means to start over, but of course, I lost sentimental things. Framed photos that I never stored in my phone or backed up in the cloud (for security purposes), all the Post-it notes Thatcher wrote me, chunky heels my mom gifted me after the FanCon tour, and much more.

But I feel immensely grateful to have Thatcher here—and that no one else was hurt. All the material items seem far less important and unnecessary in the end.

"Are you ready?" Thatcher asks.

We've been moving hurriedly. We have somewhere to be, you see.

"Almost." I dispose the cut tags into a trash bin and crouch down to a cat carrier. "I have something for you before we go."

I can feel his confusion mount behind me.

My purple tulle skirt catches in the carrier's zipper. "Merde," I mutter and tear the fabric. *So it shall be.*

Thatcher suddenly squats down. He helps me unstick the zipper, and my cheeks hurt, my smile overpowering my face.

"Merci," I say.

But his face has already fallen, seeing what's inside the carrier.

"The night of the fire," I explain, pulling out the item. "I saw this on the vanity and I shoved it inside with Ophelia, before you put Licorice with her."

Thatcher takes the old library book out of my hand. The cover of *The Outsiders* is worn, and his chest rises as he flips to the list of names, eyeing the last one written.

Skylar Moretti

Thatcher started with less than me. I have possessions strewn throughout my childhood house. His whole life was in a bag, and it went up in flames.

I just wanted to preserve something for him.

He kisses the top of my head. "Thank you, Jane." He pinches his eyes for a half a second, then stands and slips *The Outsiders* on my teenage bookshelf.

He could've tucked the book into his bag, and I find a lot of love in the fact that he set his childhood possession next to mine.

I smile. "Now I'm ready."

We leave the regal mansion, entering a late-March warmth. Spring has come very early this year, and we bathe in the temperate weather.

He slips his hand in mine, and we walk past a baby blue Land Rover, parked near the fountain.

My Volkswagen Beetle was too damaged in the fire to salvage, and so yesterday, I bought Thatcher a car for his Christmas present, and he chose the color for me.

Our vehicle sits very pretty, I think.

We descend the driveway. Pink tulip trees blooming on either side, and I glance up at Thatcher, his flannel shirt hiding the burn on his shoulder.

It'll scar, but he's said the pain has lessened. And I take comfort in that fact. Tony was released from the hospital at the same time as Thatcher, and the rumor is that he's being transferred to Security Force Alpha.

Where he'll be the bodyguard to Connor Cobalt—my brilliant, cutthroat dad. Who can make the tallest men feel infinitesimally microscopic and tiny.

With that behind us and so much ahead, the air sings with a newfound happiness. We reach the neighborhood street and stroll towards the music and voices at the end of the cul-de-sac.

We're not the only ones en route.

Farrow and Maximoff step onto the road with Kinney perched on Moffy's shoulders, her black combat boots thudding his chest. They leave the Hale house along with Luna and Xander. Like us, they've chosen to temporarily reside at our childhood homes. Just until we choose a new place to live.

They smile at Thatcher and me.

Luna waves a neon-green pompom, one I made for her long ago, growing up, and I realize Moffy, Xander and Kinney have their makeshift pompoms in hand too.

I laugh into a tearful smile, and I look up to Thatcher, who has such light in his eyes. And he's the one to tell me, "Today is a happy day."

"It is," I nod.

We trek forward, and I hear Kinney ask her older brother, "Why are you so slow? Walk faster."

"I could run, Kinney, but you'd scream—"

"Huh, I'm afraid of *nothing*."

He sprints forward, whooshing past me, and Kinney shrieks.

We all laugh, and that laughter blends into the packed cul-de-sac where Thatcher's big Italian-American family is among all of mine—

parents, siblings, aunts, uncles and cousins. Plus, Omega bodyguards are here as friends. Grilling out burgers and cheesesteaks, music flowing into the bright blue sky. Beers are chilled and sipped.

They turn and smile at our entrance.

This is our engagement party.

Thatcher and I exchange another readying look. We go around and greet all his relatives and all of mine. My parents congratulate us, both near tears, though my mom will vehemently deny it, and then my dad tells me that I was quicker than him. To accept love. He rarely admits to being second-best at anything, so his words swell my heart.

I squeeze Thatcher's mom, stepmom and grandma tight, and they kiss my cheek. I even meet his dad, who flew in from Coronado where he trains Navy Seal recruits.

He hugs Thatcher, and as they catch up, I find my little sister at a dessert table, a lacy umbrella shielding the sun from her fair skin.

Near the end of the table, Winona and Sulli burst into laughter, cupcake frosting smudged on their noses and cheeks. I smile. It's not a real party until the Meadows sisters shove cupcakes in each other's faces.

Audrey drops a pink pompom and the parasol once I clasp her hands. We jump up and down and chant to each other, "Beautiful, gorgeous, ravishing." We kiss each other's cheeks, and when we slow, I take her pompom and touch her nose.

"This was orchestrated?" I wonder, referring to the pompom. I've quickly realized that all the ones I made specifically for my cousins and siblings are in their possession today.

"Yes, we had to create a new mega-group chat, one without you, but it all went according to plan. Except for *Eliot*. He says he lost his pompom somewhere." She leans in close to whisper, "I think he burned it years ago, and he just doesn't have the heart to say. Especially since Tom's ribbon is singed."

Sure enough, Tom has been enthusiastically waving around a charred pompom. Nearby, Beckett gives him a *what the fuck* look. Ben holds his mustard yellow pompom by his side, and Charlie makes an effort to casually shake his in the air like he's ringing a bell.

"We love them anyway," I note.

She nods proudly in agreement, and her gaze drifts behind me. She lets out a breathy sigh. "I swear, Jane, you're the luckiest girl in the world. To have such a beauty like him. Don't ever let him go."

My sister's love of Thatcher is a rising tide inside my heart, and I turn to see him approaching.

Two beer bottles in one hand. His bold, quiet dominance lures me, even as he stops and passes me the alcohol.

"Thank you." I run my lips together and flush. I will always be flushing around Thatcher Moretti. I crane my neck more to meet his eyes, and for some odd reason, I greet him. "Thatcher."

"Jane." He swigs his beer, and without speaking more, he takes my hand and guides me into the masses. My heart pitter-patters. My smile can't wane.

Everyone is dancing, jumping—and we join in. He hoists me up on his body. My legs around his waist and one hand on his neck, and his grip is beneath my ass.

He slyly passes his beer to Banks as he walks by, and then he peels my fingers off his neck and holds my left hand.

I eye him curiously.

He slips off the paperclip and slips on a pink sapphire ring, multi-colored gemstones set around the teardrop-cut.

My lips part. "How did you…?" The ring looks like someone went deep-sea diving into my soul and returned with *this*. It's so terribly me that my eyes begin to water on instinct.

"There's this jewelry boutique in Paris you used to visit as a kid." He fixes a strand of my hair that blows in my face.

"You didn't go to…?"

"I went to Paris," he confirms.

My eyes pop out. "How? When?" *For me,* he went to Pairs for me, for this ring. Knowing how special it'd be for me, even though I was willing to wear the paperclip for the rest of my life.

"I had a day off in February," Thatcher explains. "Your mom, sister, and I took a private plane, and it was the quickest trip I've ever been on, but it was worth every second."

My heart swells, and I smile through tears. "You realize, you're becoming as dramatic and over-the-top as the rest of us."

He cups my cheek. "I'm happy to be here."

The way he stares into my eyes brings crashing waves to shore. It feels like someone folding me up in their soul.

I kiss him—I kiss him so fiercely and wholeheartedly. He kisses me back like this is the beginning, not the end.

Thatcher is smiling against my lips.

I clasp his jaw more strongly, my smile rising.

Cheers and applause explode around us, pompoms waving, and loving faces and bodies jump in glee. Thatcher and I sip beers and kiss and dance, me in his arms. We are all mad, beautiful synchronous chaos.

"I love you," I say so often now.

I never want to leave his embrace, happiness is right here in his arms. And if we're strong enough to survive ice and fire together, we can survive anything.

Sempre toujours.

Always always.

ACKNOWLEDGEMENTS

First, we want to thank our Grandma Lou. Though she's no longer with us, she had a large hand in Thatcher's story. She spent hours on the phone with us, talking about Italian words, culture, and her childhood, knowing these things would be incorporated into *Tangled Like Us* and *Sinful Like Us*. Before that, before we were writers, she quilted us baby blankets for the "one day" when we'd have children. Before that, she would keep reminding us about how she would be gone soon. And like Thatcher, we disbelieved. Because she was healthy. Because she was happy. Because family has the power to seem immortal.

Even though she never got to see these two books, she's so much a part of them. And we're just so very grateful for all her help and to have had someone so strong in our lives. As Thatcher would say, *"Brave. Bold. Strong women rule my world, and I love them."* For us, that's never been truer.

Thank you to the other brave, bold, strong woman in our lives. Our mom. Thank you for all of your editing prowess and your constant encouragement. Your love lights our way. During the darkest times of our lives, you've picked us back up. Thank you from the bottom of our hearts. Thank you.

Kimberly, thank you for your support and for helping get these beauties into audio. We're not only grateful, but we know all our audio listeners are so very happy too.

Lanie, Jenn, and Shea, our powerhouse FB admins and truly great friends. Thank you for all the work you put into promoting these books just because you love them. We adore you three and wish you all the fairy dust and magic the world has to offer.

Marie, thank you for your epic French translations. The Cobalts wouldn't be the same without your touch and expertise, and we're so thankful for all your help. Lily Calloway would definitely believe you have magic and belong with the Cobalt Empire.

Thank you to our brother, dad, aunts, uncles, and cousins for all your unwavering support and love. Family is such a huge part of this novel, and we wouldn't know how to write these large loving families without having one of our own.

Lastly, but definitely not least, thank you to the bloggers, reviewers, and readers who picked up this book. We are so very honored that you've chosen to read Jane & Thatcher's story when so many other stories exist in the world. Thank you so much for taking this journey with us. As Jane would say, *"Merci."*

All the love in every universe,

Xoxo Krista & Becca

PRONUNCIATION GLOSSARY

The Italian used in this book is an Italian-American language developed by Italian immigrants. It is an incomplete language and uses Italian, English, or both. Different Italians speak different dialects in certain areas, and what is used in the Like Us series is prominent on the East Coast. Words may vary in pronunciation and spelling in different communities.

braggiol': pronounced BRAAJH-oel (Origin: bracciole)

che cozz'?: prounounced KAY-kaatz (Origin: che cazzo fai?)

cornic': pronounced kor-neek (Origin: cornicello)

gabbadost': pronounced gaa-baa-dahst
(Origin: capa dura/capa tosta)

mannaggia: pronounced MAA-NAA-juh
(Origin: male ne aggia/male ne abbia)

menzamenz: pronounced mehnz-AA-mehnz
(Origin: mezza mezza)

mortadafam': pronounced moart-aa-daa-faam
(Origin: morta da fame)

paesan': pai-ZAAN (Origin: paesano)

pasta vasul': pronounced pasta-faa-ZOOL (Origin: pasta fagioli)

statazitt'!: pronounced stah-tuh-JEET (Origin: stai zitto)

stunad: pronounced stoo-NAAD (Origin: stonato)

CPSIA information can be obtained
at www.ICGtesting.com
Printed in the USA
BVHW031149231221
624751BV00012B/35